KISSING THE SAVAGE

Katerina had just reached the opening to her chamber when Lucas stepped into her path. There was a look in his silvery-blue eyes that made her insides clench with need; and that angered her. She scowled at him as he neatly pinned her between his hard body and the stone wall.

Katerina did not need to feel the thick ridge of his shaft pressing against her to know what Lucas wanted. It was there to read in the taut lines of his face. Despite the pain he had caused her, she wanted it, too. It was too soon, however. She had not yet decided if the pleasure he could give her was worth all the risks that came with it.

"I believe ye have a pallet readied for ye in the hall with the other men," she said, proud of the chill in her voice for there was only searing, welcoming heat in her body.

"Your bed would be warmer."

"There are plenty of blankets about. Seek their warmth."

"Are ye sure that is what ye want me to do?"

Before she could reply, he kissed her. It was no gentle kiss, no soft coaxing of a lover. Lucas ravished her mouth. His kiss stirred her hunger into a fierce craving . . .

Books by Hannah Howell

Only for You
My Valiant Knight
Unconquered
Wild Roses
A Taste of Fire
Highland Destiny
Highland Honor
Highland Promise
A Stockingful of Joy
Highland Vow
Highland Knight
Highland Hearts
Highland Bride
Highland Angel
Highland Groom
Highland Warrior
Reckless
Highland Conquerer
Highland Champion
Highland Lover
Highland Vampire
Conqueror's Kiss
Highland Barbarian
Beauty and the Beast
Highland Savage

Published by Zebra Books

HANNAH HOWELL

HIGHLAND SAVAGE

ZEBRA BOOKS
Kensington Publishing Corp.
www.kensingtonbooks.com

ZEBRA BOOKS are published by

Kensington Publishing Corp.
850 Third Avenue
New York, NY 10022

ISBN-13: 978-0-8217-7999-6
ISBN-10: 0-8217-7999-0

First Printing: May 2007
10 9 8 7 6 5 4 3

Printed in the United States of America

Chapter One

Scotland
Spring 1481

His robes itched. Lucas gritted his teeth against the urge to throw them off and vigorously scratch every inch of his body he could reach. He did not know how his cousin Matthew endured wearing the things day in and day out. Since the man had happily dedicated his life to the service of God, Lucas did not think Matthew deserved such an excruciating penance. A man willing to sacrifice so much for God ought to able to do so in more comfortable garb.

"This may have been a bad idea, Eachann," Lucas murmured to his mount as he paused on a small rise to stare down at the village of Dunlochan.

His big brown gelding snorted and began to graze on the grass at his hooves.

"Weel, there is nay turning back now. Nay, I am but suffering a moment of uncertainty and it shames me. I have just ne'er been verra skilled in subterfuge, aye? 'Tis a blunt mon I am and this shall require me to be subtle and sly. But, 'tis nay a worry for I have been practicing."

Lucas frowned at his horse and sternly told himself that the animal only sounded as if it had just snickered. On the other hand, if the animal could understand what he said, snickering would probably be an appropriate response. Yet, he had no choice. He needed revenge. It was a hunger inside him that demanded feeding. It was not something he could ask his family to risk themselves for, either, although they had been more than willing to do so. That willingness was one reason he had had to slip away under cover of night, telling no one where he was going, not even his twin.

This was his fight and his alone. Surrounded by the strong, skilled fighting men of his clan, he knew he would feel deprived of satisfying the other need he had. He needed to prove to himself that his injuries had not left him incapable of being the warrior he had been before he had been beaten. He needed to defeat the men who had tried to destroy him and defeat them all by himself. His family had not fully understood that need. They had not fully understood his need to work so hard, so continuously, to regain his skills after he had recovered from the beating either. He knew the praise they had given him as he had slowly progressed from invalid to fighting man had, in part, been an attempt to stop him from striving so hard to regain his former abilities, to overcome the stiffness and pain in his leg. He desperately needed to see that he was as good as he had been, that he had not been robbed of the one true strength he had. He had to prove himself worthy of being the heir to Donncoill.

"Artan would understand," he said, stroking Eachann's strong neck as he slowly rode down the hill toward the village.

He felt a pang of lingering grief. His twin had his own life now, one separate from the one they had shared since the womb. Artan had a wife, his own lands, and a family of his own. Lucas was happy for his twin yet he was still grieved by the loss of the other half of himself. In his heart Lucas knew he and Artan could never be fully separated but now Artan shared himself with others as he had only ever shared himself with Lucas. It would take some getting used to.

"And I have no one."

Lucas grimaced. He sounded like a small sulky child yet that feeling of being completely alone was one he could not shake. It disgusted him, but he knew part of it was that he had lost not only Artan; he had lost Katerina. She had betrayed him and did not deserve his grief, yet it lingered. No other woman could banish the emptiness left by her loss. No other woman could ease the coldness left by her vicious betrayal. He could still see her watching as he was beaten nigh unto death. She had made no sound, no move to save him. She had not even shed a tear.

He shook aside those dark memories and the pain they still brought him. Lucas decided that once he had proven to himself that he was the man he used to be he would find himself a woman and rut himself blind. He would exhaust himself in soft, welcoming arms and sweat out the poison of Katerina. Even though it was not fully a fidelity to Katerina that had kept him almost celibate, he knew a lingering hunger for her, for the passion they had shared, was one reason he found it difficult to satisfy his needs elsewhere. In his mind he was done with her, but it was obvious his heart and body were still enslaved. He would overcome his reluctance to reveal his scars and occasional awkwardness to a woman and find himself a lover when he returned to Donncoill. Maybe even a wife, he mused as he reined in before the small inn in the heart of the village. All too clearly recalling Katerina's dark blue eyes and honey-blond hair, he decided that woman would be dark. It was time to make the cut sharp and complete.

Dismounting, Lucas gave the care of Eachann over to a bone-thin youth who quickly appeared at his side. The lad stared at him with wide blue eyes, looking much as if he had just seen a ghost, and that look made Lucas uneasy. Subtly he checked to make certain that his cowl still covered the hair he had been unable to cut. Although he had told himself he would need the cowl up at all times to shadow his far too recognizable face, Lucas knew it was vanity that had made him reluctant to cut off his long black hair and his warrior braids. Deciding the boy might just be a little simple, Lucas collected his saddle-packs, then gave the lad a coin before making his way into the inn.

After taking only two steps into the building, Lucas felt the chill of fear speed down his spine and stopped to look around. This was where he had been captured, dragged away to be savagely beaten and then left for dead. Despite the nightmares he still suffered on occasion he had thought he had conquered the unreasonable fear his beating had left him with.

Annoyance over such a weakness helped him quell that fear. Standing straighter he made his way to a table set in a shadowy corner at the back of the room. He had barely sat down when a buxom fair-haired maid hurried over to greet him. If he recalled right, her name was Annie.

"Father," she began.

"Nay, my child. I am nay tonsured yet," Lucas said, hoping such a tale would help explain away any mistakes he might make. "I am on pilgrimage ere I return to the monastery and take my final vows."

"Oh." Annie sighed. "I was hoping ye were looking for a place to serve God's will." She briefly glared at the men drinking ale near the large fireplace. "We could certainly use a holy mon here. Dunlochan has become steeped in sin and evil."

"I will be certain to tell my brothers of your need when I return to them, child."

"Thank ye, Father. Ah, I mean, sir. How can I serve ye?"

"Food, ale, and a bed for the night, lass."

In but moments Lucas was enjoying a rich ale, a hearty mutton stew, and thick warm bread. The good food served by the inn was one reason he had lingered in Dunlochan long enough to meet Katerina. His stomach had certainly led him astray that day, he thought sourly. In truth, his stomach may have kept him at Dunlochan long enough to meet Katerina, but it was another heedless part of him that had truly led him astray. One look at her lithe body, her long thick hair the color of sweet clover honey, and her wide deep blue eyes and all his wits had sunk right down into his groin. He had thought he had met his mate and all he had found was betrayal and pain.

Lucas cursed silently. The woman would not get out of his life, out of his mind, or out of his heart. That would not stop him from getting his revenge on her, however. He was not quite sure how he would accomplish that yet, but he would. First the men who had tried to kill him and then the woman who had given the order.

Another casualty of that dark night was his trust in people, in his ability to judge them as friend or foe. Lucas had believed Katerina was his mate, the woman he had been born to be with. Instead she had nearly been his death. It was hard to trust his own judgment after such a near-fatal error and an ability to discern whom to trust was important to a warrior. How could he ever be a good laird to the people of Donncoill if he could not even tell friend from foe?

He sipped his ale and studied the men near the fireplace. Lucas was sure that at least one of them had been there that night, but the shadows cast by the fire made it difficult to see the man clearly. One of the things he recalled clearly was that few of the men had been fair as most of the Haldanes were. It had puzzled him that Katerina would hire mercenaries, but, perhaps, her own people would never have obeyed such an order from her. If those men were no more than hired swords it would make the killing of them easier for few would call out for vengeance when they died.

Six men suddenly entered the inn and Lucas stiffened. No shadows hid their faces and he recognized each one. It was hard to control the urge to immediately draw his sword and set after them. He shuddered faintly, the memory of the beating flaring crisp and clear in his mind and body. Lucas rubbed his left leg, the ache of shattered bones sharpened by those dark memories. His right hand throbbed as if it recalled each and every slam of a boot on it. The scar that now ran raggedly over his right cheek itched and Lucas could almost feel the pain of the knife's blade cutting through the flesh there.

He drew in a deep breath and let it out slowly. Lucas knew he needed to push those memories aside if he was to think clearly. The revenge he hungered for could not be accomplished if he acted too quickly or if he gave in to the fierce urge to immediately draw his sword and attack these men. When he realized part of his ability to hold back was because he did not think he could defeat the six men with a direct attack, he silently cursed again. His confidence in his newly regained battle skills was obviously not as strong as he had thought it was.

"Annie!" bellowed one of the men as he and his companions sat down. "Get your arse o'er here and pour us some ale, wench!"

There was an obvious caution in Annie's steps as

she approached the men with tankards and a ewer of ale. "Hush, Ranald," she said. "I saw ye come in and was ready. There is nay need to bellow so."

Lucas watched as the young woman did her best to pour each man a tankard of ale even as she tried to avoid their grasping hands. Unlike many another lass who worked in such a place, Annie was no whore easily gained by a coin or two, but the men treated her as if she was. By the time she was able to get away from their table, she was flushed with anger and her eyes were shining with tears of shame. Lucas had to take a deep drink of the strong ale to quell the urge to leap to her defense. He gave her a small smile when she paused by his table to refill his tankard and wondered why that made her eyes narrow and cause a frown to tighten her full mouth.

"Have ye been here before, sir?" she asked as she suddenly sat down across the scarred table from him.

"Nay, why should ye think so, child?" he asked.

"There was something about your smile," she said then shrugged. "'Twas familiar."

Lucas had no idea how a smile could be familiar but told himself to remember to be more cautious about doing so again. "Mayhap ye just see too few, aye?"

"Certainly too few that show me such fine, white teeth."

"A blessing I got from my family and God. That and cleaning them regularly."

She nodded. "The Lady Katerina taught me the value of cleaning my teeth."

"A good and Godly woman is she?"

"She was, aye."

"Was?"

"Aye, she died last spring, poor wee lass." She glared at the men who had treated her so badly. "They and the ladies at the keep say my lady killed herself, but I dinnae believe it. She would ne'er have done such a thing. Aye, and the lovely mon who was courting her disappeared on the verra same day. No one has an answer for where he went." She suddenly looked straight at Lucas. "That is who your smile reminded me of, I am thinking. A bonnie lad he was. He did make my lady happy, he did."

Lucas was too shocked to do more than nod. He could not even think of something to say to turn aside the dangerous comparison Annie had just made. Katerina was dead. The news hit him like a sound blow to the chest and it took him a moment to catch his breath. He told himself that the sharp grief that swept over him was born of the fact that he had lost all chance to exact his revenge upon the woman for her betrayal, but a small voice in his mind scoffed at that explanation. He ruthlessly silenced it.

"Is it a sin to visit her grave e'en though she is buried in unconsecrated ground?" Annie asked.

"Nay, lass," he replied, his voice a little hoarse from the feelings he was fighting. "Her soul needs your prayers e'en more than another's, aye?"

The thought of Katerina resting in the cold ground was more than Lucas could bear and he hastily pushed it aside. He also ignored the questions swirling in his mind, ones that demanded answers. He could not believe Katerina would kill herself either, but this was not the time to solve that puzzle. As he sought his revenge on the men who had beaten him he could ask a few questions, but that revenge had to be the first thing on his mind for now. When that was done he would discover the truth about Katerina's death. No matter what she had done to him, he knew he would never be able to rest easy with the thought of her lovely body rotting in unconsecrated soil.

"Do ye think ye could pray for her, sir? Would that be a sin?"

Lucas had no idea and fumbled for an answer. "'Tis my duty to pray for lost souls, child."

"I could take ye to where she is buried," Annie began and then scowled when Ranald and two of his companions came up to the table. "If ye want more ale, ye just needed to ask."

"I came to see why ye are sitting here and talking so cozily with this monk," said Ranald.

"What business is it of yours, eh?"

"Ye waste your time wooing a monk, lass. If ye are hungry for a mon, I am more than willing to see to your needs." He grinned when his companions laughed.

"I but wished to talk to someone who has traveled beyond the boundaries of Haldane land," she snapped. "Someone who doesnae smell or curse or try to lift my skirts." Annie suddenly blushed and looked at Lucas. "Pardon me for speaking so, sir."

"'Tis nay ye who must beg pardon, child, but the men who compel ye to speak so," Lucas said, watching Ranald closely.

"Here now, I but woo the lass," said Ranald, glaring at Lucas.

"Is that what ye call it?"

"What would ye ken about it, eh? Ye have given it all up for God, aye? Or have ye? Are ye one of those who says vows to God out of one side of his mouth whilst wooing the lasses out the other?"

"Ye insult my honor," Lucas said coldly, wishing the man would leave for the urge to make him pay now, and pay dearly, for every twinge of pain Lucas had suffered over the last year was growing too strong to ignore. "I but question your skill at wooing."

"Do ye now. And just what are ye doing in Dunlochan? There is no monastery near here."

"He is on a pilgrimage ere he takes his vows," said Annie. "Leave him be and go back to your friends and your ale."

"Ye defend him most prettily, lass. I have to wonder why." Ranald scowled at Lucas. "What is he hiding under those robes?"

Even as Lucas became aware of the sudden danger he was in, Ranald yanked back his cowl and exposed the hair Lucas had been too vain to cut. For a brief moment, everyone just stared at Lucas, their eyes wide and their mouths gaping. Lucas actually considered attacking the man Ranald immediately but good sense intervened. The man's friends were already rising from their seats and inching closer.

Taking advantage of everyone's shock at seeing what they thought was a ghost, Lucas leapt to his feet, grabbed his saddle-packs, and bolted for the door. He gained the outside and turned toward the stable only to stumble to a halt as someone grabbed his robe from behind. Cursing, he turned and kicked the man in the face. Knowing he would not make it to his horse in time, Lucas tossed aside his saddle-packs and yanked off his robes. By the time Ranald and his friends had finished stumbling out of the inn, Lucas was facing them with a sword in one hand and a dagger in the other.

"So, it *is* ye," said Ranald as he drew his sword and he and his companions moved to stand facing Lucas. "Ye are supposed to be dead. We threw ye off the cliff and saw ye just lying there."

"And ye ne'er went back to see if I stayed there, did ye," Lucas said, his scorn clear to hear in his voice.

"Why trouble ourselves? We had beaten ye soundly, ye were bleeding from several wounds, and we threw ye off a cliff."

Lucas shrugged. "I got up and went home," he said,

knowing his family would groan to hear him describe the many travails he had gone through to return to Donncoill in such simple terms.

"Weel, ye willnae be crawling home this time, laddie."

"Nay, I intend to ride home in triumph, leaving your bodies behind me to rot in the dirt."

"I dinnae think so." Ranald sneered as he glanced at Lucas's left leg. "I watched ye run out of the inn and ye limp and stumble like an old mon. We left ye a cripple, didnae we."

Lucas fought down the rage that threatened to consume him. He had to exact his revenge coldly, had to fight with a clear head and think out every move he made. It was this man's fault that Lucas could no longer move with the speed and grace he had before, and it was hard not to just lunge at the man and cut him down. Before the beating he would have not been all that concerned about the other men, knowing he could turn on them with equal speed and have a good chance of defeating them all. Now, because of these men, he had to weigh his every move carefully if he had any hope of coming out of this alive.

"E'en that wee wound willnae stop me from killing ye," Lucas said, his voice almost cheerful even as he noted with a twinge of dismay how the men began to slowly encircle him.

"Still arrogant," said Ranald, grinning as he shook his head. "Weel, soon ye will be joining your wee whore in the cold clay."

"So, Annie spoke true when she said Lady Katerina was dead."

"Aye, she joined ye or so we thought. Tossed her right o'er the cliff and into the water with ye."

That made no sense to Lucas, but he pushed his sudden confusion and all the questions it raised aside.

How and why Katerina had died was of no importance at the moment. Staying alive had to be his only priority. A quick glance toward the inn revealed a white-faced Annie and several other Haldanes watching and listening, but Ranald spoke too low for them to hear what was a clear confession. Lucas had to hope that, if he failed to win this fight, they would find out what happened to Katerina, although why he should care about that was just another puzzle he had no time to solve.

"I dinnae suppose ye have the courage to face me mon to mon, without all your men to protect your worthless hide," Lucas said as he braced himself for the battle to come.

"Are ye calling me a coward?" Ranald snarled.

"Ye needed near a dozen men to capture me, beat me nigh unto death, and toss me off a cliff, and then ye murdered a wee unarmed lass. Aye, I believe I am calling ye a coward and weel do ye deserve the name."

"'Twill be a joy to kill ye, fool."

Glancing around at the men encircling him, Lucas had the sinking feeling that it would also be a quick killing, but then he stiffened his backbone. He had been in such tight spots before and come out nearly unscathed. All he needed to do was regain that arrogance Ranald found so irritating. Lucas was a little concerned that he would fail at that. It seemed his heart was beating so hard and fast that he could actually hear it. Telling himself he was imagining things, he readied himself to win and, failing that, to take as many of these men with him as he could. This time, killing him was going to cost them dearly.

Chapter Two

"He is alive?!"

Katerina stared at young Thomas, certain she had misheard him, that his breathlessness had garbled his words. Lucas could not be alive. He had been bleeding and broken when Ranald and his men had thrown him off the cliff. The fall would only have added to his already serious injuries. Just before they had tossed her off as well she had caught a fleeting glimpse of Lucas's limp body being dragged off the rocky shores by the rough, wind-tossed waters of the loch. She had barely survived being tossed into those waters herself and she had not been beaten first. Even as she struggled to keep from drowning in those cold, dark waters, she had looked for Lucas and seen nothing.

"The mon has those same eyes, m'lady," Thomas said. "Aye, and e'en the same voice. I recall both verra clearly, although he didnae seem to remember me. It has to be him."

"Weel, ye have grown a fair bit in the last year," she muttered, still fighting her shock.

"Did Sir Lucas nay tell us once that he has a twin?" asked William as he stepped up to stand close by

Katerina's side and place a comforting hand upon her shoulder.

A wave of sharp disappointment swept through Katerina at her second-in-command's words, but she just nodded in silent agreement with his recollection. "Aye, Cousin, he did. Artan was his twin's name and Lucas said they were alike in looks, voice, and sword skill. This must be Lucas's twin. His family has finally come to find him or to seek revenge."

"But, m'lady, did ye nay tell us that Ranald and his dogs had cut Sir Lucas's face?" asked Thomas.

"Aye," Katerina whispered, unable to halt the searing memories of that day from flooding her mind.

"Weel, this mon has a scar upon his face and he also limps a wee bit, as if his leg is a wee bit stiff."

"It could still be his twin brother." That both men would suffer such similar wounds was too great a coincidence to be plausible, but Katerina was afraid to let herself hope that Lucas had survived and had returned to her.

"Ranald and his dogs believe it is Sir Lucas and they mean to be certain that he dies this time."

"Then, whoe'er this mon may be, 'tis best if we pull him free of this trouble ere those curs kill him. We can sort out this puzzle of who he is later. Thomas, ye best spread the word that we are riding so that all is ready for us."

Pushing aside the fierce, tangled emotions raging through her, Katerina selected six of her men to ride with her. They all donned their long, black cloaks, wrapped a wide strip of dark blue linen over their mouths and noses to better hide their faces, secured their hoods over their heads, and mounted their waiting horses. This was not what they had planned to do when they had gathered this night, but Ranald and his men could not be allowed to murder another man.

As she led her men on a swift race toward the village, Katerina fought to kill the hope young Thomas's words had stirred in her heart. She had done her best to kill all hope when Lucas's body had not even washed up onto the rocky shores of the loch so that she could give him a proper burial. It had taken a long, wretched time to silence all the questions that had kept her from fully accepting his loss, ones such as why his family had never come searching for him. Those unanswered and long ignored questions were all creeping back into her mind now and she struggled to silence them again. All that should matter to her right now was that Ranald and his men were about to kill again and she had sworn on her father's soul that she would put an end to Ranald's brutality.

Even more important, she had yet to prove who gave the man his orders. Katerina was certain it was her half-sister Agnes, but she needed indisputable proof of the woman's crimes and that was proving very hard to come by. She never would have thought her half-sister was so clever, so cunning. Katerina's only moments of satisfaction, fleeting and shallow though they were, came when she thought of how Agnes had to be feeling as trapped, as cornered and frustrated, as she was. Agnes had not yet found her rogue of a husband, the man their father had so disliked. Until the man was found and Agnes was made a widow, she could not lay claim to Dunlochan either. They were both locked into this battle, which was draining all the joy and prosperity from Dunlochan.

The conditions set by her father's last wishes had been demeaning. The results had thus far been disastrous. Katerina loathed the thought that five old men chosen by her father had the final say on whether any

man she chose to wed was suitable or not. That sorely
stung her pride. The fact that she and any who supported her were marked for death before her father
was even cold in the ground made her wonder just
what her father had been thinking of. Either he had
been utterly blind to Agnes's true nature and thus saw
no danger, or his general scorn for women had made
it impossible to even consider the possibility that
there would be a battle over the lands and money he
had left behind. Her father may not have been an af-
fectionate man, but she had always considered him a
good laird and a clever man. His instructions concerning the settlement of Dunlochan after he died
made her wonder if his illness had badly disordered
his wits.

The sound of sword hitting sword abruptly pulled
her from her thoughts and she signaled her men to
slow their pace. Even in the gray light of day's end she
could see the men in front of the inn—one man encircled by seven. Ranald never did like to fight fairly,
she mused as, using hand signals, she silently instructed her men on how they should proceed. Their
biggest advantage in the coming confrontation would
be their horses. Few men could stand fast before a
charging horse. Satisfied that her men understood
what she planned, Katerina fixed her gaze upon the
man in the middle of the circle and struggled to
ignore how much his long black hair reminded her of
Lucas's as she kicked her horse into a gallop.

Lucas cursed as one of the men behind him managed to get close enough to score his lower back with
his sword. He saved himself from a more dangerous
wound, but only barely. There was some comfort to be
found in the fact that he had bloodied his foes, but

Lucas could not ignore the fact that he, too, was
bloodied. That he was still alive proved how much of
his old skill he had recovered, but it was not enough.

Even as he knocked the sword from the man's hand
Lucas suddenly realized that the pounding he had
heard was not in his heart or his head. The man he
had just disarmed had halted abruptly in rushing to
retrieve his weapon, his eyes widening as he stared at
something behind Lucas and his face turning parchment white. The men flanking him looked the same.
Even as Lucas strove to keep a close watch on the men
surrounding him, he looked in the direction they all
did and gaped.

Seven horsemen were galloping straight toward
them, their horses large and holding steady. One male
rode slightly in the lead, the others in a neat line right
behind him. Lucas watched that straight line slowly
curve around and realized they moved to encircle his
attackers and cut off their escape. The only hesitation
in that awe-inspiring maneuver was when one of the
horsemen smoothly leaned down and caught up the
pack Lucas had dropped. The leader never wavered,
but continued on in a straight line, one that led
straight for him.

For a moment it was as if time itself had slowed to
a crawl. Lucas saw his enemies react to this attack as if
they moved through thick mud. He saw everything
clearly, from the fact that the rider headed for him
was a lot smaller than the rest to the eerie sight of
their black cloaks flowing out behind them and the
dark blue cloth that covered most of their faces. It was
all a beautifully graceful yet utterly terrifying sight.
Then his enemies started to try to flee and Lucas's
ears were assaulted by the sound of swords clashing.

Lucas was also looking for a route of escape when
he realized the lead horseman had slowed. The huge

black gelding the man rode reared to a halt at his side
and the rider held out a surprisingly small gauntleted
hand. It appeared he was about to be rescued, Lucas
thought.

"Get on ere one of these cowards realizes I am a
verra easy target here," snapped the rider.

Despite the way the rider's voice was muffled by the
cloth wrapped around his face, Lucas felt a twinge of
recognition. He tried to see the rider's eyes but the
hood of the black cloak shadowed all of the face not
masked by that blue cloth. Grabbing the rider's ex-
tended forearm, Lucas used the hold to help swing
himself up into the saddle behind the man. A soft
grunt escaped the man and the struggle he had to
stay in the saddle was obvious, but Lucas was impressed by the strength of what he now assumed was
little more than a boy.

"My horse . . ." Lucas began.

"Will be weel cared for," the rider replied even as he
kicked the horse into a gallop.

Lucas wrapped his arms around the waist of his rescuer and hung on. His rescuer was astonishingly slender. He frowned for there was something tantalizingly
familiar about the youth. Even the scent of the slim
rider teased at his memories. It left him with a puzzle
he hoped would soon be solved.

For one brief moment Lucas feared he had escaped
one danger and blindly stumbled into another. He
quickly shook aside his suspicions. If these people
meant him any harm they only needed to have left him
where he was. Why they had exerted themselves to
rescue him he did not know, but he suspected that, too,
would be made clear once they got to wherever they
were headed. And, mayhap, he had just found some
allies in his quest for revenge. He had not wanted his
family entangled in his search for vengeance, but, since

these people seemed to be the enemies of his enemies, he saw no reason not to either join with them or seek their aid.

Katerina tried to concentrate on riding safely through the trees in the fading light of day's end. Fixing all of her attention on that chore was the only way she could control the maelstrom of emotions tearing through her. If she faltered in that rigid discipline she knew she would halt so that she could reassure herself that it was truly Lucas who was seated behind her, and that indulgence could put them all in danger. She had no doubt that Ranald and their men were already chasing them.

When she had seen Lucas standing there fighting for his life, she had nearly screamed out her joy. Fortunately good sense had prevailed. Ranald might now know that Lucas had survived, but the man still thought that she was dead. That deception was vital to any chance she had of winning this war with Agnes.

A strong thread of disbelief still twisted itself around her mind and heart. It was difficult to believe that Lucas had survived the vicious beating he had suffered and being thrown into the loch. She knew his leg had been broken, so how had he saved himself from drowning? Yet her eyes told her that it was indeed Lucas Murray she had just yanked out of Ranald's deadly grasp. Everything from the sound of his voice to the feel of his body pressed close to hers as they rode told her that it was him.

One question kept pounding in her mind even as she and her men scattered, only William continuing to ride with her, giving their pursuers half a dozen trails to try and follow. Why had Lucas not tried to find her, to at least let her know that he was alive?

From the brief look she had gotten of the man he had obviously needed a long time to heal, but that only explained why he had not returned to Dunlochan. It did not explain why he had left her to grieve for him as he must have known she would. The possible answers to that question, which slipped so insidiously into her mind, were chilling and she quickly shook them away. Lucas knew her, knew her very well. He could not possibly believe she had had anything to do with the attack upon him.

Seeing Old Ian up ahead, Katerina quickly reined to a halt and dismounted. She resisted the urge to help Lucas when she noticed the slight awkwardness in his dismount. Turning her whole attention to Old Ian, she handed him the reins to her horse, William swiftly doing the same.

"I heard the mon had returned," said Old Ian after studying Lucas closely for a moment.

"Aye, and gave Ranald yet another chance to kill him," said Katerina and then she grimaced. "'Tis why we had need of ye tonight. I hope we didnae pull ye away from your meal."

"My woman will keep it warm for me. Get ye gone now ere those swine catch sight of ye."

Seeing that William had already begun to brush away their trail with a leafy branch, Katerina nodded. "As soon as the pursuit has ended someone will come to fetch these beasties."

"Nay trouble. I have feed enough. Godspeed."

"And to ye, too."

Even as Old Ian led the horses away William followed, brushing away the trail left behind them. Knowing he would catch up to her, Katerina silently waved to Lucas to follow her and began to jog toward the old kirk that had become one of her hiding places for far too long. Only once did she chance a look at

Lucas to make certain he had no trouble in following her. There was an odd hitch to his gait but he
moved quickly and showed no signs of pain. They
would be able to savor their reunion later.

Lucas was impressed by the group's actions. Multi-
ple trails for an enemy to follow, people readied to
hide the horses, trails brushed away, and utter silence
for most of the time. He realized these people had
been at their work—whatever that work was—for
quite a long time. It was also obvious that they had the
full support of most of the people of Dunlochan.
Lucas had the feeling he had become involved in
something far more than simple reiving, something
that may have even been behind that attempt to kill
him. If they were just reivers, he had to wonder why
they stayed so close to the ones they raided and
fought with. It was that alone that made him think it
was all something far more complicated and more
dangerous than simply raiding for food and coin.

His eyes widened as they approached a ruined
stone kirk. Lucas glanced back at the man who trot-
ted along behind them dragging a branch to disguise
their trail. The man's gaze was fixed upon the kirk
whenever he was not glancing around, looking for
any hint that their enemy had found them. It seemed
they were indeed headed for that roofless stone building. He held silent, reminding himself that these
people had snatched him from Ranald's murderous
grasp with an awe-inspiring skill, and had, thus far, revealed meticulous planning in their every move. Such
people did not choose hiding places too obvious or
too difficult to defend or escape from.

The moment they entered the kirk, his two cloaked
companions stopped and Lucas joined them in taking

a moment to catch his breath. His leg throbbed with pain but he forced himself to ignore it. Glancing around, Lucas realized the kirk was an ancient one and built to last for a very long time even without a roof. The stone walls had been decorated with a vast array of carvings that were obviously Christian yet carried a lingering flavor of paganism. Lucas watched as the larger of the two men moved to a shadowed corner and pressed his palm against the face of what looked to be one of the twelve apostles and pushed hard. A grating sound assaulted his ears and Lucas nearly gaped as the carving began to move, opening inward like a door. There was no room behind it, however, just what appeared to be a large black hole in the floor.

"Catacombs?" he asked softly as he edged closer.

"Aye," the small reiver replied, almost grunting out the reply as he lit a torch. "A veritable maze of them."

"Is this the only way in or out of them?" Lucas felt compelled to ask.

"Nay, there are two other routes."

That was good news but did not fully soothe the unease Lucas felt. He hated small, enclosed spaces. He suspected he was about to discover that large enclosed spaces with no fast route of escape would disturb him almost as much. Stiffening his spine he followed his short savior into the dark, struggling to climb down a wooden ladder without displaying too much awkwardness. When the larger man shut the door and followed him, Lucas smothered the urge to run back up that ladder and out into the open air.

The torch the small raider carried did not do much to cut the oppressive dark that enfolded them all. Lucas breathed a silent prayer of gratitude when the larger man lit a second torch and handed it to his small companion. He inwardly cursed when he looked around to find himself in a large burial chamber. Although not a particularly superstitious man he hoped this was not where they were going to be staying. Despite his distaste for small dark places Lucas was almost relieved when yet another hidden door was revealed and they started down some steep, narrow stone steps.

At the bottom of the steps they traveled several yards along a narrow tunnel before coming to yet another chamber. Here were tables and benches, a central hearth, and bedding. Glancing up as his companions lit several wall torches, Lucas saw two holes in the solid rock ceiling that allowed smoke out and air in. Either these people had worked very hard to make themselves a comfortable lair or the ancient holy men who had once occupied the kirk had done so.

Lucas looked at his companions and immediately forgot about asking where the other ways out of this tomb were located. They had removed their cloaks and the cloth masking their faces. The smaller one was no youth. He recognized that long, thick, honey-gold hair all too well. For a moment he felt choked with joy as he looked upon Katerina's sweet face and saw her smile, her wide dark blue eyes alight with welcome and happiness. Memories of their time together, the warmth of her kisses, and the softness of her skin swept over him. And it was all a lie, he thought, abruptly banishing every trace of pleasure he felt over the sight of her standing there alive and well and pretending she was glad to see him.

"They told me ye were dead," he said.

Something cold and hard in his voice halted Katerina's rush to hold him in her arms. For just a moment she had seen joy, wonder, and heated welcome in his beautiful silvery-blue eyes, but that was all gone now. Now Lucas looked distant, cold, and even angry. She began to feel increasingly uneasy. This re-union was not going as she had imagined it would.

"Aye, but those bastards didnae succeed in killing me, either," she said.

"And why would they e'en want to? Ye refused to pay them for a job weel done, did ye?"

"A job weel done? Ye think *I* ordered them to beat ye?"

Lucas shrugged. "Ye certainly seemed to be enjoying the show."

"They caught me as they caught you. They told me that if I stood there and said naught, did naught, they wouldnae kill you." The scornful noise he made cut her deeply.

"Ye made nary a whisper of protest e'en as they threw me o'er the cliff."

"I was too shocked! By the time I realized they truly meant to kill ye, it was too late to do anything, e'en protest. Ye were gone."

There was a catch in her husky voice that sliced through his fury and that made Lucas even angrier. He would not weaken again, would not allow the tears welling in her beautiful eyes to soften his heart and make him a fool. The important thing to find out now was just why she had saved him this time when a year ago she had tried to kill him.

"I cannae believe ye would think *I* had anything to do with that attack upon you. What reason could I have had to do such a thing?"

"The usual—jealousy."

"Jealousy? Ye think I would have a mon killed for that?"

"Ye had made it verra clear but a few hours earlier that ye were furious about the way Agnes wouldnae leave me be, that ye believed I was welcoming her fawning attentions."

"I would ne'er have ye beaten and killed for that!"

"Then what was your reason?"

Katerina just stared at him, unable to understand how he could believe such things about her. Then the pain she felt over his suspicions turned to anger. She had grieved for this man. All the time she had wept until she was weak and ill, he had thought her the cause of his pain and near death, judgments reached without any proof.

"Ye dinnae deserve this, but I will tell ye the truth this once. I had naught to do with what happened to you. 'Twas Agnes's order the men followed. They told me that if I stood silent, did not plead or weep or try anything to help you, they wouldnae kill ye. I did exactly as they asked because I wanted ye alive. Then they tossed ye over the cliff. Ere I had fully accepted the truth, that they had ne'er intended to let ye live, they threw me o'er after ye. Agnes didnae just want ye dead for spurning her, but me as weel."

"It appears ye recovered weel enough."

The way Katerina stared at him as if he was a complete stranger to her made Lucas uneasy. He had the unsettling feeling that he had just dealt her a heart-deep wound, but that made no sense. He had seen her, seen her standing there silent, dry-eyed, and unprotesting as he had been beaten and cut.

"Mayhap it just went further than ye had planned for," he began, abruptly silenced by the slashing movement she made with her hand.

"And mayhap ye ne'er kenned me at all. Mayhap I have spent all these months grieving o'er the loss of something that ne'er truly existed."

Before he could respond and hurt her even more, Katerina walked out of the chamber, leaving him alone with the other man, who watched him as if he was a complete lunatic.

Chapter Three

Lucas scowled at the man who sat across the fire from him. The only thing the man had said since Katerina had walked out was *I am William and I think ye may be too witless to live.* Although the insult stung, Lucas could only admire loyalty. This unrelenting silence, however, was becoming unendurable. Lucas had questions that needed answering and it was becoming obvious that Katerina was not soon to return to answer them.

"Where did she go?" Lucas finally asked.

"Away from ye," William answered, not even glancing up from his carving.

"I ken that weel enough, but where did that take her? Are there more rooms like this one?"

"There are a lot of rooms down here. Some are a goodly size, some nay more than a niche in the rock. There are passages and hollows running throughout this hill, right up to the back of Dunlochan keep itself."

"'Tis one great bolt-hole."

"Aye, for the holy men who used to abide here and for those within the keep. I am thinking 'tis a mixture of what has always been here, what was natural, and hundreds of years of hard work. This land certainly gives a mon many a reason to want a secure place to hide for a wee while."

"True. So, why are ye hiding here now?"

"Weel," William briefly looked at him and the look in his dark eyes was not particularly friendly, "it certainly isnae because of ye or what ye think she did."

"Ye didnae see her that day, didnae see how still and calm she was as Ranald and his dogs beat, kicked, and cut me. They told me she had ordered it done. Ranald himself whispered it in my ear as he cut my face. Said it was Katerina's plan to make sure I wasnae so bonnie any more and wouldnae find it so easy to play with a lassie's heart."

"And ye would believe a mon like Ranald o'er Lady Katerina? Wheesht, I think the bastards kicked ye in the head one too many times for 'tis certain that your wits are sadly scattered."

"If Katerina was so innocent why didnae she send word to my clan about what had happened to me?"

"And bring their wrath down upon the people of Dunlochan, most of whom had naught to do with it? She thought ye were dead and kenned that the Murray clan might seek blood to pay for the killing of ye. M'lady was fair surprised when nary a one of them came looking for ye." William paused in his carving to look at Lucas more closely. "Just how did ye survive and get away?"

"I can swim."

"Ah, the lass was that sure your leg had been broken."

"It was, but a mon can abide almost any pain if it means he doesnae drown. I crawled out of the water and kept right on crawling. Stopped only long enough to tend my wounds as best as I could and then headed home. There were good people along the way to give me aid." Lucas shrugged, loath to think much about pain-filled days and nights, the terror of feeling so help-less, and all the travails of traveling unarmed and unable to even hunt for food. He also did not want to explain how his twin had found him because of a dream because too many people found that bond be-tween twins a little hard to believe or tolerate. "I didnae notice Katerina looking for me either, and I would have been easy enough to track down and catch."

William shook his head. "She is right to say that ye ne'er truly kenned her. Did ye nay hear her say that they threw her in the loch as weel? Ah, I can see ye doubt the truth of it, but I will tell ye the tale anyway. They threw her in right after ye. Being that she is such a wee lass they were able to throw her farther than they did ye and she landed in the water, hitting only a few rocks when she went under. She nearly drowned. Ken-ning that she couldnae let the bastards see that she could swim and mayhap save herself, she swam be-neath the water as much as she could and made her way to a sheltered cove. Poor lass was fair battered to death upon the rocks there ere she could get to shore. We found her two days later, weak and feverish. Call-ing for ye, she was, but, of course, that must have been her just wanting to make certain ye were dead."

Lucas just cocked one eyebrow, ignoring the man's sarcasm and silently urging him to continue with his tale.

"She sent us all out to look for ye," William contin-ued, "but we couldnae find ye. It was nigh on two months ere she was healed of her wounds and the fever that nearly killed her. S'truth, for three weeks nearly the only sensible things she uttered were orders to find ye and let everyone believe she was dead."

"Why play that game?"

"Mayhap because someone obviously wants her dead?"

The man's continuing sarcasm truly grated on Lucas's temper, but he fought to endure it. He was finally getting some answers. They might not be the right ones or even the truth, but he could decide on all that later. Right now he needed to know just what he had stumbled into.

"Who does she think wants her dead?" Lucas asked William.

"That bitch of a half-sister she was cursed with, Agnes. She wants it all, ye ken."

"All what?"

"Did Lady Katerina nay tell ye about her father's will, his dying wishes and commands?"

"Nay, she didnae."

William sighed and shook his head. "Mayhap if she had ye wouldnae be so quick to think her guilty. The old laird, Katerina's father, chose five men to act as a council after he died, to hold final approval of any mon chosen by her or her half-sister. If the men dinnae approve of the mon and the lass chooses to wed him anyway, she loses. All she gets is a wee bothy and a bit of land on the far western edges of Dunlochan lands, and a verra wee dowry. The other lass gets all the rest. There is nary a doubt that the council would have approved of ye as a husband for our lady so Agnes had to be rid of ye. Can ye nay see now that our lady had no cause to do ye harm, that 'twas only to her benefit to keep ye alive so that ye might choose her as your wife?"

"Aye, but I can also see that, if Katerina thought I was turning to Agnes, it would be to her benefit to see me dead and gone."

A sharp curse escaped William, but then he shrugged and turned all of his attention back to his carving. "As I said, I begin to think ye too daft to live. After all, if the lass truly wished ye dead, all she had to do today was leave ye to Ranald and his dogs and just let the bastard finish what he had started a year ago. Mayhap ye ought to think on that for a wee while."

Lucas was thinking on it, but he would never admit it to William. It was the one thing that kept his doubts about Katerina's guilt alive and pestering him. What she had done for him today did not change what had happened that long ago night, he told himself firmly. Perhaps she had been tormented by guilt and regret while they had been apart and could no longer condone his murder. Lucas knew he would be staying with Katerina and her men for now and intended to use the time to find the answers he needed to uncover all the truth.

Wearied from weeping, Katerina slowly dragged herself off her bed and bathed her face in cold water. The very last thing she wanted was for Lucas to see that she had been weeping. She still felt stunned by his accusations, but she refused to let him know how deeply they had hurt her.

Her stomach rumbled, demanding food, and she knew she would have to return to the hall to get something to eat. That meant facing Lucas again and she dreaded it. The pain was still too fresh. So, too, she realized, was the anger his accusations had stirred within her. It was clear that all his sweet kisses, his passion, had been false or he never would have condemned her so. A little doubt she could understand and forgive, but not this cold condemnation. He did not even give her denials a moment of consideration. Katerina doubted that even showing him the many scars she had gathered that day would sway him. She would have trusted him with her very life, but it was now clear that he had never trusted her at all.

The problem was what to do now, she mused as she poured herself some wine. Sipping the wine, Katerina paced her small bedchamber and thought about the best way to handle Lucas. Her first inclination was to just ignore the man, to cut him from her heart and treat him as a complete stranger. It was a good plan, if only because she knew it would annoy him to be completely ignored, but Katerina decided she would not be able to hold to that plan for very long. She had never even been able to ignore Agnes for long and no one angered her as her half-sister did.

That left her with the choices of spitting his anger and mistrust right back at him or trying to convince him that he was utterly wrong in his suspicions. The former might relieve her of any bile stirred up by being thought so poorly of by the man she had given her heart and innocence to, but it would make life very difficult for her men. The latter sharply stung her pride. Why should she have to convince him of the truth just because he was too witless to see it? Of course, when he did finally see the truth, she would have the pleasure of gloating. Men did so hate to be wrong, she thought, and suspected Lucas would suffer even more because of what they had once meant to each other.

"And that is something it would be wise to forget," she muttered.

Especially since she may well have been utterly deceived in what she believed they had shared, she thought, and felt like weeping all over again. She ruthlessly buried the pain and tried to face the truth. The love she had thought she and Lucas shared may well have been a lie. Katerina knew she had loved him, and still did, fool that she was. However, what she had thought she had seen in Lucas may well have been no more than passion and they had certainly given in to that, short and glorious as it had been. Yet, even if she had discovered that Lucas did not love her and would soon leave her, she still would never have had him murdered and Lucas should know that. The fact that he could know her so little after what they had shared hurt, if only because it put all of his soft words and heated kisses into doubt, the memories of which she had treasured in the vain hope of easing her grief.

"Curse it, I but go round and round and make no decision," she snapped and abruptly finished off her wine.

Before she faced Lucas again she definitely needed a plan, however. Proving him wrong and having him have to apologize was a good plan but it was really not enough. After all, that left her with no plan for what to do after he had groveled in abject remorse. The battle against Agnes, Ranald, and their minions might not be over and she and Lucas might still have to deal with each other as well as the lust they had shared.

She still loved the fool, still wanted him, and she could not ignore that or try to lie to herself about it. Although she could no longer trust in her judgment about what Lucas felt for her, Katerina was certain that the hurt he had dealt her had not killed her love or desire for him. She had the chilling feeling that she was incurable. Even now a part of her hoped it was all some horrible mistake and when she met with Lucas again he would apologize and take her into his arms to kiss away the pain.

"Fool," she muttered and glared in the direction of the hall.

Then again, in his arms was where she truly wanted to be, she admitted to herself. If he finally saw the truth and gave her a pretty apology, there was no reason why she could not enjoy the passion they had shared so briefly once again. After all, she was no longer a maiden.

Katerina nodded and started out of her room. If Lucas came to see the truth and displayed an appropriate remorse, she would allow him to become her lover. She hesitated in her walk to the hall long enough to silence that fearful voice in her head that whispered that Lucas might no longer desire her. There was a year's worth of unsatisfied hunger in her and she wanted it fed. Katerina also knew that she still wanted Lucas to be so much more than her lover. It would just take time to see if she could trust in him again, in his passion, and in all his soft words of desire. It would also take time to trust in her own judgment again and to forgive him, she decided as she entered the hall and met his narrowed gaze.

The man was too handsome for any woman's peace of mind, she decided crossly as she approached the hearth and sat down next to William. A faintly ragged scar ran over his right cheek but it only added a touch of danger to his looks. He was still tall, lean, and strong despite the stiffness in his left leg that she had fleetingly noticed during the escape from Ranald and his men. The only real difference she could see at the moment was that there was no warmth in his silvery-blue eyes as he looked at her and no beguiling smile curved his sensuous mouth. When she realized she was staring at his slightly full bottom lip, thinking of how she would like to nibble on it, she gave herself a mental slap and scowled at him.

"Why are ye still here?" she demanded, accepting the bowl of rabbit stew William served her and refusing to acknowledge, even to herself, that she would have been devastated if Lucas had left while she had been indulging in self-pity and grief.

Lucas scowled right back at her and helped himself

to a bowl of stew. It annoyed him that upon seeing the faint evidence that Katerina had been crying, he had immediately wanted to take her into his arms and comfort her. If her guilt and shame troubled her it was none of his concern.

"It appears that ye and I have the same goal this time," he replied. "We both want Ranald dead."

Katerina inwardly winced at that blunt truth. She loathed the fact that she wanted a man dead, but could not deny that, in many ways, she did. The only way to be safe from Ranald was to bury the man. Ranald was not the sort of man to meekly accept any loss and, when she won the battle against Agnes, Ranald lost. The man liked the power he now wielded far too much to give it up without at least seeking revenge upon the ones who took that power away from him.

"True. If there is to be peace in Dunlochan again then Ranald must be slain."

"Because he betrayed you? Who does he obey now?"

"The same one he has always obeyed—Agnes. 'Tis because of her and all of her plots that Dunlochan is now under siege and we must hide inside this hill."

"Ye expect me to believe that Agnes has kept ye and your men running and hiding for a year? That lass hasnae the wit to do that. The only thing that lass can think about is men and gowns."

"Agnes rules Ranald and the two of them are cunning and cruel." Katerina shook her head. "I suspect my father thought as ye do, that Agnes was naught more than a witless girl whose only thoughts were for teasing and luring men and spending too much of his coin on gowns. To be certain, Agnes does spend far too much of her time pondering such useless things, but she is also cold and cruel. There is a hard, cold viciousness in Agnes that she hides weel from the men she seeks to enthrall. Her husband was bewitched for a while but he finally saw her for what she truly is. Sadly, it took the death of a maid he had flirted with to open his eyes."

"He saw Agnes kill a maid?"

"Nay, but he had nay doubt it was her doing. He hadnae e'en been unfaithful, had just exchanged a few smiles with the maid and a jest or two, but it cost the poor lass her life. I think Agnes had Ranald do it, that she and Ranald were already lovers. So did her husband Robbie. Robbie left soon after and hasnae been back since. Agnes has been hunting him, but I dinnae think it is for a loving reunion. Nay, she wants Robbie dead."

"Because the men your father chose as advisors dinnae approve of him?"

"Ye and William had a nice wee talk whilst I was gone, didnae ye."

Lucas found himself almost smiling at the look Katerina gave William, a look that cried the man a traitor. He quickly pushed aside that feeling. Katerina had always been able to make him smile, but Lucas now felt that was one reason he had never seen a hint of warning concerning her betrayal of him.

"He told me what *he* believes, aye," Lucas drawled.

That hurt, but Katerina just turned her scowl back on him. "Nay, they dinnae approve of Robbie. My father didnae, either. Robbie isnae a bad mon, but he isnae exactly what a father would want for his daughter. He is poor, a wee bit feckless, and a mon who would much rather talk or buy himself out of trouble than pick up a sword. I think their judgment harsh. There is good in Robbie and I believe he would have made Agnes a verra good husband if she had actually been interested in having one."

"Aye," agreed William, "but, mayhap, nay such a good laird for Dunlochan. Robbie didnae really want to be one, either. Far too much work for the lad."

"True." Katerina smiled briefly. "Far too much work. Unfortunately Robbie's lack of ambition is one reason Agnes now wants to be a widow. I e'en think she might be considering making Ranald her next husband."

"And the council would approve of such a mon?" Lucas asked in surprise.

"They might," replied Katerina, "but I am nay sure why. Fear, mayhap. They have to ken that Ranald would nay hesitate to kill them or their families if they tried to stop him from grasping the laird's seat. 'Tis easy to say aye or nay to a lass's choice of husband when the mon is no true threat to ye, isnae it."

"True. So why doesnae Agnes just claim that her husband is dead?"

"Because the council would require proof of it, if only the word of someone they dinnae recognize as one of Agnes's minions. The fact that Ranald hasnae been able to rid the area of those treacherous masked reivers," Katerina exchanged a fleeting grin with William, "has also made Agnes hesitate, I think. Ranald hasnae really proved his worth to her yet."

"Except in her bedchamber," William muttered.

"From what little I ken of it all, Robbie also proved his worth there but it didnae keep Agnes faithful to him nor has it made her hesitate in wanting him dead now." Katerina frowned as she thought over the whole situation with Agnes and Ranald for a moment. "I think Agnes is hoping she can wed with Ranald and grab hold of Dunlochan ere the council can make its objections heard."

"Then silence them so that their objections can ne'er be heard?" Lucas asked.

"Something like that. Although it wouldnae be easy, for they are weel born men and have important friends and kinsmen."

It was almost impossible for Lucas to believe the fair-haired, giggling Agnes could be capable of such cold cunning. He had not spent much time with the woman, had actually done his best to avoid her, but he had seen no hint of such a cold, vicious nature. Then again, he had never suspected such a nature in Katerina and that blindness had nearly cost him his life. Or, he was utterly wrong in what he thought had happened that long ago day by the loch, a soft, coaxing voice whispered in his mind. Lucas ruthlessly silenced that voice. No one had yet shown him any reason to believe Katerina was innocent, that she was, perhaps, as much a victim as he had been.

"Are the others coming here tonight, William?" Katerina asked her cousin.

"Nay, not until much later," William replied. "Ranald is taking longer and longer to give up the hunt when he pursues us and we dinnae want him finding our bolt-hole."

Katerina nodded, grateful for such caution, yet deeply disturbed by the need for it. Ranald was becoming far more tenacious than he had ever been in the beginning of this battle. The man's determination to put an end to their forays against him had grown with each defeat he had suffered at their hands. Katerina did not need to hear the man's threats and curses to know that Ranald wanted them all dead. Agnes undoubtedly had the same desire. The danger for her and her men, even their allies, grew each time they rode out yet Katerina knew there was no choice. The battle for Dunlochan had not been won yet. Katerina was growing fearful that it could never be won.

As she took the men's now empty bowls to clean

them, Katerina thought about the last year. It had been one long, hard, continuous battle, first to survive Ranald's attempt to murder her, and then to try and regain all that had been stolen from her by the endlessly greedy Agnes. An anger born of the grief she had felt over Lucas had sustained her, but now she knew Lucas had not died and she felt weary of it all.

"If everyone thinks ye are dead, why hasnae Agnes just grabbed hold of Dunlochan?" asked Lucas when Katerina returned to the hearth bringing a full wineskin with her.

"She has," Katerina replied. "She and Ranald. Only the council my father chose ere he died stops Agnes from openly declaring herself laird of it all and doing everything a laird can. The council uses the fact that our father didnae approve of Robbie as the reason they cannae declare her the laird. A woman cannae truly be a laird, can she, not in the eyes of most men, and they rule the world. Agnes needs the mon, a husband, to help her hold fast to her inheritance and wield the power she hungers for. E'en the king wouldnae take her side in this. So, a lot of power still rests in the council's hands, although they dinnae really seem to use it to rid us of Ranald."

"Mayhap they ken that, if they push too hard, they will sign their own death warrants."

"I suspicion that is just what they think."

"Then I think ye must needs do more than just irritate the mon as ye have been doing."

"Ye dinnae ken anything about what we have been doing here."

"Ye ride out to stop the mon from killing someone and to harass him and Agnes with thieving, aye?"

Katerina had the strong urge to hit Lucas with something very heavy. He had just reduced all their efforts to what sounded like a child's game. She knew they were simply holding steady, simply staying alive and saving a few people here and there, but there was little else they could do until she got proof of Agnes and Ranald's crimes.

"I need to prove that Agnes and Ranald are guilty of more than simply making life miserable for everyone. I need to prove they have blood on their hands. 'Tis no easy thing to do. At best I may yet catch them at something that will bestir the council to act."

"Ye need to push harder. Ye strike and run and he chases. Ye need to make the mon bleed."

Out of the corner of her eye she could see William nodding in agreement. "He could easily make us bleed," she said. "'Tis something I must consider every step of the way."

"There is that risk. Howbeit, unless ye push him hard and unrelentingly, he willnae make that mistake ye are waiting for. Ye need to lessen the number of men he has at his command and in a way that makes fewer and fewer men want to stand with him. Ye need to set him and Agnes against each other, e'en if it is only by making her openly question his competency. Ye need to corner the beast. Ye need to push his back hard against a wall and keep a blade at his throat."

"Until he impales himself on it?"

"Aye."

"How clever of ye. Weel, while ye make your fine plans, I believe I will make up a list of the supplies we need and go fetch them."

"From where?"

"Why, straight from the lair of the beast. Where else?"

Lucas heard the word *fool* as clearly as if Katerina shouted it.

Chapter Four

"I dinnae believe I asked ye to accompany me."

Lucas lifted his gaze from watching Katerina's hips sway as she walked and almost smiled. The lad's clothes she wore could not disguise her almost voluptuous curves. She might be small in stature, almost a foot shorter than his six feet plus, but she was all woman. He had resented the desire he still felt for her at first but no longer. Any man would desire Katerina. It was only a man's natural inclination he suffered from, he told himself firmly. Perhaps if he ceased accusing her of trying to kill him, they could revisit that passion they had shared for far too brief a time. He would, of course, make sure she was not armed when they indulged themselves.

"Ye cannae go into the lion's den alone," he said, "and William has to wait for the others to return." He thought about how Ranald was searching for the reivers, searching hard enough to keep the rest of Katerina's men from seeking the shelter of the caves. "Are ye sure this is a good time to go into the keep and steal some food?"

"Ranald would ne'er think to look for us right inside the keep."

"But if someone sees—" He barely stopped himself from walking into her when she abruptly stopped and whirled around to glare at him.

"Listen, Sir Murray, I and my men have done fine without your aid for a year." Katerina knew she was spitting her words out from between tightly gritted teeth, but there was no chance that she could conceal her anger from him this time. "We thank ye for deciding to join with us, to contribute your great strength and fighting skills, but I dinnae believe any of us declared ye the leader of us all. So, mayhap ye could keep your opinions to yourself."

Lucas had the inane thought that Katerina was lovely when she was angry, and then quickly shook it out of his head. "Ye havenae won, have ye?"

"We havenae lost, either."

"And ye are content to let this battle continue to drag on like this? To continue to nip at Ranald and flee his retribution until ye destroy Dunlochan?"

Katerina desperately wanted to hit him—repeatedly. Instead of her anger causing the man to back down, he pummeled her with hard questions. Worse, his questions revealed that he could clearly see all that was wrong with the fight she was locked into. It *was* destroying Dunlochan. A quick, decisive win was desperately needed, but she could not see any way to get one, not without causing far more bloodshed than she could stomach. She ruefully admitted to herself that, if Lucas gave her that much-needed decisive victory, a part of her would be eternally grateful. Another part of her, one ruled quite firmly by her pride, would undoubtedly want to inflict some severe, painful injury upon him.

"We are doing our best to stop Ranald from destroying Dunlochan and benefiting from it." She turned away from him and started on her way again. "When this fight is over he and Agnes will have nothing, mayhap not e'en their lives, but I will hold Dunlochan and my men will still be alive."

"'Tis admirable that ye dinnae wish the men who fight with ye to suffer or die, but no battle can be completely bloodless. Nay, not if it is to be won."

That was a hard cold truth she had no wish to study too closely. The men who rode with her were her people, her kinsmen, and her friends. Several times, as she had tended to wounds received during a raid, she had seriously considered giving it all up. The burden of keeping her men alive and trying to rid Dunlochan of men like Ranald often grew so heavy Katerina felt crushed by it. The only thing that kept her struggling onward was the certainty that Agnes and Ranald would never let her rest. They would never trust her to simply accept her meager inheritance, accept all her losses, or accept their attempt to kill her. They would never believe that she would simply live peacefully on the little piece of land and the small cottage her father had left to the loser in the battle for the rule over Dunlochan. They would kill her and anyone foolish enough to stand with her.

And why that thought should suddenly make her so afraid for Lucas, Katerina did not know. The man did not deserve her concern. He was obviously one of those men who believed that, if anything went wrong in his life, it had to be the fault of some woman. She was surprised she had not seen that in him until now, but suspected his fine looks and her desire for him had hidden a lot of his faults from her.

"I fully intend to win this battle, Sir Murray, *and* without turning the land red with the blood of my kinsmen or friends," she said, once she was sure he would not hear any of her own lack of confidence in her voice. "Mayhap we have just been testing Ranald's strengths and the skill of his hirelings ere we make our final strike against him."

Lucas snorted, his disbelief clear to hear in the rude sound. He could tell by the way Katerina clenched her small hands into tight, white-knuckled fists that she was furious, but when she just continued to walk, he decided it was safe to ignore her anger. It was undoubtedly foolish of him to join Katerina's small army, but since he was now part of it, he was eager for the battle to be won. Katerina was very skilled at slapping Ranald swiftly and sharply, but she had yet to succeed in knocking the man down. Her men had to be as eager to put an end to the battle as he was, yet Lucas suspected few complained openly, so the plans never changed. It was past time they did so.

What angered him at the moment was *what* fed his eagerness to get Katerina to heed him and start fighting Ranald, *really* fighting the man. Lucas's own deep need to make Ranald pay for beating him and trying to kill him was definitely part of his eagerness, but not all of it. He had to face the fact that he did not like Katerina constantly putting her life at risk, and that angered him. Part of his reason for returning to Dunlochan was to make her suffer for her part in what had happened to him. It hardly made sense to then start worrying that she might get hurt. A desire for her that he could not kill had obviously rattled his wits.

"Where does Ranald hide when he isnae chasing ye or grinding the people of Dunlochan under his boot?" he asked even as he noticed that the passage they traveled in was beginning to slowly wind upward. He struggled not to think too much on how deep in the earth they were.

"With Agnes, of course," Katerina replied after sternly telling herself it would be childish to ignore the man when he had asked a very reasonable question.

"They openly commit adultery?"

"Weel, they arenae rolling about in the heather for all to see, but they arenae really secretive. Agnes declares herself a widow e'en though near everyone about here kens verra weel that her husband fled her side. They also ken that no one has actually brought word that the mon is dead."

"And no one acts against her or Ranald for sinning so openly?"

"Wheesht, dinnae ye sound so verra pious," Katerina murmured, casting a fleeting glance at Lucas over her shoulder.

"My family frowns upon such a thing, true enough, but I was speaking of ones like the men on that council, or the women who consider themselves the righteous ones. Every village has some of those and they dinnae abide anything that e'en hints at sin."

"Ah, aye, *those* women. Nay, few here speak on the matter aloud. The fear Ranald likes to breed in people has spread wide and settled in deep and hard. There are many who see Agnes as being just as bad, just as dangerous, as Ranald. So, nay, naught is said and naught is done, e'en when Agnes turns her lustful gaze upon another mon, and then another, and then—"

"I believe I understand. Although I am a wee bit surprised that Agnes would dare to be unfaithful to Ranald. It could prove verra dangerous."

"Oh, he doesnae like it, but he can have no power in Dunlochan without her. He isnae faithful to her, either. Ne'er was. Ranald feels it his right to take any woman he wants. I worry about Annie at the alehouse. Ranald wants her, but, so far, he has not taken her as he has others."

Although Katerina did not say the word *rape*, Lucas had no trouble understanding that that was what she meant. He had a deep loathing for men who brutalized women. It was just another reason to make very certain that Ranald did not escape justice. Lucas was a little surprised that Agnes had anything to do with the man, but he was beginning to realize he had misjudged the woman. For reasons he could not understand he believed most of what Katerina said about her half-sister. The only thing he doubted was that Agnes could be as cunning as Katerina believed her to be. The few times he had dealt with the woman he had certainly not gained any sense that there was much intelligence behind Agnes's big blue eyes.

The insidious thought that some of Katerina's anger at Agnes might be due to the fact that the woman was bedding Ranald slipped into Lucas's mind and he inwardly cringed. Despite all he suspected Katerina of, he found that hard to believe. The ugly surge of jealousy that gripped him at the thought of Katerina and Ranald together surprised and dismayed him. Lucas did not want to care who Katerina gave her favors to.

A soft noise yanked him from his dark thoughts. Instinct ruling him, Lucas grabbed Katerina by the arm, yanked her back, and shoved her between him and the rocky side of the passage, even as he drew his sword. Someone was moving stealthily toward them down the passageway. Katerina and her men had been safe within all the caverns and passages for a full year, but it only took one mistake to steal that safety away. The man who came into view a moment later was tall, almost too thin, and looked as alarmed as Lucas had briefly felt. Lucas did nothing to stop the man from drawing his sword.

"'Tis only Patrick," Katerina said, pushing at Lucas's back and softly cursing when the man did not move an inch.

"*Only* Patrick?" the young man muttered and peered around Lucas to look at Katerina. "Are ye unharmed, m'lady?"

"Aside from being pressed right into the rock by this hulking brute, aye," Katerina replied.

"One of your men, is he?" asked Lucas.

"Aye, one of mine," Katerina answered. "Now, would ye please move? I cannae breathe."

Lucas kept a close watch on Patrick all the while he slowly sheathed his sword. Patrick returned the compliment by keeping a close eye on Lucas as he did the same. The man's dark blue eyes held the same wariness Lucas felt. It was only Katerina pushing hard at his back and cursing him softly that ended the silent weighing of strengths and weaknesses between him and Patrick. Lucas wondered why the man's tall, fair-haired handsomeness should irritate him so much.

A heartbeat later he knew exactly why when Patrick smiled at Katerina. Worse, Katerina smiled back at Patrick. The feelings stirring to life inside of Lucas carried the strong taint of jealousy and the very last thing he wanted was to feel possessive toward Katerina. The fact that he had felt the same way only moments ago told him he might be losing that battle. Lucas struggled to fix his mind on the fight against Ranald and Agnes and only that.

"'Tis good to see that ye have returned safely. And unharmed?" asked Katerina.

"Quite unharmed," replied Patrick, and then he cast a quick look at Lucas. "It appears Sir Murray wasnae quite dead yet."

Katerina laughed and shook her head. "Nay, not yet. He is thinking he will join us in our fight against Ranald."

"Nay *thinking*," said Lucas, "but *planning* to. As I have said, I too want Ranald dead."

Seeing how Katerina winced at that blunt statement, Patrick patted her on the arm. "It has to be done, m'lady. Ye ken it weel e'en if we do all avoid saying so bluntly. Who else has returned?"

"None that we saw. Ye are the first. William waits in the hall for the others."

"And what are ye about to do? Ye are nay thinking of going out and looking for any of the others, are ye? If they are staying away 'tis because it is still too dangerous to come here, the risk of being seen and captured too high."

"Nay, I dinnae plan to venture outside. I go to gather us some much-needed supplies, that is all, so ye may cease bristling and go join William."

The moment Patrick left, Katerina started on her way again. She desperately needed to put some distance between herself and Lucas. Despite the roughness of his actions in his efforts to protect her, she had been deeply stirred by the feel of his body pressed so close to hers. Even the hard, cold stone wall against her back had not cooled the sudden rush of heat in her veins. It was sad, she decided, when a woman could be aroused by being pressed hard against rock by a man who thought her capable of brutally murdering him just because she was jealous.

Suddenly, it did not seem such a good idea to accept Lucas as her lover. The feelings she had for him were still so fierce, ran so bone deep, Katerina knew she would be risking a great deal of pain. She should not have forgotten how she had felt when she had believed he was dead. It had torn her apart, left a gaping wound where her heart should be, and it had been many long months before she had been able to push some of that pain aside. If Lucas and she became lovers and he continued to believe she had had some part in the attack upon him, then they would just be using each other to scratch an itch. She might find that acceptable, despite the punishment her pride would have to endure, but she now suspected that would not last long and she would soon be wallowing in her own pain again. Lucas, on the other hand, could simply walk away at any time.

And, yet, what choice did she have? She thought as she eased open the door to the storerooms deep beneath Dunlochan keep. Despite wanting to do violence to the man for his insulting accusations, Katerina knew she would not be able to resist another taste of the desire that had always flared between them. She inwardly shrugged. She had survived all attempts to kill her; she had survived thinking the only man she had ever loved had died and left her alone; she would survive the fact that the man she loved and desired was a blind idiot who might just use her and walk away. If they did become lovers, she would try to gather up as many heated memories as she could and then stand dry of eye as he walked away. It was all she could do to salvage her pride. That was one thing she would not allow Lucas Murray to destroy.

"Are we below Dunlochan now?" Lucas whispered as he followed her into the room lit by only one small torch set high on the stone wall.

"Aye. What we want should be over here."

Lucas followed her into a shadowy corner of the room and nearly gaped. Piled there was a very large collection of food and drink. Someone inside the keep was obviously helping Katerina by secretly setting aside some supplies, probably little by little every day. As a warrior, Lucas could not stop himself from wondering exactly how they might use such allies to defeat Ranald and Agnes.

Seeing how Lucas scowled at her supplies, Katerina carefully placed her list of things she needed in the hiding place she and the cook had agreed on so long ago. Neither of them had thought it would take so long for Katerina to win back Dunlochan. Poor old Hilda still believed in her, probably more than Katerina believed in herself, but she suspected the woman was growing weary of waiting to be free of Agnes's harsh rule.

"Just how has this come to be here ready for ye to walk away with it all?" Lucas asked, keeping his voice as soft as Katerina kept hers.

"Ah, weel, Old Hilda, the cook, and a few others slowly gather it up. When we take it we always leave a wee message telling them what we think we might need soon."

"Doesnae anyone notice how much is going missing from the stores?"

"Nay. Can ye truly see Agnes or Ranald keeping records or tallying anything at all save for the money in their purses? I doubt they e'en think on where it all comes from. Not e'en Agnes's woman, Freda, tends to *how* the things they want are acquired, only that they are delivered into her hands exactly when she wants them. 'Tis *my* people who diligently tend to such things as these stores and the ledgers. 'Tis another good reason for me to continue to play dead. If Agnes or Ranald kenned that I was still alive, a lot of my people would be in grave danger. They would immediately come under suspicion and that could easily mean their deaths."

"Ye have planned for that, havenae ye." Lucas did not make it a question for he knew she would have made meticulous plans for the safety of such people. Considering what he believed she had done to him such confidence did not make much sense, but he shrugged aside that puzzle as he picked up a heavy sack of food. "There is a lot here. Ye could ne'er have carried it all back on your own."

"Nay, not in one journey, true enough." Katerina shrugged. "I had little else to do aside from waiting for my men to return. A few trips back and forth 'twixt here and the hall wouldnae hurt me."

"The people who do this for ye could be verra useful in other ways."

Katerina sighed, all too aware of what he was thinking of for she had often considered the very same thing. "They could be, but using them for anything aside from gathering food and information for us could get them killed. Most of them are verra young or old. They arenae warriors and some have no ability to become ones. They are cooks, clerks, pot boys, and the like. Verra good at listening since people like Agnes ne'er e'en see them, and verra good at making ten meat pies but serving only eight, slipping the other two aside for us. E'en that small but valuable service puts them at risk."

Lucas nodded in agreement. "There may come a time, however," he began.

"When the risk is worth it," she finished for him. "I ken it and so do they."

The sound of a foot sliding over stone drew Lucas's attention. Again he pushed Katerina behind him as they both crouched behind the stacked barrels. Afraid the sound of him drawing his sword would echo too loudly in the room, he slowly drew his dagger. The glow of candlelight came first followed by a plump, gray-haired woman who paused in the entrance to the room and nervously looked around.

"'Tis Hilda the cook," Katerina whispered even as she wriggled out from behind Lucas and stood up. "O'er here, Hilda."

"Oh, bless ye, child," Hilda said as she hurried over and gave Katerina a brief, one-armed hug. "I have been slipping down here whene'er possible just hoping to catch ye. I was getting ready to try and hunt ye down." Hilda's eyes widened as Lucas stood up and stepped closer to Katerina. "Oh, have mercy, he is alive!"

Quickly putting an arm around Hilda's shoulders to steady the woman when she swayed, Katerina said, "Aye, and he means to make Ranald pay for what he did to him."

Katerina knew Lucas intended to make her pay, too, but she did not say so. She needed full cooperation amongst her allies. Telling Hilda, who had been like a mother to her, about Lucas's suspicions would set the woman firmly against him. That was a trouble she did not want to deal with at the moment.

"Weel, how wondrous, and it ne'er hurts to have another strong sword arm when ye are in such a hard fight." Hilda eyed the monk's robes Lucas wore. "Unless—have ye joined the church?"

"Nay," replied Lucas. "I thought it a good disguise." He could tell by the woman's expression that she most certainly did not agree with him.

"Weel, 'tis God's blessing that ye survived those bastards."

"Verra true," Katerina agreed. "What did ye need to see me for, Hilda?"

"Ranald is suspicious about young Thomas, I fear. The lad disappears a lot and does it when ye ride. Ranald has finally taken notice of that. He feels he ought to bring the laddie here and beat some truth out of him."

Already planning on how to bring young Thomas to safety, Katerina asked, "But Ranald hasnae decided on doing that just yet?"

"*He* has, but Agnes hasnae. She isnae sure Ranald is right and she frets o'er how acting against the lad could rouse people's anger against her. Fool woman doesnae seem to see that almost every mon, woman, and bairn at Dunlochan already loathes and mistrusts her. I but needed to warn ye for I think Ranald will soon convince her of the need to grab Thomas. Especially if, weel," she looked at Lucas, "if she learns that this mon is still alive."

"She will learn that as soon as Ranald returns this night, for he tried to kill Lucas again and we snatched away his prize." Katerina kissed Hilda on the cheek. "Thank ye, Hilda. I must go quickly now and see to Thomas's safety."

"Godspeed, child."

Grabbing up all they could carry, Lucas and Katerina hurried back to the hall. Lucas could almost feel Katerina's fear as she nearly ran through the passages. He was not sure what could be done to help the boy but he knew she would try something. Lucas also knew that he would not let her go alone. That need to keep her safe made no sense to him, but he was beginning to think a lot of what he felt and thought concerning Katerina Haldane made no sense.

"What has happened?" William demanded, alarmed by the way Katerina and Lucas rushed into the hall.

"Ranald has become suspicious of Thomas," Katerina replied as she set aside the sacks of supplies.

William and Patrick cursed. "Then we have to try to get to the boy before he does," William said.

"There are only four of us," Patrick pointed out quietly.

"It will have to be enough," said Katerina. "We cannae let Ranald get his hands on the boy."

"Nay, of course we cannae, but do we have a plan?"

Katerina rubbed at her forehead, trying to ease the

ache that was beginning there. "Nay, and I am nay sure we can make one until we ken where Thomas is and if Ranald is already hunting him. Hilda said Agnes hadnae agreed with Ranald's plan to grab Thomas and beat some truth out of him, but after what happened tonight, Ranald may nay care about that."

"Where does Thomas live?" asked Lucas.

"At the inn," replied Katerina. "He is Annie's brother and they both live at the inn. She has a wee room in the eaves, but, unless 'tis verra cold, Thomas stays in the stables with his beloved horses."

"'Tis nay the easiest place to creep up on, but 'tisnae impossible. The night can hide a great deal. I walked into Ranald's hands, foolishly thinking my disguise was good enough to hide me. This time we all ken that our enemy may be there."

"True, but so will many of his men, I suspect."

"Is there any choice?"

"Nay, there isnae. I but wonder about Annie. Hilda didnae say Annie was in trouble, but if Ranald cannae get his hands on Thomas—"

"Then he will grab Annie and use her to bring the boy to him."

"That is what I am afraid of."

"It is probably just what will happen," said Patrick. "I can get Annie if the rest of ye go after Thomas."

"Ye can get into the inn unseen?" Katerina's eyes widened with surprise when Patrick blushed.

"I can. I used to be verra friendly with Morag ere she ran off with that traveler last spring. I ken just how to get into the inn without being seen." He shrugged. "She didnae want anyone to ken that she had lovers so she always made the men she bedded down with creep about like thieves. Sorry, m'lady," he mumbled.

"Dinnae apologize. I kenned what Morag was. I just

didnae ken ye were one of her lovers. Weel, it will serve us weel now. Ye get Annie out of there and we will do what we can to get Thomas."

"Ye dinnae think we should wait until more of our men return?" asked William even as he collected his sword.

"I dinnae think we can afford to waste any time e'en in such a good cause. Ranald is going to be enraged o'er the fact that he lost the chance to kill Lucas again."

"And he will be eager to take that rage out on someone." William sighed. "Ah, weel, Thomas has been a great help, as has Annie. We cannae let them suffer for it."

"Agreed. So, 'tis back to the village, only this time we cannae make such a fine show of it."

"I hope ye arenae suggesting we walk to the village."

"Nay all the way."

Katerina actually found herself smiling when she heard the three men groan, but it was a fleeting moment of lightheartedness. Her heart felt as if it was cramped with fear for young Thomas and his sister. Until she got them safely out of the reach of the brutal Ranald she doubted she would be able to breathe easily. Too many had already paid dearly in this battle with Agnes and she refused to let her half-sister and her lover claim another life.

Chapter Five

Katerina watched Patrick slip away into the shadows near the inn and bit back the urge to call him back. This was dangerous, more dangerous than anything they had attempted before. She had to keep reminding herself that it would be much more dangerous if they had to try and rescue Thomas or Annie from Dunlochan keep, perhaps even impossible. The storerooms and a few hidden passages she had discovered as a child were the only places she could reach unseen. Beyond that, moving about Dunlochan keep became very perilous indeed.

The hardest thing about being a warrior, she decided, was trying not to fear for each and every man under her command. Katerina knew she was going to be happy beyond words to give up that command. William could take full control of such things once she regained possession of Dunlochan and do so with her full blessing. She did find some strength in the knowledge that, if he was the one giving the orders, he would be doing just what she was doing now. No one with any conscience could allow Thomas and Annie to fall into Ranald's brutal grasp.

"If Patrick says he can slip in and out of the inn without being seen, then he can," William said quietly.

Smiling fleetingly over his attempt to soothe her, Katerina nodded. "I ken it. It doesnae stop me from fearing something could go wrong, however. But, now, 'tis best if we turn our attention to the matter of getting into the stables unseen."

"And getting out with Thomas the same way."

"Aye, that would be best." She glanced at Lucas, who crouched next to her, pressed a little too closely on her right. "Can ye run fast, Sir Murray?"

Lucas winced, even though every instinct detected no mockery or contempt of his limp in her tone, just a need for facts as she planned her next move. "For a short distance and with little grace," he answered bluntly.

"A short distance will do, Sir Murray."

The way she kept calling him *Sir Murray* was beginning to make his teeth hurt from clenching them in rising aggravation. It was an attempt to make him feel a complete stranger, and, perhaps, to make her feel that he was as well. Lucas knew it should not trouble him if she wanted to play that game, but it did. Worse, it stung in a way he did not feel it ought to. He could all too clearly recall the way she had spoken his name when desire held her tight in its grip and he wanted to hear it again.

He inwardly shook his head as if to cast such thoughts aside. If they did become lovers, Lucas was determined to keep it all a simple matter of a man scratching an itch. Thoughts of how she had once breathed his name against his skin, how that had warmed his blood nearly to boiling, would make that impossible.

Forcing his thoughts back to the matter at hand, he asked, "Are ye expecting Ranald to come soon?"

"Aye," Katerina replied. "He has become more persistent in trying to track us down, but his temper makes it hard for him to be truly patient. If he hasnae already given up the chase, he will soon. Then he will be after Thomas. Usually he and Agnes agree on what must be done, or she orders it done, but I dinnae think we can count on that now. Ranald must ken that he is losing his place in Agnes's plans, that every time he lets the reivers escape, she doubts him even more. He will be eager for something to help him hold fast to his place in her plans, anything, nay matter how small or what crimes he might have to commit to get it."

"Then let us hurry and get the lad out of danger."

Silently they crept through the shadows toward the stables. Katerina prayed this was not one of the few nights Thomas decided he did not want to sleep with the horses. Despite their dark clothes and staying in the shadows, Katerina felt as if they were in clear view of anyone who wished to look their way. She could feel a thin line of sweat trail down her spine and was heartily grateful when they finally slipped into the stable without anyone crying out in recognition or alarm.

"Since the two of ye are far better with a sword than I, I will go up into the loft and get Thomas," Katerina whispered. "Ye can guard my back."

Lucas watched her nimbly climb the rough ladder to the loft. His body tightened with desire as he watched the way her taut, nicely rounded backside moved with each step. He was glad of the robes he still wore as they hid the blatant evidence of his desire. No matter how often he considered the risks of becoming involved with Katerina in any way, his body continued to make its interest painfully clear. If he was going to stay with her and her men for any length of time, he knew he had better come to some decision about her and his attraction for her or he would undoubtedly do something foolish.

Katerina heard Thomas before she saw him. The boy snored softly and she crept toward the sound. Cautiously placing a hand on his shoulder, knowing how some people could wake from a sound sleep with fists flying, she gave him a little shake. She almost smiled when he opened his eyes, stared at her blindly for a moment, and then blushed. Since he was obviously fully dressed beneath a thin blanket, she suspected he had been pulled out of the sort of dream he did not want her to even guess at.

"M'lady, what is wrong?" he asked as he sat up and pushed his thick, fair hair out of his face. "Is Annie hurt?"

She knew he had long feared that Ranald or one of his men would rape Annie as they had other women, and Katerina hurried to reassure him. "Nay, but 'tis time for ye and your sister to hide away, Thomas. Ranald has become suspicious of you." Although his only response to that was to grow very pale, she nodded as if he had spoken aloud. "Naught was said about Annie, but, if Ranald cannae get hold of ye, we fear he may try to get her."

Thomas nodded vigorously as he stood up and rolled up his blanket. When he stuck his hands beneath the hay that had served as his bed and tugged out a sack of belongings, Katerina realized the boy had clearly foreseen a time when he might have to leave quickly. It saddened her that any of her people should have to live in readiness of fleeing his home, but, at the moment, she was glad of the boy's preparations.

"I can fetch Annie in but a moment," Thomas said.

"There is nay need. Patrick has gone to get her as

he said he could slip in and out of the inn without being seen."

"Ah, aye. He used to come to see Morag."

"So, he obviously wasnae completely unseen."

"Oh, I suspicion he was. I only saw him once when he was leaving. Kenned he was visiting Morag because she liked to boast about it." He waited until Katerina started down the ladder before tossing his sack down to William and then following her. "Does Sir Murray want to take his horse back now?" he asked as he nimbly jumped down the last few rungs of the ladder the moment Katerina had stepped off it.

"Aye, Sir Murray would verra much like to take his horse back," replied Lucas before Katerina could reply or even consider the matter.

Katerina looked toward Lucas, who was leading his now saddled horse out of its stall. "I dinnae think we can slip something that size out of here without being seen."

"Eachann can be verra quiet."

"Eachann cannae be *small* and quiet. A small shadow can escape the eye. A shadow the size of a gelding isnae so easy to ignore."

"If Ranald isnae right outside the inn, I can show Sir Murray a way to slip the horse out of the village," said Thomas.

"Are ye certain of that, Thomas?" Katerina asked. "We have come to save ye from Ranald. I dinnae want ye to fall into his brutal hands just because Sir Murray wants his horse."

"I willnae. I have slipped a horse or two out of the village before."

"I willnae ask why ye would do so."

"Might be best," Thomas murmured, but he grinned.

Katerina looked at Lucas and could tell that he was

determined to take his horse with him. She had learned at a very young age that men could be very attached to their horses. It was also clear that he was not really waiting for her to say aye or nay, but readying himself to leave. She supposed now was not the time to remind him of who was the leader of this band.

"We shall meet at the place where Old Ian met us earlier," she finally said. "By then I will have thought of some place where we can put the beast. Take care," she said to Thomas as he eagerly swung up into the saddle behind Lucas.

She watched Lucas leave through the back of the stable and wondered why she felt like sighing heavily. The concern she felt over Thomas and Annie had obviously disordered her mind. Katerina followed William out of the stable, annoyed at the way she continuously listened for some sound that would indicate Lucas and Thomas were in trouble and might need her help.

Patrick and Annie were waiting for them at the edge of the village, drawing Katerina's thoughts away from Lucas. Annie needed to be reassured that Thomas was safe with Lucas and Katerina began to feel tense, knowing they were taking a lot longer to accomplish their task than she wanted to. When they were finally headed back toward what she now had to call home, she breathed a sigh of relief only to nearly choke on it when she heard the approach of several riders.

Some of her fear eased as both Patrick and William acted swiftly, silently, and competently. Patrick grabbed the reins of Annie's horse and William moved to ride with Katerina. Going in two directions, they all moved deeper into the shadows afforded by the many trees allowed to grow at the far end of the village. Katerina watched a group of seven men ride toward the village and knew they were Ranald and his men even before she heard his voice.

"I grow verra weary of chasing these bastards all o'er Dunlochan," Ranald said, his voice hoarse with anger.

"They are verra good at hiding their trail," said Colin, Ranald's closest companion in arms.

"No one can be that good without help, Colin. No one. These bastards are getting help and I mean to find out who and how."

"Ye think someone in the village is helping the reivers?"

"Aye, more than one and I also think these curs are far more than just reivers. If that little bitch was still alive I would think she was behind all this."

"Lady Katerina? But, a woman—"

"A woman can be as cunning as any mon. Dinnae forget whom we work for. Mayhap some fools do this in her memory. I dinnae ken but I mean to find out. I intend to start with that little cur Thomas."

"I thought Lady Agnes didnae want ye to do anything to the boy."

"She will change her mind once the little bastard starts telling us all he kens about these reivers. Aye, and mayhap I can use him to make his sister lift her skirts."

Katerina was tempted to follow the men when they rode past, moving out of her hearing. It was not often that she had such a good chance of finding out Ranald's plans. The man was surprisingly incautious about where he talked about his and Agnes's plans. Common sense ruled, however, and she joined the others in silently slipping away. She noticed that Annie looked very pale, a few tears visible on her cheeks in the faint light cast by a shrinking moon. The young woman may have come with them simply because Patrick had said she should, but now Annie fully understood the danger her brother was in and, quite rightly, it obviously terrified her.

Lucas and Thomas were waiting at the arranged meeting place, as was Old Ian. Leaving the horses to the care of the old man and his sons, Katerina led the others into the caves. It was not going to be easy having a youth and a pretty woman staying with them, but there was no choice. The moment they entered the well-lit hall, Katerina also realized that someone should have told Annie that she was not dead, for the moment Katerina pushed back the hood of her cloak, the young woman took one horrified look at her and fainted into Patrick's arms. Patrick, the rogue, grinned like a fool.

"Thomas!" Katerina hurried to get some cloths and water to bathe Annie's face after Patrick settled the unconscious woman on the table. "Didnae ye tell your sister that I hadnae died?"

"Nay, ye said it was a secret," he replied as he moved close to the table to stare at his sister in concern. "I gave my word to tell no one and my sister is someone, aye?"

"I hadnae meant your own sister."

"When I talked to her at the inn, she spoke of ye as dead," said Lucas. He smiled faintly at Thomas. "It might have been a kindness to tell your sister, lad, if only to save her from going to Lady Katerina's grave. Still, 'tis good that ye ken how to keep your word."

"She went to my grave?" Katerina asked in shock even as she gently bathed Annie's pretty round face with cool water.

"Aye," replied Lucas. "When she thought me a holy mon, she asked if 'twas a sin to say prayers o'er the unconsecrated grave of a suicide. She didnae really believe ye had killed yourself, though."

"'Tis odd, but that is one of the things that angers

me the most about all of this. How dare Agnes let people think I committed such a sin."

"Myself, I think I would be more annoyed by being tossed o'er a cliff into a loch," drawled William.

Katerina had to fight a smile and ignored the way Thomas and the men all grinned. It was difficult, however, not to stare at Lucas. With the grin on his face and the light of laughter in his fine eyes, he looked so much like the man she had fallen in love with that it hurt. The way his somber, almost angry expression returned so quickly, hurt even more, for she knew now that part of it was caused by his belief that she had betrayed him.

A soft groan from Annie drew her full attention, and Katerina gladly accepted the tankard of wine William handed her knowing Annie would probably need it. For a brief moment after Annie opened her eyes, she looked confused, but then her gaze settled on Katerina again and she turned even paler. With her free hand, Katerina grabbed Annie's hand and held it tightly, hoping that touch would reassure the woman.

"Dinnae ye faint on me again, Annie," Katerina said sternly. "Drink this," she ordered and handed the woman the wine.

"Ye arenae dead," Annie said in a soft, unsteady voice before she gulped down nearly half the wine. "Why would everyone say ye are dead when ye arenae?" She gasped. "And who did they bury?"

Katerina rocked back on her heels and stared at Annie for a moment, all too aware of how everyone was staring at her and waiting for an answer. She tried to think of her grave as little as possible, for it gave her the chills. Agnes had put up a very nice stone and played the grieving sister with skill according to some of the others. Katerina had never wondered if anything or anyone had actually been put beneath that stone, however.

"I am shamed to say that I ne'er gave it much thought," Katerina finally replied. "I assume 'tis an empty grave, Annie. Rocks, mayhap, if they needed to give the coffin some weight. Unless there is someone who went missing at the same time—" she began, but Annie shook her head.

"Nay, no one save Robbie," Annie said as she slowly sat up.

"I cannae think Robbie came back to Dunlochan and died so conveniently, just when Agnes needed a body. If naught else, Robbie would be appalled at becoming a pawn in Agnes's treacherous plots."

Annie nodded slowly. "And so easily, too."

Katerina grinned. "Verra true. Nay, I doubt anyone rests in my grave."

The relief on Annie's face came and went so quickly, Katerina knew she had been lucky to see it. She hid her shock. Had she been wrong about Robbie? Had he been unfaithful to Agnes even before Agnes had broken the vows said between them? Even as doubt about the man and her own judgment crept into her mind, she was able to banish it. Robbie might be quick with a smile for the lasses, but he held true to his vows until he realized the woman he had given them to did not do the same, that Agnes had fooled him in all ways as to the woman she truly was. He had left too quickly after that to have already begun an affair with Annie. Annie was also an innocent and somewhat pious. She would never have fallen into a love affair with a married man. That did not mean, however, that Annie could not be enamored of the far too charming Robbie. Katerina inwardly sighed, hoping the young woman had not given her heart away foolishly. She was all too aware of how much that could hurt.

"What do Thomas and I do now, m'lady?" Annie asked as she shyly accepted a little more wine from Patrick.

"Stay here."

"Here? For how long?"

Katerina tried not to grimace, knowing Annie would not like her answer. "I fear I dinnae ken. Ranald willnae give up wanting to get his hands on ye and Thomas. Weel, Thomas is the one he sought, but ye heard how he began to plot pulling ye into his grasp as weel, aye?"

Annie shivered in obvious distaste. "Aye, I did and it fair turned my insides to ice."

"So, I fear ye and Thomas must now hide away with us until Ranald is no longer a threat."

"Just what do ye need to defeat that cur and Lady Agnes?"

"Proof of their crimes. That is what is proving so hard to get hold of. I need clear, hard proof to show the council."

Annie muttered something that sounded very much like a curse. "Old fools, the lot of them. They ken what she is and what she and Ranald have done and still do. They ken the crimes that unholy pair has committed. I think their hesitation has naught to do with what fulfills your da's wishes. Nay, I think they sit back and let this bloody game continue because they dinnae want to give up the power they hold as guardians of Dunlochan." She blushed when she realized everyone was staring at her. "Pardon. I was disrespectful."

"Nay, ye just put the hard truth into words, something the rest of us have hesitated to do." Katerina took Annie by the hand. "Come, I will show ye where ye can sleep. Thomas can share with ye or stay here with the men."

"I should like to stay with the men, of course," said Thomas.

Katerina hid her smile as she led Annie away. A quick glance at Annie revealed that woman was doing the same. When she reached the small chamber she had chosen for Annie, Katerina helped the woman set up a pallet to sleep on and hang a blanket over the door. With both of them working it did not take long to make the small stone chamber relatively comfortable and a lot less like the cave it was.

"'Twill be strange to live under a hill like the fairies," said Annie as she looked around, "although 'tis finer than my wee niche at the inn." She smiled at Katerina. "'Tis wondrous that Sir Lucas still lives, is it not? Ye must be so happy to have him back."

"Weel, I *am* glad that Ranald didnae kill him. 'Twould be verra fine indeed if Sir Lucas didnae think I had a hand in it all, however." She inwardly cursed her loose tongue and shrugged when Annie stared at her in shock before giving the woman a succinct account of what had happened a year ago.

"He thinks *ye* tried to kill him?" When Katerina nodded, Annie began to look very angry and shook her head. "Men can be such blind, stubborn fools. I am sorry, m'lady. I had thought—" She shook her head again.

"Ah, weel, so had I. It appears we were both wrong."

"Ye will soon prove to him that he is a fool to think such a thing. Aye, ye will soon make him choke on his foolish suspicions."

"'Tis a pleasant thought."

"But ye dinnae ken what to do after that, do ye?"

"Nay, I dinnae. But I suspicion I will think of something. Get some rest, Annie."

"I willnae be a burden, m'lady. I cannae fight, but I can surely find work to do to help ye. I can cook and clean."

"Such help will be greatly appreciated. Good sleep, Annie."

"Good sleep to ye, m'lady, and my thanks for saving me and Thomas."

"Ye and Thomas have both been a help to us, although ye didnae really ken it. I couldnae have lived with myself if I had left ye to Ranald's untender mercies."

Katerina left Annie to seek her own bed, her whole body aching with weariness. She had just reached the opening to her chamber when Lucas stepped into her path. There was a look in his silvery-blue eyes that made her insides clench with need and that angered her. She scowled at him as he neatly pinned her between his hard body and the stone wall.

Katerina did not need to feel the thick ridge of his shaft pressing against her to know what Lucas wanted. It was there to read in the taut lines of his face. Despite the pain he had caused her she wanted it, too. It was too soon, however. She had not yet decided if the pleasure he could give her was worth all the risks that came with it.

"I believe ye have a pallet readied for ye in the hall with the other men," she said, proud of the chill in her voice for there was only searing, welcoming heat in her body.

"Your bed would be warmer." Lucas told himself it was the lingering excitement of a battle and a rescue that had stirred such need in him, and that he had only sought out Katerina to ease it because she was close at hand. He ruthlessly ignored the voice in his head that called him a liar.

"There are plenty of blankets about. Seek their warmth."

"Are ye sure that is what ye want me to do?"

Before she could reply, he kissed her. It was no gentle kiss, no soft coaxing of a lover. Lucas ravished her mouth. His kiss stirred her hunger into a fierce craving. Katerina clutched at his robe, fighting the urge to rip the coarse wool from his body and crawl all over him. Her need was a living thing inside her, but she fought it with all her strength. The moment his lips left hers, she grasped the shredded tethers of her control and pushed him back. Her whole body felt chilled by the loss of his heat, but she ignored it. It was too soon. She had no control over her emotions, and if she did decide to take him as her lover, she knew she would need some if only to shield her heart from the pain he could inflict on it.

"Kissing a woman ye think guilty of attempting to murder ye isnae wise. Doing it whilst dressed as a monk might be considered blasphemy. I suggest ye leave. Now."

Katerina did not flinch from his hard, searching stare. If he had been looking for a weakness in her, he had undoubtedly found at least a hint of one in the way she had responded to his kiss. It did not matter. She was in control now and she intended to hold fast to it. There was a glint of anger in his eyes and she was pleased to se it. If she was going to suffer the un-quenched fires of desire tonight, he ought to suffer in some way as well.

Lucas could see the strength of her resolve to send him away and knew he would not get what he craved tonight. Her desire for him was still there, however. He had tasted it in the kiss they had shared. He could wait, no matter how uncomfortable waiting was going to be. Bowing slightly, he left her and began to try to recall all the ways he could ease the hunger in his body so that he could get some much-needed rest. He would need his strength for the campaign ahead. Coaxing Katerina back into his arms so that they could wallow in the passion they shared, at least for a while, would take every scrap of patience and guile he could muster. He *could* wait, but he had no intention of waiting for too long.

The moment Lucas was gone, Katerina staggered to her bed and collapsed onto it, her whole body trembling as she fought to control the desire that kiss had brought to life. She was glad Lucas had not argued with her, for her control was tenuous at best. A little push from him and she might well have fallen straight into his arms. Something in the way he had looked at her, even in the way he had bowed, told her that he *would* push. She would have to make her decision about him soon, for every instinct she had told her that Lucas was now on the hunt and she was his prey.

Chapter Six

It was a trap. Katerina could see no proof of that, could hear nothing to indicate they were riding into danger, could not even smell it in the air, but her insides were clenching with fear. It was the same feeling she used to get as a child when she had to go somewhere where she knew Agnes could be lying in wait for her, only much, much worse. A quick glance at the faces of the men with her told her they shared her uneasiness, but she knew their wariness could be born of different causes.

When the feeling had first swept over her, she had looked to Lucas as the cause. For three long days now he had been haunting her thoughts, the warmth of his kiss still lingering on her mouth. He had also been stalking her, always near, always touching her in some way, always watching her with desire darkening his eyes, and always trying to steal a kiss, something he accomplished far too often for her peace of mind. The moment the feeling had grown stronger, however, she had known he was not the one causing it.

Old Ian had sent word that someone had taken the horses. True reivers having always been a problem, though thankfully rare, they had set out to track them down. Now Katerina began to think it was not so simple. Although she always felt tense before a battle, this feeling was even stronger, deeper, and carried a strong hint of foreboding.

"I dinnae like this," she muttered as she stared at the horses and men slowly, suspiciously so, crossing an open field.

"Nay, it smells wrong," agreed William, and several of her men grunted softly in agreement.

"Like a trap."

"Aye, verra like a trap, a weel laid trap."

Lucas nodded slowly, his gaze never leaving the men and horses they had been pursuing most of the night. "Open, but with a lot of places for men to hide all round the edges of the field."

"Just waiting for us to come out into the open," she said, "and then moving to cut off our retreat."

"Unfortunately, we need the horses."

Katerina hated to admit it but he was right. The six horses they now rode were all they had left if they did not retrieve the ones in the field. They were not all the best horses, either. To replace the ones stolen from them, they would actually have to steal some and Katerina was very reluctant to do so. She was trying to prove Agnes guilty of various crimes and did not think that committing some herself was the best way to do that. There were also the risks to consider. She might not suffer much for stealing horses simply because she was the daughter of a laird, but her men most certainly would. Katerina suspected that, if given a choice in the matter, her men would much rather ride into what they all suspected was a trap than risk hanging for stealing.

"The best way to do this is swift and hard, Kat," said Lucas. "Go out there, grab what we can as fast as we can, and get out."

She tried to ignore the warmth that stirred within her over the use of the name Kat, one he had used often when they had been happy together. Now was a very bad time to be growing sentimental. She had horses to retrieve and men to protect. The part of her that resented Lucas offering plans and assuming some authority was ruthlessly smothered. A good plan was needed if they were all to get out of this trap alive and she would not argue over where that plan came from.

"I think that is the way to do this, Cousin," said William. "If this really is a trap, we cannae take time to fight with those men and retrieve all the horses. We can, however, ride in fast, grab some, and hie away, giving whoe'er might be lying in wait for us little chance to launch their attack on us."

"Agreed then," she said, adjusting the slip of blue linen wrapped around her face to make sure it hid her face well. "No fighting unless ye need to. Just grab a horse and get out of there. We ken that no one lurks in hiding here so this will be our escape route."

"And we will all set off in different directions as usual once we are hidden by these trees."

"Let us pray there are no archers hiding out there," she muttered softly when William moved closer to her.

"Few can hit a swiftly moving target. And, if Ranald is behind this, most of his men couldnae hit the side of Dunlochan keep on a clear day with no wind."

Katerina smiled as the men all chuckled over William's insult, but the good humor was fleeting. The men were waiting for her signal to move. After praying for their safety, she gave it and immediately spurred her horse into a gallop. She bent low over the horse's strong neck to make herself as small a target

as possible as she rode straight toward the men herding her horses across the field.

She was in reach of one of the horses when she saw
men on horseback rushing out of the trees, swords
drawn, and heading right for her and her men. It did
not please her at all to see that she was right, that it
was indeed a trap. When one of the men herding the
horses tried to grab her, she slammed her cudgel into
the side of his head, sending him tumbling to the
ground. Katerina then grabbed hold of the reins of
the horse nearest her and turned to flee, hoping to
make it to the safety of the trees before Ranald or his
men could reach her.

A grunt escaped her as something slammed into her
back. The pain hit her a heartbeat later with such
force her vision clouded. Instinctively, she reached for
what was causing her such pain, releasing the reins of
both her own horse and the one she was trying to retrieve. Both horses reacted badly to the sudden lack of
a hand upon the reins, jostling her as they faltered and
tried to decide what to do next. Realizing her precarious position as she reeled in the saddle, Katerina
reached for the reins, but it was too late to save herself.
Her hood fell back, dislodged by her frantic attempts
to grab the reins and stay in the saddle, revealing her
long hair. Despite the cloth that still covered most of
her face, Katerina suspected that several of Ranald's
men would recognize her thick fair hair; Ranald certainly would. She hit the ground hard, pain shooting
through her hip and back and, for a moment, her full
attention was fixed upon trying to breathe again.

Lucas glanced toward Katerina only to see her flail-
ing in her saddle and he cursed. Even as she fell, he
caught sight of the arrow protruding from her back
and he felt a chill run through his body. The fact that
her hood fell back, revealing her distinctive hair and

revealing her identity as clearly as any banner, concerned him far less than her welfare. They could deal with the consequences of Ranald knowing she was alive later. The only thing that mattered now was saving her life.

He thrust the reins of the mount he had retrieved toward William. "Take these and get out of here."

"But Katerina—" William began to protest even as he grabbed the reins and secured them to his saddle.

"I will get her and meet with ye at the caves."

William hesitated for only a moment longer and then raced away, following the rest of Katerina's men into the trees. He paused only once in his flight to grab the reins of the horse Katerina had lost hold of. Lucas raced toward where Katerina was struggling to get to her feet. Ranald obviously had the same idea, but he was caught up in a confused melee of men and panicked horses that were all trying to go in different directions. To his relief, Lucas reached Katerina first, reaching out for her and pulling her up behind him before grabbing the reins of her horse and securing them to his saddle.

"The other horse," Katerina choked out even as she wondered why she was so concerned about the beast when she was close to being captured and was in pain.

"William grabbed it. Can ye hold on tight?"

"Aye," was all she managed to say before Lucas kicked his horse into a gallop.

The ride to their hiding place was little more than a befogged sense of speed and excruciating pain to Katerina. She was barely conscious when Lucas stopped to tie her to him with the linen strip he had worn over his face. When they stopped a second time, she roused from her pain-filled stupor enough to try to see where they were, but pain blurred her vision. As Lucas took her into his arms she caught a glimpse of

Thomas and Patrick leading the horses away while William did his best to obscure their trail. That sign that everyone was doing exactly what they should ended all need Katerina had to try to hold on to consciousness and she gave herself over to the blackness that had been fighting to claim her.

"Oh, sweet Jesu, is she dead?" Annie cried from the opening to the hall.

Lucas did not hesitate, but kept striding toward Katerina's bedchamber. "Nay, but she needs tending to as swiftly as possible. She needs this arrow out and may have broken something when she fell from her horse. I need water, rags, and anything else ye may have for healing wounds."

"Aye, I will be but a step behind ye."

The moment Lucas got Katerina settled on her side on her bed, he began to cut away the clothes the arrow had pierced. He struggled to calm the emotions roiling through him. It made no sense that he should be so upset, so chillingly afraid for Katerina. Had he not planned to avenge her part in the brutal beating he had suffered? Although he had not made any specific plans for his revenge against her, the very words *avenge* and *revenge* implied that some violence and pain would ensue. It was obvious now that he would never have been able to do Katerina any physical harm.

Thinking on it, he realized he had thus far failed to exact any revenge on her. He had even joined in her fight against Ranald and Agnes. About all he had accomplished was to irritate and insult her and continuously try to seduce her. It was not the sort of revenge ballads were written about.

When Annie arrived, setting all she had brought on

the chest next to the bed, Lucas began to prepare himself for the gruesome task of removing the arrow from Katerina's back. "Are ye strong, Annie?"

"Aye," she replied. "Of body and stomach."

"Good. Ye will need to be both for what happens next. I must needs remove this arrow."

She frowned, obviously confused by his hesitation. "Do ye wish me to pull it out?"

"Nay, I need ye to hold her still. First I must push it through so that the tip comes out the front of her." He ignored Annie's horrified gasp, and continued, "Then I will cut the arrowhead off. Only then can I pull it out of her body."

"That will be an agony for her," Annie whispered.

"Aye, it will, and, e'en though she is unconscious, she will fight the pain."

"Why cannae ye just pull it out?"

"Because it will make the wound worse, tearing into far more coming out than did going in. The head of the arrow must come off first. Now, the more she moves the longer it will take to get this cursed thing free of her body. Are ye ready? Ye willnae swoon, will ye?"

Annie shook her head and moved to hold Katerina firmly in place. The scream that escaped Katerina as he shoved the arrowhead the rest of the way through her body made Lucas's stomach churn. He suspected he was as pale as Annie was. He cut off the arrowhead and then, after taking a deep breath to steady himself, yanked the shaft of the arrow out of her slender body as swiftly as he could. Katerina screamed again and tried to twist away from the pain he caused her but a softly praying Annie held her firmly in place. Lucas was heartily relieved when Katerina lay silent and limp after the ordeal and he prayed she was so deeply unconscious now that the rest of the work he had to do would not reach her.

Struggling to recall all he had learned while growing up in a family of healers, Lucas cleaned the wounds and then stitched them closed. The salve Annie gave him was unfamiliar to him, but he had a sensitive nose and easily picked out the various herbs in it, judging it safe if not as good as some of the women in his family could make. He put the salve on Katerina's wounds and then bandaged them. Relieved that he was done with that chore, he stretched until some of the tension in his body eased and he felt he could continue.

"Are ye a healer?" asked Annie.

"Nay, but many of the women in my family are renowned healers and every child is taught at least some of those skills," Lucas replied. He looked down at Katerina's pale face and sighed. "We are nay done yet."

"She has more wounds?"

"She fell off her horse. I dinnae think she has broken anything, but we must be sure."

Although Annie was obviously uncomfortable with Lucas seeing Katerina naked, she said nothing as they stripped off the rest of Katerina's clothing. Lucas was relieved to find no broken bones, but there were a lot of bruises marring her fair skin. He helped Annie bathe Katerina with cloths soaked in lavender-scented water and put some salve on the worst of the bruises.

"She has a lot of scars," he murmured, lightly tracing a long, ragged one on Katerina's slim leg.

"William said she was badly injured when she was thrown into the loch and had to save herself."

While Annie fetched a night shift for Katerina, Lucas studied the scars marring Katerina's body. Some were small, more the result of a somewhat un-skilled healer tending to her wounds, but there were several large ones, the result of serious wounds. The scars supported most of William's tale of what happened a year ago. Katerina was very lucky to have survived such large, deep wounds.

Doubt about Katerina's guilt inched into his mind and this time refused to be pushed aside. Perhaps she truly had not intended to have him killed. Ranald and Agnes could have used Katerina's jealous need to punish him for their own purposes. Once Katerina realized they meant to murder him she had finally tried to stop what she had started but it had been too late to save him or herself.

He inwardly shook his head as he helped Annie put Katerina into a night shift. Tired and worried about Katerina as he was, Lucas knew it was a very bad time to try to sort out anything, let alone exactly what had happened a year ago. He finally admitted to himself that pain might have clouded his judgments, made him recall only pieces of what had happened. Lucas was not ready to believe Katerina was completely innocent, but he was now prepared to start looking for some answers, even to consider that he may not have the full truth.

William strode into the room just as Annie pulled the covers up over Katerina. "How does she fare?"

"The arrow wound was bad, but I dinnae believe 'tis a mortal wound," Lucas replied. He espied a jug and tankard on a small table in the corner of the room and moved to pour himself a drink. "Ah, wine," he murmured after peering into the jug. "Just what I need."

"She looks verra pale," William said as he moved closer to the side of the bed and studied Katerina's face.

"Loss of blood and pain will often leach all the color out of a person. She didnae lose too much blood, however." After hastily downing a whole tankard of wine,

Lucas poured himself another one and moved back to stand at Katerina's bedside.

"Did she break anything when she fell off her horse?"

"Nay, but she will be bruised from head to toe and verra sore."

"Ah, weel, mayhap that will serve to keep her abed until she heals enough to rise safely."

"She isnae an amiable invalid then, aye?"

William rolled his eyes. "The moment she isnae feverish or in too much pain to move, she thinks she is healed."

"Weel, if she becomes too much trouble we will simply tie her to the bed." Lucas winked at Annie when she gasped.

"'Twill work, but only if ye can tie better knots than I can."

Lucas stared at William in shock for a moment and then laughed. "Ye tied her to the bed?"

"She wouldnae lie still and had reopened her wounds several times. Also had to do it when she grew feverish as she kept trying to return to the loch to look for ye." William looked at Lucas and cocked one brow. "Only God kens why."

The knowledge that Katerina had tried to find him soothed Lucas in some way and that irritated him. "Guilt?" he murmured and just shrugged when both William and Annie glared at him. Deciding it might be wise to change the subject, he asked William, "Exactly how are ye related to Kat? Ye are her cousin, aye?"

"Aye," William answered. "I am her uncle's bastard. He had a lot of us. He liked the lasses."

"Too much so," said Annie, her expression one of utter feminine disgust. "'Tis what got the fool killed.

Everyone told him to stay away from the blacksmith's wife, but he wouldnae heed that bit of good advice."

"Ah, so the blacksmith caught the mon cuckolding him and killed him, did he?" Lucas realized he was gently stroking Katerina's pale cheek, told himself he was just checking to see if she was feverish, and yanked his hand back.

"Beat him badly, but didnae kill him, 'though I still think that beating led to his death."

"Aye," agreed William. "He acted verra odd for about a week and then just fell down dead."

"I suspicion he was bleeding inside, mayhap e'en inside his head," Lucas said. "So, if ye are such a close relation, why didnae the old laird choose ye to be the laird after he died?"

"Because the old laird hated his brother and the feeling was fully returned. I ne'er heard the full tale, but it had something to do with a woman. I suspicion it was the laird's wife. She was a good woman so I cannae believe she did anything wrong, but I fear I cannae say the same about my father. So, any child of my father's wasnae good enough in the old laird's eyes."

Lucas shook his head. "'Tis sad when there are feuds between the verra people who should stand firmly together. And the council the old laird selected didnae argue with him about it all, I suspect."

"Nay. I fear my father didnae make as many friends as he did enemies."

"Because he liked the lasses?"

William nodded. "Several of the men here are my brothers. Agnes and Ranald see us as threats and, weel, Katerina was always good to us. She didnae care who bred us, or that we were bastards, only that we were blood kin. That meant a lot to us, so when she was in trouble, we stood with her. Ye see, Agnes also hates us, always has. The fact that she, too, is a bastard doesnae seem to have made her verra sympathetic."

"How could I have misjudged that woman so?" Lucas muttered.

"Ye seem to make a lot of misjudgments about people."

Before an argument could begin between the two men now glaring at each other, Annie said, "Agnes is verra good at playing the sweet, somewhat witless woman that men seem to think they want. All smiles and titters, caring only about being admired by men and dressing in fine clothes. 'Tis mostly women who see through that guise quickly, if only because Agnes doesnae much like other women and cannae hold fast to her mask of sweet idiocy. E'en her own husband was fooled for months and he is a canny fellow. I think she fooled the old laird, too, because I cannae believe he would have done anything to place Katerina or the weelbeing of the people of Dunlochan at risk. Yet, his dying wishes have done just that."

"Aye," agreed William. "He may have made it too plain to see that he was disappointed he could only breed daughters whilst his brother scattered bastard sons all over the countryside, but he loved his child as best he could. His illness came on him sudden and it didnae give him much chance to think long and hard about what he was doing. Katerina was furious that he made no plans for any of us, for all his nieces and nephews."

"Especially since ye and a few others had served him weel as men at arms," said Annie.

William shrugged. "We didnae really do any of that for him. Nay, 'twas for Dunlochan and Katerina." He looked closely at Lucas. "Do ye think Ranald recognized her when her hood slipped back?"

"I feel certain he did," replied Lucas. "The mon was

struggling to get to her, e'en striking out at some of his own men when they got in his way."

After cursing softly and viciously for a moment, William noticed Annie's bright blushes and took a deep breath to calm himself. "Pardon, Annie."

"Nay, ye dinnae need to ask for it," she said. "'Tis just that I have ne'er heard ye curse so much," she suddenly grinned, "or so verra colorfully. This situation almost demands a mouthful of curses, I am thinking."

William smiled faintly and then looked at Lucas. "Ranald hates Katerina. If the mon truly believes she survived, he will tear apart all of Dunlochan to find her."

"Why does he hate her so much?" Lucas asked,

"Because she told him *nay*," said Annie. "E'en worse, he kenned that she probably didnae say *nay* to ye."

"And since ye seemed to be most serious in your wooing of her," continued William, "there was a chance ye and Katerina might wed. Ranald kens that fool council would approve of ye and that will take away what power Agnes has granted him. If Ranald gets his filthy hands on Katerina, she will die and it willnae be an easy death he gives her."

"Then we had best make verra sure the bastard doesnae get her," said Lucas.

It took some persuasion, but Lucas finally got William and Annie to go to bed and allow him to stay with Katerina. Lucas pulled a rough-hewn chair up to the side of the bed, rested his feet on the bed, and studied Katerina. Her father had obviously been a cold, hard man and made his disappointment over her not being a son all too clear to her at times. Her half-sister was apparently a vicious little witch and had undoubtedly made Katerina's life a misery as often as possible. Now she had people trying to kill her so that she could not claim what was hers by right of birth, something that should never have been in doubt. Lucas felt sympathy for her despite his reluctance to do so.

Sipping his wine, he decided it was time to search out the whole ugly truth. He refused to believe he was completely wrong about Katerina, but thought he might find something that would make it easier to forgive her part in the beating he had suffered. Lucas suspected he was close to forgiving her anyway, but some justification for doing so would be a comfort, would make him feel less like some lovesick fool.

He also needed as much information about Dunlochan, Ranald, Agnes, and the battle for the right to rule Dunlochan as he could get if he was going to keep Katerina safe. Even though he did not want to look too closely at what he might still feel for her besides desire, he knew he could never let her come to harm. Recalling the look upon Ranald's face as he had struggled to get to Katerina, Lucas knew William was right. Now that Ranald knew that Katerina was still alive, the man would never stop hunting her. It seemed that Lucas was soon to get the hard, fierce battle and bloodletting he had argued for.

"What do ye mean she is still alive?"

Ranald looked at Agnes, idly thinking that her usually soft, sweet voice could sound painfully shrewish at times. "Just what I said—she is alive. I saw her hair when the hood of her cloak slipped down."

"A lot of people at Dunlochan have fair hair."

"Nay like Katerina's. 'Twas her, Agnes, and arguing with me o'er it willnae change that. We need to plan what to do next. Both Murray and your sister are alive and that means a lot of trouble is soon to come our way."

Agnes watched her lover pace her solar, a tankard of ale clutched tightly in his big hand. Ranald was not a very handsome man, his features too coarse and his nose too large, but he was big and strong. He was also mean and devious, two things she admired in a man. Her husband had possessed neither quality and had quickly bored her. Neither did her sister and so it puzzled Agnes that Katerina could have fooled them for so long.

The fact that Sir Lucas Murray was still alive both pleased and dismayed her. Lucas was a man who made her mouth water and her stomach clench with lust despite his rough manners. She had been enraged when he had shown no interest in her, but had continued to woo Katerina. Even though she had ordered his death, Agnes now wondered if she might have a second chance to seduce him into her bed. He would still have to die, but, mayhap, she could have a little taste of him first. If she could do so while Katerina watched, it would be even more exciting, and satisfying.

"I dinnae ken what ye are thinking of, Agnes, but ye best stop," said Ranald. "That smile ye now wear would send chills down the spine of even the bravest of men."

"Ye flatter me. I was but thinking of what to do about these people who refuse to stay dead."

Ranald studied his lover. She was beautiful, as many of the Haldane women were, with thick fair hair, big blue eyes, unblemished fair skin, and a body that was somehow both lithe and voluptuous. Her face was as beautiful as any he had ever seen, one that made men see sweetness and innocence in her expression, compassion in her smile. He knew she had none of those qualities. It was one reason they worked so well together. Ranald was still astonished that the old laird had been blind to the hard, cold, almost amoral woman hidden behind those sweet smiles.

"And just how do ye think we ought to deal with them?" he asked.

"Why, we must correct your mistake."

"*My* mistake? Curse it, Agnes, the Murray mon was a broken hulk when we threw him into the loch. Your sister went under when we threw her in and stayed under. 'Tis no surprise that I thought them both dead. Aye, and the fact that we havenae seen either of them for a year only made me even more certain of it."

"But we *have* seen Katerina, havenae we. She has been plaguing us and ruining our plans all along."

Ranald cursed. "Ye didnae ken the leader of those reivers was Katerina either."

"Nay, I didnae. True enough. I accept that error in judgment. 'Tis time to mend things, however."

"How?"

"Why, by finding them. Finding them and killing them. And this time I want to see the bodies."

Chapter Seven

"Ranald kens I am alive, doesnae he?"

Katerina stared at Lucas wondering why he was sprawled in a chair next to her bed. He looked tired and a little surprised by her question. Hazily recalled nightmares had prompted those first words out of her mouth, however. All those nightmares had concerned Ranald capturing her and all the painful suffering that would bring to her. She needed to know if she had been recognized, if there was any chance that some of those very chilling dreams might come true.

"Aye, he does," Lucas replied as he stood up and fetched her some mead, mixing a few herbs into the drink before bringing it to her. "Drink this," he ordered quietly as he slipped an arm behind her and held her up a little to help her drink.

Even though the strong taste of the herbs made her grimace, the mead soothed her sore, dry throat. Katerina surreptitiously studied Lucas as he helped her drink the brew. He looked *very* tired. She had a few vague memories of his presence at her bedside, along with Annie's, and wondered if he had actually helped care for her. It seemed a strange thing for a man to do for a woman he believed had tried to have him killed.

By the time she finished the drink, she felt so weak and tired she knew she would be a long time recovering from this wound. She also had more important things to worry about than whether or not Lucas had cared for her wound. It was a very bad time for her to be so helpless.

"He is looking for me then, is he?" she asked as he gently bathed her face with lavender-scented water.

"Like a mon obsessed," said Lucas. "Turning o'er every rock."

She inwardly winced at his blunt answer, but recalled that Lucas was not one to tell the truth gently. "That isnae good."

"Nay, it isnae, but he has been looking for ye and your men for a long while."

"He thought he was looking for reivers, for naught but a nuisance. Aye, the longer we plagued him, the harder he tried to catch us, but he didnae really see us as a threat to him. He felt his place at Agnes's side, as a mon of power in Dunlochan, was secure, and that only Robbie remained as a thorn in his side. Now that he kens I am alive, that we both are alive, I suspicion he recognizes the threat to him. If naught else we could get him hanged. E'en Robbie cannae do that."

Lucas sat on the edge of her bed, ignoring the cross look she gave him. Her color was good but the occasional wince she made told him that she still suffered some pain from her wounds. Despite his opinion that the wound she had suffered was not a mortal one, it had been a long, hard fight to keep her alive. Katerina had obviously not been taking very good care of herself and that had left her with little strength to fight blood loss, pain, and a raging fever. Having had most of the care of her, he felt as exhausted as she looked. He was also feeling highly emotional and knew it would be best if he got away from her as soon as possible.

"Has there been any trouble then?" she asked when Lucas did not argue her opinion on how great a threat Ranald was.

"Nay. A few beatings as Ranald searches for someone who kens that ye are alive and where ye might be hiding." Lucas saw how much that news upset her and quickly added, "He seems to have given that up quickly. At the moment your people are safe."

"How long have I been abed?" she asked, suddenly startled by the weakness in her leg when she tried to move it away from where it pressed against his body.

"Almost a week. Ye took a fever and it was slow to release ye from its grip."

Katerina cursed softly. "That is why I feel so weak then."

"Aye. Ye will need at least a week ere ye regain your strength. The only good thing about it all is that the fever kept ye abed long enough for your wounds to begin to heal weel."

"An arrow?" she asked, not sure her memory about how she was wounded was correct. She lightly touched the bandage wrapped around her upper chest. "I didnae realize it had gone all the way through."

"It didnae. The best way to remove an arrow from a body is to push it all the way through, cut off the arrowhead, and *then* take it out. Otherwise that arrowhead can do a great deal of damage as ye pull it back through the body."

Thinking on that for a moment, Katerina slowly nodded. "That makes sense. It feels as if it is healing weel."

"Thank ye."

"So it was ye who tended to my wounds?"

"I did. There are a lot of healers in my family. I am nay a true healer, but I did learn a lot about tending wounds from the women in my clan. I assume none here felt skilled enough to push me aside so that they could do the work. They left me to it. Annie helped, tending to ye when ye needed a woman's aid."

Katerina inwardly sighed with relief at that news. Knowing the sort of intimacies required in tending to a badly injured or ill person, she had begun to get alarmed as he had spoken of tending to her wounds. It was hard enough to accept Annie's care in such matters. If Lucas had tended to her more personal needs, she would never have been able to look him in the eye again. She actually felt herself blush when she suddenly realized she was going to have to ask for Annie's help right now.

"Is Annie close at hand?" she asked quietly.

Seeing how flushed she was, Lucas grinned and stood up. "Aye. I sent word that ye were waking up and she should be here verra soon." He leaned over her, ignoring the way she pressed deeper into the pillow in a vain attempt to keep some distance between them. "Ye *will* rest, Kat, and give us no trouble about it, or I will be tying ye to this bed."

"Ye wouldnae dare."

"Aye, I would." Placing his hands on either side of her head, he fixed his gaze upon her mouth. "I think I will dare one other thing, too."

Katerina was just about to protest when his mouth covered hers. Despite the weakness in her body, she blindly wrapped her arms around his neck as he kissed her. It was a slow, deep kiss, as if he was savoring the taste of her, and Katerina knew that, if she was not so very weak, she would be crawling all over the man. Every feeling she had ever felt for him came rushing back, pulled out of hiding with each stroke of his tongue. Katerina felt shaken, even a little afraid, when he finally ended the kiss and pulled away from her. This kiss had disturbed her even more than the first one and she doubted that was because she was so tired and weak.

"And here comes Annie to lend ye aid," Lucas said as he strode out of the room. "I will return later."

Much later, he thought as he barely stopped himself from running, as far and as fast as he could. Katerina still moved him, still had a tight grip on him, and it scared him to death. He had grieved for her, for the loss of all he had thought he had wanted, and for the betrayal she had dealt him. To his shame he had even wept for the loss of her. Every feeling he had thought he had killed or buried had been renewed as he had fought to keep her alive. When she had finally begun to recover he realized that every caution he had thought he had learned had been swept away. That kiss had shown him just how susceptible he still was. In fact, he feared he was still in love with her.

He cursed and headed for the hall. He would have something to eat and then find a quiet place to get some rest. After that he was going hunting for some answers even if it took him deep into Dunlochan keep itself.

"Men can be such a trial," Katerina complained as Annie helped her back into bed.

Worrying over all she still felt for Lucas and how dangerous those feelings were had actually helped her endure Annie's kind help in seeing to her personal needs. She had been so busy fretting over that kiss and all it had made her feel that she had done what she needed to, been cleaned up, and was now back in her bed without being painfully embarrassed by Annie's help. Unfortunately, she had not come up with any solution about what to do concerning Lucas and how she felt about him.

"Sir Lucas kept ye alive, m'lady," Annie felt compelled to say.

Katerina sighed. "I feared that might be the way of it. So now I must be grateful."

Annie bit back a grin over those somewhat petulant words as she helped Katerina sit up slightly, resting her against the bank of pillows Annie set behind her. "Aye, I fear ye must. Now, I have brought ye some broth. Ye should try to eat as much of it as possible."

"I ken it. I do feel verra hungry, but I also ken I cannae eat anything too rich or hearty." She was pleasantly surprised by how tasty the broth was as Annie spooned some into her mouth. "This shallnae be too hard to bear. 'Tis surprisingly tasty."

"Sir Lucas told me about some ways to make broth taste better."

"The mon can cook, too, can he? That simply isnae fair."

Annie laughed, but quickly grew serious again. "He told me that he learned about such seasonings when he was recovering from that beating. He had to have a lot of broth as his jaw was broken and he couldnae eat much of anything for a verra long while."

"The beating he thinks I ordered done out of jealousy."

"I cannae think he truly believes that, nay down deep in his heart. No mon could care for a woman as he has cared for ye this past week if he thought she had betrayed him so. Nay, not e'en if he does come from a family with a lot of healing women in it. I feel sure he was verra worried about ye and he worked the whole night through several times to keep ye alive when the fever was raging through your body."

That news stirred a hope inside Katerina that she

did not wish to feel. It could make her do something very foolish, such as give her heart into Lucas's keeping again only to get it shattered once more. He had not yet offered her an apology for his accusations and, until he did, she could not trust in the hope that he had already changed his mind about her. She had lost faith in him as well and was not sure if that could ever be fully restored.

"Ah, Annie, when I first saw that he had survived I was overjoyed and ready to run into his arms. I felt as if every prayer I had uttered had just been answered. 'Tis then that he accused me of trying to have him killed. It will be hard to forget how that hurt, how it still hurts. It will be also verra hard to trust my heart into his care again."

"What if he grovels?"

"That may soothe me a wee bit," Katerina drawled and exchanged a grin with Annie. Pleased with how that touch of humor had lightened her spirits and eager to get Lucas out of her mind for a moment, Katerina decided to change the subject. "Tell me what news there is. I cannae bear nay kenning how everyone fares."

Annie began to tell her nearly everything that had gone on since she had been wounded even as she kept spooning the broth into Katerina's mouth. Despite the fact that Ranald was hunting for her and Lucas with a vengeance, nothing of any great importance had happened. Relieved, Katerina was able to settle down for a rest once she had finished eating. She knew she was going to need all her strength to face what lay ahead and it was not just Ranald's pursuit that concerned her. Lucas and her feelings for him would have to be faced and dealt with and she knew whatever decision she made about him would affect the rest of her life. It was a daunting thought.

* * *

Lucas caught William looking at him with something approaching amusement. "Ye can laugh if ye feel so inclined," he drawled.

"'Tis a sore temptation," William said and grinned. "Might I ask what ye are planning to do?"

"I am going into Dunlochan keep and see if I can find a way to hear or see something that will help us. We cannae just keep hiding, nay with Ranald so desperate to get his hands on Katerina."

"And for that ye have to dress all in black and dirty your face?"

"Aye. It makes it easier to hide in the shadows and slip about in them. One can dress all in dark clothes but then be betrayed by the whiteness of one's face. My brother and I used to practice the many ways one could hide in the shadows and quickly discovered how the hands and face could give one away. Hence the gloves and the dirty face."

After studying Lucas for a moment, William nodded. "I can see that now. Dinnae ye think that 'tis a wee bit dangerous to go right into the keep?"

"It is that, but we can barely move now because of Ranald and his men hunting us as they are. They seem to be everywhere and ne'er rest. I also think there are ways to move about inside Dunlochan without being seen. There are passages in the walls."

"Aye, but I dinnae ken where they all are."

"Neither do I, but I have learned from Katerina where some of them are and I will start with those. Most times one passage will lead into another although there is often a trick about it." He shrugged. "It will give me something to do aside from hiding in these caves and hoping Ranald doesnae discover them."

"Weel, I wish I could go with ye, but I suspicion this

is one of those jobs best done alone. Take care. We cannae afford to have ye caught. If naught else, they would use ye to get to Katerina."

Lucas nodded even as he told himself William was wrong. Ranald and Agnes might try to use him to get to Katerina, but Katerina might not be interested in sacrificing anything to help him. After all, there was still a chance she had tried to have him killed just because she thought he was showing too much interest in Agnes.

As he made his way through the passages to the storerooms of the keep, he realized that the accusation he had flung at her and tried to cling to even now no longer felt right. Even the words in his mouth tasted wrong. At some time during the days and nights he had spent with Katerina and her men, he had begun to believe her incapable of trying to kill him. He did not know when or why, but he knew he no longer thought her guilty of wanting to see him dead. Lucas did not think she was completely innocent, but he found far too much comfort in the fact that she did not want him dead. It was somewhat alarming and made him even more determined to find out the whole truth.

After slipping along several passages and finding out nothing more than the fact that Agnes's people had very few morals, Lucas was ready to return to Katerina's hiding place. If nothing else it was growing uncomfortable to listen to so many lovers entertaining themselves when he had been celibate for so very long. Even as he turned to start his journey out of Dunlochan keep, his hand lightly sliding along the wall of the dark passage, he felt something that drew his attention. Cautiously opening his shuttered lantern a little more, he found himself staring at what looked to be a door. The mix of wood and stone that lined the passages inside the keep walls had made it hard to see at first, so perfectly did it blend with its surroundings.

Dimming his light, Lucas slowly opened the door. Seeing that it led to another passage, he quietly slipped inside and eased the door shut behind him, placing one of the small bits of wood he had carried with him in the frame of the door so that it could not shut completely. The last thing he wanted was to discover that these doors could only be opened from one side just as he was trying to make a swift escape. Silently he moved along the passage and within a few feet he began to hear the murmur of voices. Lucas followed the sound even as he tried to guess what part of the keep he was in.

"Why havenae ye found them yet, Ranald?"

The sound of Agnes's voice startled Lucas into stopping. He was surprised at how clearly he could hear and quickly shuttered his lantern. He did not want some flash of light to give him away. There had to be some sort of listening hole nearby or the thick walls would have muffled Agnes's voice. She was sounding almost shrewish, he mused as he lightly ran his fingers over the wall to try to see if there was a hole and if it was low enough for him to see as well as hear.

When he found the hole, he quickly put his eye to it. He could not see all that much of the room but suspected it was Agnes's solar. He recognized the tapestry over the fireplace and the grim-faced woman named Freda sitting in a chair to the right of the fireplace. All he could see of Agnes was the edge of her skirts. They were blue, a color she often wore because he suspected she felt it complemented her eyes. Around the edges of the hole he peered through was cloth and he felt sure he was looking through a tapestry. Not sure how safe it was to keep his eye pressed to the hole he backed away and leaned against the wall, hoping he would hear something worthwhile.

"It has only been a week, Agnes," snapped Ranald. "Ye ken as weel as I do that these bastards are verra good at disappearing. We have been chasing them for a year."

"Someone must ken where they are. Ye need to beat the truth out of some of those insolent villagers."

"I tried that and all that accomplished was to make more people angry. Ye get them too angry and ye will have more than a small group of reivers to deal with. Ye may even give the men on that council some backbone and ye cannae afford that."

The swish of skirts told Lucas that Agnes was moving and he chanced another peek through the listening hole to see that she had seated herself near Freda. Agnes did not look very sweet and witless at the moment. Her expression was one of cold, hard anger. As he returned to leaning against the wall he realized that everyone was right about the woman, and his confidence in his own judgment sank even lower.

"Mayhap it is time to do something about those foolish old men," Agnes said.

"That wouldnae be wise," said Freda, her voice strong and weighted with an authority that surprised Lucas. "They arenae poor villagers or crofters. They have important friends, ones who would ask questions, mayhap e'en seek retribution."

Agnes cursed. "I grow verra weary of having to bow to their rule."

"It willnae be for verra much longer. Word has come that Robbie may have been found."

"*May* have been? That does me no good. I need him found and then buried."

"Patience, child. Patience is often the best weapon against one's enemies."

"If Robbie has been found, he will be taken care of," said Ranald. "He isnae such a great threat. Sir Murray and your sister are of greater importance. They could put a noose around our necks."

"Sir Lucas didnae e'en send his family after us, so why should he act against us now?" asked Agnes.

"He didnae come back here to see Katerina."

"Are ye sure of that?"

"The mon thinks she tried to have him killed. E'en if he no longer believes that, he must still believe that she was the one who ordered him beaten and no mon will forgive a woman for making him a cripple."

"A cripple? Ye ne'er said he had been crippled."

"Didnae see that it mattered as ye want him dead. He has stiffness in his left leg. Ere we tossed him o'er that cliff, we broke his leg, fair crushed it, so that he couldnae do much to help himself e'en if he survived the fall."

"Weel, he managed to do both, didnae he."

"Is there any way he could have guessed the truth?" asked Freda. "I always thought too many kenned that ye forced Katerina to act as she did. Someone may have told Sir Murray."

"Nay, none of my men would tell him anything," said Ranald. "If they ever saw him they would either run or try to kill him. They certainly wouldnae pause to have a wee talk with the mon and tell him they beat him near to death and tried to drown him because Agnes told them to and they are verra sorry they let him think his lover did it."

"Ye grow verra insolent, Ranald," Freda murmured. "I ne'er much liked the plan anyway. It wasnae thought out weel. In truth, 'twas just ye striking out in a temper, Agnes, because the mon didnae fall for your charms. Ye have ne'er tried to control your temper as ye should. Doing something because ye are angry is ne'er a good idea. Things such as that attempt to kill them both should be planned coldly and with a clear mind."

"It was verra obvious that he was wooing Katerina," snapped Agnes. "When I couldnae seduce him away from her, I kenned he was serious in his pursuit of her. Ye ken as weel as I do that the council would have thoroughly approved of Sir Lucas Murray as her husband. He had to be gotten rid of."

"Dinnae try to act as if ye actually had a plan, child. Ye didnae. Ye struck out in anger as ye often do. It failed. Accept that."

"As ye wish," Agnes said tightly. "Do ye have any great, weel thought out plan for getting rid of him and Katerina now?"

The sound of a slap echoed in the passageway. "Dinnae be so disrespectful. Aye, I have a plan. Grab either Sir Lucas or Katerina."

"That is what we have been trying to do."

"Use whichever one ye capture to draw the other into a trap," Freda continued as if Agnes had not spoken. "The mon may think Katerina guilty of having him beaten near to death, but he is one of those honorable men and he willnae be able to do anything else but try to rescue her. Katerina will ne'er leave him in your hands either, Ranald. Each of them, with their honor and compassion, is the other's own worst enemy."

"'Tis much the same plan I had when I went after Thomas," Ranald said. "I had hoped to beat some information out of the boy but kenned weel that he could be used to lure Katerina into my grasp."

Agnes snorted in obvious contempt. "Ye thought to lure Annie into your grasp, Ranald. Dinnae try to fool us."

"Either one would have brought Katerina running to the rescue."

"Which is what we need her to do now," said Freda. "They must be hiding close by as they are always quick at hand when someone is in trouble. There is a hiding place on Dunlochan lands, Ranald. Find it. There may be some note of it in the ledger room. If ye cannae read, get Agnes to do it for ye."

There was the sound of a door shutting and, after a moment of heavy silence, Agnes said, "Weel, ye heard her. We are to dirty our hands and look through the papers in the ledger room."

"I will do it. I can read weel enough."

"Ye need to be out searching for Katerina or Sir Lucas. I cannae do that, can I. Ye can help me with that tedious chore from time to time, but catching Sir Lucas and Katerina is the far more important one. I still cannae believe that bitch survived being thrown into the loch or that Sir Lucas has returned to trouble us once again."

"'Tis nay their ghosties I am dealing with. The old woman was right. The last time we tried to be rid of those two we just struck out at them, didnae think it through. It wasnae a bad plan and I did have Lady Katerina convinced that she could save her lover by standing still and quiet, acting like she was watching it all with a cold eye. Yet, we failed, and it could weel be that we would have succeeded if we had thought it out and planned it more carefully. This time we will do so."

"Mayhap whilst ye are planning it all so carefully, ye can think of a way to allow me a wee bit of time with Sir Lucas ere ye kill him."

"Only if ye allow me a wee bit of time with Lady Katerina ere we kill her."

Agnes cursed softly and then sighed. "Fair enough. I suspicion ye had plans to take that time anyway."

"Cannae see wasting an opportunity."

"And I think it is time we made a few plans to rid ourselves of the burden of that cursed council."

"Aye, I think Freda is being far too cautious there."

"Thank ye, Ranald. Come with me, I have a plan as to how I might thank ye for your support of all my plans."

Chapter Eight

He was an utter ass. Lucas slowly slid down the wall until he sat upon the floor and lightly banged his head against the wall a few times. It did nothing to dislodge the distasteful truth from his mind, however. He was still an ass, a witless blind fool. Katerina was innocent. He had scoffed at her tale of what had happened that night and it had all been the truth.

How could he have ever thought otherwise? Katerina had always shown nothing but kindness to all around her and she possessed a light spirit, compassion and honor as much a part of her as the blood that ran in her veins. There had been a part of him that had constantly denied her guilt, but he had always ruthlessly silenced it whenever it stirred. Lucas did wonder if it was that part of him that had kept him unable to take another lover even after he had healed enough to feel lusty again. At least he had not been unfaithful to her despite the few times he had tried to be. It was humiliating to realize that the usually witless part of him had been the only part to show any good sense.

The problem was what did he do now? Even if he had not killed whatever love Katerina may have felt for him, he had definitely killed her trust and faith in him. Lucas was not confident that he had the skills to repair that wound. A blunt but simple apology would certainly not do it.

Groveling might help, he thought wryly. At the moment, with every deep, fierce emotion he had felt for her a year ago swamping his heart and mind, released from the prison he had forced them into, Lucas suspected he might actually be able to grovel quite abjectly. He knew himself too well, however, to believe that he would really be able to do it. By the time he reached her side again pride would have reared its head and would prevent him from doing so. Knowing that he was wrong did not mean he would admit to it easily.

Lucas carefully stood up and began to wind his way through the passages that would lead him back to the hall hidden so well in the caves. He knew he had to have Katerina back. He had known it from the beginning but until now, that need had only fed his anger at her. His mistrust of her had made him see that need as a curse, a weakness that could get him killed. In fact, if Katerina wanted him dead now, he would not blame her at all.

Idly rubbing his leg, the damp in the passages causing it to ache, Lucas suddenly cursed. He stopped and dragged his hand through his hair. What could he be thinking of? Katerina would not want him now. He was scarred and maimed. There was no ignoring the awkwardness he suffered all too often because of the stiffness in his shattered leg. Katerina deserved a man firm of limb and unmarred.

A heartbeat later, Lucas decided he was being a coward, perhaps even making excuses so that he did not have to face her or admit his wrongs. He all too easily recalled how she had looked at him that first night after rescuing him from Ranald and his men. There was no disputing the joy that had brightened her eyes just before he had snuffed it out with his baseless accusations. She had spoken of grieving for him and he winced to recall how he had scorned her claim. Even more important, she had already included him in several of her forays against Agnes and Ranald and that strongly implied that she at least trusted him to successfully carry out his part in such actions. He had to trust in those indications that he had some chance of winning her back, small though that chance might be.

"Admit it, fool," he muttered as he started on his way again, "if only to yourself. Ye dinnae have any choice but to try and mend things a-tween ye and Kat. Ye havenae truly been alive since ye lost her. Swallow your cursed pride and take your chances."

Katerina also had her own scars, he thought as he cautiously entered the storerooms. He hated to think of all the pain she must have suffered, but it might mean that she would be far less concerned with his scars than many another woman. It was a small thing, but it gave him some hope. Once in the passage that led away from the keep, he moved more quickly, suddenly eager to get to Katerina.

Wincing, Katerina struggled to sit up on her own. By the time she accomplished that simple task she was so weak she fell against the pillows at her back and had to struggle to ease her rapid breathing. She was also bathed in sweat and wished she could reach the bowl of water and cloth Annie had set down on the chest near the bed. There would be no swift recovery from this wound.

Worse, she was bored. Even trapped into hiding

from her enemies, she had still found a lot to keep her busy. Lying in a bed, too weak to do much of anything but think, was sure to make her insane in a very short time. She doubted she could even play a game of chess at the moment for her hands shook. Katerina cursed and looked around, wondering if she could call someone in to keep her company. She had a few books she had slipped out of Dunlochan and someone could read to her, she mused, and then cursed again. Katerina could not believe she had been reduced to this.

A noise at the doorway drew her attention and she tensed as Lucas entered the room. He looked so good to her that she nearly shouted at him to go away, even as she wondered why he was wearing such dark clothing. Katerina inwardly sighed. Her emotions might be in such a tangle that too much time with Lucas could be dangerous, but she was too hungry for company to care very much.

"Bored already, are ye?" he asked as he stopped by the edge of her bed.

"More than words can say."

"Ye are looking verra flushed." He touched her forehead and his brows went up at the sweat he found there. "Ye havenae gotten out of bed, have ye?"

"Nay, I merely tried to sit up all by myself. I am as weak as a newborn."

"Ye will be for a few more days." He moved to the bowl of water Annie had left and wrung out the cloth. "Ye must take care to move verra little and verra slowly," he said as he gently bathed her face. "I dinnae think ye can open your wounds, but the fever could easily return if ye allow yourself to get too tired. It nearly took ye twice. It wouldnae be wise to invite it back."

"Are ye saying that I nearly died twice?"

"Aye." Lucas did not even want to think about those harrowing hours where he had fought to keep her alive, let alone talk about them. "Ye arenae as strong as ye used to be, I think, and it was a hard struggle for ye to fight off the fever."

Katerina knew it was foolish to be so alarmed by that news, but she was. She had given little thought to how sick she might have been, had simply acknowledged that she had had a fever brought on by her wound. Now that she thought about it Annie had alluded to such a thing, but she had failed to fully understand. It was a little terrifying to realize how close death had come to her.

"Now ye look too pale," he grumbled as he tossed the cloth back into the bowl.

"Weel, ye just told me I almost died twice."

"But ye didnae die, so why fret o'er it. Just keep it in mind and take care of yourself. Rest and dinnae try to do too much too soon."

The fear of taking another fever and failing to fight it off would certainly make her be careful, Katerina mused. She knew herself too well, however, to believe it would work for very long. It was something she would have to remind herself of from time to time, when the tedium of lying in bed for hours became too much to bear. Perhaps if she arranged a tight schedule of care and attention it would help. Whenever she got so crazed with boredom she was tempted to do too much, she could ease that feeling with the sure knowledge that someone would soon come to read to her, or play chess, or help her get clean.

"Kat?"

She blinked as his voice yanked her back from making all her plans. "What?"

"Where did ye just go?"

"Oh, I was thinking of the ways I might be able to stop myself from doing anything foolish."

"And what did ye think of?"

"I need to arrange a verra tight schedule of care and companionship."

"And ye think that will help?"

"Oh, aye. When the boredom makes me want to pull out my hair, I can remind myself that in but a few minutes William will come to play chess with me or Annie will come to wash my hair. Such as that." She shrugged. "It might help."

"It will help a lot. It did for me when I was trapped in a bed for months. I had so many kin ready to fall in with my plans that there were actually moments when I wished I could have some time alone."

It was the first time he had referred to the time he had spent healing from his many injuries. Katerina was a little surprised. What surprised her even more was that there was no hint of accusation or anger in his voice or his expression. She desperately wanted to ask him to tell her more about how he had saved himself and how he had recovered so well, but she was afraid such a conversation would ruin the tentative truce they seemed to be enjoying.

Lucas watched the expressions dance across her lovely face and almost smiled. Katerina was quick of wit. She was already sensing a change in his attitude and was puzzled. He wondered if that would be enough, and inwardly grimaced. He knew he owed her an enormous apology, and had planned to give her one immediately, but the words were stuck in his throat. It might work just as well if he showed her he had changed, made it clear by his actions that he no longer thought her a threat to him. It was the coward's way out, but he was willing to try it for a while, if only to save himself from the humiliation of openly declaring himself an utter idiot.

"Ye like to play chess?" he asked.

"Aye, but I am so weak my hands are trembling a wee bit and I wouldnae be able to handle the pieces weel," she said.

"Ye could just tell me what move ye wish to make and let me move the piece for ye." He glanced at the small pile of books set neatly in a basket in the corner. "Or I could read to ye for a while."

It was sad how thrilled she was by his offer, she decided, and almost smiled. "Read to me, I think. I would like that. I dinnae believe I have the strength to think my way through an entire game of chess and I would like to at least give ye a good game."

"Which book?" he asked as he went to the basket and began to look through the books.

"It doesnae matter. Whichever one ye feel inclined to read. I have the feeling I willnae be able to stay awake for too long."

Lucas picked out a book of songs and poetry, deciding the shorter tales told by the words of the troubadours, the old songs would be best. He sat in the chair next to the bed and began to read. The faint smile that appeared on her face cheered him for he knew he had chosen the right book. It held far too many flowery sentiments for his liking, but it obviously made her happy and that was the most important thing right now.

It was not long before Katerina's eyes were closed. Lucas watched her as he continued to read, but her eyelids did not even flutter open once and he finally set the book aside. He leaned forward and lightly stroked her cheek with his fingers, fighting the urge to sigh like some foolish boy caught tight in the throes of his first infatuation. Katerina was beautiful, of that

there was no question, but it was far more than that
that had drawn him to her and he could not believe
he had forgotten it. She was strong, compassionate,
loyal, and had a quick, sharp wit.

In fact, she had been and still was everything he
had ever wanted in a woman. Despite her innocence,
even her passion was strong, matching his own in a
way that kept him hungry for her all the time. Now
that he knew the truth, Lucas could not understand
how he could ever have doubted her. He was very glad
he had never voiced his suspicions to his family. It had
been pride that had kept him silent about his belief
that he had been betrayed by the very woman he had
wanted to make his wife. He had not wanted any of his
kin to realize what an utter fool he had been. He had
kept his grief over her loss and the hurt she had dealt
a secret as well, although he suspected a few scraps
of that had escaped when he had been fevered. No
one had questioned it, however. At least he did not
have to explain to his kin why he was now pursuing a
woman he had claimed was the one who had ordered
the beating he had suffered.

Standing up, Lucas stretched, his muscles stiff from
all the creeping through damp passages he had just
indulged in. He leaned over and brushed his mouth
over Katerina's forehead. When she murmured softly
he moved his mouth down to hers. Even caught fast
in the beginnings of sleep she responded to his kiss,
her lips warm and welcoming, and her tongue lazily
toying with his when he eased it into her mouth. He
forced himself to pull away before need and temptation made him attempt to take advantage of her.

Lightly stroking her hair, he wondered if he would
ever find the words to apologize for the great wrong
he had done her. What could he say? My pardon for
thinking ye are a murderess, a woman who would kill

a mon because he smiled at another. It was not enough. Lucas was not sure any apology, no matter how elegant, would ever be enough, but that would not stop him from trying to win her back.

Hearing a soft rustle of skirts, he looked to find Annie standing in the doorway. He smiled faintly and waved her over to the bed. Although he was reluctant to leave Katerina, Lucas knew it would be best to leave her in Annie's capable hands for a while. He needed to think, to plan his campaign to bring Katerina back into his arms, and he could not do that successfully when his attention was fully taken up with Katerina, even if it was only to watch her sleep.

"She has just gone to sleep," he said quietly as Annie stepped up beside him.

"There isnae any sign of the fever returning, is there?" asked Annie.

"Nay, and I dinnae think it will return if she takes good care of herself."

"I cannae believe we almost lost her. She has always seemed so strong, so verra alive."

"She is both, but I am thinking that living in these caves for a year hasnae been verra good for her, and, nay matter how comfortable she has made them, there isnae all the food or warmth she was accustomed to before this."

Annie nodded. "Aye, and she isnae all that long recovered from all the wounds and the fever she suffered after that bastard threw her into the loch."

"Nay, she isnae." Thinking of all the scars Katerina carried, Lucas was astonished that she had recovered as well as she had. "So, we must be sure that she nay only takes care to rest but that she isnae allowed to get too bored and fretful."

"I ken it. She could try to get up or do something

else that would cause her harm. I mean to keep her verra busy and try nay to leave her alone too much."

"Exactly what she and I were discussing ere my reading sent her to sleep. Just a week more. Then I feel sure she will be strong enough to get up and e'en allow herself to get tired without having to go right to bed. I shall leave ye to it, then." He started toward the door. "And dinnae fret if ye feel the need to rest a wee bit yourself. Katerina is recovered enough to call if she needs help or feels the fever catching her in its grip again."

Lucas headed for the hall. He needed to talk to William about some of the things he had overheard. He would not tell the man everything if only because he doubted he could stand William's gloating when it became obvious that he had heard the full truth about the beating and the attempt to kill him. What the vicious pair he had just listened to said about their plans for now and in the future was all the man needed to know. That and the location of the passage within the walls next to Agnes's solar. They now had a chance to learn all of Ranald and Agnes's plans and Lucas intended to take full advantage of it.

Katerina slowly opened her eyes and looked to the side of the bed. She was annoyed at how disappointed she felt when she saw Annie there sewing a shirt for Thomas and not Lucas. She touched her lips, not sure if the kiss she had felt was a dream or had really happened, but the warmth of it lingered. Shaking aside such useless puzzles, she began to sit up, immediately drawing Annie's attention.

"Nay, Annie, let me try this myself," she said as the woman put down her sewing and moved to help her. "It isnae such a great thing yet I believe 'tis one small, harmless way to start to regain some of the strength I have lost."

"Aye, I suspicion it is. Do ye want something to drink?"

Realizing that all her effort to sit up on her own had been wasted because she was going to have to have Annie help her with her personal needs, Katerina softly cursed. "After I make room for it." She grimaced as Annie took her by the arm and carefully helped her out of the bed. "I hate this."

"I ken it, but it willnae be so verra long ere ye can do this much for yourself as weel."

Katerina hoped the woman was right because the more she healed the more embarrassing she found the need to have such help. By the time Annie got her back into bed, she needed to have the fine sheen of sweat bathed from her skin. Despite her embarrassment, however, she did feel much better by the time it was done. She gratefully accepted Annie's help in drinking some mead, yet again strengthened with some herbs, for her hands were shaking slightly again. Once that was done, Katerina rested against the pillows Annie plumped up behind her back and realized that, although she was tired, she was not really ready to go to sleep again.

Her thoughts immediately went to Lucas. There had been something different about him when he had visited her earlier. The anger in him seemed to have disappeared. He was almost like the Lucas she had fallen in love with a year ago. What Katerina could not puzzle out was why there was a change in him or how long that change would last. Was it just because he had been too weary to be angry, or had he finally begun to reconsider his accusations against her?

"I dinnae understand men at all," she muttered.

Annie smiled as she sat down and began to work on

the shirt again. "I dinnae think many women do, but then men dinnae much understand women."

"That seems a verra strange way for things to work."

"It does, doesnae it, but mayhap 'tis arranged that way so that those who wed will ne'er truly bore each other. Why are ye troubled about that now?"

For a moment Katerina said nothing, not sure she wished to share such troubles with the woman, but then she sighed. She had no one else to share them with and it would probably help to have someone to thrash it all out with. Another woman's point of view might even help to ease some of the confusion gripping her so tightly at the moment.

"Sir Murray was acting verra different when he was here earlier."

"Different? In what way?"

"Kinder. There wasnae the anger in him that he has carried about since he arrived."

"Ah, that anger. Mayhap he had finally thought things through most carefully and decided ye are nay the threat to him that he thought ye were, that ye are innocent of what he accused ye of."

"I wondered on that but why should he have changed his mind?"

"Because all of us who ken ye weel tell him he is wrong."

"And when has that e'er mattered to a mon?"

Annie laughed softly. "True. Sadly true. I cannae say, m'lady. Mayhap he has learned something, heard something from someone he cannae dismiss as just your friend or kinsmon."

"But where would he have heard anything?"

Annie shrugged. "I dinnae ken. The men dinnae tell me all that much about the battle with Ranald and Agnes. When they do talk to me, 'tis about what they heard concerning the people in the village or the like.

If anyone would ken if Sir Lucas had heard something important, or where he has been that he might have heard something important, William would. 'Tis verra clear to everyone that Sir Lucas treats William as your second-in-command."

"Which is good because that is what he will be when I have control of Dunlochan." She frowned. "I wonder how he kenned that for I dinnae believe I have e'er told him so."

"Ah, weel, men are much like dogs in that as they can always seem to sniff out the leader in a pack."

"I certainly hope they dinnae do it in the same way dogs do." Katerina grinned when Annie giggled. "No matter. At least Sir Murray chose the right mon and didnae insult William in any way."

"True, for it wouldnae be just William who felt the sting of it. There are those brothers of his who would also take insult."

"And my wee band of men would turn into a snarling pack of angry wolves, useless to me. Nay a pleasant thought." She frowned, her thoughts immediately going back to the puzzle of Lucas's change of humor. "Yet, if he heard something and kens the truth now, why didnae he tell me so?"

"Or apologize for thinking poorly of ye."

"Aye. He said naught about it. Ye would think he would at least let me ken that he was wrong and why he has changed his mind."

"Ah, weel, there ye have it."

"What do I have?"

"The reason why he has said nothing. If he has finally heard something that has made him see the truth that has been right under his nose all the time, then the only way to tell ye is to admit he is wrong. E'en Thomas, young as he is, finds it verra difficult to admit that he is wrong about something."

Katerina thought of her father and realized she could all too easily recall the same fault in him. "'Tis a peculiarity with men then, aye?"

"It would seem so. Does it matter if he doesnae come right out and say he was wrong and now he kens ye are innocent of all the wrongs he accused ye of?"

"I fear it does. He hurt me, Annie, hurt me verra badly. If 'twas but a wee sin against me I wouldnae care, but his accusing me of trying to kill him fair tore my heart right out of my chest. Aye, he needs to say something if he has changed his mind about that. It doesnae have to be pretty and he doesnae e'en have to bluntly declare that he was an idiot, but he has to say something. He has to give me some reason why he believed such an awful thing about me, try to explain how the idea e'en entered his head or I am nay sure I can trust my heart to him again."

Annie sighed and nodded. "Aye, I think I would feel the same. It revealed that he had lost faith in ye and that is a verra grave sin indeed. Unless he explains how that happened ye could spend the rest of your days fearing it would happen again. All I can say is that, if ye want the mon back, are willing to accept an apology and start again, best ye listen verra closely to what he says. 'Tis just like a mon to slip an apology into a conversation without ye e'en kenning he has done so."

"And something tells me that is exactly what Sir Murray might try to do, although he is always so bluntly honest in all else."

"But nay on something that has probably left him feeling like a fool. Then ye are dealing with a mon's pride and 'tis a powerful thing." She winked at Katerina. "Rest, m'lady. Your eyes are already more shut than open and I think ye are going to need all your wits about ye in the coming days."

Katerina smiled even as she closed her eyes. It seemed that simply waking up was enough to use up what little strength she had. And Annie was right; she was going to need her wits strong and clear to deal with Lucas in the coming days.

If he had changed his mind about her, no longer believed her capable of such a heartless crime, he would present even more of a lure for her than he did already. That meant she had to make a decision about whether or not she would allow the passion that flared between them to take hold of her again. If he had changed his mind, Lucas could well be thinking to return to where they had been before the beating. She had better be ready to say aye or nay for she knew there would be no turning back no matter which answer she gave him.

She had meant every word she had said to Annie. She needed an apology of some sort, but she needed an explanation even more. Katerina knew she had to try to understand why he had condemned her so quickly and had been unwilling to accept her claim of innocence. Until he did that to her satisfaction there would always be a shadow of doubt and fear in her heart. As sleep crept over her, dimming her thoughts, a small voice whispered that that should make no difference in the passion she and Lucas could share, that she should take what she craved and sort out the other problems later. Katerina was not sure that was the best advice she had ever given herself, but she had the feeling it might just be the only advice she heeded.

Chapter Nine

"If we dinnae get some meat soon, ye will be eating naught but oatmeal morning, noon, and night," Annie said as she served Lucas a bowl of stew.

Looking at the spoonful of stew he was about to put into his mouth and then into the bowl he held, Lucas could see very little meat in it. It looked a lot like the broth Katerina had had to eat for the last three days. Although it tasted good, it was not what he wanted to eat too often. He had had his fill of such food when he had been recovering from his injuries.

"We are that low on supplies?" he asked.

"Just on meat. William says Old Hilda told him that Ranald and his men are feasting every night, eating as if they are afraid it will all disappear tomorrow. She said that if it continues there willnae be a chicken, cow, or pig left within the walls of Dunlochan. And none of the fools has gone hunting, nay for game leastwise. She said she would try to get us some, but William told her nay to take the risk. He told her that when supplies are too tight a little thievery is much too easy to spot and she would be one of the first ones they would be looking at with suspicion."

"He is right in all he says and I pray she heeds him.

The cook is always the first one such men look at when the meal is poorly made or is too plain, or when there isnae much of it set out. Getting meat for us isnae worth the risk to the woman. Right after I check on Katerina's wounds I will go a-hunting."

"May I come with ye?" asked Thomas.

"Aye, if ye wish to," replied Lucas.

"Oh, aye, I wish to. I havenae left these caves in days. 'Twould be nice to get out of them for a wee while."

"Mayhap ye should wait until the rest of the men return from moving the horses," said Annie.

"That could be far later than ye think it will be, Annie," Lucas said. "The horses have been hidden far from here and they will be moved a fair distance from where they were last night. 'Tis a verra long walk the men must make now and made all the longer by the stealth they need to use."

"But Ranald is hunting ye."

"I ken it, but a mon and a boy can hide more easily and quickly than a large group of men can." He smiled faintly. "I shall wear a cap to hide my hair. 'Tis what caught me out last time."

She sighed and lightly bit her bottom lip. "Mayhap Hilda—"

"Nay, she cannae take the risk, Annie. The minute they suspected her of taking food, they would suspect she was giving it to us. 'Tis a wonder the fools havenae started to turn on all the ones who had been close to Katerina yet. I think they suffer that blindness that so often afflicts the people who have a lot of servants, and simply dinnae see that, say, a cook, could be any threat to them. I would like it to remain so."

"Aye, ye are right. Our friends within the keep have all been verra lucky so far and it would be careless to put that at risk for the sake of a bit of meat."

Lucas finished his meal and stood up. "All of us are being hunted, Annie. Ranald may want me, or Kat more than any other, but none of us are safe. I dislike hiding away here, but I understand the need for it. I willnae do it without a good meal, however. Dinnae fret, the game is still plentiful round here and, though it sounds vain of me to say so, I am an excellent hunter."

He strode away before Annie could think of any more arguments she could make. It was risky to go out to hunt some food, but it was also risky to go out every night to move the horses around in the hope of keeping them out of Ranald's hands. It was risky to sit in these caves so close to Dunlochan keep. Until Ranald and Agnes were no longer a threat they were all trapped by risk. It was not something he felt he should say to Annie, however, as the woman fretted over the safety of them all far too much already.

Lucas entered Katerina's bedchamber and grinned. She was struggling to sit up again and although her movements were much stronger and the hint of her former grace could easily be seen, she was still having some trouble. Katerina's need for some hearty fare to regain her strength was yet another good reason to take the risk of going out to hunt. If they were reduced to oatmeal and broth she would never regain the health stolen by her wound and the fever.

"Need some help?" he asked as he walked up to the bed. He caught a quick glimpse of a somewhat dirty foot and knew Katerina had been out of her bed but he resisted the urge to lecture her.

"Nay, 'tis getting easier," Katerina said, trying to sound pleasant when she actually felt very inclined to curse. She certainly was not about to confess that one reason she was struggling now was because she had risen and seen to her own personal needs, using up far more strength than she had thought she would.

"Aye, I can see that. Ye shall be up and dancing in but a day or two."

"Have ye come here for a reason other than to bludgeon me witless with what ye think is humor?"

"Ouch." He laughed and shook his head. "I can see that your wits are returning to their usual sharpness. Nay, I came to have a look at your wound ere I go a-hunting."

"A-hunting what? Nay Ranald and his men, I hope." She tried to see the wound he uncovered but it was in an awkward spot high on her shoulder and she could barely see more than the edges of it around Lucas's long fingers. "I wouldnae be at all surprised if that is just what Ranald would like ye to do."

"Nay, I dinnae go out hunting Ranald although I have been thinking of it. The mon has run free o'er Dunlochan lands for far too long. Nay, tonight I go to find some meat for the table."

"Has something happened to Old Hilda?"

Deciding it was time to leave the bandage off, Lucas did so, and then retied her night shift, trying hard to ignore the tempting glimpse of the soft curves of her full breasts. "Nay, Old Hilda is fine." He told her what Annie had told him. "The risk is too high now. The people still within the walls of Dunlochan are safe and I want them to stay that way."

"A wish I share wholeheartedly but 'tis verra risky for ye to go out there now. Ranald—"

"Is hunting us. Aye, I ken it weel. It doesnae matter. A number of us have to go out each night to move the horses from one hiding place to another, dinnae we. I see nay difference between that and me going out to catch us a few rabbits for the pot except that I will bring back something other than sore feet."

Katerina smiled fleetingly, but quickly grew concerned again. She knew everything he said was right and there was no argument she could make against his decision. She still felt tempted to try. Unfortunately, the only argument she had was that her stomach had knotted when he had said he was going a-hunting. It was a feeling she always got when something was wrong, but she doubted he would understand or believe her. Katerina suspected he would get the same look on his face as her father always had, that irritating expression of the superior male affectionately amused by the woman's emotional foolishness. If he did, she would probably hurt herself in her attempt to hit him repeatedly.

"I dinnae like it," she murmured.

"Although I am actually looking forward to getting out of these caves for a wee while, I am nay too fond of it either. But I am nay too fond of a regimen of oatmeal and herbal broths, either. 'Twill be just Thomas, who kens verra weel how to be quiet and stay weel hidden, and me. We willnae be easy to see or easy to catch and find if we are seen. I dinnae intend to bring down a deer and risk getting caught whilst dressing it or trying to drag it back here. I go for some rabbits. Small game. Something that willnae clearly mark that someone has been in the area hunting."

"I ken it. I ken that ye are verra skilled in all of this." She grimaced. "'Tis just that my stomach hurts."

Lucas blinked. "Your stomach hurts? Do ye think ye have eaten something that wasnae good for ye?"

"Nay. E'er since I was a little girl I get an ache in my stomach when something is wrong and it really aches now."

"Did it ache the night ye got wounded? Or the night Ranald attacked us by the loch?"

"Weel, the night I got wounded I had reason to

think it ached for a specific reason." She felt herself blush at the thought of how she had believed it was time for her monthly bleeding to begin, especially when the look in his eye told her he had guessed what she was referring to. "The night Ranald attacked me by the loch as I waited for you, I thought 'twas, weel, anticipation." She ignored his grin and continued, "'Tis neither of those things now."

"Weel, lass, I suspect ye have a wee gift for sensing trouble. I had a great uncle who could do the same. Aye and a cousin. I will heed it in such that I will be verra wary and verra careful. Unfortunately, we are surrounded by trouble and we need meat. The men willnae stand for meals without it and ye need it to regain your strength."

"I ken it. In truth, I have had the ache in my stomach now and then ever since Ranald learned that I was alive." Katerina fought to hide her pleasure over the way he so calmly accepted her strange gift and, even more important, seemed to believe in it without question.

"And that should be no surprise, aye? The mon wants ye dead. I willnae ignore the chance that ye are having a warning about something else, however." He bent over and gave her a quick hard kiss, pleased by the way her blue eyes darkened with a pleasure she could not hide. "Ye remain aware as weel. Annie remains here and the men should return in a while. Thomas and I will be back as soon as we can. I dinnae go to enjoy a hunt, simply to get what I can as fast as I can." He started out the door. "And next time ye have to use the bucket call for Annie so that ye dinnae exhaust yourself so." He hurried through the doorway and quickly stepped to the left, just in time to miss being hit by the tankard that flew after him.

Katerina heard his soft laughter fade away as he left

and she cursed. How had the man known that she had gotten up to relieve herself without calling for Annie? She suspected it was just a very clever guess on his part. Still, he was right. She had exhausted herself over that one small chore. If she had had Annie at least help her to the bucket tucked behind the privacy screen and then help her back to bed, she would not need to sleep again.

Settling herself more comfortably against the pillows, she tried not to tire herself worrying about Lucas. She idly rubbed her aching stomach and repeatedly told herself that it was simply a continuous warning about how Ranald wanted her dead. It did not mean that something bad was going to happen tonight, to Lucas or to her. Such good sense only eased her concern a little. Even though Katerina knew she would probably sleep for a while, she also knew she would hold fast to her concern for Lucas and young Thomas until they returned safe and sound.

"Wheesht, ye are good," said Thomas as he tied the third rabbit they had caught to his belt.

"Practice and patience, lad," Lucas said, idly setting another trap and wondering if three rabbits was enough for now.

"Weel, I do have a problem being patient, I confess." He watched the way Lucas tied the small noose he then hid carefully beneath the leaves before baiting it with some clover. "How do ye ken that there are a lot of hungry rabbits round here?"

"Ye look for the signs such as weel cropped clover."

"Ah, aye, I can understand that."

Once the trap was set, Lucas sat back in the shelter of some thick bushes and waited. He would not wait too long for he felt they had been outside long enough already. Yet one more rabbit might mean no one had to risk hunting tomorrow.

"Mayhap we should just steal some chickens," said Thomas, keeping his voice low, almost a whisper.

"I think Katerina would like to survive this without stooping to thievery. We cannae reach the chickens inside the keep, so we would have to steal from the crofters or villagers and I think they have as much need of such bounty as we do, mayhap more."

Thomas sighed and nodded. "Aye, they do. I was just thinking that chickens could be kept inside the caves, aye? They would also give us eggs."

"Clever lad. Ye think with your stomach. I like that in a mon." Lucas exchanged a grin with Thomas. "I am hoping we willnae be trapped in the caves for verra much longer."

"Ye have a plan to beat Ranald and Agnes? Ye can get the proof Lady Katerina needs to defeat them?"

"I am the proof needed, laddie. They both tried to kill me."

"But Lady Katerina said it has to be hard proof. Ye are her friend, aye?, so why would anyone believe ye?"

"Because I will have my verra powerful family standing behind me. I just need to puzzle out a way to get word to them and get their aid without putting any of them in danger. Right now, a Murray coming here could easily be walking to his death and I cannae have that."

"Are your people really that powerful?"

"Powerful enough. Certainly more powerful than Agnes or Ranald. Ah, here comes our rabbit."

Lucas winced when the trap did its job and he soon had another dead rabbit to add to the catch hanging from Thomas's rope belt. He preferred to hunt with a bow. Trapping an animal always made him feel as if he was cheating, if only because it was baited. This time, however, it was a necessity, for he had to make a large catch and make it quickly.

He cleared away all sign of the trapping he had done and any sign that anyone had lain in wait in the bushes. Thomas seemed unconcerned by the fact that he had four dead animals swinging from the rope belt around his thin waist. Lucas almost grinned. Thomas was one of those young lads who wanted to know everything, see everything, and do everything. Annie certainly had her hands full.

Lucas was just about to ask the boy about his family, if he had anyone besides Annie, when a soft noise caught his attention. He briefly placed his hand over Thomas's mouth to stress the need for silence and crouched down. It pleased him when Thomas did the same, keeping a firm hold on their catch so it did not brush the leaves and signal where they were. Lucas did wish the boy was far away, however, as he had the strong feeling that the trouble that made Katerina's stomach ache was about to descend upon them.

Keeping Thomas sheltered by his body Lucas slowly crept backward, seeking out the heavy undergrowth deeper in the forest. Between it and the many deep shadows in the forest Lucas felt they could hide safely from whoever it was he felt stalking them. Keeping Thomas safe was his greatest priority if only because he loathed the thought of returning to Annie and Katerina and telling them something had happened to the boy.

Just as Lucas moved to try and make the boy understand that he was to start running and keep on going no matter what he heard, a dark shadow rose up behind Thomas. Lucas lunged at it, bringing the man down before he could grab Thomas or hurt the boy in any way. While Thomas ran a little deeper into the shadows, Lucas quickly got a firm hold on the man and with equal speed, snapped his neck. The sound of the bone cracking seemed inordinately loud in the quiet forest. It was as Lucas rose to his feet intending to catch hold of Thomas and try to get him to safety that he realized he had been surrounded by Ranald and his men. Even as he cursed his bad luck and drew his sword, he had to admire the way the man had captured him.

"This grows to be a tedious habit, Ranald," he said as the man stepped out of the shadows, his smug attitude making Lucas ache to kill him.

Ranald stared down at his dead man for a moment and then looked at Lucas. "For a cripple ye are surprisingly dangerous."

"Thank ye."

Lucas could see Thomas standing in the shadows just behind the men who had captured him. The boy's very pale face was easy to see and Lucas feared one of Ranald's men would soon see the boy. With the faintest movement of his head he tried to get the boy to run, but Thomas stood as still as any statue, as if he was too terrified to even breathe. When Thomas looked as if he was going to move toward Lucas, Lucas shook his head, and hastily fixed his gaze on Ranald. His hand down at his side, he tried very hard to signal to the obviously frightened boy to run away.

"Get the boy, Harold," snapped Ranald.

"But we got the mon ye wanted," began Harold.

"Get the boy."

"Ye dinnae need him now," said Lucas. "Ye can gain naught from capturing him."

"I can gain a traitor to his laird."

"Dunlochan doesnae have a laird at the moment."

Seeing that Harold was actually going to do as Ranald ordered, Lucas opened his mouth to yell at the boy to run, only to feel something slam into his head. As Lucas fell to his knees he saw Thomas caught in the midst of starting to run, the boy's wide eyes fixed upon him as all the while Harold inched closer and closer. Even as he felt blackness closing in around his mind, Lucas caught Thomas's gaze and held it.

"Run, Thomas. Now!" Lucas ordered and then gave in to unconsciousness.

Katerina ached to get out of bed and pace her room. The only thing stopping her was the sure knowledge that she would probably fall flat on her face after only a few paces. The way Annie sat in the chair next to her bed wringing her hands did nothing to ease the tension growing ever worse inside Katerina.

"Something is wrong," Katerina muttered. "I am fair certain of it. They should have been back by now."

"Ye are fretting o'er naught," said William as he poured each woman a drink and handed it to them. "They went hunting, 'tis all. They may be trying to catch as much as they can so we dinnae have to go out hunting again for a few days."

"William, my stomach is aching. Verra badly, too."

Although William frowned in concern, he sat on the end of the bed and said, "Weel, that could because ye ate something that didnae like ye, or ye are still a wee bit sick, or it is your woman's time. It doesnae have to mean that there is trouble."

"What does your aching stomach have to do with Thomas and Sir Lucas being so late to return here?" asked Annie.

"When there is trouble, my stomach aches," Katerina replied honestly, idly rubbing at her stomach.

"It isnae always right," said William.

Annie ignored him. "And your stomach aches now?" she asked Katerina.

Katerina nodded. "It aches a lot."

"Katerina, if we werenae in such danger I would send someone out right now," said William, "but I cannae do that. I cannae go to the men and tell them that because your stomach aches we must all rush out and just pray that Ranald and his men dinnae grab us whilst we search for two people who may or may not be in trouble. Nay, especially when we have already run that risk once tonight."

When she looked at Annie, Katerina grimaced and Annie did the same. She could tell the woman shared her need to go out and find Thomas and Lucas and drag them back to the safety of the caves. Unfortunately there was no argument that could be made against William's solid good sense. Even if the men did not think she was an utter madwoman, it would be foolish to send them all out just because she *felt* something was wrong.

"Does your stomach truly hurt when there is trouble?" asked Annie.

Realizing that the woman wanted to talk, wanted to try not to worry herself sick over her young brother, Katerina nodded. "It has done so since I was a child. It isnae always a good way to judge if one is safe or nay. There is even the chance it aches now because I ken that Ranald wants me dead. That is a danger, aye? It just isnae an immediate one. The men would most certainly think I had lost my mind if I demanded they rush out into the dark where Ranald and his men are undoubtedly searching just because my stomach hurts and I *think* it might be because Sir Murray and young Thomas are in trouble."

Annie smiled, although it was a weak expression and quickly faded. "True. And e'en if they only thought us foolish women, we would ne'er hear the end of it."

"Weel, my cousins ne'er let me hear the end of it anyway." She reached out and patted Annie's clenched hands. "It sometimes takes a long time to hunt. I suspicion Lucas is trying to catch enough so that no one has to go out for a night or two just as William said. He is verra aware of how dangerous it is to be outside at the moment and he will keep a verra close eye on Thomas. I also told him about how my stomach ached and what it meant."

"Ye told Sir Lucas about that?" asked William.

Katerina nodded and forced herself not to glance at the door to her room yet again. "He accepted it without hesitation. It seems his family has a few people in it that have the same gift." She looked back at Annie. "So, he has been duly warned."

"I will wait another hour, Cousin, and then I and one other mon will set out to see what can be seen," said William. "I just dinnae believe there is any trouble. If your stomach is warning ye of something 'tis just as ye said it might be—a warning that ye arenae safe whilst Ranald hunts ye."

He frowned as a sudden commotion in the hall drew all their attention. It sounded as if everyone was running straight for Katerina's bedchamber. A moment later a breathless, filthy Thomas appeared in the doorway, four dead rabbits hanging from his rope belt.

"Ranald has Sir Lucas and he wants Katerina to come to him or he will kill him!"

Katerina looked at Thomas and then looked at William, wondering absently what was causing the strange rushing noise in her head. "Weel, it seems my stomach was right after all," she said and fell back against the pillows.

William heard a soft sound beside him and looked to find that Annie had obviously fainted as well. She finished her slide out of the chair with an admirable grace. William looked again at his unconscious cousin, a woman who never fainted, and then at Annie, before returning his gaze to the door. Thomas stared at the women with wide eyes and the men crowded behind him looked just as stunned.

Looking at Thomas, who was leaning far to the side to get a better look at his unconscious sister, William said, "Thomas, ye have done weel. We will leave these lasses to wake on their own and go to make some plans to rescue Sir Lucas. Then, when we return ye and I will have a talk about the best way to deliver distressing news to women."

Chapter Ten

The excruciating pain in his arms struck Lucas first. He bit back a groan and slowly opened his eyes. It took a moment for him to see clearly, the pounding in his head blurring his vision. Lucas took several slow, deep breaths to help himself rise above the pain in his body. It did not really surprise him to see a grinning Ranald standing in front of him the moment his vision cleared, although he had hoped the hazy memory of being captured had just been a nightmare. The only good thing he could think of was that there was no sign of Thomas.

A quick look around revealed that they were in an old crofter's home that was nearly a complete ruin, little more than the bare shell of the building still standing. It would not be a good place to defend oneself from an attack but Lucas doubted that Ranald expected one. He hoped that did not mean that Ranald was sure there were none of Katerina's men available to come after him.

"Ye should have stayed dead, Murray," said Ranald.

"We Murrays arenae easy to kill," Lucas drawled. Glancing up Lucas studied the way his wrists were tied together as he hung several inches off the floor from a thick rope attached to a beam in the ceiling. "Ye have an unusual way of entertaining your guests, Ranald." He heard the other men in the cottage snicker but a hard glare from Ranald quickly silenced them. "Did ye think I was poaching?"

"Since Agnes holds Dunlochan and didnae give ye the right to hunt on her lands, then, aye, ye were poaching. That is a hanging offense, ye ken."

"So is murder and I believe the lairdship of Dunlochan hasnae been decided yet. As for hanging," Lucas glanced at the ropes around his wrists and then looked back at Ranald, "I believe ye may need a lesson or two in the art of it." Lucas resisted the strong urge to flinch away from the point of Ranald's sword when the man cut the laces on Lucas's shirt. "Tsk, mon, have some respect. My mother made this shirt for me."

"She will be making ye a shroud soon. Just how did ye get away last time?"

"I can swim."

"Your leg was broken, near shattered. How could ye swim?"

"As I told someone recently, a mon can bear most any pain if he kens it will stop him from drowning."

"Weel, ye willnae escape this time."

"Escape what? Murder?"

"Aye," Ranald replied with a cold, blunt honesty. "But, first, we will use ye to bring that wee bitch Katerina to our door."

"And just how do ye plan to do that? Ye dinnae e'en ken where to leave a message for her."

"Dinnae need to. Thomas will bring her running to your rescue. 'Tis why he escaped so easily. We wanted him to flee."

Lucas doubted it but said nothing.

"Sent a mon after him at the start." Ranald glared at someone behind Lucas. "Thought we might find where the bastards are hiding by following the boy and then we could clean out the whole nest of those reivers, but the fool lost the little cur."

"He was fast, Ranald," protested a man with a deep husky voice. "I followed him into the trees but he was gone. Didnae e'en leave a trail to follow."

Relief swept over Lucas although he kept his face free of all expression. Thomas had taken to the trees, clever lad that he was. Lucas had once seen how nimble the boy was when he got up into the trees and he suspected that Thomas had traveled a fair distance through the forest that way before touching the ground again.

"And why do ye think Thomas will bring Katerina here?" Lucas asked Ranald.

"After ye fell into your wee sleep. I yelled out what I wanted him to do. I kenned he was near at hand. He heard me." Ranald smiled in triumph. "He will tell her that the price for your life is her surrender."

"Ye lied."

"Of course I lied. Ye and that bitch could put a noose around my neck. Agnes's too, although she is sly enough to make a mon believe she is completely innocent and might save herself." Ranald grinned even as he ran the tip of his sharp sword over Lucas's stomach, leaving a shallow, bloody trail. "Ye thought she was sweet, silly and innocent, didnae ye. Ye ne'er realized that the moment ye didnae fall victim to her bonnie smiles and coy ways ye were a dead mon. That ye would refuse her and openly show favor for her half-sister only enraged Agnes more. No one can hate as deep and hard as Agnes can."

"Weel, there is something to be so verra proud of."

"I find it so."

He would, Lucas thought, fighting the urge to cry out as Ranald used his sword to score a circle in the skin around his heart. Now that he was fully awake and aware, Lucas noticed that Ranald had been quick to put some distance between them. The man had an odd, mocking smile on his rough face that told Lucas he was one of those who truly enjoyed inflicting pain on others. That Agnes would choose such a man as her lover said a lot about the kind of woman she was and none of it was good.

Lucas wished he could see Ranald's men. He wanted to see the looks upon their faces as they watched their leader cut up a bound, unarmed man. Some of the men had to be of Ranald's ilk, cruel brutes that measured their strength and power by how much misery they could cause. There was a small chance, however, that one or two could barely stomach Ranald. One or two men willing to protest such behavior or even demand that he stop could be enough to pull Ranald's attention away from him. The cuts Ranald had made so far were shallow and did not bleed too badly, but too many of them left untended for too long could prove dangerous. A pause while Ranald dealt with a rebellion in his ranks could drastically reduce the number of wounds Ranald inflicted, leaving Lucas with enough strength not to be a burden to his rescuers.

And he would be rescued. Lucas was consoled by the knowledge that Katerina was far too weak to be a part of any rescue attempt thus keeping her out of harm's way. He could only hope that William was as cunning as he seemed and would know how to keep his men safe even as he got Lucas out of the mess he was in.

"Are ye sure they are at the old crofter's cottage, Thomas?" William asked.

"Aye, I followed them so that I could be sure Ranald wasnae lying when he said it." Thomas helped himself to one of the oatcakes Annie had made earlier and set in a bowl on the table. "I didnae think he was since he wanted our Katerina to come there, but ye cannae trust a mon like Ranald."

"Nay ye cannae and ye did weel to think of that, lad."

"So, how do we save Sir Lucas?" asked Patrick. "There are only six of us and we cannae get the horses quickly anymore."

"Do ye ken how many men were with Ranald, lad?" William asked Thomas.

"'Twas hard to see in the dark and all, but I am fair sure he had eight with him," Thomas replied. "Was nine but Sir Lucas killed one. Snapped his neck like a twig, he did."

William's eyes widened slightly but he said nothing. He frowned at the top of the rough table as he tried to think of what they could do. He could not leave Lucas with Ranald. The man would kill Lucas and Ranald liked to inflict pain. The death Lucas would suffer would not be one he would wish on any man. He had to be sure he would not be putting his men in danger, half of whom were his brothers.

"The cottage they are in is little more than the frame of a building," William said at last, looking around at his men. "Ranald and his men cannae hide in it so they willnae have a great advantage o'er us."

"Nay," agreed Patrick, "but they have Sir Lucas and he will be in grave danger if we attack too openly."

"I think we can sneak up on them. Aye, 'tis open ground right around the cottage, but we shall have plenty of hiding places until then."

"And then we rush at them?"

"I cannae see any other way. We can slip along like

ghosts until we are seen but, aye, then we will have to run at them and hope we can get to them before they can kill Sir Lucas. 'Tis just the sort of thing Ranald would do if he thought he had lost the fight."

"Aye, it is," agreed Katerina as she and Annie entered the hall.

Katerina had woken up to find herself alone with only a slowly rousing Annie. She still could not believe she had fainted. As she walked over to the table and sat down with Annie's help, she decided it was because she was still a little weak and had not been able to tolerate such worry and fear as well as she used to. Once awake, however, she had refused to be left in her bedchamber while everyone else planned how to get Lucas away from Ranald.

"Ye have to remember that Ranald wants Lucas dead. It pleases him at the moment to try and use Lucas to get to me, but in the end he stills wants him dead." She sighed. "I also think that Ranald just likes to kill."

William nodded. "I have long believed that of the mon." He reached out and patted Katerina's hand. "Dinnae fret, Cousin. We will get the mon back. I but try to ensure that none of us are hurt in the doing of it." He looked at the men. "We will don the darkest clothing we have and smear some dirt o'er our faces. 'Tis a trick Sir Lucas showed me and it makes it much harder for anyone to see ye. Everyone arm themselves with their swords and as many knives as they can carry. Donald, ye bring your bow and arrows. We may have need of your skill to even the numbers or to keep Ranald and his men from reaching Sir Lucas."

Katerina watched the men hurry off to get what they needed and then looked at William, who had risen to go to the chest where he kept his weapons and clothes. "It sounds a good plan, Cousin."

"It isnae the best but there isnae much time to come up with a truly brilliant plan," he said and he buckled on his sword. "Still, Ranald and his men are in a fairly open place and we shall have the cover of the trees until we are quite close." He looked at her and shook his head. "And ye shouldnae be out of your bed."

"I am nay as weak as I was, William, and if I dinnae move around a little bit now and then, how can I e'er regain the strength I have lost."

"Ye cannae, true enough, but dinnae do too much too quickly or ye will find yourself e'en worse off than ye were." He stopped next to her and brushed a kiss over her cheek. "Dinnae fret, Cousin, we will get him back."

"I have faith in ye, William. Godspeed."

It was not until William actually saw the cottage that he felt any real confidence in his plan. Ranald and his men were easily visible. Donald would have no trouble lessening the number of men with Ranald e'en from a safe distance. A few well-placed arrows would also stir up a panic amongst the men. The sight of Sir Lucas hanging from the rafters as a grinning Ranald tormented him with his sword was enough to make William's men eager to fight and that, too, was a good thing.

"Ranald is a vicious bastard, isnae he," murmured Patrick.

"Aye, he is and always has been. True, I have only kenned the mon since he joined forces with Agnes, but a mon like him is born and bred mean." William looked around at his men. "Keep a close watch on Sir Lucas and kill any fool that tries to get near him." When they all nodded, he signaled them to start moving toward the cottage.

* * *

A soft grunt echoed through the cottage followed by a cry of alarm. Lucas pulled himself free of his attempt to separate himself from the pain Ranald was inflicting and looked around. A man had fallen into his line of vision, an arrow sticking out of his back. Lucas immediately turned his full attention on Ranald, knowing that the man could well try to kill him before the ones who had come to rescue him could succeed.

"That bitch!" Ranald screamed even as he headed for the opening that had once been the door. "Kill him!" he ordered his men, pointing at Lucas just before he ran for his horse.

For one tense moment the men remaining in the cottage looked at Lucas. Some had the glint of resolve in their eyes but it was fleeting. When another one of the men fell with a dagger in his throat all interest in Lucas fled. Ranald's men became interested in only one thing, getting out of there alive.

It was all over before Lucas could clear his mind of the pain enough to watch the battle. One other man managed to get to his horse and follow the fleeing Ranald. Two others did not even bother to fight but flung down their swords and surrendered. The rest died trying to get to their mounts.

When William and his men entered the cottage Lucas was almost able to smile. It had occurred to him at some point during Ranald's continuous torment of him, all the little cuts and slices, that he was going to die a very slow and painful death if nothing happened to stop Ranald. Although he hurt all over, felt as if his body had been shredded into pieces and his arms pulled free of their sockets, he was still alive, and Lucas felt that was reason enough to feel jubilant.

"Wheesht, he made a mess of ye, aye?" said William as he and Patrick worked to cut Lucas free.

"Aye," agreed Lucas as he was gently lowered to the ground. "I believe I may soon feel like screaming."

"I am fair surprised ye havenae done so already. Ye must have a thousand cuts on ye."

"Actually I was thinking of how my arms are going to feel in a moment."

William grimaced. "Ah, aye."

As the feeling came back into his arms, it took every ounce of willpower Lucas had not to weep like a bairn. Even the shallow, stinging cuts covering his body disappeared from his thoughts as waves of pain washed over him. He was breathing hard and drenched in sweat by the time the pain in his arms began to ease. Sitting on the floor taking slow, deep breaths to try and steady himself, he looked around and realized William and his men had cleared away all signs of the fight and the torture Lucas had endured. He managed a faint and fleeting smile when William crouched in front of him.

"Feeling better?" William asked.

"I dinnae feel like cutting my own throat in an attempt to stop the pain anymore," Lucas replied.

"That bad, eh?"

"Worse."

"Do ye think ye can make it back to the caves? We have to walk, I fear. We werenae able to grab any of the horses Ranald's men rode here. Ranald scattered them as he fled. He didnae care that that left his men unable to flee themselves," William said in something akin to wonder. "Only that mon Colin managed to get away."

"And the ones who surrendered?"

"New men. Recently hired by Agnes. They were more than willing to swear that they would leave and ne'er come back. Seems Ranald fair sickened them with the way he acted tonight. Both by torturing ye and deserting his men to save his own hide. From what one of them said word will spread and Ranald may begin to find it difficult to get new men."

"And that can only help us." Lucas began to get to his feet and readily accepted William's aid.

"Are ye sure ye can walk back with us? We could make a litter."

"Nay, I believe I can make it."

"Ye are covered in blood."

"Many small cuts, nay more. If I fall down or slow ye down too much, then ye can make me a litter, but I would much rather make it there on my own."

Lucas walked beside William as they headed back to the caves. The other men fanned out to keep a watch for any sign of Ranald returning with more men. William was indeed a very good soldier.

"Did Thomas make it back unharmed?" he asked, hoping that talking would help to keep his mind clear and keep him on his feet.

"He did and he made a grand show of it." William told Lucas all about how the boy had burst into Katerina's room and how both women had fainted.

"That will be a fine memory for the lad."

"Aye, that it will. Just tell me when ye think ye might need a hand."

Within a few minutes Lucas knew he was not going to make it to the caves on his own. He was increasingly lightheaded and there did not seem to be one part of him that did not hurt. It was an effort just to stand upright long enough for the men to build a litter for him. The moment it was done William moved to help him get on it and Lucas knew he more fell down than lay down. Patrick and William picked up the litter and took only a few steps before Lucas let the blackness that had been creeping into his mind take him away from the pain.

* * *

"Sweet Jesu!" Katerina felt like fainting all over again when they carried Lucas into the hall where she still waited. "I hope ye killed the bastard."

"Sadly, nay we didnae. He and Colin escaped. Ranald is less about five men, however." William told her about the two men they had captured and then released. "Ranald willnae find it so verra easy to hire swords anymore."

"Good. Annie, I think it might be better if we put him in that wee niche near us. He is going to need a lot of tending. There doesnae seem to be any part of him that isnae bloody or bruised."

"Ranald had him hung up like fresh kill and was slowly carving him up with his sword. None of them are verra deep but he has bled a lot nonetheless. I think he meant to kill the mon like that, slow and painful, one drop of blood at a time."

"Ranald will surely burn in hell. Help me get him into bed so we can wash him clean and see just how bad it is."

William signaled Patrick to help him carry Lucas to the little bed that had been readied for him. After advising Katerina not to do too much and get too tired, he sought his own bed. From all he could see his cousin still held deep feelings for Sir Lucas, but he was too tired to think abut how much trouble that might bring them.

Katerina sat by the little bed and helped Annie bathe each and every cut on Lucas's body. She felt like weeping. She also felt like hunting Ranald down and gutting him.

"I cannae believe one mon could do this to another, and one who was tied up and unarmed." Katerina shook her head. "'Tis impossible to understand a mon like that."

"Aye, it is," agreed Annie. "Ranald is one of those men that sorely deserves to taste what he inflicts on others. It makes me fair sick to think that he wanted to get his hands on Thomas."

Katerina found that thought so chilling she shivered. "It doesnae bear thinking on." She studied a much cleaner Lucas closely. "I think William is right. None of these cuts are verra deep. Ranald did indeed mean to kill Lucas verra slowly and make him suffer a lot as he did it. And my half-sister has such a mon as her lover and e'en considers marrying him."

"I think she is much akin to him, m'lady."

Thinking of some of the things Agnes had done even as a child Katerina had to agree. "I cannae allow that woman to stay at Dunlochan."

"It might be best to banish her when ye hold Dunlochan again. I wouldnae want a woman like that to be living in my home."

"I couldnae e'er trust her." Katerina gently brushed the hair from Lucas's forehead. "At least William and the men are safe again and Ranald doesnae appear to have hurt Lucas too badly."

"Nay, I think he will mend just fine. Go to bed, m'lady. Ye arenae fully healed yourself and need your rest. I can tend him for now. I dinnae think he will need much more than a lot of rest and a close eye kept on these cuts to make sure they dinnae get putrid or the like."

Katrina slowly made her way back to her room, pleased that it was only a few feet away. Not only was it not too far to walk in her weakened condition but it was close enough to Lucas's bed that she would be able to hear him if he needed anything. Shedding the robe she had thrown on after fainting, she crawled into her bed. No one had lectured her, but she knew she had pushed herself a little too hard this time.

As she closed her eyes she decided that might prove to be a good thing for it would force her to sleep despite the horrible images of Lucas in her mind. It had broken her heart to see him so pale and bloody and she knew she still loved him. He was settled so deeply into her heart she doubted she would ever dig him out. It hurt to think that he did not love her, but she knew there was little she could do about it.

What she needed to decide was what she would do about him. He had been so kind to her, so much like the old Lucas, that she had softened toward him. She could not forget his accusation, however. Unless he apologized and explained himself, she knew that would always stand between them and, even if he did renew his courting, she would doubt his words and fear more hurt at his hands.

If not love, then there was the passion that flared between them. Katerina felt she could indulge herself in that pleasure if she kept her heart sheltered. If all they shared was their desire for each other then it did not matter what he believed about her. She smiled faintly as she let sleep enfold her in its arms. It would be wonderful to feel that heat again and this time she would not be held back by her innocence and a fear of the unknown. If Lucas became her lover he would be in for a few surprises.

Chapter Eleven

Lucas grimaced as he bathed his body. He was not a pretty sight. It had taken over a week for all of the wounds Ranald had inflicted upon him to finish healing. They were still visible, however. He suspected some would even leave a scar and he already had more than enough of those. Although he was not a vain man his battered body troubled him now. He had to wonder what Katerina would think if he was lucky enough to be naked with her tonight.

Nay, not if, he told himself. When. They would make love tonight. He was absolutely certain she would welcome him into her bed. The woman had been inviting him all the time he had been healing from his wounds, tempting him with her soft kisses, her smiles, and all those little touches and strokes. Lucas had the feeling she was not offering him all she had before, however. That hurt, but he accepted the full blame for her wariness. The fact that she still desired him was something he could find some hope in, however.

"Do I really want to ken why ye are here making yourself smell all sweet and nice?"

Scowling at William, who leaned against the side

of the opening to the small alcove where people could bathe if they had a wish to, Lucas asked, "Do ye really think it is any of your business?"

"She is my cousin," William said as he walked into the little room and sat down on a stool in the corner. "In truth, she is more like a sister to me."

"And why would ye think my bathing has aught to do with her?"

William snorted. "Because the two of ye have been wooing each other all week or more. Ye both fair stink of wanting each other."

"Katerina is a grown woman."

"And no longer an innocent. I ken it. I also ken it was ye who ended that innocence. And I ken that nay so long ago ye thought my cousin was the reason ye were beaten and nearly killed. Nay something I would have thought capable of stirring a mon's lust."

"I dinnae believe that about her any longer." Lucas was not about to confess that even when he had believed it she had still been able to stir his lust.

"Because ye heard someone say something about it whilst ye were creeping through the hidden passages of Dunlochan?"

Lucas sighed. "Aye. I heard Ranald and Agnes admit to it all."

"I see." William crossed his arms on his broad chest. "Katerina's word wasnae enough, nor was mine, yet ye suddenly ken the truth because ye hear those two telling the same tale?"

"Ye and Katerina made your distrust and dislike of those two verra clear. I shared what ye felt for Ranald, but I had no reason to think ill of Agnes. As far as I kenned, e'en Ranald had no reason to try to kill me unless someone paid him to and he claimed that someone was Katerina. I couldnae see the two of ye accusing the two of them of the crime as a good enough reason to cast aside what I had believed for a year."

"In some strange way that actually makes sense. Ye havenae told Katerina that though, have ye?"

Lucas shook his head. "Nay, we dinnae talk about that at all."

"So why has she been inviting ye to her bed?"

"Because, nay matter what I felt or she felt about that day by the loch or my accusations, the desire that existed between us a year ago is still there. Still strong. She cannae resist it any more than I can."

"So, like a couple of greedy bairns, ye intend to take what ye want and worry about the consequences later."

"I am hoping there willnae be any consequences, just rewards." Lucas stepped out of the heavy wooden tub and began to dry himself off.

"For ye, aye, how could there not be as ye will be bedding a beautiful woman."

"I will be bedding the woman I had intended to marry until I was beaten senseless, nearly killed, and obviously became verra confused."

"Ye truly wished to marry her?"

"Aye. I ne'er would have taken her innocence if I hadnae meant to marry her. I was certain she was my mate, my other half, and all that."

"Yet ye believed that she would try to have ye killed because ye smiled at another lass?"

"I ken it sounds mad, but I begin to think pain and confused memories had made me just a little mad." Lucas shrugged and began to get dressed. "When I can understand it I will explain it all to Katerina and I am hoping she will forgive me."

William shook his head. "I am nay sure 'tis forgiveness ye have to worry about. Katerina is a verra forgiving lass. Nay, I think your trouble is going to be that

ye didnae believe her. 'Tis that lack of faith in her that
is going to cause ye the most trouble."

Lucas sighed. "I suspicion ye are right. Yet I cannae
do anything to mend the mistakes I have made unless
she is close at hand to heed whate'er I may have to say.
In truth, I am nay going to talk about it all until I do
get it straight in my mind."

"Might be best, e'en if all ye can end up saying is
that ye havenae any idea why ye thought as ye did."
He stood up and walked to the hall with Lucas. "Ye
mean to take whatever she may offer until ye can find
a way to get what ye really want, arenae ye."

"Aye, that is about the way of it."

"I would probably do the same."

Lucas was not sure if that was a blessing of sorts or
just an agreement to what few plans he had, but he
decided not to ask. He had told William more than he
had told anyone, including his twin brother, and felt
a little uneasy about that. He did not think the man
could or would use any of it against him. He just
hoped that William did not tell Katerina everything
they had just discussed. When he and Katerina finally
faced that dark time in their past he wanted it to be at
a time and place of his choosing and he wanted to be
fully prepared for it.

"What are ye planning?" Annie asked Katerina even
as she took a deep breath, enjoying the smell of whatever Katerina had put into the water.

"Why should ye think I am planning anything?" Kat
asked as she stepped into the tub of hot water she and
Annie had spent a long time getting filled.

"Weel, despite the fact that ye bathe and wash more
than any lass I have e'er met, this is a wee bit more
than ye usually do. Ye have also been spending a great

deal of time with Sir Lucas. And ye just have this, weel, this look that tells me ye are planning something."

"I am. I am going to take Sir Lucas Murray as my lover. Tonight."

The wide-eyed look on Annie's face made Katerina a little nervous. She could not be sure if it was shock or outrage. Although she did not really care all that much if Annie approved of what she planned to do, she definitely did not want the woman to disapprove. Annie was the closest thing she had ever had to a friend and she did not wish to lose her over this.

"But ye are a lady, a laird's daughter, and a virgin."

"Aye to the first two and nay to the last." Katerina would not have thought it possible but Annie's eyes got even bigger.

"Does Sir Lucas ken that ye have bedded down with another mon?"

"Sir Lucas was the mon."

"Oh. I see. So, are ye to be married then?"

Katerina sighed and started washing her hair. "I dinnae ken. He ne'er mentioned it last year e'en though he told me some verra pretty things. Pretty things that sounded verra much like the words a mon would say to the woman he means to make his wife. He certainly hasnae mentioned it since he came back, all angry and accusing."

"Would ye like to marry the mon?"

"Ere he stood there and accused me of trying to kill him I would have said aye in a heartbeat. Now? Weel, how wise is it to marry a mon who can make love to ye, be your first lover, and then believe ye would try to have him murdered in a particularly brutal way? He has no faith in me, doesnae trust me." She shrugged. "Howbeit, he desires me and I desire him. I thought it over and decided I will take what I can get and do my best to protect my poor battered heart."

Hannah Howell

"Are ye hoping that desire will become more?"

"I would be lying to ye and to myself if I said nay. Of course I would like it to be more. I would like him to trust in me and have faith in me and love me. Howbeit, if that doesnae happen I willnae let myself grieve o'er it." She grimaced. "Weel, nay much."

Annie smiled. "Ye want it all but ye will take what he is willing to give. 'Tis something many women do. Sometimes it all works out verra weel and sometimes it doesnae work at all."

"Which is why I mean to do my best to protect my heart."

"I am nay sure that is something that can be done."

"Mayhap, but I will at least nay be expecting any more than what he gives, I willnae have any false hopes, and that is protection of a sort." Katerina stood up and began to dry herself off, wrapping her wet hair in one large cloth and using the other to gently pat the water from her skin. "Weel, are ye going to share in this bounty we worked so hard to produce or nay?"

Annie hesitated only a moment before shedding her clothes and getting into the still hot water. "Oh, this is verra nice. I will smell so lovely, too."

Katerina laughed. "'Tis the scent as much as the heat of the water that makes it so verra lovely. 'Tis just a shame that it is so much work to fill a tub with all that lovely warmed water."

"That is why lairds and ladies have servants."

"Quite true."

"Are ye nervous?"

"About taking Sir Lucas as my lover? Aye and nay. I have been with him before although it was my first time with a mon and it wasnae all such a delight. Yet, I have dreamed of it for months, all the time that I thought he was dead. And e'en though he hurt me so badly, the desire is still there. I do fear that I have re-called it all wrong and that I will be sorely disap-pointed."

"Oh, nay, I dinnae think ye will be. A mon as fine of looks as he is has had to have a lot of, er, training. He kens what to do to please a woman. I have nay doubt of that."

Katerina paused in rubbing her hair dry and frowned. "I really dinnae wish to think on that."

Annie laughed and began to wash her hair. "Nay, I suspicion not. There is one thing though. I think he will be a fierce lover. There is something in him that seems to be a little wild, a little untamed." Annie blushed. "'Tis a foolish thing to say about a mon who will be a laird one day."

"Nay," Katerina said quietly, "it isnae. 'Tis exactly right. There is something a little wild in Lucas. He looks a fine gentlemon and he speaks weel, reads, kens the ways of the world and how to be a laird but he also wears those warrior braids and if Ranald hadnae surprised him that time by the loch, Lucas could have slain the lot of them—all six men."

"Nay! Truly?"

"Aye. I saw him in a fight a few times. Nay a serious one, just men trying to prove their worth with a stranger. He can move so fast and he seems to be able to see everything at once, catching all of his attackers e'en when they try to get behind him. And he does feel a, weel, an exhilaration when he is in battle. Nay quite a savage of the verra old days, but verra close I am thinking."

"Oh, my, and now the poor mon has a limp."

"He does, but he was giving Ranald and his men a good fight when we rode in to rescue him. Nay as smooth and swift as before his leg was broken but far better than any other mon I have e'er seen. Aye, now

that I recall how the mon fights, I am most eager to
see how such strength and grace will aid him in the
bedchamber." She laughed and winked when Annie
blushed despite her own laughter.

Annie stepped out of the bath and began to dry
herself off. Having considered taking a bath after Katerina, she had brought some clean dry clothes to put
on and hastily did so. She then moved to help Katerina brush and braid her still damp hair, Katerina
then doing the same for Annie. As soon as they had
cleaned up the small room, they hurried off to the
hall to prepare the evening meal.

Lucas tried very hard not to stare at Katerina as they
all gathered in the hall for the last meal of the day.
As she moved past him to set the bread on the table
he caught the scent of lavender on her skin and felt
himself harden with anticipation and hunger. He did
not think he had ever wanted a woman the way he
wanted her, not even in his younger days when he was
just learning about the pleasures of the flesh and all
of his needs and desires were at full, untamed
strength. It took all of his self-control not to leap up
and drag her off to her bedchamber. The little smirk
he caught on William's face from time to time aided
him. He was not about to add to the man's amusement.

By the time Lucas felt he could steal away with Katerina, he was surprised he was not breathing fire. He
had had plans to walk with her for a while, talk and
steal a few kisses, but he was hard-pressed not to push
her up against the wall only feet from the hall and
take her there. Lucas found himself praying that she
felt at least partly as desperate as he did as she led him
to her bedchamber.

Katerina moved to the little table where she kept the wine. As she poured them each a full tankard, she realized that her hands were shaking slightly. The whole time she had been in the great hall, eating her meal, and conversing with the others, her mind had been filled with thoughts of what was to happen once the meal was done. She was so tense with anticipation she was not sure she could swallow the wine she had just poured for herself. When Lucas moved to stand behind her, she felt so hot and needy she was surprised she was not all a-sweat.

"Do ye really want that wine?" he asked as he kissed the side of her neck and felt a shiver go through her body.

"Are ye saying ye dinnae want a drink?" she asked, not surprised at the husky note in her voice.

"The only thing I want right now is ye, Kat. I want ye naked and in my arms. In the bed, on the floor, or against the wall. Or mayhap all three."

"Oh. I hadnae thought ye would be quite so—" She searched her rapidly befogging mind for the right word.

"Eager?" he whispered as he began to unlace her gown. "Aye, I am eager. I am nay sure about ye, but I have a whole year's worth of hunger that needs to be fed."

It took a moment for Katerina to realize what he had just said and she cursed and pulled away from him, not caring that her gown was nearly falling off her. "What do ye mean by *I am nay sure about ye?*"

Lucas held up his hands. "Nay, nay. Ye misunderstood."

"I dinnae think so. Ye were implying that I have had lovers since ye. 'Twas verra clear."

"I wasnae meaning to insult ye." He dragged a shaking hand through his hair, trying desperately to think clearly and not stare at her high, full breasts that were almost completely revealed by her sagging gown. "Sweet Jesu, Kat, ye thought I was dead and ye are a verra passionate woman. Ye are also being hunted and people want ye dead. I just thought ye may have sought some comfort or a little pleasure when ye have so little of it in this life Agnes has forced ye into." He hated to think of her with another man but he prepared himself to accept it.

Katerina studied his face. He looked as if he was about to be served poison. For some reason that made her want to smile. She was not foolish enough to think a possessive nature in a man was a sign of anything aside from a possessive nature, but it was still flattering in a small way. Then she recalled the rest of what he had said and her eyes widened.

"Ye havenae been with anyone for a whole year?"

"Nay." Lucas thanked God he could say that now, for it was the full truth and she had to be able to read it in his face and hear it in his voice. "I willnae say I didnae think on it or e'en go to the alehouse with the intention of having a woman, some faceless woman who wouldnae care or make me feel aught but a need and then satisfy it. But, nay, I couldnae e'en do that. And then there is the matter of my leg," he faltered as he felt himself blush and he inwardly cursed.

"Your leg?"

"It can be verra stiff at times and so there is an awkwardness just when ye wish there wouldnae be."

"Oh." She slowly moved back toward him. "But nay all the time."

"Nay all the time."

He gently pulled her back into his arms, suspecting it was going to be the last truly gentle thing he would do for a while. The need pounding in his veins was wild and almost uncontrolled. She had not really said whether she had had another lover during the time she thought he was dead, but her outrage was answer enough. Katerina Haldane was all his and, although she did not know it yet, he had every intention of keeping her.

Lucas kissed her and she felt the strength of his need, sensed how hard he was trying to be slow and gentle. As the kiss grew a little fiercer so did her desire. Soon she did not know who was doing what but their clothes were nearly torn off their bodies by eager hands and their mouths moved over every inch of skin as if starved for the taste.

Katerina clung to him as he moved toward the wall and pinned her there. She was unconcerned about the hard stone against her back, cared only about the hard body of the man holding her in his arms. A soft cry of surprise and then pleasure escaped her as she felt him push into her, her body at first protesting his entry and then greedily grasping hold of him, welcoming him. It was fast and furious and Katerina reveled in it. She felt her body tighten with that exhilarating feeling she remembered from so long ago and heard herself urging him on. Then she felt herself fall into the stars, pleasure rippling through her whole body until she felt consumed by her own passion. A heartbeat later she felt Lucas bury himself deep inside her and groan her name as his whole body shuddered and his seed warmed her insides.

With the return of sanity came embarrassment, but Katerina had barely begun to feel uncertain and anxious to retreat when Lucas kissed her. He held her tight in his arms as he stumbled over to her bed and fell down onto it, careful not to crush her beneath his much larger body. Her eyes widened when she felt him harden inside her.

"Lucas?"

The way she said his name, her voice husky with the lingering effects of their shared passion, made Lucas groan. He began to stroke her body, enjoying every curve and hollow as he kissed her breasts. It was going to be a long, exhausting night, he thought, and it was the last clear thought he had for a while.

Katerina finally found the strength to lift her head from Lucas's broad chest. She felt a slight chill on her body and searched for the blanket. Picking it up from the floor she spread it over them before returning to his arms. Her body felt a little sore, but she did not mind. It was a good sore, one that brought on heated memories of what had passed between her and Lucas in the past few hours. The man was insatiable and made her feel the same.

She looked over his sprawled body and began to notice the scars. The wounds from his most recent capture by Ranald were still a little raw, but she suspected only a few of them would become scars. The beating he had suffered a year ago had left a lot more. She gently tugged the blanket to the side revealing the leg Ranald had broken and she almost gasped. The scars that lingered there were ragged and ugly and she could almost see how the bone had cut through the skin. He was very lucky he had not lost the leg and she had no doubt that it was the healers in his family who had saved it for him. Suddenly the blanket was gently and firmly taken from her hand and tossed back over the leg.

"Ye dinnae want to be looking at that," Lucas said, a little embarrassed by his scars and the way he had been behaving since entering her bedchamber. "'Tisnae pretty."

"I ne'er thought it would be. My scars arenae so pretty either."

"They arenae so big and ragged. My leg looks like a dog grabbed it and chewed on it."

She wanted to ask him a lot of questions but held her tongue. They would be questions about the attack on the banks of the loch and she felt that was a subject it might be best to avoid. The very last thing she wanted to do was ruin the bliss they had found together with a talk that would certainly be tainted by his suspicions and anger. She had seen no sign of those things almost from the time she had been wounded but she could not be sure he had rid himself of them.

"I dinnae believe mine are all that much neater. William did his best but he isnae a healer. He stopped the bleeding, kept it all from going putrid, and tended me until the fever burnt itself out. I would ne'er complain that the ordeal has left me with a few scars."

He gently pushed her onto her back and, ignoring her soft protests, began to search out and kiss every scar. It was obvious that she had been thrown upon the rocks several times, each time tearing open her tender skin. Lucas wished he could have been there to help her, maybe even save her from some of the worst of the scarring, but he had been fighting for his own life and by the time he had recovered he had marked her as a deceiver and a murderess. He felt the heat of embarrassment touch his cheeks and was glad his face was hidden against her flat stomach. At some time he was going to have to talk to her about it, try to explain himself, and gain her trust and forgiveness. It would be wonderful if the wild lovemaking they shared was enough to mend the wound he had dealt her, but he knew it was not.

Katerina threaded her hands through his hair as he kissed her stomach and then licked the scar that ran down her thigh. She was just wondering if it was some sort of silent apology when he kissed the tight blond curls sheltering her womanhood. A squeak of shock escaped her and she tightened her grip on his hair. By the time she gathered enough of her wits to protest such an intimacy his stroking tongue had stolen all of her reticence away and she gave herself over to the strange new delight. By the time he joined their bodies, she was so hungry for him she did not care what he saw or did so long as the pleasure he gave her continued.

Lucas knew he was being a little rough but he could not stop himself and Katerina seemed to revel in it. He felt the start of her release deep within her body and thrust deep so that he could savor it as it grabbed hold of him and took him along with her. He collapsed on top of her, barely recalling the need to move his body a little to the side so that he did not crush her with his weight.

"Ye are going to make me an old mon a-fore my time," he murmured as he nuzzled her hair.

It took nearly all the strength she had left in her, but Katerina lifted her arm and stroked his hair. "Weel, ye may have some rest from your duties for a wee while as I am going to sleep now."

"Oh, are ye? Too weak and feeble, are ye?"

"That I am. Or, so I feel right now."

He turned onto his back and pulled her into his arms. It made him grin to think he had loved her into a stupor, but he was careful to hide his expression. Lucas suspected it would look a little too much like masculine gloating. As he idly stroked her back he felt her body go limp against his and her breathing grow soft and even.

Putting an arm beneath his head, and caressing her hair with his free hand, Lucas stared up at the smooth stone ceiling of the cave that served as her bedchamber. He knew he would never forget this place or this night. Even with the shadows that lingered over their reunion, his idiocy and false accusations, Ranald and Agnes and their murderous plans, and the fact that Katerina was exiled from her own home, it had been perfect. His body felt wonderfully heavy and sated yet he knew he could easily be stirred to passion again, and after so long and a growing fear that the beating had left him impotent, he wanted to just lie there and savor the feeling.

Closing his eyes and deciding to take a rest himself, he held Katerina a little closer and with what he admitted to himself was a touch of desperation. She was his. They belonged together, should be planning a life together and picking out names for all the children they would have. In a way he had stolen that from both of them. It would be hard work to get her to trust in him again, but he knew it was worth it. He knew he would never doubt her again. He was just going to have to work very hard to make her believe it.

Chapter Twelve

Warmth spread throughout Katerina's body. She murmured with pleasure as desire stirred to life within her. This was one of the best dreams she had ever had. She could even feel the slight roughness of Lucas's lightly calloused hands and the moist heat of his mouth. If she could have dreams like this all the time she would never get out of bed. She shifted her body as need became an ache inside her and her leg brushed against a hair-roughened thigh.

"Open your eyes, Kat, ere ye think ye are being attacked and hurt me."

That deep, laughter-filled voice was achingly familiar and Katerina relaxed. Keeping her eyes closed, she smiled and rubbed her toes against Lucas's leg. She liked the feel of that crisp hair against her skin. It was nice to wake up all wrapped in heat, she decided. There were a lot of problems facing her, many of them concerning the man now kissing her breasts, but Katerina did not want to face them yet.

Lucas nearly laughed. Katerina was sprawled beneath him with a little smile curving her full lips. She was humming softly to herself as she stroked his leg with her toes. It was very pleasant, but he had woken up hard and heavy with a need for her and he wanted her wide-awake and heartily participating as he fed that need.

"Kat," he whispered as he stroked her breasts, rubbing his thumbs over her nipples until they hardened and she wriggled against him, "open your eyes."

She slowly opened her eyes but only part of the way, just enough to see that he looked far too tempting in the morning. Katerina almost grinned. She was sorely tempted, but rather liked the feeling of being coaxed. He rubbed his shaft against her thigh and there was no doubting his interest. During their long night of lovemaking she had feared that she would wake in the morning and feel the bitter pinch of shame, but she felt none at all. The passion she and Lucas shared was all she could have hoped for and more. It was also a perfect way to make her forget all her worries and she found that she craved that delightful respite.

"Tirling at the pin rather early in the morning, arenae ye?" she murmured as she slid her hand over Lucas's hip and lightly trailed her nails up and down his shaft.

"If ye keep doing that I willnae be merely knocking on the door, lass, I will be kicking it in."

Enjoying the way his eyes closed and a light flush colored his cheeks when his desire rode him hard, Katerina encircled the hard, thick shaft with her hand and stroked him. The soft growl that escaped him made her shiver in anticipation. There was definitely something not quite tame about Lucas Murray. When he opened his eyes to look at her she saw that the silvery-blue of his eyes had darkened into an almost midnight blue and appeared just as mysterious. She smiled at him as she slid her hand down his shaft and lightly squeezed the sacs at its base. The way he shuddered gave her a delicious sense of pure feminine power.

"Temptress," he growled and kissed her.

The idea that anyone would think her a temptress was almost laughable. She might even question their sanity or think them liars. The way Lucas said the word, with such heated honesty, actually made her feel that she really was a temptress, even if she was only in his eyes. Then Lucas joined their bodies, the rhythm of the thrusts of his hips matching those of his tongue in her mouth. Very quickly Katerina forgot all about feminine power and temptresses. The only thoughts that lingered in her head for long were those of the rhythm of their bodies and midnight blue eyes.

"Ah, there ye are," said Annie as Katerina stepped into the hall.

"Aye, here I am." Katerina grinned at the look of disgust Annie gave her. "Anything I might help ye with?"

"Aye, ye could chop the leeks for me but only after ye have something to break your fast. I will make ye some porridge and Patrick brought us a jug of goat's milk."

"I am nay too fond of goat's milk," Katerina said as she sat down at the table.

"Weel, try to stomach it. Ye need to keep up your strength and put on a wee bit of weight. When ye had that fever ye lost some weight in fighting it and ye didnae really have enough to begin with. Sir Lucas was most concerned about that lack of a few more pounds to fight the fever with."

"Oh, weel, where is the milk then? I better gain those few pounds as swiftly as possible or the mon will recall that he wanted me to gain some and he will become a sore trial."

Annie quickly set a large bowl of porridge in front of Katerina and a tankard full of goat's milk. "If ye are serving everyone so much of this milk, Annie, ye will be emptying that jug within an hour."

"The jug can be refilled. Three of the four goats Patrick brought to us are female."

"We have goats?"

"Aye. It seems people are noticing that Ranald and the rest of those fools soiling Dunlochan arenae hunting their food and yet are eating as if they are kings without a worry for where the food comes from. Those who have animals are gleaning the best out and hiding them. The goats are from Patrick's sister."

"Weel, that makes sense, I think."

"The best cows from Old Wey's land are being kept with the horses and moved from place to place."

"'Tis that bad?"

"Aye, and getting worse. And, dinnae worry, Mistress Meg's chickens will be nay trouble at all and we will have fresh eggs more often now."

"Where are the chickens?"

"Two of them joined me in my bath," drawled Lucas as he strode into the hall and sat down next to Katerina. "Since they kept the messy end away from me and my water I didnae mind."

Katerina ate some more of the porridge and forced herself to drink some of the milk before she asked, "Sheep?"

"High up in the hills where there are many places to hide them if Ranald comes looking."

"Pigs?"

"Three. One with piglets. We refused to take the boar for the beast is huge and verra temperamental. Dinnae worry, m'lady, Thomas is happy to care for them all. He has always loved animals and will keep them clean and weel fed. He has e'en discovered a way to take them out to enjoy the sun now and again."

"So somewhere in these caves are chickens, goats, and pigs." Katerina watched Annie closely as she asked, "No ducks or geese?"

"Nay, not yet."

Katerina almost laughed at the way Annie kept her gaze fixed firmly on the porridge she was dishing out for Lucas and did not even twitch as she was questioned. The woman was getting verra good at not lying but not revealing any unnecessary truths, either. Although Katerina could only admire that skill, she felt sad that Annie had been forced to learn it.

"A bargain has been made, ye see," said Annie, sitting down across from Lucas and Katerina. "If we keep these much-prized animals safe we will get help in rebuilding the stock of the keep that those fools are devouring. I am thinking we may need it."

"It sounds a good bargain, Annie. I am just surprised William made it for he isnae too fond of such animals."

"Nay, he isnae, but he is fond of eating." Annie smiled when both Lucas and Katerina laughed. "'Twill be fine. Being that these animals are such fine breeders and all they are verra weel cared for, so it shouldnae be too great a trouble."

"Oh, it will be," said Katerina. "We cannae let the people lose all their source of food, can we."

"Nay, we cannae although it already begins to stink like a stable in here," snapped William as he strode into the hall.

William had obviously not had a good morning, mused Katerina as she fought to hide a smile. Her cousin did not often lose his temper completely, but he could become surly when things did not go his way.

Since they had been trapped in these caverns for almost a year it was a good thing that William's surliness was usually short-lived.

"Have ye already been out moving the horses?" she asked.

"And those cursed cows."

"Ye may be grateful for those cursed cows one day if Ranald and Agnes are being as careless with the stock as everyone says they are."

As he poured himself some ale and sat down at the table, William grunted. Katerina waited patiently while her cousin took several slow but deep drinks of the ale. When he finally looked at her over the top of his tankard, she smiled at him. He laughed and shook his head.

"I worked hard to ne'er become a farmer," he said. "It irritates me to find that I am one, at least for the nonce."

"And I am a troll." She grinned when everyone laughed, then said quietly, "'Twill pass. It has to. At some time e'en those old fools on the council will have to see that Agnes is hurting Dunlochan, hence their own ever-fattening purses."

"Do ye think the men on the council are using this trouble between ye and Agnes to fill their own coffers?" asked Lucas.

"I do although I cannae prove it. I cannae really leave here to find anyone powerful who would heed me and who those old men would then bow to, either. Aye, they were my father's friends and compatriots, but they arenae mine, and they arenae Agnes's. Oh, they dinnae break whate'er promises they made to my da as far as I can see, but they dinnae really honor them either.

"As his old friends they ken full weel that he would be screaming for them to put a stop to this or beating them about the head for making a profit on the misery of the people of Dunlochan. But they dinnae do any more than what was written in the verra terse last testament my da scratched out as he was dying. They sit like carrion birds, watching and grasping what they can, telling all who may listen that all the old laird wished was for them to be sure neither of his daughters married without their approval."

William nodded in solemn agreement. "That says it true. The old laird would be fair to shaking with fury o'er what is happening." William frowned toward the opening leading into the passage as the sound of voices and laughter drifted closer. "And here comes one reason we were a wee bit later to return here than I had planned."

Before Katerina could ask him what he meant Patrick, Thomas, Donald, and another man entered the hall. She stared at that other man and knew her mouth was hanging open even before Lucas shifted closer to her on the bench and gently closed it with his fingers on her chin. For a moment she stared at the man very hard as if a closer look would change what she was seeing, but there was no mistaking that fiery red hair, bright green eyes, or cocky grin.

"Why the devil have ye come back here, Robbie?" she demanded.

He laughed, walked over to her, and gave her a kiss on the cheek. "Why, to see ye, my dear sister."

Katerina was hard-pressed to hide her surprise when Lucas edged even closer to her, his long legs nudging Robbie until the man had to step back a little. Lucas acting so possessive was a heady thing and she told herself that later she would take the time to lecture herself about how little it meant. A man could act possessive over a tankard of ale. She kept her gaze fixed on Robbie and acted as if she had not noticed Lucas's behavior.

"I am nay your sister," she said.

"I am wed to dear, sweet Agnes, so that makes me your brother." He looked around the hall. "Very comfortable for a cave. Just why are ye living down here?"

"We are living down here because we are rather fond of staying alive. And I always thought ye were as weel."

"And I am."

"Then why have ye come back to Dunlochan?"

Robbie started to reply, but paused when a blushing Annie served him a tankard of ale. "Why, thank ye most kindly, Mistress. 'Tis glad I am to see that someone has held fast to their good manners despite living in a cave."

"If ye dinnae answer my question, ye will be buried in a cave." Katerina forced herself not to soften her expression beneath the warmth of Robbie's wide grin. "Now, sit down and answer the question."

"Weel, I decided it was time to see my wife again," he replied as he sat down across from Katerina, slipping smoothly between Annie and William. "I am married to the woman and the vows did say for better or worse. I began to wonder if I had judged her unfairly."

"The vows ye spoke also said until death do ye part and, by returning here, ye have now given Agnes the chance to fulfill that part of the vow."

"Agnes and Ranald have been searching for ye, Robbie," said William. "They want ye dead."

"Why?"

"So that she can marry Ranald, get the council to approve the marriage, and then claim Dunlochan as her own," replied Katerina. "There is a battle going on here, Robbie, and ye have just stepped right into it. And just in case ye have some idea of still going to visit with your wife, let me tell ye that anything ye thought Agnes had done, she probably has, if not a lot worse."

"But what can she gain by killing me?"

"I just told ye—Dunlochan. Ye werenae approved of by the council, the men my father chose to help us poor witless women. Agnes feels verra certain Ranald will be and I suspect she has a good reason for feeling so confident about that."

The fact that Robbie did not respond to her sharp words told Katerina just how upset he was. He had somehow convinced himself that Agnes might not be as bad as he had thought, perhaps even thought on how he had no hard proof and thus could have allowed jealousy to cloud his thinking. Agnes could cause a man to be a fool even when she was miles away. Even if he no longer loved Agnes or was even truly enthralled by her, it had to be a hard blow to realize your wife wanted you dead when you had never done anything to her to deserve such a harsh sentence.

"'Tis verra hard to believe," Robbie finally murmured and suddenly finished off his ale, but Annie was quickly close by his side to refill his tankard. "I think I hoped too hard that I was mistaken about her, but all ye have said so far only reminds me of all the reasons I left, and how clear it was then that she wasnae the woman I thought she was."

"She fools a lot of people, Robbie," Katerina said gently. "She fooled him," she added, pointing to Lucas.

"Just who is he?"

"Sir Lucas Murray of Donncoill," Lucas replied.

"I have heard of your clan. Why are ye crouched in the cave with these Haldanes?"

"Because Agnes and Ranald have already tried to

kill me twice. It has annoyed me and I wish to discuss the matter with them. They have also tried to kill Katerina."

"It has been bad here then, has it?" Robbie asked.

"It could be worse, but, aye, it has been bad," replied Katerina. "Ye are verra lucky that these men found ye and nay Ranald or his men."

"And all this is because your da gave those fools on the council the right to say who ye should marry?"

"Aye, although I feel certain that at least one mon on the council plays his own deep game."

"Probably Hay, Sorley Hay."

"Do ye ken the men on the council weel then?"

"A few of them," Robbie answered, "and I have to be surprised that your da would place any trust in them. Oh, they arenae all bad men, but they are weak. If your da was still here they would stay loyal, but he is dead. That was probably too much temptation for them."

Katerina rested her arms on the table and leaned closer to Robbie. "What I need is proof of the crimes being committed here. I need more than my word that she has tried to see me dead."

"I am nay sure my word would be much better," Robbie said quietly.

Although Katerina had suspected as much she was still disappointed. "Weel, just tell us what ye do ken about Agnes, Ranald, and e'en the council. We may see something ye dinnae."

There was a lot, from the death of the maid to rampant adultery committed by Agnes. Robbie had no real proof that Ranald and Agnes had killed the maid, however. The complete lack of morals revealed by Agnes's bedchamber activities might help, she mused, if only to get some of the more pious members of the council to deem Agnes unfit as mistress of Dunlochan.

That slowly forming plan was destroyed when Robbie spoke of finding Agnes in bed with Daniel Morrison, the leader of the council.

"Weel, that explains why they just let her continue on and didnae e'en raise an outcry when I was declared dead," muttered Katerina.

"The mon has a wife and she holds the purse-strings, ye ken," said William. "Mayhap we should try a little of the blackmail that Ranald and Agnes obviously use."

"'Tis something to consider. We have to do something soon. Before Ranald found out that Lucas and I were still alive we had at least been able to stop some of their crimes, and ease their brutality. Now we cannae e'en do that. What usefulness we had is gone. I think it may be time to confront the council. After all, I dinnae need to pretend to be dead any longer." She frowned when she saw Lucas shaking his head. "I could go to one of the few meetings they have and speak out."

"It would be too dangerous," said Lucas. "'Tis obvious Agnes has the head of the council under her command. If naught else he wouldnae want anyone to ken that he bedded down with her."

"That still leaves four others."

"None of whom have made any attempt to help ye or restrain Agnes."

Katerina knew Lucas was just speaking the truth but she still wished to hit him. The more they tried to find some solution, anything aside from open war or murder, they came up hard against a wall. It was beginning to feel as if she had been caught in this trap for years and she was beginning to be a little frantic. At least for a while it had seemed as if she was accomplishing something, but now, hiding constantly because of Ranald's searches for her or Lucas, nothing was changing and it probably never would. All they were doing now was surviving and that was just not good enough.

"I will keep thinking on it, Katerina," said Robbie. "I may yet recall something of use to ye. Mayhap if I go to the village—" He grimaced when everyone shook their heads. "Nay? A bad idea?"

"Ye are too recognizable, Robbie," Katerina said.

Feeling sorry for herself and hating it, Katerina decided she would have a bath. A nice hot bath always calmed her and then she might be able to think of something beside how defeated she felt. With Annie and Thomas helping, she soon had a full tub of steaming hot water. Sprinkling some lavender over it, she shed her clothes and climbed in. It was sinful to indulge in such a luxury so soon after the last one but she was in sore need of it. Soon she was so relaxed, so calm, she was even able to ignore the chicken sitting on the stool in the corner.

"Katerina is finding it hard right now," said William after she, Annie, and Thomas had left with the last buckets of water and he knew she would not return for a while. "It does seem as if Agnes has won right now."

"There has to be some proof of some crime," said Lucas. "No one can hide every sin they commit. Aye, and ones like Ranald and Agnes make a lot of enemies. They may kill some, but they cannae kill them all, nor can they always keep them too terrified to talk."

"We have been at this for a year," said Patrick. "We should have found something by now."

"When ye werenae raiding or trying to save someone, ye were hiding until the need to ride out came round again. 'Tis impossible to gather the sort of information ye need under those circumstances."

"Aye, true enough, yet none of us can go out openly and start seeking the information needed. Ones like myself may nay be as recognizable as ye or Robbie or William, but we have been hiding here for so long, we would appear to be strangers and that would rouse a dangerous interest."

"We do seem to be backed into a corner," said William.

"We will get out of it," said Lucas. "We still have the ability to spy on them. Aye, that can be a long, tedious way to defeat an enemy, but it works."

"Then we will make sure there is always someone listening."

"Dinnae ye have anyone in the keep already?" asked Robbie. "Katerina was weel liked and I am sure people would help."

"Oh, we have people inside," replied William, "and 'tis our good fortune that they havenae suffered because Katerina is alive. But they cannae be everywhere and they would rouse suspicion if they were seen outside certain rooms too often. We can listen anywhere the passage lets us go."

"Including Agnes's solar and her bedchamber," said Lucas. "Two places where she feels she can speak freely and has done so already. So, we shall set this out as if 'tis the watch at the gate or on the battlements, each taking a turn."

Lucas smiled faintly as he entered the tiny area where the bath was and saw Katerina nearly submerged, her eyes closed and the air scented with lavender. He shooed the chicken off the stool and moved it next to the tub. The way she opened only one eye to watch him only made him want to smile wider. Despite all the lovemaking they had indulged in last night and this morning, the way she suddenly blushed at being caught in her bath finally broke the restraints he had kept on his amusement and he grinned.

"I cannae believe ye are blushing," he said. "I have seen—" His words were halted by her wet fingers touching his lips.

"'Tis different and I cannae explain why," she said. "I dinnae suppose anyone suddenly had a cunning idea that will end all of this and rid Dunlochan of Ranald and Agnes as weel."

Taking away the scrap of linen she clutched tightly in her hands, Lucas began to scrub her back. "Nay," he replied. "We are going to watch and listen more closely than we have been, every hour in fact."

"Weel that may help. Agnes has always been one to boast." She sighed, leaned her head back against the rim of the tub, and said, "It is just that this place which was once a shelter now seems like a dungeon."

"I ken it and I havenae been here nearly as long as ye and the others have."

"So Agnes has won."

"Nay, she just hasnae lost yet."

"And ye dinnae think she can win?"

"Nay against us."

"Why? Because we are good and she is not?"

He smiled. "Nay, because she may be cunning and she may now hold Dunlochan, but she isnae truly all that smart. She also doesnae have the love for this place and its people as ye do. She just wants the comfort, whate'er money she can get her hands on, and the admiration of men."

"Aye, that sounds like Agnes, but what does that

have to do with her winning this foul game our father started?"

"There is no patience in the woman, no care for land or people, and, if worst comes to worst, we just have to wait until she finds something about Dunlochan that she cannae abide any longer."

"But what would that be?"

"Agnes is a whore. I think it time that that isnae ignored anymore."

"Ye plan to ruin her good name, nay that she has much of one."

"What do ye think Agnes will do if she can no longer control people through fear or respect? If she hears everyone whispering about her whorish ways?"

Katerina smiled faintly. "I believe she will be enraged."

"I believe she will be, too, and an enraged Agnes isnae so careful about what she does or says."

"'Tis a wee bit thin as plans go, Lucas."

"It is, but it also has a verra good chance of working."

"I hope so, Lucas, for these walls that have seemed like such a fine haven are truly starting to feel too much like a tomb."

Chapter Thirteen

"I dinnae think ye ought to go."

Katerina sighed as she secured her hair as tightly as possible. "This deadly game has to end, Annie, and those old fools hold the power to see that it does."

Annie cursed. "I ken it. I do. 'Tis just that Sir Lucas didnae think it was a good idea and he is a mon with, mayhap, more knowledge of such things."

"A lot of knowledge, but the men on the council are nay men ye face with a sword. Ye have to talk to them. We cannae bring them here, either, can we. For one thing, 'twould be like a royal procession," she muttered. "They would lead Ranald and his men right to us and we would all be slaughtered in our beds."

"Ye are in a dark humor, arenae ye."

"Aye, I am. I am tired of all of this, Annie. I am tired of living in caves, nice as they are. I am tired of my own blood and her brutal hireling trying to kill me. I am tired of watching Dunlochan slowly sink into ruin because of those fools up there." Katerina pointed in what she hoped was the direction of the keep.

"And ye think talking to these old men will help?"

"It cannae hurt."

"I am nay so sure of that. They have to ken at least

some of what has been happening and they havenae done a thing about it all."

That and the fact that Agnes had bedded at least one of the members did trouble Katerina, but she could see no other choice. It had been a fortnight since Lucas had started a continuous watch on Ranald and Agnes, but what information they did get did not help them much at all. This was one of the few nights all the men on the council would meet and she felt it was her best chance to get someone to listen to her.

"Aye, they have been almost useless and it seems they may have been enriching themselves at Dunlochan's expense, but because my father gave them authority, they are the ones I need to talk to."

"Are ye certain it wouldnae be better to wait until one of the men can go with ye?"

"It might be, but then again he might simply refuse to let me go." She caught a certain look upon Annie's face that told her that was exactly what the woman hoped would happen. "I must go, Annie. I must. We have become trapped here, helping no one. Nay, not even ourselves. These old men might be completely useless, some or all of them might e'en prove to be the enemy, but they might also help us. There is nay kenning until someone sees them and I think that someone must be me."

"I ken it. I just hope the men do. Go with God."

Katerina crouched at the corner of the tutor's home in the village staring at Daniel Morrison's home. It looked much finer than it ever had before, but Katerina tried not to let suspicion creep into her heart and mind. She sat calmly watching as each man from the committee entered Morrison's home after exchanging very formal greetings. Only one was left to arrive for the

meeting and when Katerina saw the man hurrying
down the road, struggling to untwist the long dark cloak
tangling around his legs and hold on to an over-filled
box of scrolls at the same time, she had to smile. It was
Malcolm Haldane, a distant cousin and a very dear
man. No matter what the other members of the council were like, she felt sure she could count on Malcolm.

   She decided to give the men a little time to get comfortable before going in. She would have to do it
stealthily for she suspected Agnes and Ranald would
have someone keeping an eye on the council. If they
had some hold on the men, they would want to be sure
none of the men betrayed them, and if they did not,
they would be looking very hard for one. The last
thing she needed was to be found by any of Ranald's
men right outside the council's meeting place. She
knew they wanted her dead but she saw no reason to
give them a reason to torture her for information first.

   After what she felt was sufficient time, Katerina took
a last careful look around her and slipped into Morrison's house. She paused in the entry way for a
moment, standing in a shadowed corner, and looked
at the elegance displayed there. Trying to judge what
such craftsmanship was worth and then deciding on
how or even if Morrison could afford it gave Katerina
the start of a headache. When a young servant hurried down the hall toward a heavy, elaborately carved
door, she stayed close behind him. As she slipped into
another small shadowy corner made by the irregular
walls of the house, she saw the servant simply open
the door and go in. When he left the room he did not
lock it behind him. Although the men inside could
still lock it themselves, she had a chance to just walk
in. That would give her the opportunity to surprise
them and that could prove to be to her advantage.

   Once the servant had disappeared she waited again,

listening very carefully to see if any other people were close at hand. Deeming it safe, she stepped out of the shadows and walked quietly to the door. Katerina kept her gaze fixed upon the hall the servant had come and gone from while she pressed her ear to the door. When she felt the pinch of guilt over eavesdropping she told herself that she needed to have a little information before she confronted the men and wagered her life on the mere possibility that none of them had allied themselves to Ranald and Agnes.

"I was wondering if I might have a look at the books, the ones tallying the expenses and income of the Dunlochan keep."

Katerina smiled faintly, recognizing that slightly tremulous voice. Malcolm was a brilliant but not a verra brave man.

"Why do ye need to see them? If ye are in need I shall gladly lend ye some money."

Morrison, Katerina decided. That man had obviously found Malcolm's request an insult. Either Morrison was an extremely suspicious man or he already knew Malcolm would find something amiss in those ledgers. After a few more minutes of hearing nothing but idle talk, Katerina decided she might as well go inside for little was being said that required her to listen stealthily.

She opened the door, walked in, and yanked the hood of her cloak back. Morrison looked at her as if she had committed some horrible dark sin and was even staring from her to Malcolm and back again as if the two of them had planned this. Morrison was definitely a man to watch closely, she decided. A few minutes after her entrance Malcolm finally shook free of his shock and hurried over to hug her.

"'Tis good to see ye hale and strong, lass," he said. "I was sorely grieved when all said ye had died. I ken ye would ne'er have committed such a sin as the taking of your own life," he added in what she supposed he thought was a soft voice.

"Thank ye, Malcolm," she said. "I am always pleased to find someone who had enough faith in me to ken that." She pretended not to notice how the other men in the room flushed under the rebuke that was not so well hidden in those words.

"Weel, come, come. Sit down, have something to eat and drink and ye can tell us what happened to ye, aye? And where have ye been that ye would leave us all to think ye dead? Aye, I think ye have a fine tale to tell."

By the look that crossed Morrison's face he was obviously struggling with his temper as he watched Malcolm act as if he was the host. Although the man might not be the one cheating her, he was definitely a man to watch. Morrison was enjoying his role as a guardian to the welfare of Dunlochan and would not give it up easily. Some of his anger might come from the fact that he had been leaching money out of the keep and the lands and now someone was going to be looking at all the paperwork and that could be very dangerous for him.

For a while she just talked with the men, mostly with Malcolm. As soon as she finished her ale, she set the tankard down and looked straight at Morrison, making no attempt to hide her suspicions. If he was stealing from her she wanted him so worried about the consequences that he might even attempt to put some of what he had stolen back.

"The true reason I have come here today is because there have been repeated attempts upon my life," she said and noticed that even Morrison was looking shocked. Either he was a verra good actor or he had nothing to do with the attacks, was interested only in stealing from her. "I need this matter of who will hold Dunlochan settled. Agnes is still married to a mon we all ken my father never approved of. I cannae understand why ye have left the woman and her acknowledged lover in charge. The signs of their brutality, greed, and immoral behavior are everywhere."

Malcolm shook his head, his expression one of honest, deep sorrow. "How it troubles me. Women hurt, men beaten, livestock taken. 'Tis as if we are in a war yet there are no enemy soldiers around."

"Save for Ranald's ugly hirelings," muttered Brock Heywood, watching Katerina carefully as he idly scratched his thick gray beard. "Seems a fortnight back, mayhap more, mayhap less, that fool lost six, mayhap seven men and he and the woman have been making a nuisance of themselves trying to get money for more men."

"That would have been when Ranald captured Sir Lucas Murray, hung him up like fresh kill, and began to take wee slices off him. I heard it said Ranald ran the minute he saw men coming. One of the men who surrendered said he means to let it be kenned that Ranald doesnae stand with the men he hires, but runs as soon as the enemy draws too near. I believe the mon wishes he had kenned how swiftly Ranald can change from a leader to just another mon running for his life and leaving his men to fend for themselves."

As the men indulged in a round of tales, insults, and complaints about spineless men, Katerina looked around the room. Everything in the room bespoke a man of money and yet she did not recall hearing that Morrison was wealthy. A glance at the man revealed that he was sweating a little, his eyes darting nervously around the room as if he was suddenly seeing it from her eyes.

Before returning her full attention to Malcolm, Katerina took another look around the room to try and commit it to memory. She tensed as she suddenly realized that one of the men was gone. She had neither heard nor seen him leave. Even worse, she did not know when he had left.

Katerina suddenly felt her stomach begin to ache. Something was definitely going to happen and the growing ache in her stomach meant that whatever happened it was going to be bad, at least for her. She wanted to flee, but was not sure if that was the right thing to do. She was in a room with four grown men. She should be safe enough, even if they were not all her friends and allies.

"Are ye feeling ill, child?" asked Malcolm. "Ye have gone verra pale."

"I just felt uneasy for a moment," she said. "I was just realizing that Sorley isnae here and that I hadnae e'en seen him leave."

"Why, indeed, he is gone." Malcolm looked around. "I didnae see him leave either." He looked at Morrison. "Ye dinnae think he may have taken ill, do ye?"

Morrison shook his head. "Nay. I suspicion he just needed a wee bit of air." He winked at Katerina. "He drinks a wee bit too much from time to time, ye ken."

"How sad," she murmured, thinking that someone ought to tell Morrison that kindly uncle tone of voice he was trying to affect was not verra comforting. In fact, she felt sure that he not only saw Sorley leave, but knew where he was going and why. Katerina began to feel even worse and it was difficult to fight down the urge to get up and run and keep on running.

"I hadnae realized he had such a problem," said Malcolm, frowning at Morrison. "He drinks verra little when he is in company."

"Ye are right, Malcolm," said Brock, also frowning

at Morrison. "I have ne'er heard that about Sorley. He always seems quite a sober mon, e'en a wee bit too stern and serious."

The youngest of the group at only two score years, Matthew said, "A wee bit unkind of ye to say so."

Despite the strengthening discomfort, Katerina was amused by the way Malcolm, Matthew, and Brock were arguing about the accuracy of Morrison's claim. She firmly believed that none of those had anything to do with neglecting or even stealing from Dunlochan. That left Morrison, whom she suspected more and more with each passing minute, and the mysteriously missing Sorley.

Unable to stand the ache in her stomach any longer and increasingly afraid of being caught or trapped or hurt or any of dozens of dire fates her mind was conjuring up, Katerina got to her feet intending to take an early leave. She had intended to stay a little longer, just long enough to glean some more information, but now that she had some hint of who might be guilty, she could do it later or Lucas could for she had a feeling he was going to be seriously considering locking her up in a very high tower room.

"Leaving us so soon, m'dear?" drawled a voice that gave Katerina ice-cold chills from her head to her feet. She turned to see Ranald standing in the doorway, two strong men flanking him.

"What game are ye playing here, Ranald?" demanded Matthew, who then looked around Ranald and his soldiers to see Sorley peeking into the room. "Sorley, what have ye done?"

"I brought the ones who are looking for her," replied Sorley.

"Fool," snapped Matthew.

"Ye would turn a wee lass o'er to this mon kenning

how he treats women?" asked Malcolm in a tone of utter shock.

"This wee lass could get us all hanged, could e'en take away all we have worked for."

Malcolm sighed and shook his head, casting a mournful yet furious look at the small man still hiding behind Ranald. "I worried that ye had been taking what did not belong to ye, but I didnae wish to hear my own conclusions and so I pushed them aside, letting ye raise doubts in my mind about so many things." He looked at Morrison. "And I am thinking that ye kenned exactly where he went and allowed it. For what? This?" Malcolm waved a surprisingly elegant hand around to indicate all the riches decorating the room.

"And I think ye may ken more than is good for ye," said Ranald.

"Shut up," snapped Morrison. "Just shut up and get out."

Ranald glared at the man. "We are all in this together. Best ye nay forget that."

"I am not a part of this," said Malcolm, "and I will-nae allow ye to hurt Katerina." Even though he paled alarmingly when Ranald pointed a sword at him, Malcolm did not back down.

Katerina was just about to tell Malcolm not to do anything foolish when she caught sight of Morrison stepping up behind him. Before she could cry out a warning, Morrison struck Malcolm over the head with the thick end of a walking stick. Even though he moved quickly to catch Malcolm before he hit the floor, Katerina did not feel that lessened Morrison's crime. She suspected Malcolm was going to be as out-raged as Matthew and Brock looked now.

Catching sight of a trickle of blood running down the side of Malcolm's pale face, Katerina took a step toward him. She was grabbed by the arm and yanked back to stand with Ranald. Her arm aching from the rough handling, she was prepared to protest such treatment. Something in the way Ranald looked at her made her glance around and she realized one of the two men who had entered with him was now gone. Then something slammed into her head and, as she fell to the floor, the last clear sight she had was the horrified looks on the faces of Matthew and Brock.

Matthew watched Ranald and his men carry Katerina away and then turned to look at Morrison. That man sat in a chair near the padded bench he had set Malcolm down on, bent over and burying his face in his hands. Sorley looked pale and upset but nowhere near as devastated as Morrison.

"I cannae believe this of ye, of either of ye," Matthew finally said. "Have ye given any thought to what that swine will do to that poor young woman?"

"I suspicion he means to make sure that she is really dead this time," Morrison said in a flat voice.

"Because she is a threat to him, of course. Tell me, how long do ye think it will be ere he sees us as a threat to him? I dinnae think sacrificing that poor young woman has really bought ye verra much more time with your wee treasures." He moved closer to Malcolm and stared at Morrison until the man relinquished his seat. "With a woman that bonnie, I think ye may nay need to wait until Ranald assures your silence. I wouldnae be surprised if we soon have another visitor—one who willnae be verra happy at all to discover what ye have done."

"Gone? What do ye mean? Where did she go?" Lucas felt bad that he seemed to be scaring Annie, but finding no sign of Katerina terrified him.

"She went to see that council. They had one of their meetings today in the village and she went there. 'Tis at Daniel Morrison's house." Annie had to yell, for Lucas was already running down the passage that would lead him out of the cave, William, Patrick, and Robbie right behind him. "And nary a one of them giving a thought as to hiding their faces or hair." She shook her head. "The whole village is going to be seeing them."

Lucas knew he had men following him, but he did not slow down at all to see who had decided to watch his back. He had rushed everyone back to the caves, cutting their hunting time a little, because he could not shake free of a sense of impending danger. He had tried to ignore it, tried to talk himself out of it, even tried to drown it with a hearty drink from his wineskin, but it had continued to gnaw at him. Unable to concentrate on finding meat for the table any longer, he had decided to just get back to the caves, see Katerina, and get rid of the feeling since it seemed to be born of a fear for her safety. Instead he had found her gone, off to meet with the council, and his feeling of foreboding had turned into an utter conviction that she was in trouble.

"A somewhat more cautious approach to whatever it is we are charging toward might be a good idea," said Robbie as he caught up to Lucas and kept pace at his side.

"I will use stealth when we reach Morrison's house," Lucas said. "That is where Katerina went. The council is meeting there." He heard William cursing from close behind him.

"At times that lass shows no sense at all," William said.

"Senseless to go alone, but one cannae really argue with her about the need to talk to the council."

Moving into the shadows of the house directly across the rutted road from Morrison's home, Lucas finally stopped to catch his breath. There was no sign that there was any real trouble at the house but the feeling of danger still lingered. As Patrick slipped away to get a closer look, Lucas stood waiting, feeling so tense he was surprised something did not snap.

"Morrison's house is looking much finer than it used to," murmured Robbie as he stared at the house, clearly not looking for something appropriate such as a footprint.

Lucas was still trying to just ignore that useless observation, when he suddenly realized it was not useless at all. If there had been obvious improvements to Morrison's house one had to ask why, and, more important, where had the funds come from. If Morrison was helping himself to any of the wealth of Dunlochan then Katerina was definitely in danger.

"I can only see five men in the house and all of them are men I know," said Patrick as he slipped into the shadows right beside Lucas.

"But no Katerina?"

Patrick shook his head. "Something has happened, though, for cousin Malcolm is laid out on a bench and Matthew and Brock are arguing with Morrison and Sorley. That is verra strange, for Malcolm would ne'er get in a fight, so why is he unconscious on that bench? And Matthew and Brock are calm, soft-spoken fellows who dinnae have much of a temper yet they are tearing into Morrison and Sorley. The oddest of it all is that Morrison and Sorley are just standing there accepting it, nay e'en raising their voices."

William scowled toward the house. "Aye, strange indeed, for both those men are quick with their fists."

"It has already happened," Lucas whispered and sprinted for the house.

"What has happened?" asked Robbie as he, Patrick, and William followed Lucas.

"He thinks something has happened to Katerina," replied William. "If it has, I wouldnae wish to be one of those fools right now."

Lucas slammed through the door, ignoring the pain that careened through his shoulder. He could hear raised voices and ran toward them. As when he had run out of the caves, he could hear the others close behind him, but he did not wait for them. He threw himself into the door of the room where the voices were coming from, only partly aware of how they abruptly stopped. Standing in the doorway he studied the four men gaping at him. He spared one fleeting glance at the man on the bench who was just beginning to rouse and then fixed his stare on the other four, who subtly shifted closer together.

"Where is she?" he demanded.

"Where is who?" Morrison looked at the door hanging crooked, one twisted hinge all that was keeping it from hitting the floor. "What have ye done to my door?"

"What I will do to ye if ye dinnae tell me where Katerina Haldane is. Now."

"I would be telling him if I were ye," said Patrick as he carefully stepped around the shattered door. "He isnae in a verra good humor right now."

"He will be in a worse one soon," grumbled Morrison, only to squeak in an odd high-pitched voice when Lucas was suddenly there in front of him, his hand on Morrison's throat and holding him a few inches off the ground.

"If ye wish to breathe again, I suggest ye tell me where she is," Lucas said, and, when Morrison still appeared to hesitate, slammed him up against the wall.

"Gone," Morrison managed to croak.

Patrick, William, and Robbie encircled Lucas and his captive and William said quietly, "I dinnae think it will help anything if ye strangle the fool."

"It might help me," said Lucas, his voice a soft snarling sound.

William lightly touched Lucas's arm. "Only until they hang ye."

Lucas closed his eyes and took a long, deep breath to try to push down the rage and fear that had him behaving so savagely. One by one he removed his fingers from the man's throat. Morrison collapsed to his knees, gasping for air. A little calmer, Lucas cursed his fury for it appeared it would be a while before Morrison could speak again. He felt no remorse over what he had done, just a little regret that he had not waited until he had gotten the answers he needed.

"He told me to go and get Ranald," Sorley said, pointing at Morrison, who actually gathered up enough strength to glare.

"For a mon who is always so eager to set on a fellow with his fists flying, ye seem to have a lot of the coward in ye," said Matthew after hastily introducing himself to Lucas, the one man he did not know. When Sorley leapt toward him, Matthew neatly caught the wrist of his right hand, stopping the hard fist aimed at his head. He then quickly and efficiently knocked Sorley out with a hard right to the jaw.

"Weel done, Matthew," said Brock.

"I dinnae fight, old friend, because I choose not to fight, nay because I cannae."

"A good time to fight would have been a year ago when the daughter of your good friend was killed," snapped Lucas.

"'Twas said she had killed herself because ye had left her," Matthew said quietly.

"I ne'er believed it," said Malcolm as William

helped him sit up. "I said it, but none of ye would heed me, and, coward that I am, I ceased to speak about it."

"Ach, ye are nay a coward, Malcolm," said Brock. "Ye are a scholar, nay a warrior. 'Tis your way. Aye, and ye asked Morrison for the books, letting him ken that ye smelled something wrong. Matthew and I have been sniffing that stink for a while and we ne'er got the courage to ask. Ye did." He looked at Lucas. "And, aye, we should have done something. All we did do was make sure none could claim Dunlochan. I thought it was because we shared the belief that something was wrong but," he glanced at Morrison and Sorley, "'tis easy to see now that some agreed simply because they didnae want Agnes to have full control of the purse they were dipping their greedy hands into."

"We can discuss that later," said Lucas. "Ranald has Katerina?"

Malcolm nodded and then winced. "He does. He has taken her to Dunlochan. I am nay sure how long she will survive."

"They will try to use her to draw me into their trap. I plan on snatching that bait right out of their greedy hands and then ending this threat as it should have been ended months ago." He swung around, fighting the urge to punish all the men for what Katerina had been suffering, and marched out of the room.

William watched all the men on the council wince, some of them looking far more remorseful than others, and shook his head. "Malcolm, ye, Matthew, and Brock watch these two thieves. When this is done, we will be looking for them." He hurried after Lucas suspecting that the man was going to need someone with a cool head to hold him back from making a hasty, ill-thought out, and probably fatal mistake.

Chapter Fourteen

Her head hurt so badly and pounded so loudly Kate-rina felt sure she would soon be sick. She felt very reluctant to open her eyes and she wondered why that should be so. From what she could feel beneath her hands and her body she was stretched out on a table. Keeping very still helped to control the pain in some small way, but every instinct she had was loudly demanding that she should get up and run, run as fast and as far as she could. It took a moment of careful thought before she realized why she should feel that way.

She had been betrayed. One of the men her father had trusted, had considered his friend, had handed her over to Ranald. Katerina had not been surprised to discover that some of the men on that council had been stealing from Dunlochan. She had suspected it, but she was still shocked and disappointed. She just prayed that she would live long enough to be able to have a close look at those ledgers so that she could find out exactly how much she had lost.

A hand grasped her by the shoulder so tightly Katerina could feel long, sharp fingernails begin to sink through her clothes and pierce her skin. One shake was all it took to stir up all she had just managed to calm by sheer force of will. The burning feeling in the back of her throat that always heralded a bout of nausea made her cough. She tried again to push the nausea aside, hating the feel and the taste of it, but especially hating the feeling of having no control over her own body when it hit. All she needed to do was lie very still and breathe slowly and deeply and it would fade, she told herself.

"I ken ye are awake, Katerina. Open your eyes. Now."

That punishing hand shook her again, a little harder this time. The sharp voice was painful to her ears, making her head throb even more. Katerina lost her battle with her nausea. She quickly felt around for the edge of whatever she was lying on, then leaned over, and was so sick that she heard nothing but her own misery. It was not until the retching began to ease its grip on her that she heard a man's low, mean laugh and a woman's voice uttering a stream of curses.

"The bitch has emptied her belly all over my new slippers!"

"Do be quiet, Agnes. I warned ye to stand back as I so quickly did. Ranald had to hit her hard on the head to make certain she went down and made no trouble. Such wounds often cause a person to feel sick."

Slumping back down onto what she finally realized was one of the tables in the great hall, Katerina cautiously opened her eyes. She nearly closed them again and not just because the light hurt her eyes and increased the pounding in her head. Freda and Ranald began to move closer to the table, carefully stepping around a plump maid who had already been dragged over to clean up the mess she had made. The only good thing Katerina could see before her eyes was Agnes fleeing the room.

As her vision cleared, Katerina stared at Ranald. She thought on how the man had tortured Lucas, of all the sword cuts and painful bruises he had inflicted upon Lucas's fine body, and she ached to kill the man. Some of the rage she felt must have shown itself in her eyes, for Freda and Ranald hesitated just a moment before taking those last few steps toward her. Although she did not like the taste of the anger and hatred she felt, Katerina did not fight it. She knew it was all that was holding back a great deal of fear.

"Shouldnae we wait for dear Agnes to return ere we have our loving reunion?" she asked.

"Agnes will do exactly as I tell her to do," said Freda.

"And why should Agnes do for ye as she has ne'er done for another?"

"Because she is my daughter, ye little fool."

Katerina wanted to ask the woman to repeat that, desperately wanted to have misheard her, but she hastily bit back the request. She knew she could not pretend that she was not shocked or surprised for her expression had undoubtedly given her away. Freda looked smug and Katerina wished she had the strength to sit up and slap the look off the woman's face.

Then she thought of her father and felt both hurt and angry. He had never told her and he must have known. He had demeaned the mother of his child, placing her in the position of a servant and forcing her to live a lie. Worse, he had held to that lie for years, even when Katerina's mother had been alive. Katerina did not believe her mother had ever been told the truth for the woman would never have tolerated such treatment or such a lie. There was only one reason Katerina could think of for her father to do such a thing, yet she had never heard even the softest whisper or hint that her father had lovers. A man keeping his leman in the same keep as his lawful wife was not something that could easily be kept a secret. The smile that slowly curved Freda's thin lips made Katerina fear that that was exactly what her father had done.

"Aye," said Freda as if she savored the word, and crossing her arms over her ample chest. "Your father was a hard bastard. His poor foolish wife ne'er guessed just how heartless he was."

Ranald snorted. "If ye are trying to make her think the old laird had her mother *and* ye, best forget playing that game. Aye, I have heard that he was a hard mon, but, nay, he wouldnae do that, and he certainly couldnae have kept it a secret for so long. The mon wasnae your lover save for that one time." Ranald laughed. "Jesu, woman, he barely recalled who ye were from one day to the next. If his friend hadnae confirmed your tale and Agnes didnae look so much like a Haldane, he ne'er would have recognized Agnes, either."

Katerina almost gaped at Ranald, but then she caught the look in his eyes. He had not ended Freda's attempt to lie about her relationship to the old laird out of some sudden, strange twist of sympathy. He just wanted to strike out at Freda. Obviously the two were allies but not friends. Katerina suspected Freda gave the orders and Ranald found some of them hard to tolerate, or he just loathed being commanded by a woman.

"So what game do we play here?" asked Katerina, speaking up before Freda could strike out at Ranald as she so clearly wanted to. A fight between the pair could be useful but not until she had recovered from the blow to her head enough to at least stand up. "'Tis the same as when ye captured Lucas, isnae it." Katerina made a soft tsk-tsk. "Too lazy to think of something different, are ye? Something that might actually work?"

"This will work," snapped Freda. "Sir Murray will come for ye and then we will have both of ye in our grasp. This time there will be no mistakes. Nay, I will kill ye both myself if I must."

"And ye dinnae think that anyone will become suspicious?"

"Why should they? Everyone at Dunlochan thinks ye and Sir Murray are dead."

It annoyed Katerina beyond words that Freda had seen the one true weakness in her plan. By letting everyone think she was dead, Katerina had known that she was making it easy for her enemies to kill her without fear of any consequences if they got hold of her. It had seemed simple enough to avoid capture, but, as Katerina glanced around, she decided that might have been a dangerous arrogance on her part.

"The council now kens that I am alive," she said.

"The council must be careful in how it acts against us. They have their own sins to hide."

"Nay all of them. Only Morrison and Sorley."

Freda cocked just one brow. "Are ye so certain of that?"

"Oh, I suspicion Matthew and Brock, and mayhap e'en Malcolm, may have a few wee sins ye have discovered, but I doubt ye found enough to make them accept taking a part in a murder. Two murders. They didnae e'en ken that Morrison and Sorley were stealing from Dunlochan and were appalled when they learned of it. They were also appalled that Morrison and Sorley handed me over to Ranald as they ken now that he wants me dead."

"I dinnae care if ye die or nay," Ranald said. "'Tis just easier and the surest way to keep ye from coming back to try to claim Dunlochan."

That was said in such a calm, almost amiable tone of voice that it reached out and grabbed hold of the fear Katerina was struggling to keep at bay. She had to fight to keep it from swamping her. The way the man spoke of killing made her very certain that there would be no mercy to be found in him. Even if she tried to bargain with him, she would not win. He would agree with the bargain, take what he wanted, and then kill her.

"Why isnae she dead?" demanded Agnes as she came back into the hall, marched over to the table, and glared at Katerina. "If neither of ye have the stomach for it, just give me the knife."

"Ah, my loving sister, blood of my blood, how good it is to see ye again," murmured Katerina.

"We cannae kill her now," said Freda. "We need her to bring Sir Murray here."

"Why should he come here, put his own life at risk, just for her?"

"Because he is a knight, an honorable mon who will feel it is what he must do to maintain his honor."

"Such nonsense." Agnes gave Ranald a seductive smile before glaring at Katerina again. "Must she lie there like that?"

"Nay, I was just about to have her moved to a chair by the fireplace and tie her to it. It isnae wise to leave her free as she could interfere when Sir Lucas comes or use some small moment of distraction to flee. If ye would be so kind, Ranald?" Freda asked, her voice a chill parody of courtesy.

Katerina bit back a cry of pain as Ranald grabbed her by the arm and yanked her off the table. When her feet touched the floor she nearly collapsed, dizziness and nausea swamping her. She wished she could fight him as he dragged her over to the chair near the fire, but she was too consumed with simply trying to remain conscious. Before she had gained enough control to just see clearly again, he already had her tightly bound to the chair. Katerina let her head rest against the back of the chair, closed her eyes, and fought to soften the pain and quell the nausea assaulting her. She knew she needed her wits strong and clear, but feeling the way she did at the moment made her unable to think of anything except how miserable she felt.

A tug on her hair brought her out of her stupor and she opened her eyes. Freda stood by the side of the chair holding her hair, an alarmingly large knife in her other hand. Katerina took a long, deep breath and then let it out slowly as she reached for calm and, she prayed, courage enough to see her through the ordeal ahead.

"Feeling a need for some small token?" she asked.

"This is to be taken to the inn from whence I am certain it will get to Sir Murray. A small missive will be with it telling him exactly where to come and how to behave if he wishes to see ye alive."

"Ah, let me guess. He is to come here alone and unarmed."

"Aye."

"Whereupon ye will let him see me alive and then kill him."

"Aye."

"Nay!" cried Agnes as she hurried over to glare at her mother. "Ranald said I could have him first."

For a moment Katerina thought Freda was going to hit Agnes. There was such a fierce, furious look on the woman's face that Agnes actually took a few steps back until she was pressed close to Ranald. Then the look faded, slowly changing to one that could only be called cunning. Katerina fought the urge to shiver when the woman looked at her again.

"It could well torment ye to see your lover with my daughter," Freda murmured. "I suspicion it could cut ye more deeply than any knife's blade."

"And why would ye think the mon is my lover?"

"Because he believed ye were the one who had him beaten and nearly killed yet he fights with ye now."

"And I ken weel that he willnae like to see Ranald take his woman," Agnes said, as if she had such a clever plan to begin with and had not just been thinking of her own wants and needs.

Freda slowly nodded. She took a small piece of parchment from a pocket in her black gown and wrapped the hair in it before giving it to Ranald. "See that this goes to the inn and that it is made verra clear that Sir Lucas Murray must receive it as soon as possible. Make sure the mon ye send understands that he must nay try to follow the one who will take it to Sir Murray. It would be good to ken where these reivers have been hiding so that we could rid ourselves of them at last, but getting Sir Murray here is of more importance now."

"Are ye certain of that?" Ranald asked.

"Verra certain. He is a warrior. He undoubtedly leads them now and could make them stronger and more dangerous. In truth, once this one and Sir Murray are dead, there is a verra good chance the rest of them will slowly fade away into the mists."

Ranald shrugged and went to find a messenger. Katerina could not be sure he would obey Freda in this as he really wanted the rest of her men. She had to have confidence in the cunning of her people to keep Ranald from finding them. Not only would worrying about them distract her when she needed to be watching every move her enemies made, but there was nothing she could do to help them now.

"Ye really believe ye can win, dinnae ye," she said.

"Why not?" asked Freda. "I have accomplished all I wanted until now. Ye have proven a sore trial and far more clever than I had anticipated, but I kenned I would win in the end. Your father ne'er kenned that about me. He thought me some fool woman who had spread her legs for a mon and would be willing to accept any scraps he offered after that. He thought recognizing Agnes as his daughter should be more than enough to please me, that I wouldnae feel the sting of shame when he made me her nurse and refused to let anyone ken what I had once been to him. The bastard threatened me with sending me away and keeping Agnes with him if I told anyone who I was."

Katerina thought that Agnes might have fared better, been a better person, if her father had done that at the start. He had not been a particularly loving man, but he had still been a good one in most ways. Freda was a woman twisted by anger, an anger strengthened by thwarted ambitions. Katerina was both surprised and ashamed that she had never noticed that about Freda until now.

"Of course, I made him pay for that arrogance."

The look on Freda's face made Katerina wish she could suppress the need to ask any questions, but it was impossible. She felt a strong sense of foreboding about what she might learn, but even that was not enough to make her hold her tongue. She felt almost compelled to dig out the truth no matter how chilling and ugly it might be.

"Just how do ye think ye made him pay, Freda?" she asked.

"First I took his wife."

Katerina just stared at the woman. She hoped she looked no more than curious, perhaps a little disbelieving. Inside she wanted to scream, knowing the woman was telling the truth. Freda believed she would win this game and that Katerina would take these confessions to the grave with her.

"She wasnae having an easy time with the bairn she carried and the right mixture of herbs was all that was needed to rid her of it. Then one just had to be sure she kept getting the potion that would keep her bleeding her life away."

"So ye feel all clever and strong because ye killed a bairn in the womb and a woman on her childbed, neither of whom had ever done ye any harm?"

"It was because of your mother that I wasnae made the lady of Dunlochan as was my right." Freda took a deep breath as if to calm herself and continued. "I allowed the old fool one more chance to live. He could have married me once his mourning was done but he didnae. He hardly e'er looked at me and was cold and cutting whene'er I tried to approach him."

"So ye killed him, too."

"Aye." She frowned. "He took a lot longer to die than I had felt he should."

"How inconsiderate of him."

Freda gave her a look of disgust and then took Agnes by the hand to lead her over to the table. When the woman ordered some food and drink brought for her, Agnes, and the returning Ranald, Katerina nearly screamed. Freda had murdered her family and after confessing her horrible, cold-blooded crime, she sat down to dine. Katerina found that it both frightened and enraged her.

"Here, lass, I have brought ye something to drink and a wee bit of broth."

Katerina looked up into Old Hilda's kindly face and suddenly wanted to weep. It seemed strange to her that simply learning that her parents had been murdered should make her grieve for them all over again. She supposed it was because she now knew it had not had to happen. That it had not been some illness or the all-too-common risk of childbearing, things one could not fight against, but the act of a bitter woman. If someone had known, if someone had really looked at Freda, it may all have been avoided.

"What are ye doing?" demanded Freda in a shrill voice although she did not make any move to stop Hilda.

"I thought that when ye called for food and drink ye meant me to see to the lass," Hilda said.

"Oh, do as ye wish. It matters little either way."

Katerina watched Hilda breathe a sigh of relief and then whispered, "She killed them."

"Aye, lass, I heard." Hilda helped Katerina drink some of the cider. "She will pay for her crimes."

"Are ye sure? She hasnae yet and it has been years."

"Your mother was too sweet to sense danger or see a threat from another woman and your da was too arrogant to see any woman as a threat. Ye are neither." She carefully spooned the well-spiced broth into Katerina's mouth. "Ye have the strength your dear mother ne'er had and the wit your da often didnae. Ye also have Sir Lucas Murray and a lot of good men on your side."

"Da had good men."

"But he wasnae so verra good at winning the sort of loyalty ye can. He commanded it yet he gave the men no real reason to care, if ye see what I mean."

"I think I do. Da expected things just because he was the laird, but he ne'er actually did much to earn such things as loyalty and respect. He just was the laird."

"Exactly. His people love Dunlochan, but didnae really love him, if ye will forgive me for saying so."

"Of course. Still, he didnae deserve to die that way."

"Nay, he didnae." After glancing toward Freda and

the others, Hilda gently patted Katerina's cheek. "Dinnae ye worry, lass. Ye willnae be losing this battle."

Keeping a close watch on Freda and the others, Katerina said, "Dinnae do anything that will put ye at risk, Hilda."

"I willnae, lass. Ye just worry about yourself."

The moment Hilda finished feeding Katerina she gave her a wink and hurried back to the kitchen. Katerina had the feeling that the woman was going to do something to try to help her and Lucas. Although she was grateful, and would be even more so if Hilda did successfully help them, she did not like the thought that yet another one of her people was about to be in danger.

For a moment she felt as if she was drowning in guilt. She had never seen the threat Freda posed to her parents, had never questioned the cause of their deaths. She had not really seen the threat to herself until she and Lucas had been nearly killed. Now she had all her most loyal people risking their lives to try and keep her alive. And they had all been brought to this point because she had never looked too closely at Freda. It had to be her own blindness that had brought all this tragedy down on Dunlochan.

It was a while before Katerina began to pull herself out of the deep well of self-recrimination and self-pity she had sunk into. A soft voice of common sense began to grow louder and louder, drowning out the voice that wanted to blame herself for everything that had ever gone wrong at Dunlochan. It was foolish because many of the things that had gone wrong had occurred when she was still a child. The first step on the path to the tragedy that had struck down her parents had been taken when she was not yet born.

Katerina sighed and realized that some of her

desire to blame herself was born of not wanting to blame her parents. Her father had bedded Freda. He was the one who had treated the woman so shamefully. And it was Freda who had turned her anger into something vicious and deadly. The only one of the adults involved in the tragedy who could be said to have been completely innocent was her mother. Katerina hated to blame her father for her mother's death and that of the child she had carried but he was partly responsible. If nothing else, his arrogance and his belief that women were neither strong nor clever, that they could never be a threat to any man, had allowed Freda the freedom to take her deadly revenge. Even when he had been so ill, even when he realized he was dying of a disease none of the healers could understand or cure, her father had not once looked at his scorned lover with suspicion.

"Weel, we will soon see an end to all of this," said Freda as she walked up to stand next to Katerina. "We just got word that the missive is on its way to Sir Murray."

"Do ye have any idea of who he is?" Katerina asked, even as she struggled to recall all the tales Lucas had told her of his clan during the time he had been recovering from the wounds Ranald had given him.

"He is your lover and your champion. It makes him vulnerable. What else must I ken about the mon?"

"His clan is verra important. After he, er, died, I fully expected them to show up here in force to find him and then make us all pay for his death."

"They didnae e'en show up to make us pay for his injuries and they were verra bad from all I hear. Why should I worry about them now?"

"Lucas was the reason they didnae come here to raze Dunlochan to the ground. He wouldnae allow it.

But they will do it if they wish to. If ye kill him this time, ye willnae be able to enjoy your victory for long."

"They willnae be able to prove we were at fault."

"Are ye certain of that? Mayhap Lucas told them about all of us, about Ranald's part in his beating and the attempt to murder him. Mayhap they ken exactly where Lucas is now and are simply allowing him the honor of exacting his own revenge. If that is so, then the moment he doesnae come home when he should or they hear he is dead, they will ken exactly where to come and who to look for."

Agnes stepped up to glare at Katerina. "If they are so powerful and important why havenae we heard of them?"

"Because ye dinnae trouble yourself to leave the little kingdom ye have made for yourself here. If ye had e'er gone to court ye would have heard all about them. Many of their kin have gone there and they are weel respected and trusted. Few wish to challenge them."

"Ranald, have ye heard of these Murrays?" demanded Freda.

"Some. They dinnae like to fight."

Katerina almost laughed, but she forced herself to just keep staring at Freda. Ranald's opinion of the Murrays was clear to hear in the few words he had uttered. The Murrays preferred to talk, to try to make peace and alliances, a fight being their last resort. To a man like Ranald that made them cowards and no one to fear. Freda looked a little doubtful, but Katerina expected she was of much the same opinion. Katerina saw power and intelligence in the way the Murrays made alliances instead of enemies. Freda and Ranald saw weakness. She prayed that would make them underestimate Lucas.

"I think Sir Lucas was probably a good fighter, but he is crippled now," added Ranald.

"Then we have nothing to worry about." Freda looked at Agnes. "Ye want to bed a cripple?"

Agnes shrugged. "I dinnae intend to ask him to dance, do I. If he can still walk, he can give me what I want."

Freda sighed. "And just why do ye want him? Because Katerina has had him?"

Agnes shrugged. "As good a reason as any." Agnes then smiled at Katerina. "At least he will ken what it means to have a real woman ere he dies."

"Too late. He already has." She bit back a cry of pain when Agnes slapped her.

"Let us see just how much he appreciates ye after he watches Ranald have ye."

"Agnes, he willnae be appreciating or nay appreciating anything after that as ye mean to kill him." She spoke as if she was trying to explain something to a very small child and could see that it enraged Agnes, but Freda stopped her daughter from delivering another slap.

"Dinnae say ye are now protecting her?" Agnes asked her mother.

"I am protecting us," Freda said. "I always consider the possibility that something will go wrong. If it does, I would rather not have to explain why she is bruised and bleeding."

"Ye told her all ye have done, Freda," said Ranald as he strolled up with a tankard of ale in his hand. "If this goes wrong, I think a few bruises on Katerina will be the verra least of your troubles. This one will see ye hang for her family's deaths."

"Then ye had best be verra wary and ready to kill the mon."

"If ye dinnae mind, I believe I will bring a few men in here to help ensure our victory."

"Are ye afraid of Sir Murray? The cripple? The mon ye have thrice had at your mercy and yet failed to kill?"

"As ye say, thrice I have failed to kill him. Mayhap this time I just wish to be sure his cursed luck doesnae save him a fourth time."

Katerina watched Ranald walk away and tried not to let his words frighten her. She would not believe that it was only luck that had saved Lucas each time Ranald had tried to kill him. She had seen Lucas fight before he had been injured and after. He was a little slower than he had been, but if Ranald faced him squarely, one on one, she had no doubt that Lucas would slaughter him. Lucas could deal with even more than one man, of that she had no doubt. She did not like the thought of him walking alone and unarmed into this nest of vipers but, if anyone could walk away the victor, Lucas could. He had one advantage they did not. He had the passages he could use and Katerina was sure that, even at that moment, Lucas was making his plans to use them to their fullest advantage.

She relaxed a little, her fear nearly gone. Lucas would come for her. He would seem to do as ordered but he would have a plan that would finally sweep these villains out of her life. These people were not clever enough or strong enough to defeat Lucas. He would come and he would be calm, cold justice, one that was long overdue.

Chapter Fifteen

"We can use the hidden passages in Dunlochan to reach her."

Lucas started into the passageway only to be grabbed by William and Patrick and dragged right out. For a moment he was prepared to fight their hold, to roar out his fury and race into Dunlochan. It was a struggle, but he finally subdued that mad urge. The men holding him obviously felt that change in him for they cautiously released him although they stayed close by him. When Annie thrust a tankard of ale at him, Lucas did not hesitate to take it and tried to ignore everyone watching him as he drank it all down.

"Did it clear your head?" asked William when Lucas was finished.

"It did." Lucas handed Annie the empty tankard with a nod of thanks.

"So, ye willnae be charging off, sword waving like some ancient berserker?"

"Nay, not just yet."

"Ah, good. Now we can actually make a plan. Could be useful, aye?"

"It could be," agreed Lucas as he started toward the

hall. "We shall make our plan, then we shall rescue Katerina and slaughter our enemies, and then I shall beat ye into the mud for being such an impertinent bastard."

"Sounds like a plan to me," William said, grinning as the others laughed.

Once back in the hall where he had been given the message from Ranald and Katerina's lock of hair that had set him off in such a rage, Lucas had to struggle constantly not to feel as if every passing minute put Katerina's life in danger. She could be badly hurt, even tortured as he had been, but her life was not yet at immediate risk. Ranald and Agnes needed Katerina alive to bring him to them. She was the bait in their trap. When a small voice in his head reminded him of how Ranald lusted after Katerina, of how he might use her now that she was in his grasp, Lucas shoved all thought of that as far back into the dark depths of his mind as he could. Thinking of Ranald touching Katerina could drive him mad and make him act recklessly. He had to think only about keeping her alive and planning a rescue that would not cost her men too dearly.

Even though he was not hungry, he accepted the plate of food Annie set down in front of him. He knew he would need the strength it could give him. As he ate and waited for the others to be served and start eating Lucas tried to think calmly and coldly about the best way to free Katerina.

"The passages are still the best way for us to get into Dunlochan," he said.

William nodded. "Aye, they are. We just need to have a plan for what we must do when we get in there—beside slaughtering our enemies."

Robbie cleared his throat and then blushed faintly

when everyone looked at him. "I think Lucas ought to do exactly as they told him to do."

"Walk in there alone and unarmed?" Patrick asked, outraged. "He will be dead ere we can reach him. They both will."

"Nay, I dinnae think that is true. Lucas himself heard Ranald and Agnes agree that they would have Lucas and Katerina first. They will try to do just that. Freda may nay like it, but she will do naught to stop them."

"Why would Freda e'en think she could stop them?" asked Lucas, suddenly recalling how forceful that woman had sounded and how both Ranald and Agnes had acted as if the woman was far more to them than a mere servant.

"I dinnae ken, but she could if she really wanted to. Freda has always had power over Agnes. So, Ranald and Agnes will wish to indulge themselves. They are like spoiled children in that way. There may be an argument amongst the three of them as weel, as 'tis unwise and Freda will ken it. All of that will hold their attention firmly on Lucas whilst we slip into Dunlochan."

"'Tis a good plan except that we dinnae ken what we will find once we get in there. We dinnae ken how many men they have with them, where in the keep they are holding Katerina, and if Katerina could be in danger the moment the others realize I have not come meekly into their grasp and that they are being attacked."

"There are three men with them, they are all in the great hall, and Katerina is tied to a chair in front of the fireplace in there." Hilda smiled faintly when everyone looked at her, not all of them able to hide their surprise. "'Tis much finer down here than I e'er could have imagined."

"Come sit here, Hilda," Lucas said as he stood and helped her to the seat next to him. He smiled his gratitude at Annie, who hastily set some food and drink in front of the woman. "Do ye need to hurry back so that ye are nay discovered missing?"

"Nay. I have retired for the night." Hilda took a drink and ate a little food, smiling at Annie to show her approval of the fare. "I gave Katerina something to eat and drink. She took a sore knock upon the head, but I believe she is already recovering from that. If she were freed, she would have enough strength to watch out for herself and be no hindrance to whate'er ye need to do. I am certain of it."

"Do ye think ye can cut her free?"

"Oh, aye, but I will tell ye about that in a moment. They all want ye dead, ye ken. Ye *and* Katerina. I heard what Robbie said about what Agnes and Ranald want to do and he is right—they willnae kill ye until they get what they want. Freda was furious at first, but then she decided she liked the idea, could see how it was as good as torturing each of ye."

"Freda wields some power over them, doesnae she."

"Och, aye, that she does. Freda is Agnes's mother." She nodded at the looks of shock on everyone's face and proceeded to tell them all that she had overheard Freda confess to. "I think the woman is mad."

"Aye," Lucas said quietly, wondering how such news would affect Katerina, "and that madwoman holds Katerina."

Hilda patted him on the arm. "Nay for long, aye? Ye will set her free and send that woman to hell where she belongs."

Lucas prayed the woman's faith in him was deserved. "It willnae be easy. Nay with a keep full of armed men."

"Weel, mayhap nay so full. There are ones who are

loyal to Dunlochan but loathe Agnes and Ranald. They also all like our Katerina. Once they were told what was going on they slipped away, nay wanting to be forced to hold to their oaths of service to Agnes. They gave them when they thought Katerina was dead and Agnes was to be the one to hold Dunlochan. There is another group of men who will soon be fighting each other to get to the garderobe." She blushed a little when the men grinned. "And there are a few more who will find that they cannae get out of their quarters to go to Ranald's aid."

"Hilda, ye are our miracle. Now all we must do is find a way to get Katerina free of her bonds so that she isnae still trapped in that chair when the fighting begins. Ye said ye had a plan that might accomplish that?"

"I do. I will need one of your men. Mayhap Robbie or e'en Thomas, as they are slender and nay as tall as the rest of ye."

"And being slender and wee bit short is necessary?"

"Aye, for none of the maid's gowns would fit a truly big mon."

"Explain it all a wee bit more clearly if ye could, Hilda," Lucas said gently, feeling a tug of hope for the first time in hours.

"A maid can slip into the great hall without anyone paying her much heed at all. The hearth is always cleaned out after the last meal of the day. If I can dress one of your men as a maid who has been sent to clean the hearth he can easily cut Katerina's bonds whilst ye, Sir Lucas, hold fast to the attention of Freda and the others. That mon can also linger close at hand to give my lady help if she is in need of it."

"Ye could lead armies, Hilda," Lucas said and he kissed her on the cheek. "There is one thing to consider— mayhap it would be best to send Annie to be the maid.

A kerchief for her hair and a bit of dirt upon her face and I dinnae think Ranald will notice her."

"Nay," said Robbie so quickly and sharply that everyone stared at him in surprise, but he just blushed a little before continuing. "I will do it. E'en if freed from her bonds it sounds as if Katerina willnae be able to fight or defend herself. Annie has no skill with a sword and, ere ye mention it, neither does Thomas. I do. I shudder at the thought of donning a gown, but I can do it."

"Then so ye shall."

For a little while they talked with Hilda, gleaning all the information they could and telling her exactly what she needed to do. The moment she and Robbie left, Lucas turned to the others. "Weel, do ye think we have a plan that will work?"

"Oh, aye. Old Hilda is a treasure," said William.

"That she is. S'truth, I believe the woman has been watching and gathering information, mayhap e'en planning things, just for this moment."

"Thanks be to God that Agnes and the others are the sort to pay little heed to the servants."

"True. I believe their arrogance there is our saving grace." Lucas idly stroked the lock of Katerina's hair that he had slipped into the pocket of his coat. "I had best go and do my part."

"Be careful," said Patrick. "They are expecting to see a gallant fool come to give his life for a woman. Ye dinnae want them to guess that they may have misjudged ye and become wary."

"I ken it. I also ken that I could stir their suspicion if I play the part too weel. Ranald has come close to killing me three times and willnae believe it if I am too meek and self-sacrificing."

"True," agreed William. "I hope Robbie keeps that

hair of his weel hidden, too. Agnes will recognize it immediately."

"Somehow I think Robbie will play his part with ease." Lucas stood up. "Weel, Godspeed to ye all. I pray the next time we have to speak it will be o'er the dead bodies of our enemies."

Patrick watched the doorway until he could neither see nor hear Sir Lucas and then looked at William. "Do ye think he meant that? About the dead bodies of our enemies and all?"

"Oh, aye," said William as he stood up and began to arm himself. "There is only one way we can put a stop to Agnes, Ranald, and Freda, and that is to bury them."

Lucas hid his smile as the man escorted him into the great hall of Dunlochan. The man had not searched him for weapons other than a curt and far too light brush of his hands over the usual places one hid a knife. He had not found one of the five knives Lucas had hidden away. A sword would have suited him better but Lucas was pleased that he would not be facing his enemy unarmed.

Once inside the great hall, he looked for Katerina and tensed with fury when he saw her. He studied her carefully and used the fact that she had no more than one red mark on her cheek and a hint of blood from her head wound in her hair to calm his sudden rage. He did not hide all of it, however, as he faced Ranald, Agnes, and Freda.

"I believe ye are supposed to release her now," he said in a cold, hard voice.

"Is that what ye believe?" said Freda and she laughed softly. "Nay, my gallant fool. I said ye could *see* her alive. There she is—alive. I have now met my part of the bargain."

"I wish I could say I am surprised. So, is it Ranald who gets to kill us?" He glanced back at the three men lurking near the door. "I dinnae think he will need all three to kill a woman tied to a chair and an unarmed mon, do ye?"

Freda held up her hand to stop a growling Ranald's advance on Lucas. "Ye are verra arrogant for a mon in your precarious position, Sir Murray."

He shrugged. "I have naught left to lose so what does it matter?"

"It could make a difference in how easily ye die." She glanced over at Katerina. "Or who dies first."

"Ah, so that is how ye mean to play the game. And ye willnae accept any bargain offered, will ye. No vow that I will take Katerina with me and we shall ne'er darken your threshold again or something like that."

"Nay, I dinnae think so. I have little faith in the word of men."

"Considering the men ye deal with now, I am nay surprised."

"But ye willnae die right away," said Agnes as she walked up to Lucas and laid a hand on his chest. "If ye are verra good to me, mayhap I can offer ye a re-prieve."

Lucas looked down at Agnes. He wondered how he had ever thought her sweet but witless. He could see the cold cunning in her eyes. She was willing to walk over as many bodies as were needed for her to reach her goal. The fact that she would think she could take him into her bed and he would perform just to try to save his life revealed just how cold she was. It surprised him a little that she was the whore she was re-puted to be, but he had to wonder if she sought the warmth she herself could never feel. He took her hand in his, saw the glint of malicious satisfaction in her lovely eyes, and then dropped her hand.

"Ye would refuse me?" she said, her fury growing fast, and she clenched her hands into tight little fists at her sides.

"I believe the threat of death if I dinnae please may weel make an adequate performance difficult." He looked at Ranald when the man laughed. "If ye are still planning to wed with this woman, I wouldst ne'er sleep without a dagger at the ready."

"I ne'er intended to do so," Ranald said.

Lucas saw Agnes move and easily caught her by the wrist, stopping her palm from connecting with his cheek. "I think ye have marked that cheek enough for now, mistress."

"'Tis m'lady, ye fool," she snapped as she tried to wriggle free of his grasp.

Lucas smiled faintly as he saw how tense Freda and Ranald had grown. They could see what Agnes in her blind fury could not. He now held one of theirs. It was tempting to taunt them with that, to threaten them as they threatened him and Katerina, but he could not. Robbie was now near Katerina's seat and he could not afford to have either Freda or Ranald move toward Katerina now.

"I could just snap her wee neck," he murmured and saw Agnes pale as she suddenly realized the dangerous position she was in.

"Aye, ye could, and I begin to think she is such a stupid woman it might be best, but ye willnae," said Freda.

"Ye sound so certain of that."

"I am. Ye are a knight and I believe ye actually hold to the vows knights are supposed to take—such as bringing no harm to women."

"I am nay sure I recall that one." He threw Agnes's

hand down. "Howbeit, I cannae think that killing her is worth blackening my soul."

Agnes moved to huddle near Ranald and glare at Lucas. "Ye are a fool. I could have saved ye."

"Nay, ye couldnae. I believe ye have too grand an idea of the power ye wield o'er these two." Lucas was pleased to see that their attention remained on him. He hoped Robbie hurried and finished what he was doing and that William and the others were even now moving into position, as Lucas was tired of trying to talk these fools to death. He itched to fight them.

"I suspect ye dinnae e'en understand why ye must die, do ye," Freda said.

"Oh, I have a few ideas."

Katerina could not believe Freda was taking so long in acting out her plans. The woman seemed compelled to gloat now that she felt sure she had victory in her grasp. It was a faint tug at her wrists that drew Katerina's attention away from Freda, Agnes, and Ranald facing Lucas. Trying to look as if she kept her full attention on the murderous group now confronting Lucas, she cast a fleeting glance at the maid and nearly gave them both away by laughing.

Robbie winked at her and hurriedly continued to cut away the ropes holding her to the chair. Her hopes rose as she realized there was a plan to get her free. She hoped that plan did not stop there but would also free Lucas and put an end to Freda and her allies. It appalled her that she would think such a thing, but she knew those three had to die or she and Lucas and anyone who helped them would die. They just had to figure out how they had such a hold on people so that their deaths really did end all threat to them and Dunlochan.

The moment the last of the ropes was gone, Katerina had to concentrate to sit still and act as if she was still tied up. She used the time to muster her strength so that she could get out of the reach of Freda and Ranald. Although she knew Agnes was just as guilty as her mother and lover, they were the truly dangerous ones for they had killed and had no qualms about doing so again and again.

Sensing that Robbie was watching someone in the kitchens, Katerina glanced that way. Hilda stood there in plain sight and peering over her shoulder was Patrick. He grinned and winked at her and the last of Katerina's fear faded. She knew there was still some danger but she would not let it prey on her mind. She would have faith in her lover and her men.

A moment later the doors to the great hall were thrust open, slamming into the three men Ranald had put on guard there. William leapt into the room followed by four of her men. He tossed a sword at Lucas, who easily caught it and then turned to help fight the three guards. Lucas turned to face Ranald and grinned. That grin was a chilling sight and Katerina knew Ranald would not be given any choice save to fight and die. She stood up and was immediately shoved behind Robbie, who stood between her and the others with his sword in his hand.

"Do I want to ken where ye were hiding that?" she asked.

He flashed her a quick grin. "Might be best if ye dinnae. Can ye take this cursed thing off my head? I cannae do it with one hand and I would rather nay drop my sword."

"I would rather ye kept it pointed at the enemy as weel."

Freda stood watching Ranald and Lucas fight, her face twisted into an expression of fury. Agnes looked around for a place to flee to. She started toward the kitchen only to stumble to a halt when Patrick moved to stand in front of Hilda. Agnes pulled a dagger out of her sleeve and Katerina feared she meant to throw it at Patrick. One thing Agnes could do surprisingly well was throw a knife with deadly accuracy. Instead Agnes turned toward Katerina, clearly intending to kill her or try to use her as a means to get free. At that exact moment Katerina yanked the kerchief from Robbie's head, revealing his very distinctive bright hair.

"Robbie! What are *ye* doing here?" demanded Agnes.

Katerina thought it a little ridiculous that Agnes would act so outraged to see Robbie fighting against her murderous plans—ones that had included him. It was evident that Agnes just did not think like most people. Katerina kept her eye on Agnes's dagger and breathed a sigh of relief when she felt Robbie slip his into her hand.

"I believe I am trying to keep your sister alive, my dear murderous wife," Robbie replied.

"When did ye come back?"

"Weeks ago."

"And ye didnae come to see me?"

"Nay, I felt a strong inclination to keep on breathing and ye didnae seem to share that with me."

Katerina was pleased that Robbie had accepted the truth about Agnes. She had feared that if he ever saw his wife again he might waver in that belief and that could have cost him his life. She felt sorry for any pain he might be suffering over finding out the truth, but it was better he suffer a little heartache than die at the hands of his wife. She felt him tense and wondered if he had seen some move by Agnes that warned of a coming attack.

"Dear Mama has finally noticed us," Robbie said.

"I should have guessed as Agnes suddenly looks

smug," Katerina said. "Agnes doesnae seem to recall
that Patrick stands only a few feet away with a sword in
his hand."

"Weel, 'tis a good thing as Patrick gets far more attention from the lasses than is good for him."

It was hard to believe she could feel like laughing,
but she did. Katerina suddenly recalled that that was
one of the things she had always liked about Robbie.
He had always made her laugh even when it was the
very last thing she felt like doing.

"So ye came back, did ye?" asked Freda as she slowly
approached Robbie and Katerina.

A quick glance at Freda revealed that the woman
now held a long knife in her hand. The look on her
face told Katerina that she had every intention of
using it on someone. Katerina suspected it was her
Freda wanted to kill, but that the woman would have
no qualms about taking down Robbie to do it. When
she saw that Patrick had crept up close behind Agnes,
Katerina decided there was no longer a threat from
that direction and turned her full attention onto
Freda.

"Aye," replied Robbie. "I had thought to reconcile
with my wife, but it seemed she did not feel as ten-
derly toward me as I had hoped."

"Ye are a fool and ye have always been a fool."

"I appear to be on the winning and righteous side,
Maman, so who is really the fool here?"

"If ye had stood with us ye could have been the laird
here."

"Nay, that seat isnae yours to fill with whome'er ye
want and I want nothing that has been gained with
the blood of innocent people."

Freda shrugged. "Then ye may as weel die as ye are
of no use to me."

Katerina felt Robbie tense although she was not

sure if it was to shield her from the knife with his own body or to judge which way they should jump when Freda threw the knife. Then Freda abruptly stood very straight and her eyes widened. Katerina followed the woman's gaze down to her stomach and saw the tip of a sword sticking out. Slowly Freda raised her gaze and glared at Katerina, before crumpling to the floor. Behind her stood a blood-soaked Ranald and behind him stood Lucas, sword in hand and looking beautifully unharmed.

Agnes stopped struggling with Patrick and gaped at her mother's body before staring at Ranald. "Ranald, ye have killed *Maman*."

"Aye, I have. Just as she has killed me with all her plots and plans." He slowly sank to his knees and gave Agnes a gruesome smile, blood running from his mouth. "Dinnae fret, my bonnie bitch. I suspicion I will soon see ye again in Hell."

Patrick snatched the dagger from Agnes's suddenly limp grasp and let her go. Katerina looked to see that the fighting was over and stepped out from behind Robbie as Agnes slowly walked over to where her mother and her lover lay dead on the floor. For a moment Agnes's bottom lip quivered and Katerina waited for a loud outpouring of grief, even considered going over to try and comfort her half-sister. But then Agnes took a deep breath, and turned to look at Lucas.

"I must thank ye for freeing me from these two people," she said, her voice all soft and coaxing. "I could ne'er get free and they continued to drag me deeper and deeper into their plots."

Robbie made a sound of utter disgust. "Ye are surrounded by the dead and have openly spoken of your plans to kill people and ye have the audacity to act as if ye are naught but a victim? E'en ye arenae good enough to make that work, Agnes. Be an adult for once in your life and accept your own guilt in all of this."

She glared at him for a moment, before recalling that her plan had been to try and save her own skin. Immediately, she turned her big, blue tear-washed eyes on Katerina. "Sister, ye cannae mean to have me killed, can ye? I am of your blood. We shared a father."

"Aye, until your mother murdered him," said Katerina and then she ran to Lucas, who opened his arms wide, then held her close. "And ye tried to have Lucas murdered just because he didnae crawl into your bed. Nay, *Sister*, dinnae look for forgiveness here."

"What do ye mean to do with me?"

Katerina looked up at Lucas, but he just kissed her on the forehead. "'Tis your decision, Kat. Ye must have given some thought to this."

She had, but she had often thought that Agnes would not survive the final confrontation. In some way she was glad she had, for no matter what the woman had tried to do, Katerina had never been able to completely forget that Agnes was her sister. She took a deep breath to steady herself, and turned to face Agnes, leaning against Lucas for support and the strength to do what she had to do.

"I cannae bring myself to hang ye as ye deserve. E'en if ye ne'er wielded the weapon yourself ye have too much blood on your hands to simply set ye free. Nay, I will send ye to the nunnery at Dunbarton. I will give them a fine dowry for ye and make sure they understand that ye are to ne'er leave there."

"Nay, Katerina, ye cannae do that. I cannae live in a nunnery!"

"Aye, ye can and ye will."

"But, they dress in coarse wool gowns and do naught but pray all the day long."

"'Twill do ye good. I suggest ye gather up a few

things to wear for the journey and for whate'er time they allow ye to wear your own clothes before ye have to don a habit."

"They will cut off my hair."

Katerina had to fight to keep herself from backing down. For once Agnes looked honestly shocked. "Ye have had people killed, Agnes. By rights I should have ye hanged and a lot of people will think me a fool for nay doing so. 'Tis a nunnery or the gallows. 'Tis the truth, if ye dinnae get to a nunnery, others may see to it that ye pay for your crimes at the end of a rope. The judgment in this could easily be taken out of my hands by someone more powerful than I." She watched Agnes walk away, her step halting and her head down, a picture of utter defeat, William falling silently into step behind her.

"Dinnae falter, lass," murmured Lucas as he kissed the top of her head.

"Nay, 'tis a kinder judgment than she deserved," said Robbie as he moved to stand beside her.

"Ah, Robbie, I fear I gave nary a thought to what this means to ye," said Katerina. "Ye are still wed to her."

"She will be in a nunnery. If I choose, I believe I can get special dispensation and end it."

A bellow from upstairs drew their attention and a moment later they were all running up the stairs. The moment she ran into Agnes's room Katerina knew what had happened. Even though she did not want to see, she found herself walking to the window where a pale William stood. Lucas quickly wrapped her in his arms as she leaned slightly out of the window and looked down. Agnes lay broken on the ground, an ominous dark stain spreading beneath her shattered body. Katerina had told her sister that her choices were the gallows or the nunnery. Agnes had obviously found a third choice.

Chapter Sixteen

"I still think no one believed your tale that Agnes was killed in the confusion of battle," Katerina said as she placed some violets on her half-sister's grave.

"Probably not, but they will ne'er question it. She is gone. 'Tis sad, but that is all they care about," Lucas said quietly, still not certain how Katerina felt about it all. "Ye offered her what was a merciful reprieve from the gallows; she chose to die instead. That is all there is to it." He watched as she frowned at Agnes's grave. "Do ye grieve for her still? It has been a month now."

Lucas thought it had been the longest month of his life, but he did not say so. Katerina had not sent him away as he had feared she would, but she had set him aside. He could understand why she kept him out of her bed. She feared losing the respect of her people, feared appearing to be no better than Agnes. There was no convincing her that no one would ever think such a thing about her, and so he slept alone. All the work that had needed to be done had helped a little by making him so tired at the end of the day that he slept despite the need that made his body ache. Unfortunately, the work had begun to ease. His need for Katerina had not and he doubted it ever would.

If they got married it would solve everything, but he had not found the right opportunity to broach the subject. He had been wooing her, trying to win back her affection and trust, but he was not very good at wooing. He had brought her flowers, but they always seemed to get sadly wilted and crushed by the time he gave them to her. The few times he had tried to write her a love letter as it was said courtiers did, he had hastily burned the attempts. He knew a lot of songs said to be favored by women, but his singing voice was enough to send anyone fleeing the room with their hands clapped tightly over their ears. Lucas was not sure what else to do, as the one thing he knew might sway her to his side was lovemaking, but she was not letting him near enough most times to even try to stir her passion.

Katerina turned to face Lucas and idly wondered what had him looking so low of spirit. He never said so, but he had no regrets over the death of Agnes and she could not blame him. He had not killed the woman and probably would not have unless she had actually threatened his life, or hers. Agnes had chosen to end her own life and Katerina suspected Lucas thought it had been a good solution to the problem.

She ached for him, would like nothing more than to have him take her into his arms and let her soak up his strength, but she had to resist that temptation. It would not stop with a comforting hug and she knew it. Soon she would have to decide what to do about him, but she was still feeling too much the coward.

"Agnes was young and beautiful," she began, deciding to turn both their thoughts to her half-sister.

"Kat, she was also completely without morals," Lucas said.

"I ken it. Ye asked me if I still grieved for her. The sad thing is, and what has troubled me, is that I dinnae grieve for her at all. For a brief moment, when I first saw what she had done, I felt a grief, but I cannae say if it was for her, for the fact that the last of my closest kin was dead, or just over the horrible sin she had just committed. I have been coming here to see if, once the shock of it had faded, I would feel something. I have not. Just the occasional pinch of sorrow over a life so badly wasted."

Lucas took her hand and tugged until she started back to the keep with him. "That isnae your fault."

"She was my sister. Somehow I ought to feel something."

"She ne'er allowed ye to. I suspect in the beginning ye were willing to have her as your sister, ready to be a good sister to her, and she pushed ye aside time and time again, or worse. She is to blame for what ye do or dinnae feel. Let it go, Kat. No one would e'er think badly of ye because ye cannae grieve for Agnes."

She nodded. "I believe I will still visit her grave from time to time, though, if only out of respect for what might have been if she had had a different mother and we both had had a more loving father."

"I have always believed that every grave should be visited now and again. Keeps the spirits restful."

"Lucas Murray, dinnae say ye believe in ghosts."

"Oh, aye, I do. With some of the kin I have I can do naught else."

"Oh! Do ye mean to say that one of those *gifts* ye said your clan has is seeing ghosts?"

"I have a cousin who can see them, but I think we shall have to save that tale for another time as the guests are arriving for Robbie's wedding."

Katerina shook her head as Lucas led her around to the rear of the keep so that she did not have to meet their guests right away. "I kenned that Annie was verra enamored of Robbie, but ne'er realized that he felt the same for her."

"I guessed it right before we came to rescue ye from Freda. I thought Annie might be the best one to play the maid and he leapt in, offering himself so quickly and vehemently, I kenned it was because he didnae want Annie anywhere near the danger we were about to walk into."

"Weel, 'tis good, for Annie does love the fool."

"Ah, dinnae call your new steward a fool."

"Steward. Robbie. Two words I would ne'er have guessed could fit together so perfectly. He loves working with numbers, doesnae he."

"He does and he works verra weel with them. We now have an accounting of how much Morrison and Sorley helped themselves to. We shall give them the accounting ere they leave for home after the wedding."

She paused at the door to her bedchamber. "Do ye really think they will give it back?"

Lucas nodded. "I do, although Sorley will hate every minute of it and grieve o'er every penny."

Katerina laughed and lightly pushed him away. "Go. Ready yourself for the wedding. I will meet ye in the great hall in an hour."

The moment she was inside her bedchamber, the door shut behind her, Katerina slumped against the door and closed her eyes. She was not going to be able to keep pushing him away. Every single part of her ached for him. She slept poorly, missing the warmth of his big strong body next to hers even though they had shared a bed for such a short time. It was time to stop being a coward and decide what to do about Lucas. The fact that he was still at Dunlochan, showed no sign of wanting to leave, and was wooing her, implied that he wanted her as he had before. The only thing stopping them from being together was her own fear of being hurt. Katerina knew she was going to have to overcome that. If nothing else, she found no relief from pain by being away from him, so why not take her chance and reach out for him?

"Good question, Katerina," she mumbled as she moved to the bowl of water and began to strip off her gown so she could wash.

Annie and Robbie were getting married in a very short time and she would fix her mind on that for the moment. She refused to drag her troubles into the midst of their celebration. Later, when she was yet again all alone in her big bed, she would confront her fears and make up her mind. If nothing else it was not fair to Lucas to keep them both apart yet not apart.

Katerina leaned against the wall and watched the dancers, tapping her foot to the music. She had danced, had even danced with Lucas, but knew she had to be careful. Dancing had made her dangerously light-headed. The last thing she wanted to do was collapse on the floor of the great hall in the middle of Robbie and Annie's wedding celebrations. There would undoubtedly be some very awkward questions asked.

"Kat, m'dear," called Malcolm as he hurried over to her.

"Greetings, Malcolm," she said and smiled at him before kissing his cheek. "I am glad to see that ye have fully recovered from that knock on the head."

"Aye, aye. I thought I had a verra hard head, but it seems I was mistaken. Morrison has been most apologetic."

"So he should be. Ye were his friend."

"Still am. He acted out of fear, Katerina. Not right, of course, but understandable. I actually have come to tender my most sincere apologies."

"Ye have naught to apologize for, Malcolm."

"Och, aye, I do. I should have tried harder to find out exactly what happened to ye. I kenned ye would ne'er have done what they said, but I didnae have the courage to speak out, to ask questions. 'Tis the same concerning the money. I sensed something was wrong, but I ne'er looked too closely. It took me months to simply get up the courage to ask Morrison if I might have a look at the books."

"Malcolm, what happened here at Dunlochan wasnae something anyone could imagine. 'Tis nay your fault ye didnae see each and every crime. And, as ye just said, Morrison was your friend. Of course ye were reluctant to think that he was doing anything wrong. I am glad ye didnae grow too curious, for ye would have been killed. That is how Ranald and Freda silenced all talk about what crimes may have been committed. I have nay doubt they would have killed ye without hesitation or remorse. They talked about how the whole council was a threat to them whilst they held me captive and their solution to that was the same as it was when they felt threatened by anything—kill it."

His slender shoulders slumped a little. "Still, it would nay have gone on for so long if I had been braver."

"Ye cannae ken that for a fact. Yet I do ken that if ye had started accusing anyone of murder or theft or starting looking at the books, I would have had yet another grave to visit."

Malcolm smiled at her. "Thank ye for making an old mon feel nay quite so useless."

"Wheesht, ye arenae that old." She nodded to where Hilda was wending her way toward them. "Our

Hilda certainly doesnae think so. Malcolm, are ye running away?"

"Aye," he said even as he tried to wriggle through the crowd standing at the edges of the great hall, "and as quickly as I can."

Feeling mischievous, Katerina pointed out the direction Malcolm had gone when Hilda came close and saw that he was no longer at Katerina's side. Laughing softly, she looked around at the people of Dunlochan and felt truly content for the first time in a long time. This was what life should be like at Dunlochan and she realized that, although things had gotten very bad while Freda was in control, they had not been all that good in those last few years that her father had been alive.

One other thing that had definitely been set right was that her cousins were now in their proper place. William was her second-in-command and had many of his brothers as his men-at-arms. Katerina suspected it would take a long time before she could forgive her father for the way he had treated William and his siblings. For a man who had so often bemoaned not having a son, he had all too easily turned aside a whole lot of nephews, one of whom could have made him a very fine heir.

Signaling a page, she had the boy refill her tankard of wine. Katerina knew she was feeling quite heady with drink already, but did not care. It was a celebration and she intended to celebrate until she had to be carried to bed.

It did not surprise her when Lucas suddenly came to mind. She would like nothing better than to have him carry her to her bed. Caught up in thoughts of all they could do once they reached her bed, Katerina felt a hot blush sting her cheeks when a grinning Annie suddenly appeared at her side.

"Has my wedding got ye dreaming of your own?" asked Annie.

"Certainly not," she replied, wishing that she sounded more adamant than she did. "'Tis just verra warm in here."

Annie rolled her eyes. "Of course it is. Why dinnae ye just drag that verra bonnie mon off to your bedchamber and cure what ails ye?"

"Naught ails me."

"Och, aye, it does." Annie shook her head. "Ye need to cease being afraid, Katerina." Annie blushed, for she was still not accustomed to calling the lady of Dunlochan by her Christian name. "That mon has stayed here and helped ye without much more than a wee smile from ye from time to time. Do ye think he just needs something to do? There is only one reason he is still here and 'tis because of ye. I think ye need to find out what he wants."

"I ken exactly what he wants."

"Weel, of course he wants *that*. All men want that. They dinnae hang about a keep fixing stables to get it, though. Nay, not when they are as handsome as he is and will be a laird in their own right one day." She patted Katerina on the arm. "I see my mon looking for me and I see yours looking for ye. The only one who still refuses to see that he *is* your mon is ye. Think on that."

Katerina watched Annie hurry over to Robbie's side. For a moment Katerina felt the sting of envy and hastily pushed it away. Robbie and Annie deserved their happiness. They had risked their lives to help her regain what belonged to her. If she was not happy the only one she could really blame was herself.

She felt Lucas was near even before he slid his arm around her waist. Knowing anyone who glanced their way would see how familiarly he was touching her, she almost pulled away from him. Then some still sensible part of her realized that that would hurt him, if only in his pride. After all he had done for her, she would not humiliate him by pulling away as if he had some disease she might catch from him.

He touched his lips to her ear and she shivered, desire roaring to life inside of her. Katerina cast a look at her tankard of wine, then inwardly sighed. It was foolish to blame the drink, especially since no one had forced her to drink it. It was not the wine that was making her feel as if her blood was on fire; it was Lucas.

"Ye havenae danced again," he said. "I will dance with ye if ye like."

Katerina took a hasty drink of wine to hide her grin. Lucas sounded as if he had just offered to let her pull out his fingernails. She knew he would dance with her if she wished it just as she knew he would hate every minute of it. He would do it because it would make her happy.

For some reason that made her feel like she was the biggest idiot of all. He had wronged her, hurt her more than she cared to think about, but was she punishing him now or herself? And, she decided, trying to come to some conclusion and clouding her mind with weighty thoughts after downing far too much wine was foolish. What she wanted to do, needed to do more desperately than she had ever wanted anything else, was take Lucas up to her bedchamber and make love to him until his eyes rolled back into his head. Then she might throw a little cold water on him and do it again.

She turned around and looked up at him. Lucas Murray had to be the handsomest man she had ever seen and he wanted her. Whether it was just lust or not, at that moment she did not care. Katerina slowly ran her finger down the scar on his face and heard him catch his breath.

There was a look in Katerina's fine blue eyes that had Lucas feeling as if he had just run from here to Donncoill and back again. He glanced at her tankard and wondered just how much wine she had drunk. It could be the wine that had her looking at him in the way she used to. Then she leaned her body into his, her full breasts pushing against his chest.

"Lucas," she whispered.

Suddenly he did not care if it was the wine. The way she said his name, her voice low and husky, made him as hard as iron before she had even finished saying it. She was making him sweat and he was debating the right and wrong of taking her to bed. His brother Artan would think he had gone insane.

"Katerina, best ye be verra careful," he said, not surprised to hear the tremor in his voice. He was astounded that his whole body was not shaking. "If ye say my name like that again I will be racing up the stairs with ye in my arms and headed for your bedchamber. And this time I willnae let ye shut me out."

For just a moment Katerina was tempted to see if he would do that, but a faint glimmer of good sense prevailed. Lucas did not make empty threats, or, she thought with an inner grin, promises. She slid her hand down his arm and threaded her fingers through his. Ignoring his slightly puzzled look she led him out of the great hall. Near the stairs she took a last good look around to make sure no one was there to see what happened next, and then she looked up at him and smiled.

"Lucas," she whispered.

She had to bite back a squeal of laughter when he growled and picked her up, tossing her over his shoulder. What made her want to laugh was that she knew he was not completely jesting, that a part of him was feeling just like this and it thrilled her. Katerina was glad that no one saw them as he raced to her bedchamber. Somehow this did not seem as if this was the way the lady of the keep ought to act.

Lucas went into her bedchamber and then set her on the floor, letting her lush little body slide down his as he did so. He was ready to tear off their clothes and have her up against the door, but he needed to give her one more chance to get away. The very last thing he wanted to face in the morning was her suffering from regret and embarrassment.

"This is a dangerous place for me to be," he said, struggling to catch his breath and sound like a man courting a woman instead of one who was ready to go down on his knees and beg her to let him stay just this one night. Then she could go back to being proper and he would try to go back to courting her.

"Is it now? Dangerous for whom?"

"Dangerous for ye."

"Oh, nay, I dinnae think so." There was a part of Katerina that was shocked at how much she was enjoying herself. She kicked the door shut and then latched it, all the while staring at him with a little smile on her face. "I think ye may be the one in danger tonight, Sir Lucas."

"Oh, thank God," he breathed and reached for her.

Katerina finally found the strength to lift her head and looked around the bedchamber. Her and Lucas's clothes were scattered everywhere. She hoped they had not ripped too many things or the laundry women would have a hearty chuckle.

"Ye are a wild mon, Sir Murray," she murmured.

"Thank ye, m'lady," he said as he nuzzled her breasts.

Humming her pleasure over his touch, Katerina knew she ought to send him directly to his own bed-chamber. Sleeping wrapped in his arms held an allure that she might find too hard to give up again. Waking to him in the morning could also prove very risky indeed. She shivered with pleasure as he dragged his tongue over her hardened nipple and lightly nipped it.

"Savage."

"Ye flatter me."

She laughed and then squirmed a little when he drew the tip of her breast deep into his mouth and suckled her as if had all the time in the world and was not driving her mad. Katerina threaded her fingers through his thick hair and held him close, closing her eyes as pleasure washed over her. She had missed this, missed him. Surely for just one night, one short night she would end before morning came, she could indulge herself.

Lucas looked at her as he slid his hand down to her stomach and idly stroked her soft skin. She was so beautiful when her passion was running hot. She was even more beautiful when she was tearing his clothes off as fast as he was tearing hers off, he thought with a satisfied grin. Katerina could be as wild as he was and he was more grateful for that than he could say.

"Katerina, are ye certain ye arenae drunk?" he asked, suddenly feeling a pang of guilt as he wondered yet again if he had taken advantage of her.

"Aye, I am certain. A wee bit mayhap, but ye need not thrash yourself about taking advantage. I do believe I, er, pushed ye a wee bit."

A soft gasp escaped her when he slid his hand between her legs and began to caress her. She was not sure if that gasp was from a lingering shock at such an intimate touch or delight and soon she did not care. She clung to him as he tormented her with his caress.

When he began to kiss his way down her body, she tensed a little and blushed a little when she realized it was with anticipation. The first touch of his warm mouth made her shudder, pure fire racing through her body. Even as she thought that she ought to pull away from something so intimate and shocking, she no longer wanted to.

Lucas grasped her by the hips to hold her steady as he loved her with his mouth. He savored her soft cries and the way she slowly opened for him, her body reveling in his intimate kisses. When he felt her begin to tense, her release nearly upon her, he quickly joined their bodies. He kissed her as he thrust deep inside her and caught her cry in his mouth. A moment later he fell into passion's abyss with her, his body shuddering from the force of his release as he poured his seed deep into her body.

As soon as he could move, he rolled onto his back and pulled her into his arms. Lucas was still uneasy for this was too big a change from what she had been even a few hours ago. He prepared himself for being sent away and, perhaps, finding himself right back where he had been come the morning. The fact that she still felt the same fierce need he did, that her passion still ran hot and wild for him would be some consolation, but it would also make it a lot harder to go to bed alone again.

"Woman, I think ye are trying your best to drive me mad," he muttered.

Katerina smiled against his chest and then slowly licked it. "Mayhap I was suddenly verra tired of being good," she said softly.

"Ah, weel, I think ye are being verra good right now."

"Do ye?" She slid down a little and licked his stomach. "And this?"

"Even better."

For a little while she idly kissed him and stroked him with her tongue. Tasting his skin, teasing his belly-hole with her tongue and savoring the hair-covered roughness of his legs. She could tell by the growing tension in his body that he was waiting to see if she would bless one certain very prominent part of him with a kiss or two, but she teased him just a little more.

"How about this?" she asked and dragged her tongue very slowly up his shaft.

"I think this may be the best," he said, not surprised that his voice was hoarse and unsteady. He was surprised he could speak at all.

"*May* be? Weel, I shall have to see if I change that into an *is*."

For as long as he could Lucas savored the way she loved him with her mouth. He was surprised that having made love to her twice was not enough to give him a lot of control, but he decided he had been too long without her. Only a few minutes passed before he knew he had to be inside her. He grasped her under the arms and brought her up his body. She immediately guessed what he wanted and lowered her body down onto his with a tantalizing slowness. The way she rode him, as if every glide of her body over his sent shivers through her, soon had him as crazed as he had been when he had first entered her bedchamber. Lucas grasped her by the hips and urged her on to a faster speed.

They soared together and the feeling was so rich and fine, Lucas quickly gave up his plan to linger on the edge of release for as long as possible. When they came together, their cries blending as their releases tore through them, Lucas decided that it was the sweetest music he had ever heard. He held her close when she collapsed into his arms and could tell by the way she seemed boneless but heavy that this time she would probably have to sleep for a while. He had to admit, if only to himself, that he could also use a rest.

He gently eased their bodies apart but kept her in his arms, her soft body sprawled on top of him. For a while he just held her, stroking her hair and savoring the feeling of being completely sated. Lucas knew this was what he wanted, what he needed, but he was having a difficult time convincing her. It might be time to get in touch with one of his cousins who had a way with words and knew what a woman liked. Aside from this, he thought, and grinned.

Lucas wanted a wife *and* a lover, the perfect blend in one little woman with big blue eyes and hair the color of clover honey. He had known it a year ago and he knew it now. For some reason he had lost sight of that, gone a little mad for a while, but he had to convince Katerina that he would never do that again. It was a huge problem for a man who had little skill with soft words and explanations. He had not even been able to spit out a proper apology yet.

"Lucas, ye need to seek out your own bed," Katerina mumbled against his chest.

That stung, but he had been expecting it.

"We cannae have anyone in the keep seeing ye leaving my bedchamber." She hastily covered her mouth when a huge yawn shook her. "They would guess what we have been doing."

He was tempted to tell her that, with all the noise they had been making, he doubted many were unaware of what they had been doing. Lucas knew it was important to her not to be seen as anything like Agnes, however. She knew what they did together was nothing like what her half-sister had indulged in, but she was right in thinking others would not see much difference. He did not care what people thought, knew that the ones who mattered would never condemn them. Yet, despite how much he wanted to stay with her, he would go seek out his own bed because he did not want to ruin this night, or end it on a note of disagreement.

"In a wee while, Kat. 'Tis hours before dawn and I suspicion a few hours before all the guests have left or sought out a place to sleep."

"Oh, aye, I hadnae thought of that."

It was only a few moments later when he felt her body go completely limp and he knew she was sound asleep. It was tempting to just join her in sleep and claim that as an excuse for still being in her bed in the morning, but he was determined not to give in to that temptation. He would wait until all was quiet and there were no more unsteady footsteps passing by the door and then he would slip away to his own bed and hope no one had fallen into it while he was gone. Tomorrow, however, he would sit Katerina down and they would have a talk. He could not abide this anymore and he did not want to wake up one more morning without her in his arms.

Chapter Seventeen

Katerina opened one eye and stared at the broad chest she was sprawled over. Her stomach knotted and then began to churn. The foul burning was creeping up into her throat. She knew what was going to happen next. It had happened every morning for a fortnight. It was why she had ignored her growing need for Lucas, stayed firm in her decision to keep him out of her bed long after she began to ache to invite him back in. It was why she should have made certain he had returned to his own bed last night. Groaning softly, she leapt from the bed, uncaring about her nakedness, and raced for the bucket in the far corner of the room.

Lucas frowned as he woke up to the sound of someone retching. For a moment he feared some guest had come into his room in the night and was now paying dearly for having drunk too much at the wedding. He hoped they had at least found the bucket. Then he recalled where he had been last night and he cautiously looked around. A soft curse escaped him as he realized he had gone to sleep and, if the light by the window was any indication, he had slept late into the day.

Which meant the retching he heard had to be from Katerina, he thought with alarm. He sat up and immediately saw her. She crouched by an old bucket, nearly hugging the thing, and she was completely naked. He knew he would have enjoyed the view if she had not been emptying her stomach and, if he was hearing correctly, crying and cursing at the same time. Lucas suspected she would not appreciate him commenting on how he would have thought that was impossible.

He got out of bed and hurried to her side. When he reached out to touch her, she swatted at him. Cautiously he caught her hair in his hands to hold it out of the way and, although she snarled at him, she did not try to hit him again. After several minutes he began to grow alarmed. He was sure she should not be this sick simply because she ate something that disagreed with her or drank more wine than she was accustomed to.

When she collapsed back against him, he ignored her weak insistence that she could take care of herself and carried her back to the bed. He fetched her some water and held a bowl while she rinsed her mouth out several times. She collapsed back onto the pillows and closed her eyes. Lucas dampened a rag in her bowl of wash water and, after warily sitting on the side of the bed, he began to gently bathe her face. She looked very pale and a whisper of a moan escaped her now and then.

"Too much wine?" he asked softly, as he inched his way beneath the covers and slowly took her into his arms, relieved when she allowed him to comfort her.

"Nay."

Lucas stared down at her. Her response had been more of a grunt than a word. Slowly her body grew heavy and her breathing eased. He relaxed as he realized she was going to sleep. If she was ill from more than drinking too much wine or eating too much rich food, he did not think she could go to sleep so easily. Such fierce retching troubled him, however, and he was determined to make her rest until he was sure it was no more than just her body violently ridding itself of something it did not want.

"See, Kat? Ye need someone to take care of ye," he murmured.

Thinking on that, Lucas decided he liked the idea of having someone to care for. What made it even more appealing was the sure knowledge that Katerina would not need such care all that often. She was healthy, strong, and a woman who did not need a man to tell her how to do everything. It was what would make caring for her when she needed it a privilege instead of a chore.

His mind quickly returned to the problem of her retching. He had been living with Katerina for weeks and she had shown no sign of having a sensitive stomach. In fact there were a few times when he had expected her to suffer from what she ate, not because the food was spoiled but because of what she ate together. As far as Lucas was concerned there were just some foods that should never be put into one's mouth or stomach at the same time.

The latch on the door was wriggled and he tensed, but then recalled that Katerina had secured the latch. For a moment he remained still, knowing she did not want anyone to learn that he had come to her bed. It would be a lot easier to explain a locked door than a naked man in her bed.

"M'lady, I have brought ye your dry toasted bread and some weak cider. 'Tis what Annie says ye have every morning. Shall I just leave it here by the door?"

Dry toasted bread and weak cider? Lucas thought. There was something familiar about that filled his

head with alarums. He eased out of the bed, donned
his braies and his shirt, and went to the door. He recognized Megan's voice and felt he could trust the
woman not to tell the whole keep about him being in
Katerina's room. As quietly as he could, he opened the
door and held a finger to his lips to silence Megan.
She stared at him wide-eyed for a moment then appeared to be biting back a grin as she handed him the
tray. Lucas stared at the unappetizing fare and then
looked back at Megan, who was not even trying to hide
her grin this time.

"Ye willnae say anything, will ye?" he asked.

"Wheesht, I am nay a rattle-tongue," she said.

"I didnae think so." He looked at the tray again and
shrugged. "Weel, thank ye for taking o'er Annie's
chores for now."

"'Tis my pleasure, laird."

Before he could correct her and tell her that he was
not a laird and, God willing, would not become the
laird of Donncoill for many a long year, she had hurried away down the hall. Suddenly realizing that he
was standing in the hall half-dressed where anyone
might see him, Lucas quickly ducked back into Katerina's bedchamber. He shut the door with his hip and
took the tray to the small table near the bed. Shedding his clothes, he crawled back into bed and took
Katerina back into his arms.

After a few moments of fruitlessly trying to go back
to sleep, Lucas looked at the tray again. There was
something he needed to remember but it was proving
to be an elusive memory. Dry toasted bread. He
frowned. He realized it was his brother Artan who had
mentioned it, but Lucas was sure Artan would never
accept such fare to break his fast. He tensed. Cecily,
Artan's wife, had eaten such fare every morning for
several months as it seemed to ease her morning

nausea. Morning nausea. Not wine. Not bad food. A child. Katerina was carrying his child and she had obviously known it for a while.

It took every ounce of willpower he had not to shake her awake and demand the truth. Lucas took several deep breaths to calm himself. He recognized that he was hurt that she had not told him and decided he better be rid of that emotion before he faced her again. There were some good reasons for her to have remained silent. To be fair, he did not know how long she had known. She could still be trying to decide what she should do, even worrying over how he might react. Those fears he could ease. The others would have to be soothed as she confessed them.

And they would deal with them after they were married. His child would carry his name. Lucas had the sinking feeling he faced a battle, but he would win. Whatever problems they had could be dealt with after they got married. He knew he would get no sleep now and so he held her, waiting for her to wake up, and sorted through what he had to do in order to marry her.

The first thing he would do was write to his brother Artan. Artan had dealt with a reluctant wife and now had a good marriage. Although it galled him to have to look to Artan for advice, especially about women, Lucas knew he would rather it was his twin he had to confess his trouble to than any other one in his family. He just hoped Artan had a few sensible answers.

Katerina woke up and wondered if she was having a dream. She could vaguely recall waking up with her cheek pressed against this very same chest not all that long ago. She struggled to recall the rest of that dream, or memory. When she recalled emptying her belly into a bucket as she had done nearly every morning for too long, she also recalled Lucas there. If this was a memory, then she had not welcomed his assistance, even grudgingly accepting his holding her hair and getting her water to rinse out her mouth. The way he had bathed her face with cool water had been a kindness she had not expected and then he had held her until she fell asleep. Now it all made sense. Unfortunately, it meant that Luca was still in her bedchamber and that he had been a witness to her illness.

Well, she thought as she braced herself to look at him, he was a man and men did not understand that much about the workings of a woman's body. Katerina was sure she could think of something that would explain away her illness. Then she looked up, saw the look in his very silver eyes, and the smile she had started to give him froze right on her face.

"When is the bairn due?" he asked.

Obviously some men took the time to learn a few things, she thought and knew she ought to find that a good thing. At the moment she wanted to kick him. "I dinnae ken."

"Katerina, I hope ye arenae going to try and tell me that ye arenae carrying my child."

She had considered it, but was not about to admit to that.

"Ye are sick in the morning, retching as if ye are trying to bring up all your innards and have a look at them. Then, despite looking like a corpse, ye crawl back into bed and sleep like the dead for a few hours. Now ye are awake and ye look just fine. Also your lady Megan brought ye some dry toasted bread and weak cider. I recently heard about this sort of appalling breakfast. It was all my brother Artan's wife could hold down in the morning until her nausea passed."

"Weel, I guess I am with child then," she muttered as

she reached for her dry toasted bread wondering if any man had made a woman feel quite so wretched. A corpse, he said. "I wasnae too sure about it until the last week. Kept thinking it was because of all that has happened during the last few weeks. That would upset anyone's belly."

Lucas tried not to look too disgusted as she crunched her way through the dry toasted bread and sipped her weak cider. "Then our bairn shouldnae be born too early and raise too many questions about our marriage." He waited, knowing it would not be that easy.

Katerina felt her heart jump with excitement and joy only to come thudding down in the next breath. He wanted the child. He had never spoken of marriage before, not even when he had been courting her a year ago. She had only assumed it. This time, because he had been staying around and apparently courting her again, she had begun to think he was wooing her with an eye toward marriage. But, now, as he finally spoke of the thing she seemed to have been waiting for forever, it was because she carried his child. She had a strong urge to kick him right out of her bed.

"I dinnae see any reason for us to be married."

"That bairn is a verra good reason."

She looked at his finger pointing at her stomach and then noticed that she was still naked. Cursing softly, she got out of bed, dragging the blanket along to cover herself, and hunted for her shift. Finding it draped over the chest at the far end of the room, she tried putting it on without dropping the blanket. Irritated beyond words when that proved impossible she just dropped the blanket, yanked on her shift, and turned to glare at him.

"Out of here," she said. "I dinnae want to get

married for a bairn. This bairn is a Haldane and that is good enough."

Realizing that she was in no mood to discuss the matter sensibly, Lucas got out of bed and finished dressing. "That bairn is a Murray and it might be a son. If it is, 'tis an heir to Donncoill. Ye might wish to think of what ye are denying him by being so stubborn."

"He is also the heir to Dunlochan," she snapped.

Knowing he was growing angry as well, Lucas opened the door and looked back at her. "I will start planning the marriage as I think ye might have a few wits in your bonnie head and will decide I am right and that we should be married. No need to delay it all while ye sulk."

A look came into her eyes that told Lucas this was one of those times when retreat was in order. He stepped into the hall and shut the door. When he turned around he found William, Patrick, and Robbie all staring at him. Lucas just glared at them, daring them to say something.

"A wee bit of trouble with the lass?" asked William.

Lucas sighed. He should have known that William would not be intimidated. "I have told her that we will be married as soon as possible."

"Ye *told* her?"

"Aye, and she isnae being verra cooperative."

"I cannae imagine why when ye told her what she must do."

"She is carrying my bairn." He jumped slightly when something heavy slammed into the door behind him. Katerina obviously did not like him telling anyone. "I dinnae see any reason to wait."

William frowned at the door. "Still, ye might have tried to be a wee bit, weel, romantic."

"I have been wooing the woman for a month or

more and I dinnae think she has e'en noticed. 'Tis clear that I dinnae have the knack. Fine. I am verra good at giving orders. Now, if ye will excuse me, I need to clean up, write a letter to my brother, and then speak to the priest."

After watching Lucas walk away, William stared at the door. "So, Cousin, are ye really with bairn?" He took a cautious step back when the door opened. The way Katerina was glaring at him made him seriously consider leaving, quickly. "I think we had best have us a wee talk."

"Wheesht, ye are a brave mon, William," murmured Patrick even as he hurried away, a grinning Robbie right behind him.

"I really do think we need to talk, Cousin," William said.

Katerina rolled her eyes but waved him into her room. She really did not want to talk about it but should have guessed that William, who considered himself the head of the Haldane family, was obviously prepared to be the elder now. She finished lacing up her gown as she waited for him to decide what he wanted to say.

"I ken that ye dinnae like orders, but I think ye must heed this one."

"Why? Because he wants the bairn?"

"Wheesht, lass, ye have to ken that he wants ye, too. The mon could have been home by now. He certainly wasnae lurking about here because ye were welcoming him into your bed."

She gaped at him. "Does everyone ken my business?"

"Verra little is secret round here, Cousin. Now, are ye going to tell me ye dinnae want the mon? Because if ye do, I will be verra disappointed." He shrugged. "I had ne'er realized ye thought me lacking in wits."

Katerina sat down on the chest at the foot of the bed. "Aye, of course I want him. I have wanted him from the moment I first saw him. But I want him to want to spend the rest of his life with *me* nay my womb. He didnae e'en ask. He just told me that we would be married."

"Nay, that wasnae weel done of him but might I ask how he found out?" William studied her for a moment. "Ye are nay showing so I cannae think that is it."

"Nay, I fear he was still here when it was time for me to hang my head o'er a bucket." She saw his lips twitch. "If ye laugh, I will throw something at ye."

"And then he told ye that the two of ye would be married?"

"Only after I had crawled to bed and slept for a few hours. Oh, and Megan brought in my dry toasted bread and weak cider. 'Tis all I can manage to hold down. Then I woke up and he was there watching me and daring me to tell him I wasnae with bairn."

William nodded and sat down on the edge of the bed nearest her, reaching out to lightly tug at her hair. "He found out whilst ye were asleep. Probably started to add up the sickness and the toasted bread and I suspect he thought ye werenae intending to tell him. That can make a mon angry, lass, especially if he cares for the woman."

"We dinnae ken if Lucas cares for me or nay."

"He is a seasoned warrior, Cousin, yet we had to fight to keep him from running right off to get ye like some crazed berserker. A mon doesnae act as crazed as he did if he doesnae care. Mayhap he doesnae feel as ye want him to yet, but that doesnae mean he willnae. Ye are carrying his child, he is the heir to Donncoill, and if the child is a boy, then he becomes an heir. 'Tis no small thing for a mon. He will make ye a fine husband."

"But he is the heir to Donncoill and I must stay here at Dunlochan."

"That is for ye and your mon to discuss, lass, but I ask ye to think on this—I am a bastard and I promise ye, it isnae a nice thing to be. E'en the church has doubts about ones like me. If ye have this child without marrying Lucas, he will be a bastard. So, one thing ye may need to learn if ye decide to nay marry Sir Lucas is how to fix broken noses, for your wee laddie will be getting into a lot of fights."

She sighed after William left. He was right. She had seen all too clearly how hard life was for William and his siblings. For reasons she had never been able to understand, the child was often treated as if his bastardy was all his own fault. She placed a hand over her stomach. She could not allow that to happen to her child.

A knock sounded on her door and she silently cursed. It did not really surprise her to find Annie there. The fact that Annie did not look very sympathetic did annoy her a little. It was not as if she got herself with child on purpose or all by herself.

"Ye have been sent by Robbie, havenae ye," she said as she waved Annie to a seat by the fire and shut the door before joining her.

"He thought ye might be tired of being ordered about by men," Annie said.

"So now I am to be ordered about by women?"

Annie just grinned. "Weel, Hilda has threatened to come up and knock some sense into ye with one of her cooking tools. She just isnae sure which one yet."

"They already ken about this down in the kitchen?"

"I think some people heard ye and Lucas talking."

"Yelling."

"Weel, aye, ye were rather loud." Annie leaned forward and grasped Katerina's hands. "Marry him.

Marry him because ye love him and ye dinnae want to sleep alone and he will make a wonderful father."

"And why is he marrying me?"

"I cannae say, but then why has he lingered here? Ye werenae exactly encouraging him. 'Tis something ye shall have to sort out after ye are married."

"That really isnae the best thing to do."

"Ye start out with far more than many women, especially one like ye—an heiress. Most of those marriages are arranged and the lass doesnae get much say at all in who she ends up with. Ye have had far more freedom. Ye have chosen Lucas. Aye, mayhap he has finally said the word *marriage* because of the bairn, but I think that has been his aim right from the start. He just isnae verra good at wooing a lass. Also, if ye havenae spoken of love, he may be reticent to speak what is in his heart."

"I suppose ye are all right and of course I dinnae really wish Hilda to come and hit me with a spoon or pan, do I."

Annie laughed and, despite all her troubles, Katerina did as well.

Lucas sat at the worktable in the ledger room pretending he was studying the plans for a new stable. Instead he was wondering, yet again, why Katerina was being stubborn about marrying him. He knew he had handled it all wrong but when she woke up and looked at him so warily, the anger he had thought he had controlled had flared back to life. Now he was planning a marriage and did not yet know if the bride would attend. Artan would laugh himself sick over this.

The door to the room slowly opened and he tensed. Katerina walked in and his heart sank because she did not look like a happy, willing bride. He told himself sternly that so long as she said yes, he would be satisfied. He would have her back in his bed again and they could grow closer together as they waited for their child.

He stood up and offered her the chair that faced the worktable. When he offered her a drink, she just shook her head, and so he sat down facing her. Lucas felt awkward and he hated the feeling. Then she looked right at him and he relaxed a little although he did not know why. She looked irritated.

"Ye are the heir to Donncoill," she said. "I am the heir to Dunlochan. I am needed here."

"Ah, that is no problem. I dinnae plan on or wish to be the laird of Donncoill for many a long year. My father is still hale and strong and we are a long-lived group. Lots of healers, ye ken. We can stay here."

Katerina blinked. "That was easy."

He reached across the table and took her hand in his. "I think a lot of what ye fear will be easily solved. Ye must ken that I am nay marrying ye just because ye carry my bairn. I didnae say it right. I had been lying there waiting for ye to wake up and, weel, thinking too much on why ye hadnae told me."

"As I said, I had only recently realized I was with child. And I was sure that the moment I told ye, ye would speak of marriage and I didnae want to be wed because of what I carried in my womb."

"I am nay marrying ye for that, but I cannae wait until we sort out everything, can I? If I do the child could weel be a bastard and there is no reason for him to be. Or her."

Katerina took a deep breath, knowing she was about to plunge into some deep waters, but that she had little choice. She loved him and she carried his child. By not marrying him, she would only be hurting herself.

"Then we shall be married."

"In three days' time. I wish my brother to attend."

"Three days' time then."

He stood up and moved around to lean over her. "May I kiss the bride then?"

"Aye."

Lucas kissed her, trying to show her how he felt with the kiss. He was not sure how well he had succeeded but they were both breathing heavily when he lifted his head. He stared down at her, enjoying the warmth in her eyes and the hint of a blush on her cheeks.

"May I take the bride back to her bedchamber?"

Katerina laughed and stood up. "Nay, ye may not. Ye may stay to your own bed until we are married."

"Weel, mayhap I really dinnae need my brother to come at all." He grinned when she laughed again and hoped the future would hold a lot of that for him.

Chapter Eighteen

"Where did Lucas go this morning?"

Katerina looked at Annie, who was staring out the window. "Nowhere. Why would ye think he had gone somewhere?"

"Because he is riding in through the gates right now. I dinnae recognize the two big men with him. Mayhap they are family."

Moving to stand next to Annie, Katerina stared at the man on the horse. It certainly looked like Lucas, but something was different. It was hard to see at such a distance what that difference was, however. Then he dismounted and she knew. Lucas's limp, the stiffness in his leg that he often fretted about, was not there.

"'Tis his brother Artan," she said. "He has arrived just in time. We are to be married in an hour."

"Oh, my. They do look alike." Annie looked at Katerina's stomach. "Do ye think ye will have twins?"

"If I do I shall geld Lucas."

Annie laughed and looked back out the window. Katerina watched as Lucas came out to greet his brother. For one brief moment, they embraced. A tender greeting so short-lived that she was sure she would have missed it if she had blinked. Then Artan clapped Lucas on the back so hard Lucas staggered. Lucas immediately returned the blow.

"Men can be such children," she murmured.

"Aye," agreed Annie. "Weel, Lucas will be pleased." Annie grinned. "I ne'er imagined I would be calling a laird and a lady by their Christian names. It will take a long time for me to get used to it."

"Oh, of course, Lucas will be considered the laird now. The council approved of him."

"As if they would dare not to. Robbie says they were verra greedy and it will be a long time ere we can get it back. I dinnae understand how they could steal from ye when they were supposed to be the guardians of Dunlochan."

"I think they soothed their consciences by saying they were stealing from Agnes."

"It still wasnae right."

"Nay, it wasnae, but they are going to pay it back so there is nay need to do any more than that."

Katerina put on her deep blue gown and, as Annie laced it up, she studied herself in the looking-glass. She decided it was a very good color for her, flattering her eyes and her skin. Her hair hung loose, decorated with deep blue ribbons and, although she feared she sounded vain, she thought it looked lovely. It had been a long time since she had dressed in anything so fine. For almost a year she had dressed as a boy. She hoped Lucas liked it.

"Oh, m'lady, ye are a verra beautiful bride," said Annie softly.

"Ye were beautiful as weel, Annie."

"I think all brides are beautiful. 'Tis the day when they wear their verra best clothes and they walk toward their future." Annie blushed and shrugged when Katerina looked at her. "I feel wicked sometimes because I have Robbie and a woman had to die for that to happen."

"Agnes didnae have to die, Annie," Katerina said and briefly hugged the woman. "She chose to die. I had offered her life and she couldnae bear the thought of living without men to seduce and gowns to wear. 'Twas a verra silly reason to hurl oneself out of the window. So, dinnae feel at all guilty about having Robbie. If Agnes had gone to the nunnery, he intended to get special dispensation and free himself of her. It just would have taken a verra long time. And money."

"Thank ye. I didnae ken he was going to try to end his marriage. It makes a difference."

"And, of course, being a mon, Robbie didnae ken that it might."

"Nay, of course not."

"Weel, time to go down to the great hall. I best meet Lucas's brother ere the wedding is already under way. I have a feeling he is going to take some getting accustomed to."

Lucas tugged at his doublet. He had thought to wear his plaid but decided he should not wear his clan's colors when he was marrying the heiress to the Haldane lands. Artan stood next to him looking every inch the Highland laird with his plaid and all his weapons. Lucas felt a brief pang of loss for the life he had had at Glascreag but he had no regrets about marrying Katerina and staying at Dunlochan.

"'Tis a good piece of land ye have here," said Artan. "Although ye dinnae need it."

"Weel, as I told Katerina, I dinnae wish to take the laird's chair at Donncoill for many a year."

"Please God that is so. But, if ye did find yourself needing to choose, do ye ken which it would be?"

"Nay, 'tis too soon. If many years pass, as I hope they do, I may weel say that the lairdship of Donncoill should go to one of my brothers. Ye?"

"Nay, nay me. I have Glascreag and that is all I want."

"I thought that might be the way if it." He tugged on his doublet again.

"Cease that. Ye wished to marry this lass, didnae ye?"

"Aye, since I first met her a year ago."

"I cannae believe ye didnae call for me when ye finally set out to fulfill your need for revenge."

Lucas sighed. "I needed to do it alone. I needed to show myself that I could do it alone." He reached down and rubbed at his leg. "I will ne'er fight as I used to, but I now ken that I can fight weel and that I can solve a problem as big as the one we had here as weel as keep my woman safe."

Artan nodded. "Aye, I can understand that and here is your woman. She is a bonnie lass, Lucas. Ye chose weel."

"Thank ye. I certainly think so. Come, we have a few minutes ere the wedding begins and ye can meet her now."

"Because ye are intending to desert me as soon as ye can whilst the feasting is going on."

"Ye ken me too weel."

Lucas smiled at Katerina and introduced her to Artan. He felt pride swell his chest. She had always been beautiful in his eyes, but dressed in all her finery, she made him feel short of breath. He draped his arm over her shoulders and kissed her on the cheek.

"Just remember that I am the handsome one," he said.

Katerina laughed. "Aye, I can see that." She looked him over. "Ye have certainly dressed yourself up verra fine. I am most impressed." She took a deep breath and tried not to be flustered by the way his gaze rested on her chest. "The men have something for ye, but they wished me to speak to ye about it first as they ken ye are a Murray and will one day be a laird of Donncoill, a Murray laird."

"Ah, 'tis something that may mark me as a Haldane?"

"Aye, but they wanted to give ye something to mark ye as the mon who leads them."

"I will be honored. We still have some time if they wish to give it to me now. Is it something they might wish me to wear as we are married?"

"Aye, but ye willnae have to change your clothes." Katerina waved over William, Patrick, Robbie, and Donald. Thomas walked proudly at their side carrying a length of plaid that most of the Haldanes wore. "He says he will be pleased to accept what ye offer."

Katerina watched as the men draped the Haldane plaid over Lucas's broad shoulder and carefully arranged it. William secured it with a pin of silver and garnets that formed the Haldane badge. She knew Lucas was a Murray and would always be a Murray, but he was obviously touched by this sign of complete acceptance by the Haldane men. They could not have found a clearer way to tell him that they accepted him as their laird. She had to bite the inside of her cheek to keep from crying like some bairn.

The moment the men moved away, Lucas wrapped his arm around her shoulders again and held her close against his side. "I wondered if they would accept me, as this is really your land and keep. It is good that they do."

"It has always been kenned that the mon I wed would be seen as the laird. 'Tis why the council had to approve of him. And, we wouldnae have regained Dunlochan without ye," she said.

"Och, aye, I think ye would have. Ye and your men were causing Agnes a lot of grief and ye did help allow the council to deny her full control. All I did was stir things up a bit by coming back. I was supposed to be dead. That made our enemies act rashly. As I said, get their backs to the wall and keep them there. Ye had gotten them close. My being alive just pushed them hard up against it."

"Modest, isnae he?" drawled Artan.

"Aye, 'tis most admirable," Katerina said and laughed when Artan grinned.

"'Tis time," said Annie as she hurried over and grasped Katerina by the hand.

Katerina felt her first twinge of unease. She loved Lucas and she wanted to marry him, wanted the baby she carried to have his father's name. Yet, she was still so uncertain of him. Her trust in him had been badly tattered and she did not think he had been completely restored yet. As she knelt beside him before the priest, she prayed she was not letting her heart lead her into danger. Without even knowing it, Lucas could hurt her more than Ranald or Agnes ever could have.

Katerina could tell that Lucas was growing weary of the celebration. She got the feeling that his brother was purposely dragging out the toasts to bedevil him. It was a little embarrassing to know Artan was doing it because he knew Lucas wished to take her to bed, but somehow she still found the way he tormented Lucas amusing. There was a devil in Artan and she suspected she could grow to enjoy that.

She had to admit, however, that she was tired of it all as well. She wanted to get her husband alone. She doubted they would do much talking but she was not really in the mood for that anyway. Any talk they had, and one was very much overdue, would need to be carefully planned. She wanted his passion tonight. After their brief reunion three days ago all she could think of nearly every minute of the day and night of was how much she needed him, how good he felt in her arms, and how she loved to wake up to feel his warmth around her. Well, at least she did before she had to empty her stomach in a bucket every morning, but that would ease soon.

What she wanted to do was go to the bedchamber that was now theirs, not hers. She wanted to make love in the big bed with the man she could now call husband. Despite the fact that they had been lovers and she now carried his child, she knew she would not feel as if the marriage was a true one until it was well . . . consummated.

Suddenly William distracted Artan and Lucas took quick advantage of it. He grabbed Katerina by the hand and rushed out of the hall, amidst a great deal of laughter and a few ribald remarks. Artan's deep voice rang out over the others and he made it clear that he knew he had been cleverly thwarted in his game. Katerina just laughed, finding Lucas's eagerness both flattering and exciting. It was impossible not to be flattered when such a beautiful man was so eager to get her alone. It was so nice to be so wanted she did not even blush at some of the remarks made before the doors of the great hall smothered them.

The moment they entered the bedchamber they both stopped and looked around. There were flowers everywhere. Rose petals were sprinkled on the bed. In the corner on a small table were a jug of wine, a tray of small cakes, and some bread and cheese. Katerina looked at him and raised one brow.

"It wasnae me," he said. "I think Annie has been busy."
He sighed and looked around again. "It should have
been me, aye? I am just nay good at this sort of thing."

She wrapped her arms around his neck and gently
kissed his cheek. "And why should ye be?"

"'Tis the sort of thing a mon ought to do for his
wife, for the woman who will bear his bairns."

It was such a lovely thought that Katerina felt her
hopes for the future rise. He may not understand her
at all times or whisper sweet bits of poetry in her ear
or even say those three little words, but he was a man
who would value her. Katerina had spent most of her
life with a father who did not value her or any woman
and she knew how important that was. She kissed him
and the kiss soon grew hot and greedy. Even as he
rushed to unlace her gown she was taking off his plaid
and she knew their first time together tonight was not
going to be sweet and gentle.

Lucas muttered apologies against her skin as he
nearly tore her clothes off. Looking at her for so long,
seeing how beautiful she was in all ways, had kept him
tied up in lustful knots. He knew Artan had guessed
at his state and tried to torture him by dragging out
the toasts and it had worked. He felt as if he did not
bury himself in her very soon he would die. It was an
insane thought but the need he felt at the moment
was a sort of madness.

Katerina stumbled as she tried to tear off his braies
and they both fell to the floor. She was still laughing
about that when he buried himself deep in her body.
Her laughter quickly turned to cries of delight mixed
with incoherent demands as he drove them both in a
mad race for their releases. They fell over that blissful
cliff together and she heard their cries blend in the air.
For a while it was the last thing she was clearly aware of.

"I cannae believe I took my new wife on the floor," Lucas groaned as he slowly came back to his senses.

"I cannae believe I fell over," said Katerina. "Blame Artan. I saw what game he played."

"Aye, I will make him pay for that later. And I will be sure to thank William for putting an end to it." He looked down at her when she groaned. "What? Does the floor hurt?" he asked as he quickly helped her get to her feet.

"Nay, I was but thinking of how everyone down there kens what we are doing."

"We just got married," he said as he carried her to the bed. "'Tis expected. But, I suspect they would ne'er guess that we didnae e'en make it to the bed."

She laughed as he nearly tossed her down and then sprawled on top of her. It suddenly occurred to her that one thing Lucas had fretted over was that the stiffness in his leg would make him an awkward lover. She trailed her fingers down his spine and wondered if she should tell him that he had worried for nothing. She could only be grateful that it had helped keep him faithful. Katerina could not believe that the man still thought he might falter in his lovemaking, but she decided to wait to tell him he showed no awkwardness at all. There might come a time when he needed to be told. Right now, after the wild lovemaking they had just indulged in, he did not need to be flattered.

"I will make ye a good husband," he murmured as he slowly kissed his way down to her breasts, ready to savor her now that the madness had eased.

"I suspicion ye will, Lucas. I but hope ye will find me the sort of wife ye need."

"Ye are. Ye nay only put up with me leaping on ye like a beast, but ye leap right back. What mon could ask for anything more."

"I suppose that is a compliment," she said, grinning at him as he peeked up at her from between her breasts.

"The best any mon can give his woman." He lapped at the hardened tips of her breasts. "Ye are so sweet to taste. I cannae get enough."

"Ye dinnae taste so bad, either," she murmured and slowly ran her hands over his taut buttocks.

Lucas soon lost the ability to talk as he kissed his way down her lithe body. The taste of her drove him wild. The feel of her soft hands stroking his body as he made love to her had him aching for each and every touch. He did not think he would ever get tired of her. The heat of the passion, the near madness of his need at times, would probably ease, but he would always want more.

The little sounds she made as he kissed his way down to the soft curls between her legs were the sweetest compliments he could ever receive. When he reached his goal, he loved her with his mouth until she was crying out his name. Slowly, he kissed his way back up her body. Even as he took the hardened nipple of her breast deep into his mouth, he eased their bodies together. For a moment he rested his forehead against her heated skin and savored the feel of her tight heat surrounding him.

"Ah, Lucas, I need ye to move," she whispered.

"I ken it, but I love the feel of ye and was trying verra hard not to turn into a crazed, lustful beast."

Katerina could not believe that she could actually laugh. The feel of it with their bodies united as they were made them both gasp. She wrapped her legs around him and slowly thrust her body against his. It was all the encouragement he needed and he was soon thrusting inside her with all the fierce greed she could want. Her release swept over her so swiftly and forcefully, she banged her heels against his back. She was still shaking from it when he he pushed deep inside her and filled her with his seed.

"I think ye may have killed me," she murmured, barely able to move her arms, yet still hearing her self murmur in protest when he eased out of her body.

"I hope no one sees me naked in the next few days because I willnae be able to explain those heel marks on my back." He grinned when she pinched him.

Lucas rolled onto his back and pulled her into his arms. He loved the way she curled up against him, her body warm and soft against his. He would be able to hold her close all night for the rest of his life. It surprised him that the mere thought of that could make him feel so content. There were still so many things they needed to sort out between them, but he knew they would do it, knew it would all come right in the end. She was his mate. She just did not know it yet.

He slid his hand down to her stomach, knowing it was too soon to feel the child they had created, but wanting to feel where it rested. "Do ye wish a boy or a girl?" he asked her.

"I thought all men wanted a son?" she murmured sleepily.

"Weel, aye, but the Murrays have a multitude of sons. We dinnae need one to have an heir. So a daughter would be nice. A wee lass with fair hair and big blue eyes."

"I just want a healthy child."

"Aye, so do I." He kissed her on the forehead. "Rest, Love. Ye need your rest for the sake of that healthy child we will have."

He had called her love, Katerina thought as she closed her eyes. It would be wondrous if she really was his love. She told herself she was happy. She had a good man who would care for her and her child and made her blood boil when he touched her. As Annie had said, few women had that much. She had to learn not to be greedy, to accept what she had and count her blessings.

There was always the chance that, as they worked together and built a family together he would grow to love her. She would do her best to make him happy and that might bring him closer to her. She sensed that he was a believer in the sanctity of marriage. His voice had carried the weight of truth and belief when he had said his vows. That too was no small thing when so many men believed it was their right to have any woman they wanted, to have a wife and a leman.

She sleepily stroked his chest, thinking of how she could rest her head on it every night from now on. He was her husband and despite the things that still troubled her and the things she wanted but did not yet have, she was happy with that. In truth, she would not have it any other way.

Lucas smiled and covered her hand with his when it finally stopped stroking his chest and fell limp against his skin. He was going to have to tell his family everything that had happened and they would all wish to meet her. Somehow he was going to have to put that off without raising questions or hurting anyone's feelings. He did not want to bring her to his family until he knew he had won her heart and, even more important, her trust. There were far too many people in his family who would be able to sense if there were some problems in his marriage.

He closed his eyes and smiled. He had her now. She could not slip away as he had feared she might. Now that they were bound together before God and the law, he had time, time to mend the hurts he had dealt her and time to win her heart. It would be enough for now.

Chapter Nineteen

"Women can be puzzling creatures."

Lucas stared at his brother Artan. After the evening meal they had both slipped away to the ledger room. Seated before a fire, sipping at their tankards of wine, neither of them had said a word for almost an hour. Lucas was not sure Artan's pronouncement was worth the wait.

"And ye have discovered this great truth after only one year of marriage?" he drawled.

"If I werenae so comfortable right now I would pound ye into the floor."

"Ye and whose army?"

"Do ye want my opinion on how to mend things with your wife or nay?"

"Why do ye think things need mending?" Lucas did not like the idea that matters were so unsettled between him and Katerina that even Artan had noticed.

Artan gave him a look of utter disgust. "Mayhap because ye are sitting here with me instead of being upstairs with your new wife? Mayhap because the two of ye didnae say much at all to each other whilst we ate? Mayhap because both of ye look at each other only when ye are certain the other willnae notice it? Shall I continue?"

"I suppose ye ne'er had any trouble with your wife, that all went smoothly between the two of ye from the moment ye met her."

"It might have if I hadnae kidnapped her from her wedding celebration and she hadnae had her bonnie head filled with all sorts of strange ideas about what a perfect wife should be." Artan shrugged. "I suspicion I am nay an easy mon to live with, either."

"Nor am I." Lucas grimaced. "I certainly didnae help matters by accusing her of being the one who tried to have me murdered."

Artan cocked one dark brow. "That wee lass?"

"Not on her own. Thought she had Ranald do it for her. Even briefly wondered if she and the mon were lovers or planning to be. By the time I found out the truth, I had been lashing her with my accusations and suspicions for quite a while. I didnae find the truth all on my own, in my own mind and heart, either. I had to hear it said by others. When I think about it now, I wonder if I was caught in some kind of madness. I am certain she will ne'er trust me again."

"Of course she will. Might do so already. She is here and married to ye, isnae she? Carrying your bairn as weel. Ye just have to find the right words."

"And those would be?"

"I have no idea."

"Ye must have some idea. Ye have obviously settled your own troubles with your wife."

"I ne'er accused her of trying to kill me. I can certainly tell ye what *not* to say. Dinnae tell her she is being silly."

Lucas rolled his eyes. "I didnae need your great wisdom to tell me that would be unwise. No lass likes to be told she is being silly, especially when it concerns some emotion she is suffering from." He stared at Artan wide-eyed when his brother suddenly blushed. "What is it?"

Artan grimaced and took a deep drink of wine, before clearing his throat and saying, "Ye have to tell her what ye feel for her."

"Oh. I am nay sure Katerina will believe me. About the only thing she believes is that I desire her and I am nay sure she believes that will last all that long."

"Ye have to tell her ye love her and make her believe it. Dinnae just think she will ken it all on her own. I cannae understand it, but women need to hear ye say it aloud now and again."

Lucas suddenly grinned. "And ye dinnae like to hear your wife tell ye that she loves ye?"

"Of course I do, ye daft fool, but women like to talk all about how they feel. 'Tisnae so easy for a mon. But the rewards for spitting the words out are verra fine indeed. And ye might try to explain to her how ye could think her guilty of what ye accused her of and why ye didnae believe her when she told ye the truth."

Lucas nodded and sipped at his wine. He would certainly like to hear Katerina tell him she loved him. He had felt almost certain she did before that night by the loch when everything had gone so wrong, but she had never actually said so. She had given him her innocence, however, and a woman like Katerina did not do something like that unless her feelings ran very deep indeed. Unfortunately, he could all too easily recall how quickly the joy that had shown in her eyes when she had discovered he was alive had turned to pain when he had spat his accusations at her. He knew it had been a deep cut he had delivered and it probably still pained her. He was not sure he could explain his actions for he did not completely understand them himself.

"I will be leaving on the morrow," Artan announced.

"Such a short visit? Ye have only been here for two days."

"I think ye and your wife need to be alone, or as much as ye can be in a keep full of people. Ye certainly dinnae need me lurking about. Sort things out ere the bad feelings harden too much. 'Tis ne'er good when that happens. Then I will come back for a longer stay and bring my wife and bairns. Or, ye and Katerina can come to visit us. Angus would certainly like that. 'Twould give him someone else to argue with for a wee while and that will make him happy."

Lucas laughed and nodded. "Aye, I think I would like to have an argument or two with Angus again and I certainly wish to see what ye and Cecily bred. So, ere ye retire to rest up for your journey, shall I beat ye at chess again?"

"Too early for ye to be joining your wee wife, is it?"

"Until I can figure out what to say and how to say it, it might be best if we dinnae spend too much time alone together. I dinnae like tense silences where unsaid words choke the verra air out of the room."

"I will fetch the board and pieces."

Katerina entered the solar and smiled at Annie. The woman sat on the seat below the window doing her mending and looking very much at peace. She was pleased that Annie and Robbie had decided to stay on at the keep instead of accepting her offer of the cottage. Robbie's interest in tending to the accounts of Dunlochan had been a complete surprise to her, but a pleasant one. Lucas had certainly been more than willing to hand that work over to Robbie.

"Where is Sir Lucas?" Annie asked as Katerina sat down next to her.

Noticing how Megan looked at her with interest, Katerina blushed, even as she wondered why she should be bothered by the question. "He sits in the ledger room visiting with his brother."

"Oh, m'lady, 'tis a wonder to see the two of them together," said Megan. "Two such handsome men, so alike in every way."

"Aye they are verra much alike," said Katerina. "I am nay quite sure how I can tell them apart so easily, but I can."

"Of course ye can. Lucas has a scar."

Katerina laughed. "Aye, I ken it. 'Tis just that sometimes that scar is hidden because he is turned away, as is Artan, and sometimes they both have their hands over their right cheeks so ye cannae see them. They deny it, e'en when I threaten to rap on their heads with a boulder, but I think they were testing me to see if I could tell them apart. It doesnae matter. I ken that if they were still exactly the same, I could tell them apart."

"'Tis a good thing, too," teased Megan.

Katerina laughed but her good humor was fleeting. She was in a keep filled with her kin, loyal servants, and a husband, yet she felt painfully alone. It was nonsense of course, but she found it impossible to shake the feeling. She doubted it was all due to the emotional ups and downs people said often afflicted a woman with child. She obviously needed something from her husband, something more than he was giving her, and until she got it she would continue to feel as if a part of her was missing.

"Ye are looking verra troubled and sad for a woman with such a fine, strong, handsome husband," murmured Annie.

"A husband who thinks I am capable of having

someone murdered in a fit of jealousy." Katerina
winced as she saw how both women frowned at her.

"Ye still havenae sorted that out, have ye," said
Annie, shaking her head. "Ye cannae keep ignoring it,
ye ken."

"Why not?"

"Because it is gnawing away at both of ye. That isnae
good. He has apologized, hasnae he?"

"Nay in so many words."

"A mon doesnae do the things he has if he truly believes the woman is like that."

"Nay," agreed Megan. "He would be cold to her and
Sir Lucas isnae cold to ye, is he."

"Weel, nay, but passion doesnae have to have much
to do with liking or respecting a woman," Katerina
said.

"How can ye think he doesnae respect ye? If he
didnae respect ye, he wouldnae have wed with ye,
bairn or no. If a mon doesnae respect a woman, he
doesnae care if she is marked by having a bastard
child. He just says thank ye for the pleasure, lass, and
walks away. At best he may help her with the bairn,
either taking it into his care or sending her a wee bit
of coin now and then."

There was a lot of truth to that, but Katerina was
not sure it had much to do with the position she was
in. "I am the daughter of a laird. That may be why
Lucas felt he had to marry me."

Annie put down her mending and nearly glared at
Katerina. "The problem isnae him, is it. 'Tis ye. Ye
cannae forgive him for hurting ye, for thinking ye
could be so cold and heartless as to try and kill a mon
out of jealousy."

Katerina winced at the unwelcome truth in Annie's
words. "'Tis not an easy thing to forgive or forget."

"Nay, I shouldnae think it would be, but ye have to

do it. He kens the truth now and ye can have nay doubt about that."

"Aye, but he didnae really find that truth in his own heart or mind."

"I ken it and that is verra sad, but it shouldnae keep ye so apart from him, nay when I ken weel that ye arenae happy with matters as they stand. He is shamed by what he thought. 'Tis nay so hard to see that. Why cannae ye see that?"

"Oh, I can see it and there is a verra unkind part of me that is glad he is suffering."

Annie grinned. "Dinnae fret o'er that, I would feel the same."

"So would I," said Megan.

"However," continued Annie, "ye cannae let these feelings ruin your marriage ere it has even begun. Ye have to let go of the hurt, m'lady. Ye have a fine mon for a husband, e'en if he can be a bit of a fool at times, and ye have a bairn on the way. If ye keep holding yourself away from him in some ways, ye will soon do so in all ways, and then ye will have no true marriage at all. Is that truly how ye want this to end?"

"Nay, I dinnae want that at all, but, Annie, unless he talks on the matter as weel, I cannae see how it can be fixed. I cannae help but fear that he has no faith in me and that lack will certainly cause trouble. I think if I could understand how he could think such a thing it would help. Mayhap he could e'en tell me just how deeply he believed such a horrible thing about me and, if he had to fight to hold on to that belief, and that too would help heal the wound. I am nay sure I ken exactly what I need him to say, but he has to say something. As I told ye once before, he has to try and make me understand what was going on in his head."

"Aye, he does," said Megan, and shrugged when Annie frowned at her. "I have many brothers. We may nay have all had the same mothers, but we are close. Men can get a wrong idea in their heads and hang on to it just because they hate to admit they are wrong. And I have heard some of my brothers explain how they came to a conclusion and the way they reached it was so twisted it made my eyes cross. Also, if a mon's emotions are involved, he can be worse."

"Ye think Lucas may have made such a decision about me because he was feeling some strong emotion about me?" asked Katerina, oddly soothed by the thought yet not really understanding it.

"I think, with some men, that if ye hurt them, they can be almost unrelenting. They wouldnae like it said but 'tis as if they are afraid and will do almost anything nay to feel hurt again. If that means hanging on to a belief even when it makes no sense, they will do it.

"My brother Garrett was sure his woman had betrayed him and nothing anyone could say would make him think otherwise. He was wrong, had seen something and completely misunderstood, but it took a lot of work to get him to realize he was wrong. It had hurt him so much to think she would go to another mon that he didnae want to chance being wrong and trying again. Mayhap that is your mon's problem. If so, at least he had the sense to accept that he was wrong when he heard the truth right from the mouths of the ones who were truly guilty of the crimes against him."

Katerina considered that for a while. She tried to think of when she might be unreasonable and all too easily came up with an example. It would not be hard to be made to believe Lucas had betrayed her with another woman. She could not even say that she would believe him if he denied it yet she was not sure why she would show such a lack of faith in him. She suspected she simply had a very hard time believing such a strong, handsome man could really belong to her and her alone.

Hastily covering a yawn with her hand, Katerina decided that was enough discussion about her problems. They were the same ones she had had for weeks now and they had the very same solution that she and Annie had discussed when she had first recognized the problems. It was time to stop ignoring that huge wall that sat squarely between her and Lucas. The next discussion she had about the problem would be with Lucas himself and she would not back down.

After saying good sleep to Annie and Megan, Katerina made her way to the bedchamber she shared with Lucas. She stepped inside and took a deep breath, still pleased that she could find no hint of Agnes in the room. It had seemed foolish to demand the room be scrubbed and most of the furniture changed, but she was glad she had not faltered in her demand. Katerina knew it would have been difficult for her to be at ease in the room if too many reminders of the woman who had helped kill her parents and so many other innocent people had surrounded her. Now when she looked around all she could see were things that belonged to her or Lucas or little treasures that reminded her of her parents.

Katerina stripped off her clothes, washed, and donned her night shift. She sat on a stool before the fire and began to brush her hair. Lucas would be up soon. He seemed to always know when she came into the room to ready herself for bed. That was probably one of those little curiosities about her husband that she would never figure out.

A part of her wanted to greet him at the door with a demand that they talk about that huge wall growing between them, but she knew she would wait a little longer. If nothing else, Katerina knew she had to think of just the right words to say. She also had to build up her courage so that she did not falter at the first hint of reluctance from him, or some attempt to seduce her into forgetting what she wanted to talk about, she thought with a little smile. Lucas was very good at that and she enjoyed herself far too much to put a stop to it once he got started.

"And what are ye smiling about?" asked Lucas as he entered the bedchamber, grinning when Katerina squeaked softly in surprise. "Didnae hear me?"

"I rarely hear ye approach," she grumbled, and patted her chest as if that faint caress could slow the rapid beating of her heart. "I dinnae think I will e'er ken how such a big mon can be so verra quiet when he walks." She frowned. "Artan is the same way, isnae he."

"Aye, it takes practice and we practiced it a lot when we were lads training with Angus." He sat on the side of the bed and began to take his boots off. "Artan is leaving in the morning."

"So soon?"

"Aye. He had a lot of verra good reasons but I think he misses his wife and the bairns. He did complain about the cold, lonely bed."

Katerina laughed but she also felt a sharp twist of envy and sadness. Artan was a big, rough man who spoke bluntly and seemed to thoroughly enjoy a rough practice session in the tiltyard with anyone willing to take him on. Yet when he spoke of his wife and bairns you knew he loved them, that they were the light of his life. She wanted that and she was not sure how to get it.

"I must be sure to rise to say fareweel to him as I have a few gifts for him to take to his wife and bairns."

"That will please him."

Lucas watched her as she finished braiding her hair, walked to the side of the bed, and got under the covers. He snuffed most of the candles, shed the rest of his clothes, and slid in beside her. Until he took her into his arms he could understand what Artan meant by the cold, lonely bed. He never wanted to sleep without her near again, without her close enough to touch.

When Lucas removed her night shift and tossed it aside, Katerina almost laughed. She did not know why she kept putting it on at night for he removed it the moment he got beneath the covers. A soft sigh of pleasure escaped her when he pulled her into his arms and she felt the warmth of his skin pressed against hers. Despite the problems that still existed between them, she felt only pleasure, even comfort, when he took her into his arms every night. She almost felt cherished yet, when she was alone, she found it hard to believe that she was.

He placed his hand over her stomach and she kissed his shoulder. "I hope ye arenae wanting twins," she said.

"I am nay sure I can tolerate my brother besting me."

"He will let ye ken it all the time, will he?"

"Without hesitation."

"Poor laddie."

Lucas laughed and kissed her throat. He did not think he would ever get enough of her, of the feel of her soft skin and the taste of her mouth. All she had to do was walk into a room and he wanted her.

"Are ye tired, Kat?" he asked even as he stroked her slender back.

"Nay that tired," she murmured and grinned when he chuckled against her throat.

He made love to her slowly and she realized that was exactly what she needed at the moment and wondered how he knew. She sighed out her pleasure as he heated her skin with his warm kisses. Even the slow, gentle strokes of his lightly calloused hands made her shiver with need for him. Every kiss he gave her held only tenderness, so much so that she could almost believe he felt a lot more for her than desire.

A soft cry that was a mixture of shock and desire escaped her when he kissed his way down her body and she felt the heated stroke of his tongue against her most intimate place. He loved her with his mouth until she was crying out for him, needing him to fill her. Katerina gasped when he rolled onto his back and pulled her on top of him, but she quickly took control of the lovemaking. She rode him slowly for a while, stroking her hands over his broad chest and bending down to give him deep, leisurely kisses. He had such a fine strong body that she felt a need to just savor it for a while, enjoying that time when her desire was climbing but was not yet clamoring for release.

Lucas rose up enough to take the tip of her breast into his mouth and suckled her. At first he was almost lazy in his attentions but then he grew more aggressive, more demanding and Katerina felt her body respond swiftly to that. Heat flared inside her and her movements became more demanding as well. Lucas grasped her by her hips and urged her on to even greater speed and soon they were both almost frenzied in their movements as they sought the heights their bodies craved together.

Katerina collapsed into Lucas's arms, her body still trembling from the force of her release. She could feel a faint tremor rippling through Lucas as well and felt quite pleased with herself. Now that their need for each other had been satisfied, she could again simply enjoy the feel of his warmth and strength. The idle caress of his hands on her hips was almost relaxing.

Smothering a large yawn, she slowly moved away from him and lay curled up close by his side. For a moment or two she continued to miss the feel of him inside her, but it passed finally and she returned to simply enjoying all his different textures, from his hard smooth chest to his hair-roughened thigh. She could understand what made Artan want to get home as soon as possible. Katerina doubted she would ever be able to sleep in an empty bed again. Even the scent of Lucas had become necessary to her comfort at night.

"Sleep, Kat. It has been a busy few days and ye dinnae want to get too tired," Lucas murmured.

"Not good for the bairn," she murmured, more asleep than awake.

"Nay, it isnae and from what Artan told me, as the bairn grows ye will find sleep difficult at times."

"That seems most unfair."

Lucas laughed and kissed the top of her head. "Mayhap it is practice for when the bairn comes for he said one doesnae get much sleep then, either."

"Then I best get as much as I can now."

Katerina pressed her cheek against his chest and listened to the comforting beat of his heart as she allowed sleep to creep over her. She ached to tell him everything that rested in her heart but she was terrified at the same time. If he did not return her words of love she was certain it would crush her and there would be no taking back the moment. Somehow she was going to have to find the strength and courage to grasp what she so desperately needed—Lucas's love. There had to be a way for her to find a firm place in his heart.

Lucas idly ran his fingers over her thick hair, tempted to undo her neat braid. He could not complain about their lovemaking or the many pleasures they found together in their bed, but he wanted more. He wanted that woman who had looked at him with such joy, as if the fact that he had survived Ranald's attempt to kill him was the answer to all her prayers. At times he felt he was being unduly punished for his error in judgment concerning her guilt, but he knew he would have behaved much worse if she had done the same thing to him.

What he needed to do was just what his brother had told him to. Tell her everything even if it made him look like a complete idiot. It was galling to think that Artan may have found the solution to what was wrong with his marriage. His only comfort was that Artan had not done so well in the beginning of his marriage, either. Lucas felt he ought to be able to do better than Artan. All he had to do was open his mouth and utter the words that had been lodged in his heart almost from the moment he had met her.

He almost laughed, but did not want to wake Katerina. It was ironic that the one thing that might fix the problems in his marriage was the very thing that had caused the problems in the first place. If he had not loved Katerina, he might not have been so devastated by what he thought was her betrayal and might not have tried so hard to keep her out of his heart and mind. It had all ensured that he had done his best never to think on the beating, or consider what might have been real and what a lie.

On the morrow he would gird his loins and do his best to mend matters. They would talk about that horrible time and he would make her understand how it had been for him, physically and emotionally. Katerina was a compassionate woman. If he was honest, she would understand.

Praying he was right about that, Lucas decided he needed his rest, too. Revealing what an idiot he could be was not going to be an easy task. He would just force himself to recall something else Artan had said—the rewards are well worth it.

Chapter Twenty

Katerina handed Artan the gifts she wished him to give to his wife and children. Although she knew his leaving was probably for the best at this time, she was sorry to see him go. He was a rough man, quick with his fists and blunt of speech, but she liked him. She was eager to meet the woman who had married him, too.

"Thank ye for these, lass." He bent to kiss her cheek and said quietly, "Dinnae keep the fool dancing on hot stones for too long. He has been an idiot and he kens it."

"He hasnae told me so," she said in an equally soft voice.

"There are a lot of things a mon finds hard to say, lass. *I am an idiot* is but one of them." He winked at her and then turned to slap Lucas on the back.

Lucas staggered, regained his balance, and then glared at Artan. "What were the two of ye whispering about?"

"We werenae whispering," said Artan as he put the gifts Katerina had given him into his saddle-packs. "I was just speaking softly because I was speaking so close to her ears. I feared my strong, monly voice might hurt those wee, bonnie ears, is all."

Katerina laughed, threw a grinning Artan a kiss, and hurried back inside the keep before the rain weighting the air began to fall. Artan was definitely a bit odd, but still a likable fellow. She knew that his family and whatever one she and Lucas might build together would be close. In fact, the thought of that was enough to give her the courage to confront Lucas as soon as she was sure she could find him alone. She just prayed that the results of the coming confrontation would be a firm start on that family they would build together.

"She is a good lass, Lucas," said Artan as he mounted his horse, the two men riding with him waiting in silence a few feet away. "Clear away what stands between ye."

"I will although it willnae be easy," Lucas said.

"It ne'er is when it comes to dealing with women. I thought o'er the matter a wee bit more ere I fell asleep in my cold, lonely bed." He ignored Lucas's mocking sound of sympathy. "One thing I have learned is that ye dinnae need pretty words. Ye just need to speak from the heart, painful as that is. Aye, and if the lass truly cares for ye, as I believe yours does, it doesnae e'en matter if sometimes ye sound like a complete idiot as long as ye are an honest one."

Lucas grinned. "Sounds like advice our mother once gave us."

"It probably is. Be weel, brother."

"Godspeed, Artan."

After watching Artan until he was out of sight, Lucas made his way back into the keep. There was a lot of work for him to do, but he intended to see it done as quickly as possible. Artan and he were much alike and if his brother had succeeded in making a firm, loving marriage despite all the mistakes he had made in the beginning, then Lucas felt he could do the same. It was going to be hard, might even be painful, but he could wait no longer to talk about the beating and how he could possibly have believed, even for one brief moment, that Katerina had had any part in it. By the time they crawled into bed tonight, he intended to have the whole painful mess set firmly in the past.

Katerina nervously brushed down the skirts of her gown. She had seen Robbie leave the ledger room and knew Lucas was now alone. It had taken nearly the whole day to catch him without someone at his side, discussing work that needed to be done or asking his opinion or judgment on something. For a moment she had considered waiting until they sought their bed, but had pushed aside that idea. Once they got into bed she tended to forget everything except how good he could make her feel.

She opened the door, stepped into the room, and then closed the door firmly behind her. When Lucas looked up from the papers he was studying and smiled at her she almost turned and ran. Her courage had obviously not lasted very long, she thought with disgust. Stiffening her spine she walked over to the chair facing Lucas and sat down.

Lucas had to work to keep his welcoming smile in place once he took a good look at the expression in Katerina's blue eyes. She was looking disturbingly serious and a little nervous. He tried to think of some new crime he might have committed but none came to mind.

"Is there some trouble, love?" he asked quietly.

Katerina took a deep breath and nodded. "I fear there is, Lucas, and 'tis between us."

He felt his heart drop down to his feet. Lucas had the strong feeling that she intended to talk about the very things he had intended to discuss later and he suddenly did not feel at all prepared. Everything he had so meticulously planned to say in the vain hope that he could sound reasonable had just fled his mind.

"What trouble would that be?" He glanced at the door wondering if there was some chore he could claim he had to attend to right now. Lucas jumped when she slapped her hand down hard on the table.

"Dinnae e'en think of slipping away. I have spent weeks working up the courage for this and I mean to see it through to the end."

"This begins to sound ominous, lass. It must be something verra dire if ye have to work up the courage to speak of it."

"It is dire, Lucas. It concerns our marriage and our future. No need to look so grim. I am after all trying to fix things, to build a future nay end one."

"'Tis about my accusations, isnae it," he said and ran a hand through his hair.

"It is. There is a big wall between us because of what happened on the banks of the loch and it isnae going away. Nay, I think it may be getter bigger and thicker and harder to knock down."

"Ye truly believe there is a wall between us?"

"Aye, I do and part of it is of my own making. Ye hurt me, Lucas. Sometimes I e'en wonder if it isnae so much that ye hurt me but *when* ye hurt me. I saw that ye were alive and felt so overjoyed. All I wanted to do was run into your arms and hold ye close, touch ye until I could convince myself that it wasnae just another dream and then—"

"I knocked ye down, spit right in your eye." Lucas

moved to kneel by her feet and take her hands in his. "I ken it, love. I kenned it even as I did it and a part of me wanted to soothe that hurt the minute I saw it in your eyes. Another part of me felt ye deserved to be hurt and another part of me wanted to beg your pardon. I kept going back and forth like that until I thought I would go mad."

"But, why, Lucas? That is what I cannae understand. Why did ye think I had anything to do with that horrible beating? How could ye e'er think I would do such a thing, nay matter how jealous I was of Agnes. And I will confess right now that I *was* jealous of her. Terribly jealous each time she smiled at ye or touched your arm. I was so sure she would be able to woo ye away from me with the same ease as she had enthralled all the men who e'er came to Dunlochan. She e'en wooed my father into believing she was sweet and innocent."

Lucas stood, pulled her out of the chair, and picked her up. He carried her over to the heavily cushioned bench in the corner and sat down leaning comfortably against its high back. Ignoring her attempts to pull away, he settled her on his lap and held her close to him.

"A part of me ne'er really believed ye had anything to do with the beating I got. Unfortunately, I got it into my head that that was just my desire for ye talking, the part of me that wanted to believe only good of ye so that I could get back into your bed."

"And so ye did." Although she understood what he was saying she did not know if it was good or bad. "Aye, I wanted ye there, but every now and then I felt ashamed of myself for being so weak that I would take a mon who thought so ill of me into my bed, my body."

"Ye didnae do that, my heart. I already kenned the truth ere I joined ye in your bed."

"Ye mean ye had finally come to believe me?"

The look on her face made him want to lie to her, to tell her that was exactly what had happened, but that would only put a new wall in the place of the one they were trying to topple down now. "Nay, it wasnae that, although I wish to God I could say it was." He pressed his forehead against hers. "What happened when ye were injured was that I became utterly determined to find the truth. I couldnae tolerate the warring sides of me, the side that believed and the side that was afraid to believe. So I went into Dunlochan exploring the many passages here and came upon one that went right by Agnes's solar. There is e'en a wee hole in the wall to look through."

"So William said."

"Agnes and Ranald were talking. He had come to tell her that ye were alive. It was during that talk and all their plots and plans to kill ye and me that they spoke of the beating, how they planned it, and how they used ye. It wasnae your jealousy that got me beaten so badly and nearly killed, it was hers. She couldnae abide the fact that I wasnae interested in her, that I was interested in ye. E'en worse than that insult was that she kenned that if I wished to marry ye the council would approve of me."

"So ye had to die."

"And so did ye because she was the sort of woman who couldnae abide a rival."

It hurt to think that Lucas had never come to believe her side of the story but had had to hear the very ones who wanted him dead confess to it before he believed in her innocence. She tried to be sensible about it. If she had thought he had betrayed her she probably would not heed him saying he was the one telling the truth. The very fact that she felt him guilty ensured that she would do her best to doubt his word and keep on doubting it. He had also gone seeking the truth and she should not ignore that.

Katerina sighed. "So once ye kenned the truth ye felt it was safe to indulge your desire for me."

"Once I learned the truth I felt like the greatest of idiots."

"That seems fair," she murmured, and almost smiled when she felt him give her braid a light punitive tug. "So ye were upset that ye had made such a mistake and then what?"

"Upset? Kat, I was devastated. It was as if the clouds had cleared from the skies and I could suddenly see clearly again. Aye, hearing the truth from them made me see the truth but it wasnae that simple. It was if hearing them tell me what truly happened freed the truth inside of me. It was if their words turned the key to the cell I had locked the truth away in. I didnae just learn the truth, I learned that I had always kenned the truth but had shut it away deep inside of me and refused to look at it. What I couldnae understand was why I would do such a thing."

Katerina stroked his hair. He sounded so upset even now, weeks after this revelation had taken place, she knew he was far more than remorseful over having accused her of such a thing. "Do ye ken why ye did that?"

"Aye, I think I do although it makes me sound like a madmon." He grimaced. "It all has to do with what was done to me. I am a strong mon and a good fighter."

"Ye certainly are."

He smiled faintly at her instinctive support. "Yet I was helpless that night. All my skills couldnae save me from being beaten nearly to death, my bones broken, my—" He looked at her when she placed shaking fingers over his mouth.

"I was there and I saw it all. I have only just begun
to banish the nightmares those images gave me."

He took her hand to his mouth and kissed her palm
before placing her hand over his heart. "When Ranald
cut my face he bent low and told me that ye had ordered it done so that I wouldnae be so bonnie any more
and wouldnae break any more lassies' hearts or some
such nonsense. Sad to say that was one of the things that
stayed in my mind when so much else was lost, my
memory of the whole painful time very broken. That
and the image of ye standing there watching it all with
no expression on your face."

"Oh God."

"I cursed Him for deserting me a few times ere I recovered enough to give up such nonsense. When they
threw me into the loch—I think I hit the rocks first
and then the water—I played dead for a wee while but
was always inching my way along through the water to
try and get to the shore, whichever one was nearest
and yet away from them. I swam when I felt I was far
enough away that they wouldnae see me. I ne'er saw
them throw ye in. And my trials had only just begun.
I crawled as far away from the shore as I could and
then tended my own wounds as best I could. Then I
tried to get home. 'Tis a great mystery to me for the
most part. There was help along the way and I recall
some of them. Then Artan arrived to get me and take
me back to Donncoill."

"Artan arrived? Just like that?"

"Weel, nay just like that. He just kenned that I was
in trouble, e'en in pain, and he followed that feeling
until he found me."

Katerina got up and went to pour them each a
tankard of cider and, after serving one to Lucas,
promptly sat back down on his lap. "Ye and him are

verra closely bonded, I imagine. It happens with twins sometimes."

"Aye and I am verra grateful. I was nearly dead, my leg badly infected since the bones had come through the skin." He heard her gasp and felt her hand tighten its grip on his arm and decided there was no need to make her suffer all the gruesome details. "It was weeks before I was healed enough to even start to think about what had happened."

"And ye heard Ranald's vicious lie and saw me looking as cold as Agnes."

"Aye, I did." He kissed her briefly as if apologizing for even holding on to the memory. "A few other memories returned as time wore on but if they contradicted what I had begun to believe I paid them no heed." He set down his tankard on the small chest next to the bench and then did the same with hers before taking her hands in his. "'Tis humiliating to admit this but I began to see why I did that after I learned the real truth." He stared down at their joined hands. "I was hurt by what I saw as your betrayal. As I told ye, I wanted ye for my wife back then, was just trying to woo ye a wee bit ere I asked. I grieved for the loss of that, for the loss of ye as ye had to be as good as dead to me, and I grieved for the loss of all I had begun to plan and dream of—the bairns and all of that."

Katerina rested her cheek against his hair. "When ye say ye grieved do ye mean ye cried, Lucas?" she asked softly.

"Like a bairn," he muttered.

She hid a smile against his hair. It was becoming very clear to her now. Lucas had felt himself humiliated by his weakness for her, a weakness that had actually brought him to tears. She suspected the fact that he had not touched a woman in a year before he returned to her was also seen as a weakness caused by her. He might not see it and, if he did, he might not ever admit it but the fact that she had been there watching him beaten, defeated, and even crying out in pain a few times had also humiliated him. And she was an intricate part of every single one of those humiliations. Katerina was astounded that he had ever even come near her again.

"I understand now, Lucas," she said and touched a kiss to his forehead since he still had not lifted his face to hers.

"Och, nay, ye dinnae."

She leaned back a little when he finally looked at her. "There is more?"

"Aye, the minute I kenned the truth, I wanted ye back. I wanted ye in my bed, and in my home. But more importantly, I wanted ye back in my heart. Ye had ne'er really left it but I had pushed ye far into a corner so that ye couldnae torment me and make me think of all I had lost. My scattered memories made me see ye as guilty, my pride made me verra reluctant to set eyes on ye again, and my heart, with a great deal of effort on my part, was determined to become as hard as rock. But it wasnae an easy battle because the other thing I grieved for was the fact that I believed I loved a woman with no honor." He studied her as she sat so very still on his lap thinking over all he had just said.

"Ye love me?"

"Aye, lass. I couldnae kill it completely and that made me want to hate ye if that makes any sense."

Tears burning in her eyes, Katerina flung her arms around his neck. "It makes perfect sense."

"Weel, if ye think so 'tis fine with me as it makes me look less of an ass."

"It makes sense to me, Lucas, because I thought I

loved a mon who had no faith in me, no trust, and no respect, a mon who could believe that I would make wild love with him one night and have him cruelly beaten to death the next."

Lucas pulled her tight into his arms and pressed his face against her breasts, embarrassed by the sudden sting of unmanly tears in his eyes. "Are ye sure, lass?" He grinned when he felt her chest heave with a sigh of exasperation.

"I have been sure from the beginning. The only thing that has changed from time to time was whether I really wished to be in love with ye." She took his face between her hands and turned it up to hers. "Lucas, I swear upon my mother's grave that I would ne'er betray ye and ne'er willingly hurt ye."

He brushed a kiss over her mouth. "I ken it, love. I think I have always kenned it. I was just a wee bit mad for a while. I was like some daft child who burns himself once and after that is willing to shiver in the darkness rather than make a fire."

"Too many kicks to the head."

"A verra good excuse. I am sorry I hurt ye," he added softly.

"Ah, weel, 'tis done and mended. It would be nice to be able to go back to the start and do it right but—" She squeaked in surprise when he suddenly set her from his lap, stood up and grabbed her by the hand, then headed out of the room, dragging her behind him. "What is it? What are we doing?"

"Ye will see."

Katerina said nothing, just watched in curiosity as he gathered blankets, a basket with food and wine, and then went outside to call for his horse. She laughed a little when he tossed her up into the saddle and mounted behind her for she was beginning to get an idea of what he was up to. For just one moment when they reached the banks of the loch all she could see was the tragedy that had almost taken place there, the spot where they had both almost died. She hastily shook those ghosts away as Lucas helped her down from the horse.

"Now, I believe we were right here when we first made love," he said as he spread out the blanket on a mossy patch of ground beneath a huge pine tree.

She looked around, realized he was exactly right, and smiled at him. "Exactly right, my fine, braw knight. I can e'en see the mark ye made on the tree when ye stuck your dagger into it."

"Come here then," he said, bowing slightly and then helping her to sit down on the blanket even though she did not really need any help and they both knew it. "We shall begin again, right here, right now. Mayhap we can also banish whate'er ghosts still linger here."

"I just did," she said as she poured them each some wine.

"Clever lass."

Lucas set out the food and fed her as they talked of what needed to be done at Dunlochan, their families and their future. They even had a rousing discussion about what to name their first five children. Lucas reassured her that his decision to remain at Dunlochan was still firm and no great sacrifice as his father was still hale and would be the laird of Donncoill for many more years, God willing. Replete and made sleepy by the summer sun, they both lay back on the blanket and stared up at the unusually bright summer sky.

"That was a fine start to our new beginning," he said.

"It was indeed, husband," agreed Katerina, "although

ye did forget the one other thing we did whilst we were here."

"Ah, aye, making love."

"Quite so."

"Wild love if I recall your words correctly."

"The best kind."

"I cannae argue with that."

"Of course it was night with a big fat moon. Verra romantic." She grinned when he grunted at the word *romantic.*

"Remember, this is a new beginning. We dinnae have to do everything exactly as we did then."

"Nay? Weel, we have already made it different in a way." She rested her hand on her stomach. "I am with bairn."

He covered her hand with his. "And a good thing too as it means I have already set one mistake right."

"What mistake was that?" She sat up to remove her boots so that she could wriggle her toes in the moss and grass.

"I should have left ye pregnant back then. That would have made me come back for ye sooner and I wouldnae have let such fool ideas get set so firmly in my muddled brain."

"Were ye thinking of getting me with child when ye brought me here that night?" She gave him the fiercest scowl she could when he just grinned. "How devious of ye."

"I thought so," he said proudly.

"I cannae believe ye would e'en think of such a plan. Were ye thinking that would make it so that I would have to marry ye?"

"That was my plan. I was going to ravish ye repeatedly until my seed took root and then graciously marry ye. It was all carefully thought out."

"If it was all so carefully thought out why didnae ye do it?"

"Because I got all soft and stupid after taking your virginity. It was a bit painful for ye at first and I didnae want to give ye any more pain. So, I left ye be and made my plans for the next time."

"Ravish me?"

"Repeatedly. But ye were a virgin and I kenned I could easily hurt ye."

For moment, Katerina just sat quietly listening to the sounds of the animals that lived near the loch and watching the sun sparkle on the water. The word *ravish* kept tickling her mind stirring up some very enticing images. It was, however, the middle of the day and unusually bright out. On the other hand, she mused, she would soon start to round out with the child she carried and she would become more modest. Right now her figure was in very good shape, everything firm and in the right place. She would not be that way for too many years, why not be a little daring?

"Lucas?"

"Aye, love?"

"I am nay a virgin anymore."

It took Lucas only a moment to recognize the invitation she had just tossed at him. He grabbed the scruff of her dress and pulled her down. Once she was flat on her back, he moved on top of her.

"Savage," she murmured as she grabbed hold of his warrior braids and pulled his head down to hers.

"Your savage," he said against her lips.

"All mine. So, when does this ravishing begin?"

"Patience, woman. There is one more thing that must be done, something I wish I had done a year ago. Something that may have helped us avoid at least some of the trouble we have found ourselves in."

"And what would that be?" she asked as she began to unlace his shirt.

"Tell ye how much I love ye, how ye are the light in my soul, and my perfect mate."

"I was as big a coward as ye were, husband. So, I tell ye now, here in the place where we first joined our bodies, that I love ye, my fine silver-eyed savage, and I always shall."

He kissed her, trying to put all the beautiful words he was unable to say into his kiss.

"Oh my, but that was lovely," whispered Katerina, her heart pounding with a dangerous mixture of desire and tenderness. "Now, about that ravishing," she drawled.

Lucas laughed and kissed her again.

Epilogue

Summer, 1483

"I have this one secured. Ye can catch the other one."

Lucas laughed as he strode after his daughter Morainn. The tiny girl was moving along at an impressive speed for someone who had not been walking for very long. Her thick black curls were bouncing madly, and he knew she had a big smile on her angelic little face. He also knew that she was going to bellow as loudly as her brother was now when he caught her. Even as he reached out for Morainn, Lucas glanced back to see Katerina struggling to put a writhing Lachann back into the cart while Annie, Robbie, and Patrick all grinned. He shook his head, thinking that they should have brought more people with them on this journey just to herd the children. Lucas reached out and grasped his little daughter by the waist.

"Nay!" Morainn said, her tiny body going rigid as Lucas caught her up into his arms.

"Now, my wee lassie, *I* say aye and I am your father," said Lucas.

When Morainn looked up at him with her wide

eyes—eyes exactly like her mother's, one fat tear slowly winding its way down her cheek—Lucas sighed. He was glad Katerina was able to be stern with their daughter because he found it the most difficult thing he had ever done each time he tried. Worse, despite not having lived even two full years yet, Morainn already seemed to know exactly how to twist her father around her tiny finger. Only the fact that she also seemed to be able to do the same to every man and boy at Dunlochan saved him from feeling utterly humiliated by that weakness.

He set her down on her feet and pointed toward the cart in what he felt was a commanding manner. Morainn looked at him; looked at his finger for a long, silent moment; and then looked toward the cart. Her brother Lachann stood in the cart, finally quiet, his pale hair tousled by the wind and his thumb stuck firmly in his mouth as he watched Morainn. Morainn bellowed out her brother's name and started toward the cart at her usual curl-bouncing speed. Lucas strode after her, strongly suspecting that this was how she would approach everything in her life. *It would undoubtedly age him before his time*, he thought as he helped her up into the cart.

"'Tis my fervent hope that that wee gallop o'er the hills they just indulged in will keep them still and quiet for the rest of the journey," Katerina said as she helped Annie tuck blankets around the children.

"Still, mayhap, but ne'er quiet," Lucas said as Morainn and Lachann began to talk to each other in the language only they could understand. "Ye have to wonder just what they have to talk about."

"About how annoying their parents are?" Katerina grinned and kissed Lucas on the cheek as he helped her into the cart.

"Ah, aye, those great beasties who keep restricting

their freedom." He kissed Katerina on the forehead. "We will be at Glascreag ere the sun sets, love."

"It hasnae been such a long journey. Truly. Nay for me leastwise," she added after glancing at the twins and gently attempting to tidy Lachann's windblown curls. "I just hope your brother kens what will soon be let loose upon his household."

"Recall all the tales he has told of his own two lads Aiden and Eric, and e'en a few about Angus's wee Meghan," Lucas said as he mounted his horse. "I suspicion he is weel accustomed to it all."

As Donald started the cart moving, Katerina watched Lucas ride up to join Robbie and Patrick. She never tired of watching the man she had married. Despite the occasional stiffness in his leg, his body was a sheer joy to watch. Somehow, even when he limped a little, he appeared all that could be graceful in a big, strong man.

And he gave her healthy, strong bairns, she thought with a smile as she looked at her children. Katerina still found it hard to believe that she had been safely delivered of twins, a girl and a boy who were an intriguing mix of her and Lucas. Lachann had Katerina's fair hair and eyes like Lucas's, while Morainn had her father's thick black hair and eyes like her mother's. They were also in grave danger of being horribly spoiled by everyone at Dunlochan. Katerina hoped Lucas's brother and his wife would not find the lively pair too great a trial, for she wanted Lucas and Artan to be willing to have their families visit each other at every opportunity. Wives getting with child, work, the weather, and bairns too small for such a journey caused enough necessary separation between the brothers.

"Are ye nervous then, Katerina?" asked Annie qui-

etly after she saw that the twins were more asleep than
awake.

"A wee bit," Katerina reluctantly admitted. "I have
corresponded with Artan's wife but have yet to meet
the woman. Soon we will be face to face as will our
bairns. I want it all to be perfect, yet bairns can sometimes disrupt things."

Annie nodded. "That they can, but ye have me and
I am certain there are nursemaids aplenty at Glascreag."

"Of course there are." Katerina grimaced. "'Tis just
that I ken how eager Lucas has been to see his
brother again and I dinnae want anything to go
wrong. Work, women bearing bairns, and wee bairns
too young to travel yet cause them to be apart quite
often enough as it is. They dinnae need any added
reasons to forgo a visit now and then. And I ken that
'tis Lucas's dearest wish that our families are close—
wives and bairns as weel as he and Artan."

"'Twill be fine. Truly," Annie said when Katerina continued to frown. "Lady Cecily's missives are light, funny,
and full of warmth. I am certain the woman is the
same. And ye have met Laird Artan several times now.
The children will play and squabble as all bairns do and
that is how it should be." Annie lightly stroked the fine
red hair of her child who, at only five months of age,
still slept more than he was awake. "I cannae wait until
my wee Ian can run and play with all the others."

After making certain that her now sleeping children were warmly covered, Katerina wrapped a blanket around herself. "I ken that all ye say is true. I think
I just need to get this first meeting o'er with."

"It shallnae be long now. Then ye may be at ease
and enjoy the visit with your kin."

* * *

"There is Glascreag," Lucas said as he rode along at the side of the cart and smiled at his slowly waking wife. "Wipe the sleep from your bonnie eyes, wife, and have a look."

Katerina looked. She was not sure what she thought of Glascreag. The first word that entered her head and seemed to be stuck there was formidable. Glancing around she could see that the keep was surrounded by what looked to be good land, arable land, and a burn that sparkled even in the weakening light of a setting sun. Somehow that all made the large, dark stone keep and its high walls look even more formidable.

Then she thought about how cautiously Lucas had approached Glascreag lands, crossing over the terrain of other clans with speed and stealth, yet always careful to reveal no hint of a threat to anyone who might see them. A close guard had been set out every night, and Katerina now realized that it had not just been to protect them against the ever-present threat of thieves. Glascreag and the MacReiths might not be at war with anyone at the moment, but she suspected the MacReiths were not exactly allied with most of their neighbors, either. Suddenly the keep and its dark walls looked just right for where it was despite the tranquil glen that surrounded it.

And this was where her husband had been trained, had spent ten years of his life changing from a boy into a man, she thought as she watched Lucas look around him with an obvious affection. It explained that somewhat savage side of him that she had seen so little of in the Murrays she had met so far. This harsh, rough, yet beautiful land had shaped him, had seeped into his blood, and had honed his battle skills. In some ways, this was where the Lucas she knew had been born.

"It hasnae changed," Lucas said, his pleasure over that fact clear to hear in his voice.

"I think a place such as this changes verra little," Katerina said. "This land willnae let it."

"Aye, true enough. It can be harsh round here, although Angus has some verra good land."

"Good enough to stir up a wee bit of envy, aye?"

"Aye, though it has been a while since any blood was spilt o'er it. Artan says it has been verra peaceful of late."

The tone in Lucas's voice told Katerina that that did not necessarily please Artan and Lucas agreed with his brother's feelings. "I suspicion Lady Cecily is content that 'tis so," she murmured.

"Artan is, too, more than not. He wouldnae want his Sile or his lads in any danger."

From the way Artan often spoke of his wife and children, Katerina knew that to be true, but her own waking children drew her full attention before she could reply. With Annie's help she managed to get the children's soiled cloths changed just before they cleared the gates of Glascreag. Holding fast to little Morainn while Annie kept a firm grip on Lachann, Katerina watched as a group of people hurried down the steps of the keep to greet them.

The only person she recognized was Artan. In each strong arm he held a squirming, laughing little boy with thick black curls. One step behind him was a slender red-haired woman that could only be Lady Cecily, or, as Artan called her, *my Sile*. A tall, older man, his black hair well threaded with silver, held with one hand the arm of a plump, graying woman. That pair descended the steps very carefully for his other hand clasped that of a tiny, fair-haired girl child. Two very handsome young men slipped around the others on the steps to hurry over to greet Lucas.

The men indulged in the usual manly round of very brief embraces followed by backslapping that caused each of them to stagger slightly. A few moments later, Katerina found herself being embraced and kissed upon the cheek as she was introduced to everyone. She did not really need to hear the names, for all of Lucas's tales and Cecily's letters made it very easy for her to know just who was who. It surprised her a little that Angus MacReith was only a distant cousin to Lucas and Artan for the man could easily pass for the father of the twins. Lucas's cousins Bennet and Uilliam earned themselves a hard glare from Lucas, who obviously felt they welcomed Katerina a little too warmly. The moment Katerina greeted Cecily and Meg she knew the women would be her dearest friends, that Cecily was just as warm and light-hearted as her letters, and that Meg was exactly as Cecily had described her: loving and sharp-tongued.

"So where is this wee lassie of yours?" asked Angus.

The conversation Katerina was having with Cecily and Meg came to an abrupt halt. "Why, Morainn is right here!" she said, the last two words fading to a whisper as she looked around but did not see Morainn.

"Birdie!" bellowed an all too familiar childish voice.

Katerina looked in the direction of that voice to see her little daughter racing toward some chickens. "Lucas!"

Laughing along with his cousins, Lucas hurried after his daughter. Artan was so busy taunting Lucas about not being able to control his children that he had failed to keep a close watch on his own. Eric and Aiden quickly ran after their little cousin, loudly informing Morainn that the animals now fleeing in a raucous panic were not birdies, but chickens. Lachann and Angus's little girl Meghan set up a loud protest when they were prevented from running after the other children. Katerina sighed and tried to quiet Lachann. It would undoubtedly be a long time before she could have that much anticipated woman-to-woman talk with Artan's Sile.

"At last all is quiet," said Cecily as she sat on a cushioned bench next to Meg.

Already seated comfortably before the fire on the bench facing the other two women, Katerina smiled. "Quiet for us, but I suspicion the nursemaids will be busy for a while yet."

Cecily laughed along with Meg. "Aye, verra true."

Katerina glanced toward the men seated at the head table, drinking ale and arguing. "I wonder what they are arguing about."

"Anything and everything."

Meg nodded. "Angus loves a good argument."

"Lucas often said so, but I fear I thought he was jesting." Katerina glanced at the men again, shook her head, and laughed. "'Tis verra clear he was telling the simple truth." She looked around the great hall once before returning her gaze to Cecily and Meg. "I have long wanted to see this place. Lucas has told me so many tales about his years here, his training, and Angus. I kenned it figured largely in making him the mon he is."

"Aye," agreed Cecily. "I think he and Artan were born to this life. The Murrays are Highlanders, but they live in a quieter, softer land, much nearer the borders of the places Angus so loves to curse. Artan and Lucas are the sons he ne'er had. 'Tis why he has all the bairns call him *Pere*." Cecily smiled at Katerina. "Ye have gained a verra large family by marrying Lucas."

"I began to realize that when the Murrays began to visit in twos, threes, and more. I do have a dozen cousins that I am aware of. May have more, just have-nae found them yet. My late uncle was verra fond of the lasses," she said when both women looked at her curiously. "I thought that was a lot until I began to hear about and meet Lucas's family. 'Tis good. My bairns will always have someone to turn to if they are in need."

"Aye, and ones we can be certain will protect them and that is theirs. 'Tis a great comfort."

Looking at her husband again, Katerina said quietly, "There are times when I look at that mon and wonder how he has come to be mine."

"And how can ye hold fast to him?" Cecily smiled in complete understanding.

"Aye, and yet that seems as if I question the vows he has made and I then feel guilty for that."

"I ken the feeling all too weel."

"'Tis just a passing thing and of no great conse-quence," Meg said. "'Tis naught but a natural fear of losing something precious. Only God can take those two laddies away from ye, their wives. They love deep and hard and believe a vow should be kept nay matter who ye give it to, be they mon, woman, or bairn. Ye are two verra lucky lassies and I am a verra lucky old woman."

Katerina was about to dispute the word *old* when an all too familiar childish voice bellowed, "Da!"

She looked toward the doors of the great hall to see her daughter standing there in her sleep shirt. Morainn looked around the room, saw her father, and started running toward him. A moment later a breathless young maid appeared in the doorway. Katerina hurried over to the young woman.

"How did she get out of the nursery?" Katerina asked even as Cecily hurried to stand at her side.

"Och, m'ladies, I just dinnae ken," the woman replied. "We thought all the bairns were asleep. Annie went to take her bairn to visit with her mon and I was talking with—"

"Da! Kiss!"

Glancing over her shoulder to see that her daughter had reached her far too amused father and his kin, Katerina said, "Ne'ermind. No harm has come of it this time, but ye must ne'er take your eyes off her again. Morainn needs to be in a verra secure bed. If ye dinnae have such a one then a nursemaid must sleep right next to her. And, 'tis best if she has leashed the child to her in some way so that she can be roused the moment Morainn tries to escape."

"Annie said I must do that, but I thought the bairn asleep. I was about to secure the doors to the nursery as we always do when I saw that the wee lass was gone from her bed."

"Securing the door works weel, too." Katerina grinned at Cecily, who looked as if she was trying very hard not to laugh like the men were. "Morainn is a wee bit wild."

"Och, aye, just a wee bit." Cecily laughed along with Katerina and then looked toward the head table. "Best get her ere she kisses every mon in the hall."

Katerina watched the young nursemaid hurry after Morainn. "Aye, for those laughing fools willnae restrain the lass at all." When the nursemaid started to hurry past her a moment later with a scowling Morainn in her arms, Katerina halted her and kissed her daughter on the cheek even as she scolded, "Naughty lassie. Ye ken verra weel that ye are nay to go up or down the stairs alone."

Morainn gave her mother a wet kiss on her cheek

and then leaned over to give her Aunt Cecily one too. "Kiss." She stuck her thumb in her mouth, rested her head against the nursemaid's shoulder, and closed her eyes. "Mo' sleep now."

It was difficult to restrain the urge to laugh until the doors closed behind her daughter, but Katerina managed. She then laughed along with Cecily. "I think that child is going to leave me with white hair ere she grows and leaves to begin her own family."

Cecily lightly touched her flat stomach. "I wish to have a daughter and I pray she is just as full of life and spirit as wee Morainn." She put her finger to her lips when Katerina made to offer her congratulations. "Hush. 'Tis still a secret. One more week and I shall tell my husband and he will quickly tell everyone else."

"No one shall hear it from me," Katerina swore as she and Cecily went back to sit with Meg.

"Did ye ken that Cecily is with bairn again?" asked Lucas as he slid into bed beside Katerina.

"How did ye ken that?" Katerina asked in shock even as Lucas yanked off her night shift and tossed it aside. "Cecily isnae planning to say anything for a week."

Lucas grinned and kissed her on the nose. "A lass may be able to keep such a thing a secret from a Murray lad once, but ne'er twice. Artan is just waiting for her to tell him. The way he is boasting, howbeit, I dinnae think there will be a soul left at Glascreag that doesnae ken it already by the time she says something."

"She wants a lass like Morainn."

"That would be just punishment for my boastful brother."

Katerina laughed. "Nay, the two of ye will just spend

many an hour commiserating with each other whene'er ye are together."

"Aye, we can watch to see whose hair turns white first."

"And are ye thinking ye best get about breeding another bairn so that Artan isnae too far ahead of ye?"

Lucas stopped kissing his wife's soft neck and looked at her. "Are ye saying ye are ready to try for another?"

"I think I am. The twins are nearly weaned and when Cecily told me her news I felt both verra happy for her and a wee twinge of longing. 'Twould seem that my heart and body are ready for another try."

Moving to sprawl on top of her, Lucas gave her a slow, hungry kiss. "Another wee lass?"

Running her hands up and down his spine and enjoying the way his body hardened with need when she touched him, Katerina smiled. "A lass or a lad. I am nay particular. Just healthy is all I ask. Healthy, bright-eyed, and a wee savage just like our bellowing Morainn."

"Are ye calling my wee bonnie daughter, the fruit of my loins, a savage?"

"Just like her da."

"Beware, lass, or I will be showing ye just how savage I can be."

"Oh, aye, please."

Lucas laughed and then kissed her. "I love ye, my impertinent wife."

"And I love ye. Now—where is my savage?"

"Ne'er let it be said that Lucas Murray didnae give his wife all she required."

"And needed."

"Aye."

"And wanted with every breath she takes."

"Oh, aye."

"So, shall ye cease talking and get about it?"

He did.

From New York Times *bestselling author Hannah Howell comes a spellbinding tale set in the majestic Highlands, where an arranged marriage becomes a true joining of hearts . . .*

The vivid scar that spans Sir Iain MacLagan's cheek is a daily reminder of the wife he lost—and of the enemy that still stalks him. Commanded by Scotland's king to remarry in order to unite two powerful border clans, Iain reluctantly weds Islaen MacRoth, a woman whose delicate appearance belies a playful, seductive nature that proves dangerously attractive to a man who has vowed never to jeopardize his heart, or his loved ones, again . . .

Raised with eleven boisterous brothers, Islaen has little time for foolish romantic notions. Even so, she had hoped for more than a forced marriage to a man who shares her bed, but not her life. Step by step, Islaen sets out to wear down Iain's defenses. But can her ruggedly handsome husband learn to give her his love as freely as he bestows his passion?

Please turn the page for an exciting sneak peek of Hannah Howell's
Highland Wedding,
coming in November 2007!

Chapter One

She turned the corner and he was there, sitting and staring at the roses as if they could talk and would at any moment. That sad, lost look was on his scarred face again. Sometimes she would allow herself to pretend that he revealed that side of himself to her willingly, then savored the glow that gave her. It never lasted long for she was too practical. Soon she would tartly remind herself that the only reason she had seen it was because she was lurking around, catching him when he thought he was alone.

This night she would be presented at court. She had been brought in hopes of forming an alliance through marriage, preferably one that would further the family's favor with the king. From the moment she had laid eyes on the man she had fought against hoping that he would be the one chosen for her. He had all the right qualifications, but her luck had never been that good. Instead of a man her heart ached for, she would no doubt get some mincing courtier or even a man past his prime and probably past all else.

At nineteen years she was late in wedding but her father had held off finding her a husband, hoping that she would fill out to look more like a woman than

a child. It was not to be. She was small and no amount
of potions and porridge would change that. Only she
and Meg knew that she was perhaps not as unwom-
anly as she appeared. All that, however, did not alter
the fact that she thought she was not comely. She had
been told that often enough to know it was so. With
so little to offer a man, one like Iain MacLagan was
not for her.

Her hair was the color of claret wine, such a deep
red that many swore it ran with a purple hue despite
her adament denials of such an oddity. It was of such
thickness with a strong tendency to curl that it was
always slipping its bonds, looking untidy. Her eyes
were a deep brown with flecks of gold set beneath
finely arched dark brows and ringed with such long,
curled dark lashes that she was always denying accusations of their being unnatural. Though she knew her
skin was lovely and pale, she had been cursed with
freckles which, though faint and few, would not be removed. She sighed.

Whether it was that soft sigh or just a sense of being
watched she was not sure but Iain MacLagan suddenly
looked her way. She stood like a terrified hare, pinned
to the spot by turquoise eyes that shone bright yet
emotionless in his harsh dark face. At any moment
she expected him to verbally flay her with his cold,
remote voice, so well-known in court, for being so insolent as to invade his privacy.

Iain had thought to lash her with words but she
looked so much like a frightened child that he could
not. She was sadly disheveled with a vast amount of
wine-red hair easing free of her headdress. Her eyes
were huge dark pools in her small ivory face, a dainty
visage that wavered between being heart-shaped and
triangular. Perfect white teeth worried the bottom lip
of her full mouth. There were few curves to indicate

she was a grown woman, but he could see she was at least past her first flux. She was also rather lacking in height and flesh elsewhere on her body for her neck and arms were slender nearly to frailty.

He wondered what fool let her wander about unattended. Her youth was no protection. Although he himself felt it abhorrent to lust after and bed a girl barely past her first flux, he could think of others who did not. There were also those men who would care little that she was obviously well-born and innocent. For all her daintiness, she was rather pretty.

"There is no need to quail so, mistress."

"I didnae mean to disturb your privacy, Sir MacLagan." She willed her body to disappear but it did not happen.

"The garden is to be enjoyed by all. Come, sit. Ye ken my name but I ken not yours. Come."

Tentatively, she did so, sitting beside him as if she expected the bench to singe her backside. "I am Islaen MacRoth."

"Islaen. 'Tis fitting," he murmured for her voice was soft, low and slightly husky with the attraction of fine music. "I have not seen ye here before. Newly arrived?"

"Aye. I am to be put forward this eve." She saw his winged dark brows quirk and knew he thought her too young. "I am newly turned nineteen. Fither kept me at home in hopes I would grow. He gave up."

A smile ghosted over Iain's face for even with her headdress and painfully straight posture she barely rose to his shoulder. The hands that plucked at her skirts were small, delicate, and long-fingered. Except for the huge dark eyes that stared up at him everything about Islaen MacRoth was small, including her lightly freckled, modestly upturned nose. He could not help but wonder how she would find a husband, which was undoubtedly the reason she had been brought to court.

"I have a sizeable purse, some verra sweet property near the border, and an excellent bloodline."

"Ye read minds, do ye? 'Tis a verra uncomplimentary thought ye put in my head."

Guilt gave his voice the sternness he sought in order to sound convincing. It was an insult to a woman to think her unweddable and he had no real wish to insult her. She looked a sweet child.

Inwardly he cursed for his body was reacting to her as a man's did when in the presence of a lovely woman. His loins did not doubt her age. It was a feeling he fought, although he found it not as easy as it had become since Catalina's death. That troubled him deeply for he felt it vital that he keep his passion under firm control.

"Nay, only the truth and 'tis your look I read for oft have I seen it. 'Tis the ones who gape or snicker that I consider rude."

"So ye should." His face hardened suddenly. "'Twould be wrong for any mon to wed ye and make ye bear his bairn."

Unaware of what prompted his statement or put the harshness in his voice, she drew herself up to her full, inconsiderable height. "And just why do ye say that? I am a woman and ye wed women and get them with bairn. I can do it as weel as any other."

"Nay, ye cannae. Ye havenae got any hips, ye foolish wee lass."

"Pray tell me then what it is I am sitting on?"

"Your backside and cursed little there is of it."

"My mither looked much as I do and she bore a dozen bairns, healthy bairns. She didnae die bearing them either. Went fishing for salmon and drowned when I was five. If she could then I can."

"Ye cannae recall your mither exact, child." He stood up to glare at her. "Ye are a wee thing not made for childbearing."

To counter the effects of his towering over her, she stood on the bench. "Then what did God put me here for?"

"Only He kens. Aye, and only He kens how I got into this discussion. Ye'd be wise to join a nunnery and forget the bairns."

"Ye be a mon. What do ye ken about it?" she asked scornfully and squeaked when he roughly grasped her shoulders.

He did not really frighten her with his sudden fierce intensity. She found that she had a deep, abiding trust in him. What she did not understand was why he was so fierce. Their conversation had taken a strange turn that left her confused. It was certainly not like any she had dreamt they would have when she finally got to talk to him. *Although,* she mused with an inner smile over her own foolishness, *it is no stranger than if he began to spout flowery phrases of undying love as I have so often imagined him doing.* In truth, next to that fantasy, this strange discussion seemed quite reasonable.

"I ken more than I like, little one. To get a wee lass like ye with bairn is much as cutting her throat. Aye, she will do naught but scream while day fades into night and back again, only to spill out a dead bairn and her life's blood. I ken all too weel."

She staggered when he released her abruptly. "That fate can visit a woman with hips as wide as a loch," she said calmly, knowing from the brief glance she had had of remembered horror in his eyes that he spoke of something very personal.

"Suit yourself, lass," he said coldly, his calm restored. "Aye, I will. I will wed and by a year's end I will have me a bairn. Nay, I will have twins and ye can come to the christening, Sir MacLagan," she retorted with a mixture of confidence and childish defiance.

That haughty declaration almost made him smile. She looked belligerent and confident. That made him feel certain that she had little idea of what she spoke of. Some women could be kept very sheltered, knowing little or nothing of life until they found themselves wed and thrust from their family home.

"'Tis your life, mistress. Toss it away as ye please."

The reply forming on her lips was never made for she spotted a familiar shape in the distance. "I must go now, Sir MacLagan."

With that she was off and running even as a farewell formed on his tongue. Her skirts were well hiked up and, even as he noted that her legs were slim as well, he deemed them very fine legs indeed. He then looked to see what had sent her off.

Marching down the path was a tall, thin woman adorned wholly in black. Her hawkish features made him think of a carrion bird. The impression was not lessened when she paused before him, fixing him with a cold, gray stare.

The woman was so completely the opposite of the woman-child that Iain almost smiled. He mused with a touch of humor that they made a strange pair. Then again, he mused, such a stern guardian was probably just what the minx needed to keep her from getting completely out of hand.

"Did ye see a wee lass aboot, m'laird? Most like she was disheveled and without an escort."

In a courtly manner that never failed to impress, Iain replied that he had indeed seen just such a lass. In the same way he politely sent the woman in the wrong direction. As he strolled back to the castle he wondered why he had done that.

After just a few moments of conversation with the girl he was already acting strangely. Since she was going to be around often now, he decided that was something he had to watch out for. His cold, hard pose had been hard won and he had no intention of losing it to some tiny lady with wild, wine-red hair. It had worked and no knight worth his armor gave up a successful defense.

He fought down his emotions as he saw her in his mind's eye. She was daintier and smaller than Catalina had been. The only reason he could find for speaking out so bluntly was that he could see her meeting the same fate. She would go to her marriage bed, get with child, and die to be buried beside her babe, two innocents lost in one stroke. Iain shook his head wishing there could be some sort of law against letting such tiny, frail ladies wed. It was tantamount to a death sentence.

Islaen suffered no concerns about childbirth once she left Iain. Her only worry was surviving Meg's scolding, which had duly fallen on her moments after she had reached her room. A distant cousin of her father's, Meg had been hired to raise her after the death of her mother. The woman set about her job with admirable vigor. Making use of the tender spot her father and eleven brothers had for her did not deter her at all.

Each of the men in Islaen's family treated the girl with amused and loving tolerance. Sometimes Meg suspected they forgot Islaen was a girl. She had dragged the girl from wrestling matches, riding contests, knife hurlings. That Islaen seemed ill-equipped to be a fine lady was no help either. Not only ill-equipped but none too interested either, Meg feared, as was illustrated by an incident just a week past. Fine ladies did not get on their hands and knees to join in a dice game.

Meg had no sense of failing with the girl. Improvements had been made. When the laird had first brought her to care for Islaen, the girl had been as wild as any lad. With determination Meg had smoothed away many a rough edge.

"Is he not the bonniest man ye have e'er seen?" Islaen sighed after Meg soundly denounced Iain MacLagan's trick.

Meg's sharp eyes grew even sharper as they rested upon her charge sprawled somewhat ungracefully in her bath. "He is scarred."

"'Tis just a wee one," Islaen retorted defensively. "Ye hardly e'en see it."

Thinking of the scar that ran from the man's right temple nearly to his lip, Meg drawled, "Oh, aye, barely visible. A wee nick in the skin."

With no trouble at all, Islaen ignored Meg's sarcasm. She had never found it hard to do that. Long before Meg had arrived Islaen had learned that, as well as how to return it in equal measure, for her family had sharp tongues.

"I wonder how he came by it. Something gallant, I wager. A duel o'er a fair lady's honor or heart." She let her imagination take hold of her.

The noise Meg made was highly derisive. "Or bed. 'Tis the sort o' thing that puts most men in a lather. They wield one sword and hack aboot at each other just tae win the chance to wield their other sword. Men have but twa thoughts in their heads."

"Aye," Islaen sighed, "fighting and wenching, blood and flesh, violence and lust, swords and seduction, rampaging and rutting . . ."

"I ken that covers it, ye wicked girl." Meg met

Islaen's dancing gaze without expression. "Out o' the bath ere ye wrinkle."

"Heaven forbid that I should add wrinkles to the freckles," Islaen murmured as she stood up and stepped out of the bath. "I wish I could have such a husband as Sir Iain. Would we not have bonnie wee ones? And strong, like my brothers and fither. 'Twould be verra nice."

As instructed by her kin, Meg took note of Islaen's stated preference. At the first opportunity she would tell the laird. It would be nice if the child could have a husband she fancied, but none of them hoped too hard. She was a wee lass that many a man would fear to break. It had been the same when the laird had married the lass's mother only to have everyone proven very wrong indeed. The trouble was that few recalled the girl's mother, so few would believe that Islaen could prove as strong or as prolific. Then too, Islaen was a bit more delicate and not quite as lovely, her mother having been highly praised for her beauty.

Meg could not help but wonder if she had erred in keeping Islaen's true looks a secret from her family. There was no chance that a husband could remain ignorant. She had only tried to ensure that the girl did not become an object of ridicule and looked her loveliest. Perhaps that would be enough to gain forgiveness for the deception she had practiced, and forced Islaen to, when the truth was finally revealed. As she began to help Islaen dress she hoped the girl would not suffer from her own husband the very scorn and ridicule she had tried so hard to protect the girl from. It would cut the child deeply, inflict a wound that might never heal.

Islaen was dressed in her finest. Her father was a wealthy man and no expense had been spared. Her chemise was of the finest silk, as were the braies she insisted upon wearing. The corset was a rich brown velvet with elaborate embroidery on the sleeves that matched the gold surcote. Shoes of the finest gold velvet adorned her small feet. The houppelande that was becoming more and more popular was left off for Islaen had not yet mastered wearing the voluminous robe with any grace, having difficulty with the draping sleeves and the way it trailed on the ground. After placing the fine couverchef upon Islaen's head, Meg surveyed the results with a very critical eye.

After a final check to make sure that there were no lumps, bumps, or wrinkles and that the errant hair was still neatly contained, Meg declared Islaen ready. She then took her charge to join the men in the great hall where the search for a husband would begin and Islaen would meet the king.

Islaen fought to control her nerves. She did not want to do anything silly or stupid. Her pride quailed at the very thought of it.

She did not like the situation but had decided to forbear. It was far past time she had a husband. Coming to court allowed a greater choice. She simply wished the choice would be more in her hands than it would be.

The resentment that tried to gnaw at her was fairly easily put aside. This was the way such matters were settled. She was grateful she had not been betrothed at cradleside. There had been the opportunity for her to find a man and there were plenty to choose from around home. When she had reached the age of nineteen still unattached, it was no surprise that her father would take matters into his own hands. She could not blame him for that. Even if she did not really agree with his methods, she knew he was doing it out of love, because he wanted to see her happy. The political, defensive, or monetary arrangements that could come out of her betrothal were only pleasant additions, not necessities. Glancing toward her father, who was talking to Meg, she hoped he would give her some pleasant surprise in his choice of groom that would ease the sting of not having Iain MacLagan.

"The lass has an eye for Sir Iain MacLagan," Meg informed Alaistair MacRoth at the very first opportunity. "Do ye ken the mon?"

"Aye." Alaistair adjusted his long, broad-shouldered frame more comfortably upon the bench. "Widowed for o'er a year. Said he is still grieving sore as he doesnae pursue the lasses, doesnae show an interest in them at all. Said he is cold, that his emotions lie with his late wife. Be a good match, for the land Islaen would bring him lies near his kin, but I cannae think there will be any move made there." He frowned at his cousin. "Are ye sure? 'Tis a hard face on the mon that isnae helped by that gruesome scar etched upon his cheek."

"The lass claims ye hardly see it, 'tis a mere nick. Cast an eye on your wee daughter, cousin, and watch where her eyes linger."

It was an easy thing to confirm, for Islaen's whole face radiated her admiration for the man who sat at the king's table. She would seem to come to her senses, conceal the look and act nonchalant, but it did not last long. Within moments her control slipped again.

"Och, weel, I will give it a try but I cannae think it will lead anywhere. 'Tis said that a murderer stalks him, a mon who blames him for the death of Catalina, his late wife. Some old lover, I would wager. Could be he takes no wife for fear she will soon be made a widow." He shook his head and ran a hand through his graying auburn hair. "Still, best she be happy for a short while than unhappy for a long while. If ye can,

turn her eye to Ronald MacDubh. That mon is godson
to the king and he has expressed an interest in our
Islaen."

"Ye mean in her purse. Coin flows through his
hands like water, hands that cannae keep off o' the
lasses."

"He is young and nay hard to look upon. He is also
close to the king. After him they grow older and less
fair to the eye. There are too many full-bodied women
about. The young men want a wife that willnae be lost
beneath the covers, some curves to hold."

Alaistair wished his words were not true but, though
Islaen's dowry put many men to thinking, there was
money and land to be found in other places. So too
would there be some flesh to hold on to and make a
soft bed with. Delicacy of looks only aroused brotherly
feelings when it was unaccompanied by full breasts
and well-rounded hips. Their eyes would light up over
the dowry, only to flicker and die when they closely
observed what went with it. What interest could be
stirred was not held long. A little less dowry for a lot
more woman was a sacrifice most of the young men
were willing to make.

Islaen had not expected much interest, so was not
disappointed when there was so little. Her menfolk did
all the work while she entertained herself watching
Iain MacLagan. Assuming that her family would soon
find her a husband, she decided that she should soak
up as much about the man as she could. A multitude
of memories could come in handy later. It was highly
possible that her marriage could use a great deal of
imagination and dreaming to make it tolerable.

She knew that few men could equal the image she
had of Iain MacLagan. It was going to be difficult not
to constantly compare others, whatever husband she
gained, to him. That was something she was going to

have to try very hard not to do. It would be very foolish indeed to ruin her chances for happiness with another man because she was unable to let go of a dream. It would also be unfair to her husband.

That was true, of course, only if she was blessed with a husband who was also willing to try for the best marriage possible, full, rich, and lasting. There was, however, far too great a chance that she would not get a husband like that, no matter how carefully her father chose for her. She knew enough of the world to know that not all men considered marriage a sacred trust or a wife of any importance save that of a breeder of legitimate heirs. With a husband like that, memories of Iain MacLagan might well be her only source of joy aside from whatever children she might have.

Despite her admirable reasoning for her steady perusal of Iain MacLagan, she admitted that she simply liked to look at him. He was a feast for her eyes. Even when she knew she was being too blatant and fought to turn her attentions elsewhere, her gaze was drawn back to him and she was yet again lost in the pleasure of watching him.

He was dressed in dark blue and maroon. Long, well-shaped muscular legs were snugly encased in maroon hose. The tight sleeves of his deep blue jupon revealed strong arms. Broad shoulders, a trim waist, and slim hips completed what was a fine figure of a man. He was taller than most yet moved with a lithe grace that belied his strength and size. Many a woman's eye touched upon him in approval. It did not seem to matter all that much that he returned neither inviting looks nor friendly smiles, remaining impervious to all ploys and flirtations.

Facially he was somewhat daunting. His was a lean face with harsh lines not enhanced by either the jagged white scar or remote expression he wore. Grief had made his high cheekbones more prominent, the hollows in his smooth-shaven cheeks deeper. His mouth was well formed although his lips were on the thin side, something made more noticeable by their grim set. A long straight nose and proud jaw were more delineated than on other men. A dark complexion only added to what seemed a formidable and constant darkness of expression. Rich brown hair was cut neatly, framing the remarkable face. It was also shot with strands of white, unusual in a man of only four-and-thirty.

It was all food for her imagination. She wondered at his loss, the grief that had left such a mark upon him. From there it was easy to imagine herself as the one who could return love and laughter to his life. As she dreamed, there were more people than she knew working toward giving her dream a chance.

New York Times *bestselling author Hannah Howell
returns to the breathtaking Scottish Highlands
with the unforgettable Murray clan and the
stunning Annora MacKay, who cannot resist
the desire an alluring stranger offers . . .*

Annora MacKay senses a disturbing evil in
Dunncraig Keep, the estate acquired by her cousin, a
cruel and ruthless man. Only her affection for the tiny
girl he claims is his daughter stops her from fleeing.
Then a mysterious woodcarver arrives at the castle,
and she cannot thinking—or longing—for him . . .

James Drummond, once a laird now an outcast,
wants what was stolen from him—his good name,
his lands, and his child. His disguise for getting
into Dunncraig is step one of his plan, but the
enticing raven-haired woman who cares for
his daughter is an unwelcome surprise. For he
has come seeking justice, not love . . .

**Please turn the page for an exciting sneak peek of
Hannah Howell's**

Highland Wolf,

coming in December 2007!

Prologue

Scotland
Spring, 1477

Sir James Drummond, once laird of Dunncraig, once a husband and a loving father, crawled out of his hiding place deep in the Highlands' most remote mountains and slowly stood up. He felt the hint of spring in the air, the promise of warmth in the moist dawn breeze, and took a deep, slow breath. He felt like some beast waking from a long winter's sleep, only his had lasted for three long hard years. He was ragged, filthy, and hungry, but he was determined not to spend another season slipping from hollow to hollow, afraid to venture near friends or kinsmen because he had death at his heels and afraid to pass even the most fleeting of greetings with another person because they might be the one who would recognize and kill him. It was time to stop running.

He clenched his hands into tight fists as he thought on his enemy, Sir Donnell MacKay. Even though he had never liked or fully trusted Donnell, he had allowed the man to come and go from Dunncraig as he pleased, for he was Mary's kinsman. That simple act of

courtesy and his wife Mary's own sweet innocence, the
sort that never saw evil in anyone, had cost her her life.
James had barely finished burying his wife and was
thinking how he could prove that Donnell had killed
her when the man had made his next move. James had
found himself declared guilty of murdering his wife;
soon after that he was declared an outlaw; and then
Donnell had claimed both Dunncraig and little Margaret, James's only child. The few people who had
tried to help him had been killed and that was when
James had begun to run, to hide, and to keep himself
as far away from those he cared about as possible.

Today the running stopped. James collected the
sack holding his few meager belongings and started
down the rocky slope. As he had struggled to survive
the winter, living no better than the beasts he had
hunted for food, James had come up with a plan. He
needed to get back to Dunncraig and find enough
proof to hang Donnell MacKay and free himself.
There was still one man at Dunncraig that James felt
he could trust with his life, and he would need that
man's aid in beginning his search for the truth and
the justice he craved. He would either succeed and
then reclaim his good name, his lands, and his
child—or he would lose it all, including his life. Either
way, at least he would not be running anymore.

At the base of the hill, he paused and stared off in
the direction of Dunncraig. It was a long, arduous
journey, one that would take him weeks because he
had no horse; but he could see it clearly in his mind's
eye. He could also see his little Meggie with her fat
blond curls and big brown eyes, eyes so like her
mother's. Meggie would be five now, he realized, and
felt his anger swell as he thought of all he had missed
of his child's growing because of Donnell's greed. He
also felt the stab of guilt born from how he had

thought mostly of saving his own life and not what his daughter might be suffering under Donnell's rule.

"Dinnae fret, my Meggie, I will come home soon and free us both," he whispered into the breeze. James straightened his shoulders and began the long walk home.

Chapter One

Dunncraig
Summer, 1477

"Pat the dirt o'er the seed verra gently, Meggie."

Annora smiled as the little girl patted the dirt as slowly and carefully as she patted her cat, Sunny. Margaret, who stoutly preferred to be called Meggie, was all that kept Annora at Dunncraig. Her cousin Donnell had wanted someone to care for the child and her family had sent her. That was no surprise for she was poor and illegitimate, a burden every kinsman and kinswoman she had was quick to shake off whenever they could. At first she had been resigned; but then she had met little Meggie, a child of only two with huge brown eyes and thick golden curls. Despite the fact that Annora thought Donnell was a brutish man, even feared him a little, she had some doubts about his rights to claim Dunncraig. Three years later she was still at Dunncraig and not simply because she had no better place to go. She stayed for little Meggie, a child who had stolen her heart almost from the very first day.

"Seeds are precious," said Meggie.

"Aye, verra precious," Annora agreed. "Some plants just grow again every spring all by themselves," she began.

"Cursed stinking weeds."

Bending her head to hide a grin, Annora quietly said, "Young ladies shouldnae say *cursed*." Neither should ladies of four-and-twenty, she mused, fully aware of where Meggie had heard those words. "But, aye, weeds grow all by themselves in places where ye dinnae want them. Some plants, however, cannae survive the winter and we must collect the seeds or roots, storing them away so that we can plant them when it is warm again."

"'Tisnae warm yet."

Annora looked up to find Meggie scowling at the sky. "Warm enough to plants seeds, love."

"Are ye certain we shouldnae wrap them in a wee plaid first?"

"The earth is their plaid."

"Annora! The laird wants ye to go to the village and see how good that new mon makes a goblet!"

Even as Annora turned to respond to young Ian's bellow the youth was already heading back into the keep. She sighed and carefully collected up all the little bags of seeds she had intended to plant this afternoon. Ian was probably already telling Donnell that Annora was going to the village and, of course, she would. *One did not say nay to Donnell.* Taking Meggie by the hand, Annora hurried them both into the keep so that they could wash up before leaving for the village.

It was as they were about to leave that Donnell strode out of the great hall to intercept them. Annora tensed and she felt Meggie press hard against her skirts. She fought the urge to apologize for not having raced to the village without hesitation and met his dark scowl with a faint, questioning smile.

My cousin is a very handsome man, Annora thought. He had thick dark hair and fine dark eyes. His features were manly but not harsh. He even had good skin and no visible scars. Yet Donnell constantly wore such a sour or angry expression that his handsomeness was obscured. It was as if all that was bad inside of the man left some irrevocable mark upon his looks. The way Donnell looked now, Annora could not see how any woman could find him attractive.

"Why arenae ye going to the village?" he snapped.

"We are going right now, Cousin," she said, doing her best to sound sweet and obedient. "We but needed to wash the dirt of the garden off our hands."

"Ye shouldnae be working in the gardens like some common slut. Ye may be a bastard, but ye come from good blood. And ye shouldnae be teaching Margaret such things, either."

"Some day she will be the mistress of some demesne or keep with a household to rule. She will rule it much better if she kens just how much work is needed when she orders something to be done."

The way Donnell's eyes narrowed told Annora that he was trying to decide if she had just criticized him in some way. She had, all too aware of how little Donnell knew or cared about the work he ordered people to do. He never gave a thought as to how all his needs and comforts were met, except to savagely punish the ones he deemed responsible if they failed in some way. Annora kept her gaze as innocent as possible as she met his look of suspicion, breathing a silent sigh of relief when he had obviously decided that she was not clever enough to be so subtle.

"Get ye gone then," he said. "I have been hearing a great deal about what fine work this new mon does and I seek a goblet or the like so that I may see his skill with my own eyes."

Annora nodded and hurried past him, little Meggie keeping step close by her side. If the fool was so interested in this man's skill she wondered why he did not go and have a look for himself. It was the fear of saying that thought aloud that made her scurry. Donnell's response to such words would be a hard fist and she preferred to avoid those whenever possible.

"Why does the laird need a goblet?" asked Meggie the moment Annora slowed their fast pace to an almost lazy stroll.

"He wants to see if the man who carves them is as good at what he does as everyone says he is," replied Annora.

"He doesnae believe everyone?"

"Weel, nay, I suspicion he doesnae."

"Then why will he believe us?"

"A verra good question, love. I dinnae ken why he should if he doesnae heed anyone else's word, but 'tis best if we just do as he asks."

Meggie nodded, her expression surprisingly solemn for one so young. "Aye, or he will hit ye again, and I dinnae want him to do that."

Neither did Annora. Her cousin had come close to breaking her jaw and a few other bones the last time he had beaten her. She knew she ought to be grateful that Donnell's second-in-command Egan had stopped him from continuing to punch her, but she was not. Egan did not usually care who Donnell beat or how badly he did so, was in truth just as brutish as Donnell was. The fact that the man did not want her beaten, at least not too severely, made her very nervous. So did the way he always watched her. Annora did not want to owe that man anything.

"Neither do I, love," she finally murmured and

quickly distracted Meggie from such dark thoughts by pointing out the cattle grazing on the hillside.

All the way to the village Annora kept Meggie entertained by drawing her attention to every animal, person, or plant they passed. She exchanged a few greetings with a few people, yet again regretting how closely watched and confined Donnell kept her and Meggie. Although she would have preferred choosing the times and reasons she traveled to the village, Annora enjoyed the pretense of freedom, able to ignore the guards she knew were right behind her. She only wished she would be given enough time and freedom to come to the village more often and get to know the people of Dunncraig better.

Annora sighed and inwardly shook her head. She had not been given any chance to become a true part of Dunncraig, but that was only part of her regret about not getting to know the people as well as she would like. Something was not right about Donnell's place as laird, about his claim to these lands and to Meggie. Annora had sensed that wrongness from the start, but after three years, she had not uncovered any truth to give some weight to her suspicions. She knew someone at Dunncraig knew the answers to all the questions she had, but she had not yet found a way around Donnell's guard long enough to ask any of them.

Approaching the cooper's home and shop, Annora felt her spirits lighten just a little. Edmund the cooper's wife Ida might be at home and Annora knew the woman would readily sate her need to talk to another woman. Her pace grew a little faster in anticipation. She dearly loved Meggie but the child simply could not satisfy the need for a good, long woman-to-woman talk.

* * *

"Rolf, she is coming."

This time James did not hesitate to look up from his work when Edward called him by his assumed name. It had taken James longer than he had liked to become accustomed to being called Rolf. He hated to admit it but Edmund had been right when he had counseled patience, had warned him that he would need time to fully assume the guise of Rolf Larousse Lavengeance.

Then what Edmund had just said fully settled into James's mind. "Meggie?"

"Aye, but to ye she must be Lady Margaret," Edmund reminded him.

"Ah, of course. I shallnae forget. Who comes with her?"

"Mistress Annora and, a few yards behind, two of Donnell's men."

James cursed. "Does the mon think there is some danger to the woman or Meggie here?"

"Only to him, I am thinking. MacKay doesnae allow the woman to talk much with anyone. Nor the bairn. Some folk think the lass thinks herself too good for us and is teaching the bairn to be the same, but I think Mistress Annora is forced to keep to herself. E'en when she has a chance to talk to someone, there are always some of MacKay's men close at hand to try to hear all that is said."

"'Tis his own guilt making him think everyone is eager to decry him."

"I think that may be it. My Ida says the lass is clever and quick. MacKay may fear she has the wit to put a few things together and see the truth. 'Tis a big lie he is living, and it has to weigh on the mon."

"I hope it breaks his cursed back," James muttered as he tried to clean himself up just a little. "Better still, I want it to hang him."

"So does most everyone at Dunncraig," said Edmund.

James nodded. He had quickly seen how cowed his people were. Donnell was a harsh, cruel laird. He was also unskilled in the knowledge needed to keep the lands and the stock thriving. There were all too many signs that the man glutted himself on the riches of Dunncraig with little thought to how his people might survive or the fact that care must be taken to ensure that there was food in the future. The people might be afraid of the man seated in the laird's chair but they did not hold silent when they were amongst themselves, and James had heard a lot. Donnell was bleeding the lands dry to fill his belly and his purse.

Ida stuck her head into the room. "The lass says the laird sent her. He is wanting a goblet made by Rolf."

Before he could say anything, Ida was gone. For a moment James simply sat at his work table and breathed slowly and evenly to calm his excitement and anticipation. This was the first step. He had to be careful not to stumble on it. He knew Donnell spent a lot to make Dunncraig keep as fine as some French king's palace. That required a skilled wood-worker and he wanted to be the one who was hired.

"That one," said Edmund, pointing toward a tall, richly carved goblet.

"Aye, I think ye have chosen the perfect one, old friend," James said and smiled.

"I havenae seen that expression for a while."

"'Tis anticipation."

"Aye. I can fair feel it in the air. The mon is a vain swine who spends far too much of your coin on things he doesnae need, things he thinks make him look important. Ye guessed his weakness right. Do ye really think the mon would leave some proof of his guilt around though?"

It was a question Edmund had asked before and James still was not confident of his feeling that the truth was inside the keep. "I cannae be sure but I think there has to be something. He cannae be rid of all proof. Mayhap I will but hear something that will aid me." He shrugged. "I cannae say. All I do ken is that I must be inside Dunncraig if I am to have any chance of getting the truth."

"Weel, then, let us get ye in there then."

Annora looked up as Edmund and another man stepped out of the workrooms in the back of the little shop. She stared at the man with Edmund, wondering why he so captivated her attention. He was tall and lean, even looked as if he could use a few good Scratch's meals. His hair was light brown and it hung past his broad shoulders. There was a scar on his right cheek, and he wore a patch over his left eye. The right eye was such a beautiful green she felt a pang of sorrow for the loss of its mate. His features were handsome, cleanly carved yet sharpened a little by the signs of hunger and trouble. This man had known hardship and she felt a surprising tug of deep sympathy for him. Since she had no idea what sort of trouble may have put that harshness on his handsome face, she did not understand why she wanted to smooth those lines away. The way his slightly full lips made her feel a little warm alarmed her somewhat. The man was having a very strange effect upon her and she did not think she liked it.

Then she saw his gaze rest on Meggie and put her arm around the child's shoulders. There was such an intensity in his look that she wondered why it did not make her afraid. A moment later, Annora realized that the intensity held no hint of a threat or dislike. There was a hunger there, a need and a grieving; and she wondered if he had lost a child. Again she felt a need to soothe him and that need began to make her very nervous.

She looked at the goblet he held in his elegant long-fingered hands and gasped softly. "Is that the one ye wish to sell to the laird?" she asked.

"Aye," the man replied. "I am Rolf, Rolf Larousse Lavengeance."

Annora blinked and had to bite her lip not to say anything. It was a very strange name. It roughly translated to wolf, redhead, and vengeance. It was also strange for a poor working man to have such an elaborate name. There had to be a story behind it and her curiosity stirred, but she beat it down. It was not her place to question the man about his name. As a bastard, she was also all too aware of the hurt and shame that could come from such questioning; and she would never inflict that upon anyone else.

"It is verra beautiful, Master Lavengeance," she said and held her hand out. "Might I have a look?"

"Aye."

As she took the goblet into her hands, she decided the man had been in Scotland long enough to lose much of his French accent and pick up a word or two of their language. If Donnell hired the man to do some work at the keep that would make life a great deal easier. Donnell had absolutely no knowledge of French and could easily become enraged by a worker who had difficulty understanding what he said. And, looking at the beautiful carvings of a hunt on the goblet, she suspected Donnell would be very eager to have the man come and work at Dunncraig keep. The thought that she might have to see a lot of the man in order to translate orders for him made her feel a little too eager and Annora felt a sudden need to get away from this man.

"I believe this will please my cousin weel," she said. "Your work is beautiful, Master Lavengeance. The stag on this goblet looks so real one almost expects to see him toss his proud head."

James just nodded and named his price. The woman named Annora did not even blink, but paid for it and hurried Meggie out of the shop. Moving quickly to look out the door, James watched her lead his child back to the keep, two of Donnell's men in step a few yards behind them. He felt a hand rub his arm and looked to find Ida standing at his side, her blue eyes full of sympathy.

"Annora loves the wee lass," Ida said.

"Does she? Or is she but a good nursemaid?" James asked.

"Oh, aye, she loves the lass. 'Tis Lady Margaret who holds Mistress Annora at Dunncraig and naught else. The child has been loved and weel cared for whilst ye have been gone, Laird."

James nodded but he was not sure he fully believed that. Meggie had looked healthy and happy, but she had said nothing. There was also a solemnity to the child that had not been there before. Meggie had been as sweet and innocent as her mother but had had a liveliness that Mary had never possessed. There had been no sign of that liveliness, and he wondered what had smothered it. He would not lay the blame for that change at the feet of Mistress Annora yet, but he would watch the woman closely.

He inwardly grimaced, knowing he would find it no hardship to watch the woman. Mistress Annora was beautiful. Slender yet full-curved, her body caught— and held—a man's gaze. Her thick raven hair made her fair skin look an even purer shade of cream, and her wide midnight-blue eyes drew in a man like a moth to a flame. After three years alone he knew he had to be careful not to let his starved senses lead him astray, but he was definitely eager to further his acquaintance with Mistress Annora.

Suddenly he wondered if Mistress Annora was Donnell's lover; and then wondered why that possiblity enraged him. James told himself it was because he did not want such a woman caring for his child. It might be unfair to think her anything more than she seemed, but her beauty made it all too easy to think that Donnell would not be able to leave her alone. Mistress Annora's true place in Dunncraig keep was just another question needing an answer.

Stepping more fully into the open doorway of Edmund's shop, he stared up at the keep that had once been his home. He would be back there soon. He would enter the keep as a worker, but he meant to stay as the laird. For all her beauty, if Mistress Annora had any part in Donnell's schemes, she would find that her beauty did not buy her any mercy from him.

About the Author

Hannah Howell is an award-winning author who lives with her family in Massachusetts. She is the author of twenty-three Zebra historical romances, and is currently working on a new Highland historical romance, *Highland Wolf*, to be released in December 2007! Hannah loves hearing from readers, and you may visit her Web site: www.hannahhowell.com.

GREAT BOOKS,
GREAT SAVINGS!

When You Visit Our Website:
www.kensingtonbooks.com
You Can Save Money Off The Retail Price
Of Any Book You Purchase!

Visit Us Today To Start Saving!
www.kensingtonbooks.com